# The Runaway Children

ALSO BY SANDY TAYLOR
FROM CLIPPER LARGE PRINT

The Girls from See Saw Lane
Counting Chimneys
When we Danced at the End of the Pier

# The Runaway Children

## Sandy Taylor

W F HOWES LTD

This large print edition published in 2018 by
W F Howes Ltd
Unit 5, St George's House, Rearsby Business Park,
Gaddesby Lane, Rearsby, Leicester LE7 4YH

1  3  5  7  9  10  8  6  4  2

First published in the United Kingdom in 2017
by Bookouture

A CIP catalogue record for this book is available
from the British Library

ISBN 978 1 52881 719 6

Typeset by Palimpsest Book Production Limited,
Falkirk, Stirlingshire

Printed and bound by
T J International in the UK

To my wonderful agent Kate Hordern:
Thank you for everything, Kate. In the
immortal words of Tina Turner
'You're simply the best'.

# CHAPTER 1

Bermondsey, 1942

Although it was spring, it was freezing cold sitting on the stone steps leading up to our flat. It had been raining overnight and the steps were damp, moisture was seeping through my thin dress and the wind whistling along the landing chilled my bones. It felt like we'd been sitting there for hours. Mrs Ryan had shooed us out of the flat and there was nowhere else to go.

My little sister Olive was huddled against me. I could feel her shivering, so I lifted her onto my lap. The poor thing had a cold and her nose was red and sore from wiping it on the sleeve of her cardigan.

'Is someone hurtin my mummy, Nell?' she said, looking up at me with her beautiful brown eyes.

'Course not,' I said.

'Why's she screamin then?'

'Cos she's happy.'

'She don't sound happy.'

'Remember when you had to have that rotten tooth out?'

'Yes.'

'Did it hurt when they were pulling it out?'

'It nearly bloody killed me!'

'But once it was out you felt better, didn't you? Cos the toothache had gone away.'

'Is Mummy havin her tooth out then?'

'No, Olive, she's havin a baby. Mummy explained it all to you.'

'Nell?'

'Yes, Olive?'

'Where does the baby come out?'

This was getting complicated.

'Ask Mummy,' I said.

'All right, Nell.'

She put her arms around my neck. I could feel her hot breath on my cheek.

'I want to go indoors, Nell, I want to be with my mummy.'

'You'll see her soon, love,' I said.

My brother Tony, who was kicking a stone around the yard, looked back at us.

'I ain't goin in there, not while she's screamin her head off.'

'Listen, you ungrateful little git, you'd be screamin an all if you had to push a baby out of you!'

Tony was glaring at me. 'Why is she havin it? There ain't enough food for us three without havin to feed another one.'

'The baby won't cost nothin, Mum'll feed it from her titty, just like she fed you.'

At this Tony's face had gone all red and he kicked the stone hard against the wall.

'Look, Tony,' I said gently. 'It's not Mum's fault.'

'Whose fault *is* it then?' he said angrily.

'It's to do with bein married,' I said. 'If you sleeps in the same bed, you has a baby.'

I had a feeling there was more to it than that but I didn't want to think about it cos it made me feel funny inside.

Olive gave a big sniff. 'Do you think it will be a boy or a girl, Nell?' she said.

'That's up to God to decide, Olive. God counts up all the people in the world and if the world's short on boys, he sends a boy and if it's short on girls, he sends a girl.' I smoothed her hair back from her hot little forehead. She was burning up – she should be in bed, not out here in the cold. I was just about to take my coat off and wrap it around her when our neighbour, Mrs Baxter, came running down the steps.

'Any news yet, Mrs Baxter?' I asked, lifting Olive off my lap and standing up.

'Not yet, ducks, but she's doing all right. Mrs Ryan's with her and she's delivered nearly all the babies in the flats, so your mum's in good hands and thank God that there's been no air raids.'

'Olive's not well, Mrs Baxter, she should be in bed.'

'Bring her into my flat, Nell, it looks like you could all do with warming up.'

'Thanks, Mrs Baxter,' I said gratefully. 'Come on, Tony.'

But Tony hung back.

'We'll just go in for a minute to warm up.'

'I ain't cold,' he said, staring at the ground.

For all his temper, Tony was the sensitive one. He was eleven, two years younger than me and the closest to Mum. I knew that his anger came from worrying about her.

Mrs Baxter ushered Olive into her flat and I walked across to Tony. I put my arm around him; I could feel the bones of his shoulder blades jutting out from under the thin jumper.

'She's going to be all right, Tony,' I said gently. 'Our mum's as strong as an ox.'

'I know she is, Nell,' he said. 'but I hate this.'

'So do I, but it'll be all over soon and then she'll be right as rain.'

'I'd rather stay here where I can hear her.'

'I know you would, but stayin here listening to her screamin ain't gonna help Mum or you, is it?'

'I'm afraid somethin's gonna go wrong, I'm afraid she's gonna die, Nell.'

There were tears running down his face; he immediately brushed them away.

'It's okay to cry, Tony,' I said, more gently now.

'I ain't cryin,' he said angrily. 'It's just the wind.'

'Women have babies every day, Tony. Mrs O'Malley pops em out like peas and she ain't dead, is she?'

'Dad should be here,' he said. 'He should be here, lookin after her.'

'He would if he could, you know he would, but he has to fight in the war. It's not his fault.'

Sometimes when I looked at my brother it was like looking at Daddy. He had the same blue eyes and fiery red hair. Since Daddy had gone away to fight I knew that Tony was carrying a lot on his thin shoulders. He was a young boy trying to be a man. For all his bravado he cared deeply for his family and I loved him for it.

'I'll tell ya what, let's just have a bit of a warm, then we'll come out again.'

He nodded and together we went into Mrs Baxter's flat. Mr and Mrs Baxter made an odd-looking couple. Mrs Baxter was tiny. Mum said she reminded her of a little bird, always flitting here and there, running up and down the steps of Rannly Court like a young girl and lending a helping hand wherever she could. She knew everything that went on in the flats and she was everyone's friend. Mr Baxter, on the other hand, was as wide as he was tall. He only had one leg because he'd lost the last one fighting for king and country, so he didn't run anywhere, but he always had a smile on his face and he'd give you his last penny. Mum said it was a marriage made in heaven.

There was a fire burning in the grate and Olive was kneeling in front of it with her hands spread out towards the flames. Mr Baxter was asleep, his mouth was open and he was making little squeaking noises like a kitten. Tony poked me and I grinned when I saw Mr Baxter's wooden leg propped up against his chair.

Mrs Baxter nudged him and he opened one eye.

'It's Mrs Patterson's kids, Reg,' she said. 'They were sittin on the steps, freezin their little arses off.'

Mr Baxter rubbed his eyes. 'Get yourselves warm then, kids,' he said, pulling himself up in the chair and smiling at us. He picked up a poker and rattled the coals, causing warm air to waft into the room. It was lovely. 'How about some bread and scrape, they look as if they need feedin up.'

'Good idea, love,' said Mrs Baxter, bustling into the kitchen.

Olive started coughing. 'She's not well, Mr Baxter,' I said. 'She's burnin up.'

'The missus will see to her when she comes back with the bread and scrape,' he said

I looked at Olive's little red face and hoped she didn't have something real bad wrong with her. Little Betty Ormerod in the flat below ours had died of scarlet fever only a couple of months ago.

'You don't think she's got the scarlet fever, do you, Mr Baxter?'

'The missus will know, best ask the missus.'

The three of us crouched down in front of the fire and tried to get some warmth back into our bodies. Olive leaned against me and I put my arm around her. I could feel her body shaking.

'I'm cold, Nell.'

Mrs Baxter came into the room carrying a tray. 'Bread and scrape?' she said, putting it down on the table.

Me and Tony took a slice of the bread but Olive shook her head.

'I'm worried about Olive, Mrs Baxter. You don't think she's got the scarlet fever, do you?'

'I hope not,' she said. 'Or we're all for it.'

'What does scarlet fever look like?' I said.

'I think you get a red rash – has Olive got a rash?'

I lifted up Olive's cardigan. Her back was hot and clammy to the touch but she didn't have a rash.

'She ain't got no rash, Mrs Baxter.'

Olive started to cough again. 'I don't feel so good, Nell.'

'It's just a cold, love, it ain't the scarlet fever. You'll soon feel better.'

She yawned and I could see that she was finding it hard to keep her eyes open.

Mrs Baxter picked her up and put her in the armchair, then she took the blanket off Mr Baxter's lap and wrapped it round Olive, who went to sleep right away.

'Thanks, Mrs Baxter.'

'Best if she sleeps it off, Nell.'

I leaned against the chair and watched my sister as she slept, her dark lashes resting on her pale cheeks.

Everyone said that Olive was beautiful. Her hair was a dark auburn, which made her skin seem even paler, and her eyes were a soft brown, like melted chocolate. I brushed the hair away from her eyes and she stirred. I was glad that she didn't have the scarlet fever but I was still worried about her. Mr Hicks, the tallyman, said that Olive was too beautiful for this world and that frightened me. I couldn't help noticing that he didn't say the same about me.

I'd been described as a 'rasher of bacon', long and thin and wiry, with old eyes, whatever that meant. Mum said I'd grow into myself, which didn't make me feel any happier as I would much rather grow into someone else, someone beautiful. To top it off, my hair was a mass of unruly curls that were the bane of my mother's life. Old Mrs Banks from the flat above ours said that it dwarfed my face. So that was me: long and thin, old eyes and hair that dwarfed my face. Bloody perfect.

'Your day will come, my Nell,' said Mum.

*Well, I wish it would hurry up,* I thought.

I could see Tony getting restless – he wanted to go back outside and listen for Mum.

'We can't take Olive back out in the cold,' I said.

'You can leave her here with me,' said Mrs Baxter.

'Thanks, just give me a shout when she wakes up and I'll come and get her.'

'Listen,' said Mrs Baxter suddenly.

We all listened.

'I can't hear nothin,' I said.

'That's cos there's nothin to hear. Yer mother's stopped screamin, girl.'

I grinned at her. 'Do you think she's had the baby then?'

'I'd say so,' she said, grinning.

Tony was out the door like a shot – I could hear him running up the stone steps.

'Thanks for lookin after us, Mrs Baxter, and thanks for the bread and scrape.'

'You're welcome, love, and don't worry about Olive, I'll take care of her.'

I ran up the steps and into our flat. Tony was standing beside the bed, staring down at the bundle in Mum's arms, and Mrs Ryan was over at the sink.

Mum was propped up against the pillows. She looked pale and tired, but happy.

'What is it?' I asked.

She folded the blanket away from the baby's face. 'It's a boy, Nell.'

'Olive was hopin for a girl,' I said, grinning.

Mum looked behind me. 'Where is she?'

'She's asleep in the Baxters' flat, she don't feel so good. But it's not the scarlet fever, Mum, cos she ain't got no rash.'

Mum was staring down at the baby. 'Isn't he lovely, Nell?'

I stared at the wrinkled little face peering out of the blanket.

'Yes, Mum, he's lovely.'

'He's a dead ringer for Churchill,' said Mrs Ryan, turning round. 'All he needs is a cigar.'

'What you gonna call him?' I asked.

'I thought I'd call him Freddie, after your granddad.'

'Granddad was an old sod,' said Tony.

'I know he was, but it'll please yer dad and anyway, our little Freddie won't be an old sod, will he?'

'I wouldn't bank on it!' shouted Mrs Ryan from across the room, and we all started laughing.

# CHAPTER 2

I was thirteen years old and I'd lived in Rannly Court all my life. It was my home. I didn't know any different and I didn't want anything different. The court was a tenement, four storeys high, built of brick. There was a shared staircase with rooms off it and different families lived on different floors, one family on each side of the staircase, eight altogether in our block. I knew every family that ran up and down the stone steps. I heard every burst of laughter from our neighbours and every desperate cry of sadness, every fight and every celebration, through the thin walls. Our lives were played out for everyone to hear. It wasn't all good-natured but we looked out for one another, especially the women. The men came and went, looking for work, off to war or chasing their own dreams, but the women were always there: strong, matter-of-fact, making the most of it. Everyone was skint, but if you were in need they shared what little they had. And there was laughter, there was a lot of laughter.

The streets and alleyways around Rannly Court were my playground and the River Thames that flowed at the back of the flats, my very own ocean. I knew every pawn shop and every public house, every factory and every shop. I loved watching the women coming out of the custard factory covered in yellow dust. I loved watching them take off their headscarves and shake out their hair, a tiny haze of yellow around each of their faces, and their smell of vanilla and sugar. Like the other kids, I made faces at the rent man and I smiled at the rag and bone man and his mangy old horse. It was a dear old thing – he called it Bella and it had a nosebag that hung over its head when it stopped outside the pub at lunchtime, while the rag and bone man went in for his dinner. I liked to pat Bella's shoulders. She was warm and her coat was thick and woolly, and when I touched her, she shivered beneath my hand.

I said hello to the beautiful ladies who stood on the street corners with their red nails and lipstick, and they looked at me through their cigarette smoke and called me 'duck' and 'lamb'. I hoped that one day I could look as pretty as they did. I ran errands for the old people who lived in the court but who couldn't manage the steep steps. I literally ran, trying to break my own record for getting to the off-licence and back with a quarter of gin, or to the butcher's for some pork scratchings. Sometimes I wheeled snotty-nosed babies round the docks. Because I had a younger brother and sister people trusted me to look after their kids. I liked taking the babies out. I talked to them, told them stories, and those big enough to sit up in the pram listened to me instead of struggling to get out. I made sure they never got cold – I fastened up their knitted bonnets, handed down through generations of babies, and I tucked in their knitted blankets.

When we reached the docks, with their smell of oily water and rotting vegetation, the seagulls screaming in the wind, we stopped to watch bare-chested men loading heavy sacks of sugar from the Tate & Lyle factory onto barges. We had to keep our distance. The dockers were hard men, everyone knew that. My daddy was a docker before the war. He was proud of his work. The dockers were a band of brothers, he said. You had to be a good grafter to get the work, because there wasn't enough to go round and those jobs were in great demand. Daddy and his mates lived in constant fear of getting injured because if they hurt themselves and couldn't work, then the whole family would be in trouble.

I liked watching the men at their labour and looking at the barges and wondering what it would be like to go out on one, down the river. I imagined everywhere was exactly like Bermondsey – I didn't know any different. Bermondsey had everything it needed so why shouldn't everywhere else be exactly the same?

Me and Olive would take bread and dripping down to Daddy at lunchtime. He'd come to see us, away from the work and the other men. We'd sit next to him on the quayside, our legs dangling over the side, and we'd watch the barges and boats floating by on the black water, wide as a mile and deeper than we could imagine. Daddy would point out the big boats that came down the river from far-away places like Australia and New Zealand, and he'd do his best to bring those places to life for us, even though he had never been there. In my mind, all of them looked like Bermondsey, only with sunshine and kangaroos.

My brother Tony loved the river and he was often in trouble for skipping school and spending the day there. He'd trawl the mudbanks looking for treasure; pieces of coal and wood, and sometimes he'd find a bone that he'd bring home and give to one of the neighbours' dogs, or even a coin or two stuck into the thick grey-brown mud. He'd come back with his legs a dusty grey up to the knees where the mud had dried onto his skin, and Mum would send him out to wipe it off in the street because she didn't want the mud in the flats.

Mum worried about Tony spending so much time by the river. She knew that sometimes he'd wade into it and drag out larger bits of wood to bring home for the fire. We needed the wood but she was worried about him getting washed off his feet by the wake of a passing boat, or being swept out into the river and drowning. If he was late back, she feared he might have got stuck in the mud or found something valuable and been beaten up and robbed by the professional mudlarks – the

14

adults who made a living from hunting treasure at the side of the river. Sometimes they found bodies: people who'd fallen from boats or jumped off bridges or been murdered. Mum was terrified that Tony might find a body. Tony wasn't scared, though. He loved the river. He wasn't afraid of it, no matter how much Mum tried to warn him away from it. The docks were where he wanted to work when he was old enough: he wanted to be like Daddy.

We were lucky because we had the best daddy in the whole of Bermondsey, in the whole of London even. A big man with bright ginger hair and a thick ginger beard, he had bright blue eyes and a smile that lit up our world. He didn't get roaring drunk like most of the men in the flats and he never laid a finger on any of us in anger. Mum said she knew a good'n when she'd met him at the local dance and she'd been proved right. As soon as war was declared, he was the first down the town hall to join up.

I worried about him all the time, but Mum said he would be safe because there weren't many ginger men in Bermondsey so God needed him here to make up the numbers. I wasn't sure that I believed her but I clung to the hope that she was right. She didn't say out loud that she was worried about Daddy in the same way she was always worrying out loud about Tony. This should have been reassuring but I was already old enough to have noticed that Mum talked about stuff that didn't matter much more than she talked about the things that did. I didn't know what we would do if anything happened to our daddy. I just couldn't imagine it and so I tried my best not to think about it.

The River Thames flowed past the back of the flats and once the war really got going, the docks were being bombed almost every day. The council supplied Rannly Court with Morrison shelters – strong metal cages that could also be used as tables. We put ours in the hallway under the stair-well where the building was strongest and, when the warning alarm came, we'd all squash under it and Mum would sing to us in her beautiful pure voice until the all-clear went. The bombs were scary but the bombsites were the best playgrounds we'd ever had. Every day after school, kids, mostly boys, swarmed over the rubble playing war games and cowboys and Indians. The girls played mums and dads and shops in the ruins of the bombed-out houses. At the end of the day the boys came home with scraped knees and torn trousers, without a care in the world.

If there was ever any kind of trouble in the Rannly Court flats the men would deal with it. One night Mr Brown, who was always five sheets to the wind, beat his family so badly he almost killed them. No ambulance was called and no one sent for the cops. The women took care of the family and the men took care of Mr Brown – in fact, he was never seen again. Mrs Brown became happy and plump and took up with the milkman,

16

who was missing an earlobe but was kind and took care of Mrs Brown and the kids. That's the way it was. Bermondsey took care of its own and Mum said that was the way it had always been.

This was my little corner of the East End and I loved it. At night I lay in bed and listened to the sound of men staggering out of the Spread Eagle and Crown, singing at the tops of their voices, songs like 'Nellie Dean' and 'Roll Out the Barrel'. These were the lullabies of the East End that sent me to sleep.

# CHAPTER 3

Most of the kids round here had been evacuated at the start of the war. They had gone in groups, parading through the streets behind their schoolteachers, who held up banners with the name of the school. Not all of us, though. Some of us had stayed behind for whatever reason. And some had gone but then returned, making their way back home, unable to settle in the country. Bermondsey ran through them like the words in a stick of rock and the countryside was alien to them. It wasn't always the happy place they'd imagined. The evacuation had been organised so quickly and haphazardly that not all the children ended up where they should have done. Their homecoming wasn't always what they had hoped for either, and sometimes the poor little mites found themselves loaded onto the next available train by less-than-sympathetic parents.

I know that Mum worried about our safety every day, but while she was pregnant with Freddie, she had needed us nearby. She'd been ill this time, too ill to get out of bed; her ankles had swollen right up and she'd had terrible headaches.

Somebody had to look after her, make her cups of tea and do her washing, and with Dad gone that only left me and Tony. Olive wasn't exactly much help, but she refused to be evacuated on her own. Now, however, with Freddie born and the bombardment of the docks getting worse, Mum desperately wanted us to leave London and go somewhere safer. She said worrying about us kept her awake at night and she couldn't be doing with missing any more sleep because she was already missing so much with Freddie. It was true that she was tired all the time. Sometimes I'd look at her when she didn't realise I was looking and I'd see her eyelids closing, coming together. Once I saw her almost fall asleep standing up, stirring a pot on the stove. I hadn't known, until then, that human beings could fall asleep standing up.

I loved my mum and it was obvious that she couldn't go on being this tired and worried. I was old enough to understand that it would be easier for her to cope with the baby and the war and everything else if she knew us three older kids were somewhere safe.

So we had to go, but I had an idea.

'Why can't you come with us, Mum?' I'd asked.

She'd shaken her head. 'Not yet – Freddie is too small and I'm . . .'

'What?'

'I'm just too tired, Nell.'

She'd looked down at the baby in her arms. Freddie had grown into his face a bit. He didn't look so much like a grumpy old man now; he was actually quite sweet. He gazed up at Mum all squinty-eyed and moved his lips. She put the tip of her little finger into his mouth. 'I'll try to join you later when Freddie's a bit older.'

'How will you know where to find us?'

'You'll write to me when you're settled and then I'll know where you are.'

'If there's no room, you can share my bed,' I'd said.

'Thank you, Nell.'

'Or I'll go in with Olive.'

'Right.'

'So you promise you'll come?'

'I promise.' She smiled. 'This won't be forever, my love.'

None of us wanted to leave Mum but Tony, especially, was adamant that he wasn't going anywhere. He considered himself the man of the house while Dad was away and he felt responsible for Mum.

'What if she gets ill again while we're away?' he asked.

'She's got the neighbours, Tony.'

'That's not the same! They're not going to come and stay all night with her, are they?'

'I'm sure they would if it was important.'

Tony scowled. 'What's the point of us going away, anyway? It's a stupid waste of time. How can anyone be sure that the bloody countryside ain't gonna be bombed?'

'I don't suppose they can,' I said. 'But the

Germans aren't interested in farms and villages, are they? They want to drop their bombs on cities and railways and the docks. Why would they waste their bombs on a load of cows and sheep?'

'Well, I ain't goin and no one's gonna make me.'

'You're a selfish little bugger, Tony Patterson! This isn't all about you, you know. Think of Olive, she's only five and she's terrified of the bombs, she's a bag of nerves.'

'Well, let Olive go then. You go with her! I'm not stoppin her or you, am I? You two go and then Mum won't have to worry about you and I can look after her.'

'Look, Tony,' I said gently. 'I don't wanna go either but if it's what Mum wants, then I need you to come with us, I need you to help me. You're the man of the house now and I know that this is what Daddy would want you to do.'

'Bloody stinking rotten war!' he yelled.

'Think about it, Tone, for Olive's sake. Just think about it.'

He nodded and stood up, hands in pockets, shoulders hunched. He kicked a pebble and walked away down the street, the toes of his boots slapping on the pavement. There were holes in the elbows of his jumper. I hoped that he would think about it. I didn't want him being difficult, making things worse for all of us, especially Mum.

The day after this conversation, me and my best friend, Angela Townsend, were sitting in the upstairs bedroom of 59 Edison Terrace. The back wall had been blown out but an old iron bed was still all in one piece. Scraps of flowery wallpaper hung in strips and blew around in the breeze and bits of brown lino still clung to the floor. Neither me nor Angela had ever lived in a whole house and we loved it there. We made believe that it was ours. Between us we'd dragged the bed over to the gaping hole, from where we could look down on the kids climbing over the rubble and across all the gardens and allotments down to the river, where the tall cranes rose up into the sky.

Angela tucked her legs under her. 'I wonder who used to live here?' she asked.

'I haven't got a clue,' I said, 'but I don't think they were skint. Not as skint as us, anyway. Mum couldn't afford lino like this.'

'I bet it was a beautiful lady. Bet she looked like Vera Lynn, with red lips and blonde hair, and I bet she wore silk dresses with fur stoles.'

'Bet she lived here with her handsome husband.'

'Yeah. Bet he was a right looker.' Angela sighed and rested her chin on her hand. 'Bet he bought her flowers and necklaces and perfume. Bet he opened the door for her when she got in and out the taxi. Bet they took a lot of taxis.'

I smiled. 'Do you think they had kids?'

'Oh no,' said Angela. 'Her what lived here was far too busy for kids.'

'Busy doing what?'

'Working for the radio.'

I smiled. She was still thinking about Vera Lynn.

'I wonder where they are now?' Angela said. She stroked the mattress of the bed.

'They might have been killed.'

'I hope not,' she said, chewing at her nails. 'I hope they're staying in a hotel.'

Hotels were the epitome of glamour as far as me and Angela were concerned. Angela's face had gone rather sad so I said gently: 'I thought you'd stopped chewing your nails?'

'It's a habit.'

'Well, it's not a very nice one, Angela. Her as lived here wouldn't have chewed her nails.'

'It helps,' she said.

I knew that Angela tended to chew at her nails when she was worried about something.

'Is everything all right at home?' I asked gently.

Angela's eyes filled with tears. I reached across and held her hand. 'Wanna talk about it?'

'There's nothin to talk about really, Nell, because there's nothin I can do about it.'

'Sometimes it helps to talk, even if there's nothin to be done,' I said.

Angela wiped her eyes on the sleeve of her cardigan. 'Mum's not getting any better and Gran's taken to wandering the streets. We try to keep the door locked but she's a crafty old cow and any chance she gets, she's gone. The other day she was climbing over the bombsite in her nightie and her bum was showin and all the kids were laughing at her. I'm worn out with it all, Nell.'

'I'm sorry,' I said, squeezing her hand.

She wiped her eyes again. 'I'm all right really. I love my gran. She might be an old cow but she's *my* old cow,' she said, grinning.

'And your mum?'

'No one seems to know what's wrong with her – she hasn't been well since she had Mavis. She spends most of her time in bed now. It's not her fault, I know it's not, but it's hard, Nell. Sometimes I feel like a middle-aged woman with a couple of kids to look after.'

'I wish I could do something to help you.'

'You're my friend and that helps.'

'What about your lot? Have you heard from them?' I said. Angela's brothers and sister had been evacuated with all the others a while back.

'Robbie's pretty good at keeping in touch. He says the people who've taken them in are nice. Little Mavis misses Mum and Stanley's still wetting the bed. Mum's hoping by the time they come home, he'll be house trained.'

I grinned at her. 'I don't think your Stanley will ever be house trained.'

'Neither do I, but Mum lives in hope. She's not too worried though, cos they're safe and being looked after. Robbie's fallen in love with the family's two dogs, Peppa and Woody, and he says he wants a dog of his own when he comes back.'

'That's all your mum needs,' I said, smiling.

'That's all *I* need.' She sighed.

I didn't know how to say it, so I just came out with it: 'I might have to go away, Angela.'

Angela chewed at her nails again.

'What, all of you?' she asked, softly.

'Not Mum and the baby. She says Freddie's too young to be travelling all over the country and Mrs Ryan said Mum's not strong enough to travel yet.'

'What about Tony? Is he going as well?'

'Not sure about that one. He says he'll think about it.'

'I can't see him leavin your mum, Nell.'

'Neither can I, but I put him on a bit of a guilt trip, so I'm hoping he'll come round to the idea. I wish we could be evacuated together, Angela.'

'I wish we could too, but Mum would never be able to travel – neither would Gran.'

'I can't imagine leaving Bermondsey.'

'Well, right now I can't think of anything I'd rather do.'

'I know,' I said gently.

'Think of it as an adventure, girl, or a holiday.'

'It won't feel like much of a holiday without Mum.'

'I'll miss you if you go, Nell.'

'I'll miss you an all,' I said, linking my arm through hers.

We sat in silence looking out over Bermondsey until the light went from the sky and it was time to say goodbye to the glamorous ghosts of 59 Edison Terrace and make our way home. We were starting to shiver when all of a sudden the air-raid siren began wailing. I nearly jumped out of my skin. No matter how many times I heard it, it still frightened me to death. We leapt off the bed and ran down the stairs, which still had the banister on one side but was completely open on the other. In the street we joined a crowd of people hurrying towards the Underground. We soon realised we weren't going to make it; there was a massive boom as the first bomb dropped, the blast sucking the air out of our lungs and nearly knocking us off our feet. I grabbed Angela's coat and dragged her into a doorway. We flattened ourselves against the wall and covered our heads.

'Siren was a bit bloody late,' said Angela, shaking.

We clung together, terrified.

'Bloody Norah!' she added.

Just then the door behind us opened and we both fell into someone's hallway. We didn't have time to thank our saviour as a second bomb rocked the house and we were manhandled under the kitchen table and into a Morrison shelter. Me and Angela found ourselves knee to knee with Gilbert Delaney, who was in our class at school.

'Hello, Gilbert,' I said shyly.

'Hello, Nell,' he replied, grinning and scratching behind his ear.

'What were you kids doing out there in the dark?' asked Gilbert's dad, lighting up a fag.

'We were on our way home, Mr Delaney,' I said, coughing.

'What have I told you about smoking under here?' said his wife.

'It settles me nerves,' he said, winking at us.

'Well, it doesn't bloody settle mine,' she said, glaring at him.

'Would you rather I went outside and smoked, dear?'

'Don't tempt me,' she said.

We stayed under the table until the all-clear went. Then we thanked the family, said goodbye to Gilbert and made our way home through the dark streets. It was pitch-black and the air was full of smoke and bits of debris. We clung to each other like grim death as we stumbled along. Angela lived in the block of flats opposite, where we hugged and went our separate ways.

Tony was waiting for me outside the flats.

'Bloody hell!' he shouted. 'Where've you been? Mum's been doing her nut with worry! We thought you was a goner! We thought that bomb had got you!'

'I'm fine,' I said. 'It came a bit close but . . .'

'Nell!'

Mum was standing at the top of the steps. Her face was white and her eyes were round and terri-fied. I'd never seen her looking so frightened. She came running down the stairs and she grabbed hold of me and wrapped her arms around me, holding me so tightly I could hardly breathe. 'Oh, Nell!' she cried. 'My Nell, I thought I'd lost you! Where were you? What have I told you about staying out after dark?'

'I'm sorry,' I cried, 'we was out playing and it got late and . . .'

'I thought I'd lost you!' Mum screamed again. She was crying and laughing, angry and happy, hugging me and shaking me all at the same time. 'I thought I'd lost you!'

It took her a while to calm down and then we went back up the stairs. Freddie was in his drawer and Olive was kneeling beside it, looking down at him, stroking his back with her little fingers. Her face was very solemn.

'I looked after him, Mum,' she said. 'I didn't take my eyes off him for a second, like you said.'

'You're a good girl, Olive,' Mum replied.

She sat down in her chair and put her head in her hands. I saw the misery in her slumped shoulders; I saw the pain in her eyes. I knew that I'd caused this pain, by staying out so late and giving her reason to think I'd been flattened by a bomb. I felt awful about it. And I knew then that it wasn't fair on Mum, us staying: she had enough on her plate without all this worry. The best thing we could do for her was to let ourselves be evacuated after all.

# CHAPTER 4

We said goodbye to Mum in the flat because Mrs Baxter was going to come and accompany us to the station. I knew it was going to be hard saying goodbye, but I didn't realise how hard it would be. Olive, who'd been swinging between excitement about being evacuated and dreading it, had finally understood what it meant. She'd been crying all morning and now her eyes and nose were red – she looked like a hopeless little creature. Tony had been quiet; he'd hardly said a thing since he got out of bed and now he was standing with his back to us, staring out the window, looking down onto the street. He hadn't said that he wasn't coming with us, but I still wasn't sure that he was going to get on the train. On the table were three paper parcels tied up with string, holding our clothes.

'Now I've made you some bread and drippin. Don't open it until lunchtime because I don't know how long the journey will take,' said Mum.

'Why won't they tell us where we're going?' I asked.

'I suppose it's all to do with secrecy. You know, "walls have ears" and all that.'

Olive climbed onto Mum's lap and put her arms around her neck. She pressed her face into Mum's shoulder and her little body shook with sobs. I had a terrible lump in my throat but I was trying hard to swallow it down and be strong for my brother and sister. I couldn't believe we were leaving Mum and the flats and everything we knew and loved.

'Come on,' Mum said to Olive, 'it's going to be fun.'

'I don't want fun,' Olive sobbed.

'You wait and see! In a couple of days you'll have made some new friends and you'll be climbing trees and running around, and you'll have forgotten all about how sad you're feeling today.'

'No, I won't!'

I was inclined to agree.

Mum said: 'Come on now, Olive.' She eased her off her lap and beckoned me to follow her into the bedroom. She put her finger to her lips because baby Freddie was fast asleep in his drawer on the floor. She went over to the dresser and took out a black box, then sat on the bed and patted the place beside her. I sat down and watched her open the box. Inside was a beautiful silver locket hung on a slender chain.

'I want you to have this, Nell,' she said, placing it in my hands.

'But it's yours,' I said.

'And for now it's yours. You can give it back to me when next we meet.'

I weighed the locket in my hand. It felt smooth and cold in my palm.

'Open it,' she said, putting her arm around my shoulder.

I undid the little clasp and inside was a picture of Mum and Dad.

'That was taken on our wedding day, Nell. Weren't we a handsome couple?'

I gazed at the photograph; my parents looked so young. Mum's hair was dark, not streaked with grey as it was now, and my dad didn't have a beard. They were staring into the camera like two frightened rabbits.

'We were terrified,' she said, smiling.

'I think you both look very beautiful,' I said.

'Turn around, Nell.'

I did as she said and she gently lifted my hair and secured the locket around my neck.

'When you are sad,' Mum said, 'you'll know that me and Dad are close to your heart. If ever you feel lonely, you can open the locket and see my face and you'll know that I am missing you as much as you are missing me.'

'I will, Mum,' I said, and the lump in my throat that I was trying so hard to swallow threatened to choke me and I had to let it out. I sobbed and sobbed as if my heart was breaking.

Mum held me against her and smoothed my hair. She smelt of home. We sat on the bed together until the sobbing wore itself out and then she let me go. She fished a rag out from up her sleeve and gave it to me, and I dabbed at my nose and my eyes.

'I know you'll be brave, my Nell,' said Mum. 'I'm depending on you to take care of your brother and sister. Be gentle with Olive, as I know you will, and make sure Tony doesn't get himself into too much trouble.'

'I promise, Mum.'

She smiled at me. 'I'm so proud of you,' she said.

I smiled weakly back.

'We're going to be fine,' she said, 'all of us. Right?'

I nodded miserably.

'We *are*,' she insisted. 'Come on now, Nell. Mrs Baxter will be here any minute.'

She went back into the kitchen. I knelt down by the drawer to say goodbye to Freddie, I smoothed his little head but he didn't stir, I wondered when I would see him again.

I put on my coat and helped Olive, who was still sobbing, into hers. Mum had written our names on bits of paper and pinned them to our coats. Tony still hadn't moved from the window. Mum walked across to him and folded him in her arms. He tried to pull away but she held him tightly to her. And then his arms went round her. There was a desperate look on his face as he clung to her. This was bloody awful.

'There now, my strong boy,' I heard her say. 'I need you to be brave and take care of your sisters. Can you do that for me?'

He nodded. Mum smoothed the hair away from his eyes and kissed his forehead.

Just then there was a tap on the door and Mrs Baxter walked into the room. She looked round at us all and smiled.

'All ready?' she said.

'I think so,' said Mum softly.

'Have you remembered their ration books?'

'Yes, they're in Nell's parcel, tucked into her clothes.'

'Because they wouldn't be very happy if the kids turned up without them.'

'I think I've remembered everything,' said Mum.

'Best go then,' said Mrs Baxter.

Mum took me and Olive into her arms and smiled at Tony, who I could see was trying to be brave and struggling not to cry. 'It won't be for long,' she said, 'and we'll soon be together again.'

'We'll be fine, Mum,' I said.

'I know you will, my love.'

As if on cue, Freddie started to cry. I was glad, because it gave Mum something to do.

'Let's be off then,' said Mrs Baxter, and we picked up our parcels and followed her out of the door, down the steps and into the fresh air. A soft rain was falling and London looked very grey and misty, as if the whole city was as sad as we were.

When we got down to the bottom of the steps I looked up at the flats. Mum was at the window where Tony had stood earlier, holding Freddie in her arms. Me and Olive waved and blew kisses but Tony didn't look back – he just strode away in front of us.

Just then I heard my name being called and saw Angela running towards me. We put our arms around each other and hugged.

'Take care of yourself,' she said, 'and come back to me safe and sound.'

She put her hand in her pocket and took out a little pink shell. 'I got that in Margate, Nell,' she said. 'I want you to bring it back to me when the war is over.'

'I will. And Angela? Promise me that you will keep yourself safe.'

'Don't worry, Nell. Haven't you heard? Only the good die young.'

It was hard to watch her walking away. This would have been so much easier if we could have left London together. I took one last look at the flats and followed Mrs Baxter and the others out onto the road.

Although we weren't part of the main evacuation, there still seemed to be hundreds of kids on the platform, yelling and running around, making a hell of a noise. Some of the younger kids were clinging to their mothers' skirts. Olive's hand tightened in mine.

'You'll be all right, love,' I said, looking down at her. 'Me and Tony will look after you.'

'I want me mum, Nell.'

'I know you do, but she'll soon be joining us, and little Freddie too.'

A plump woman in a bright red coat was trying to shout instructions to the crowd but no one could hear her over all the noise. All we could see was her mouth opening and closing like a drowning fish. A soldier in uniform handed her a loudspeaker and she tried again with renewed enthusiasm, her voice booming out across the station.

'Mothers, you must say goodbye to your children now. We will take care of them and find them good homes, where they will be safe. Children, I need you to line up in twos, holding the hand of the child next to you.'

This piece of news brought a renewed wave of sobbing and crying as mothers tried to prise their children away from them. I was glad that Mum had stayed at home.

Mrs Baxter knelt down in front of Olive. 'Now, be a good girl, Olive, and mind what Nell says.'

'I want me mum,' said Olive again.

'I know you do, love, but you'll see her soon.'

Mrs Baxter stood up then and put her arms around me. 'I'll miss you, ducks.'

'I'll miss you an all, Mrs Baxter,' I said.

She knew better than to put her arms round Tony so she just laid her hand on his shoulder. 'Take care of your sisters, Tony,' she said.

Tony nodded and we watched her walk away across the platform. Me and Olive waved until she was out of sight. She was our last tie to home and it was hard to see her go.

We were lucky enough to find a carriage with some empty seats. I sat Olive down next to the window. I'd been on a train before but to my little sister it was all new and her eyes were wide with a mixture of excitement and worry as she looked around her.

'Are you scared of the train, Olive?' I asked gently.

'I don't think so, Nell,' she said. 'I think it smells friendly and the seat is nice and squishy. Does it go very fast?'

'It goes slow to start with and then it picks up speed and then you can see the world rushing by. It's lovely,' I said.

I put my arm around her shoulder and together we looked out the window. Children were still being herded along the platform by the worried-looking woman, shouting instructions like: 'Keep together, children! And don't go near the edge! And hold tight to your bundles!'

'Yes, I think I like the train,' said Olive. 'But I wish Mummy and Freddie was with us.'

'I know you do, love, but you're being very brave.'

'It's not easy being brave, Nell.'

'That's why I'm so proud of you, Olive, and I know Mummy would be too.'

Tony put our parcels in the rack above our heads but didn't sit down. He was rubbing his forehead with the heel of his hand, looking anxious and on edge. I was still amazed that he had actually got on the train.

'Why don't you sit down?' I said.

He didn't answer me and instead wound down the window and looked out.

Whistles started to blow and the train hissed and shuddered as it got ready to move off. Suddenly Tony reached up to the rack, grabbed his parcel, opened the carriage door and jumped down onto the platform.

I hung out the window. 'Where are you going?' I yelled after his retreating back.

'Home,' he yelled back. 'Sorry, Nell.'

I watched him disappear into the crowd. I felt sick and alone as the full realisation that I was now solely responsible for Olive's safety hit me like a hammer.

The train started to move slowly out of the station. There was nothing I could do: Tony had gone and we were on our own. I sat back down and put my arm around Olive.

'Where's Tony gone, Nell?' she said.

'He's gone back home.'

'Why isn't he coming with us?'

I shrugged my shoulders. 'You know what Tone's like, Olive.'

She nodded and said very seriously: 'He's a bugger, Nell.'

'Fraid so, love, but don't worry, we'll manage.'

'*You* won't leave me, will you, Nell?'

I smiled down at my little sister. 'Never. I'll never leave you.'

The train started gathering speed and I stared out the grubby window as it raced past streets and houses and allotments. I was leaving behind everything I loved. My beloved Bermondsey was disappearing into a cloud of smoke.

# CHAPTER 5

The journey seemed endless. As the novelty of leaving London wore off, squabbles broke out between some of the boys and a few of the little ones started crying for their parents. I looked around the carriage; we were a rum lot, that was for sure. These were kids from the East End – most of them had never been on a train before, or moved beyond the streets and alleyways surrounding their homes. And for all their toughness, even the boys looked lost and bewildered. The reality of what was happening to them was beginning to sink in.

We shared our bread and dripping with two small boys who didn't seem to have any food. They thanked us with cheeky little grins. Whoever picked these two was going to have to give them a jolly good scrub down, because it looked as if their faces had never been within a mile of water. By the way they were scratching at their heads, they were going to need de-lousing an' all.

After we'd eaten, Olive fell asleep beside me. I stared out the window at the unfamiliar country-side. Little rivers ran between green fields, and cows and sheep dotted the hillside. It was a different world, a softer world. A world that I had known nothing about until now. My whole life had been spent around the tenements and streets of Bermondsey. I'd only ever seen cows and sheep in the butcher's window and they were dead. I felt a stirring of excitement in the pit of my stomach and just for a moment I found myself almost looking forward to what was coming next.

We had to change trains twice and both times groups of children were led away to their new homes. Eventually we reached our destination, and the train slowed and stopped as we pulled into the station. I rubbed at the steamed-up window with my cardigan sleeve to try and see where we were, but all the signs had been painted over.

Our carriage door opened and a woman stuck her head inside.

'Children,' she said. 'Get all your stuff together and gather on the platform. Chop, chop!'

I nudged Olive. 'Wake up, love,' I said. 'We have to get off the train now.'

Olive rubbed sleepily at her eyes. 'Are we there?' she said.

'I'm not sure,' I told her. 'All I know is that we've got to get off.'

Her eyes were filling with tears. 'I want to go home, Nell.'

'I know you do, love, but right now we have to do as we're told and they're telling us to get off the train. Okay?'

'Okay, Nell,' she said, yawning.

I took our parcels down from the rack and I helped Olive onto the platform.

She looked around her. 'Where are we?' she said.

'I haven't a clue. We could be in Timbuktu for all I know.'

'Is that another country?'

'I think so.'

The station was small, nothing like the stations in London, which were big and bustling and dark. There were wooden barrels full of daffodils bobbing about.

The woman who had opened our carriage door seemed to be in charge.

'I want you to hold hands and form an orderly line,' she shouted. 'We are walking to the village hall, where the good people of Glengaryth are waiting to meet you.' Then she added: 'It will help considerably if you behave yourselves and try to look presentable.'

I surveyed the motley crew of children standing on the platform, looking bewildered and travel-worn, and the word 'presentable' didn't exactly spring to mind.

'Everybody follow me,' she shouted.

I held Olive's hand tightly as we walked out of the station and down through the village street. It was all so different from anywhere I'd ever been before. Bermondsey was hard – everything about it was hard – but this place was soft. Even the air felt different, sort of fresh and clean. The street was made of cobbles and Olive kept stumbling on the uneven ground and grabbing onto my coat.

'Bloody hell,' she moaned. 'Why haven't they got a proper floor?'

'Cos it ain't Bermondsey,' I said.

The houses and tenements at home were grey and dirty from all the smoke coming out of the chimneys and the mist coming off the river, but these little houses were lovely pale colours, pink and blue and yellow. It was so perfect it hardly looked real at all.

We passed a butcher's shop and a grocer's; they stood in the doorways and waved to us as we went. Everyone seemed so friendly and nice.

Kids came out of the little houses and started running beside us, making faces and calling out words we didn't understand. The woman in charge shouted at them and tried to shoo them away but they were having none of it. Instead they strutted behind her, mimicking her walk. They stayed with us all the way to the village hall, where we were herded inside and the door firmly shut behind us.

The woman in charge of us looked harassed – she was puffing away and holding her side as if she'd just walked all the way from London. 'I need a cup of tea,' she gasped to no one in particular.

There was a long table running down the length of the hall that was laden with food and drinks. There were sandwiches and buns and little cakes with icing on the top, slices of spam and loaves of bread. I couldn't remember the last time I'd seen so much food. Most of the kids had hardly eaten all day and their eyes were nearly popping out of their heads as they gazed at the feast in front of them. Men and women, mostly women, were standing around the edge of the hall, looking at us, and there was a short round woman standing on a little stage at the far end of the hall behind a loudspeaker.

'Welcome, children,' she said, so softly that we could barely hear her.

A man from the back of the hall shouted, 'Speak up, Gwyneth.'

'Silly me,' she said, giggling.

The next time she spoke, her voice boomed out over the hall, making everyone jump, including herself.

'Not doing very well, am I?' she said, smiling down at everyone.

'You're doing a grand job, love,' said the man at the back of the hall, 'and your new perm looks lovely.'

She patted her hair. 'Thank you, Dai,' she said shyly.

'Now, I know you must be tired and hungry,' she continued, 'and a little frightened, so I won't keep you long.' She cleared her throat before going on. 'On behalf of the people of Glengaryth, I would like to welcome you to our little village. We feel privileged to open up our homes to you dear children, and I hope that you will be very happy with us for the duration of your stay.'

'Why is she talking so funny, Nell?' said Olive.

'I'm not sure.'

'Do you know what I think, Nell?'

'What?'

'I think we've landed in another country.'

'Can we eat now, missus?' came a lone voice from the floor.

That broke the ice and everyone laughed.

'Of course you can eat, my lovelies,' she said. 'Tuck in and enjoy the food that the good ladies of Glengaryth have made for you.'

Olive tugged at my coat. 'What, love?' I said.

'I like it here, Nell.'

I grinned at her. 'I like it an' all.'

Olive pointed to the plump lady on the stage. 'Do you think that lady will pick us?'

'We'll have to wait and see, won't we?'

'I suppose so.'

'Well, I think they all look nice, don't you?'

'Yes, Nell, I think they all look nice – but I do hope that lady picks us.'

The kids were swarming over the food as if they hadn't eaten in weeks. They were piling it on their plates and scuttling off in all directions to eat it. I had a feeling that by the end of the day, a lot of it was going to be coming back up again.

'You hungry, Olive?'

'Starvin.'

'Let's tuck in then, or there won't be anything left.'

I noticed that the women were staring at Olive.

Well, I supposed they would, because she was beautiful. A couple of them were talking to the plump lady and pointing our way, then I saw them shake their heads. I got the feeling that they wanted Olive but not me.

We put some food on a plate and went to sit on a bench against the wall.

'This is better than bread and scrape, Nell.'

I thought so too; maybe this adventure that I had been dreading wasn't going to be so bad after all.

Children were being chosen and led away, some of them looking reluctant to leave the food behind.

'Hello?'

I looked up, and a lady was smiling down at Olive.

'How old are you?' she said.

'Dunno,' said Olive, looking up at her.

'We're sisters,' I said quickly. 'We stay together.'

'How wonderful,' said the lady. 'Dylan,' she called across the room.

A tall man walked over to us. He was wearing a dark suit and a black hat and for some reason he had a white bandage around his neck – perhaps he had been injured in the war and come home for a rest. The beautiful lady looked up at him and then back down at us.

'They're sisters,' she said.

The man crouched down in front of us and grinned. 'And do they have names?' he said.

'Oh, Dylan, of course they have names,' said the

lady, smiling at him. 'And I'm sure they are beautiful names.'

'I'm Nell,' I said. 'And this is my sister Olive.'

'I knew you would have beautiful names,' she said.

'I have a feeling my wife has fallen in love with you two,' said the man. 'Am I right, Beth?'

She nodded.

'And I always trust my wife's feelings. So, would you like to come and stay with us?'

I looked at Olive and she nodded. All thoughts of the plump lady forgotten, she gazed up at the beautiful lady in front of her.

'Yes, please,' I said.

'Can we finish our food first, missus?' said Olive.

'Of course you can,' said the lady, laughing.

Once we'd finished eating the lovely food, we picked up our parcels and followed the mister and the beautiful lady outside.

We climbed into the back of a shiny black car and sat on big squashy seats. Olive had to kneel to look out the window. The car smelled of leather and cigarettes. I'd never been in a car before; it was lovely. I touched the seats, which were cool and smooth beneath my hand. I felt like a rich kid, not a skint one from the East End.

Tony would have loved this. He was a bit of a bugger but I suddenly missed him. I missed his bony knees and holey jumper and the fact that he didn't seem to give a damn what anyone thought of him. And the way he loved Mum with a fierceness that was sometimes hard to understand and which had got worse since Daddy went away to war. I stared out the window at the little houses and the people walking along the street, the women queuing outside the butcher's. There weren't any bombsites or damaged houses – maybe there wasn't a war on in this place. It was hard to believe that only this morning me and Olive had been saying goodbye to Mum in Rannly Court and now we were in a big posh car heading to our new home. It felt funny sitting behind this man and woman who we didn't really know, but it didn't feel uncomfortable or scary. The lady kept turning round to smile at us and ask if we were all right, and to point out things that she thought we might be interested in.

'That's the village school,' she said, 'and that's the shop and that's the post office. You'll be able to post your letters home from there.'

I glanced at Olive to see if the word 'home' had upset her but she hadn't even noticed, as far as I could tell.

At the end of the village we turned into a lane that ran alongside an old stone church. At the back of the church was a field.

'What's that?' Olive asked.

'What's what, dear?' said the lady.

'That thing with legs over there. That dirty thing. And that, and that . . . Blimey! There's bloody hundreds of 'em.'

'Those are sheep, dear.'

'Sheep?'

'Yes.'

'But sheep are supposed to be white, ain't they? They're supposed to be like little white clouds on legs!'

'In picture books they are. But in real life they're out in the muddy fields and they get dirty.'

Olive pulled a face.

'That don't look right to me,' she insisted. 'That don't look like what sheep are supposed to look like.'

'Maybe it's just our Welsh sheep that are so dirty,' suggested the man.

'Maybe,' said Olive. She frowned and pressed her nose up against the car window. 'They don't look like sheep to me,' she said again, with the utmost suspicion.

'I don't suppose there are many sheep in London, dear.'

'None at all,' I said.

'Well, there you are then.'

Olive didn't look convinced and continued to scowl at the dirty sheep.

A short way up the lane we drove through some large iron gates and onto a gravelled driveway. The car stopped. 'Here we are,' said the man.

We all got out and we stood by the car, looking at our new home. It was a beautiful old house. It was *huge*!

'Which bit do you live in?' said Olive, staring at the house in awe.

The lady smiled down at her. 'All of it, I suppose.'

'Just for two of you?'

'Olive,' I said, 'that's rude.'

'Sorry, Nell,' she said.

'Well, there's four of us now,' said the lady, and we all smiled at one another. 'This house is called Pont'yr' Hirian, which means "long house in the hollow" – isn't that pretty?'

'What's a hollow?' asked Olive.

'It's a kind of dip,' said the lady.

'What's a dip?'

'You know bloody well what a dip is, Olive,' I said.

'Do I?' she said.

'Yes, you do.'

Olive didn't look convinced.

'You know that slope outside the flats?'

'The one we all slide down on our arses when it snows?'

'Yes.'

'Well, that's a dip.'

'It used to be a private house but now it's a vicarage,' the lady explained, smiling down at Olive. 'My husband is a vicar. We don't actually own it.'

'You got a landlord, same as us?'

'Exactly.'

'We're as poor as church mice, really,' said the man.

Olive giggled. 'You're just like us then.'

'Exactly like you,' said the lady, taking Olive's

hand and walking towards the front door. It was painted green and in front of it was a prickly mat, and on the mat was the word *Welcome*. Next to the mat, lined up, were boots: big boots for the man and smaller boots for the lady. There was also a pot for walking sticks and umbrellas. All this was under a small wooden porch. Olive looked up at the lady and grinned. She gave a little skip and I knew she was imagining her shoes lined up next to the lady's shoes under the porch. Suddenly I felt very tired. Happy, but tired.

I hung back and looked up at the house. I had never seen a house this big in all my life. The tenement where we lived in Bermondsey was made of red brick – well, it was once red brick but now it was grey and grimy, and you could hardly tell that it had ever been red. Although this house was made of brick, the stone was of the palest yellow. It looked at if it had been washed by the sun. Green ivy covered the walls and roof and hung down over the many windows, which sparkled in the early evening light. The roof was tiled, and I watched as a tiny bird darted into a hole in the tiles with twigs in its beak. I knew that meant it was building a nest, and soon there'd be baby birds going in and out of the roof, and we'd be there to see them.

There were chimneys at either end of the long house, and a faint wisp of smoke was curling out of each. The house would be warm. I looked up to the upstairs windows, to the curtains that hung at their sides, to the flowers on the sills, and I wanted to be inside that lovely house, looking out.

I picked up my parcel and followed the others into the porch, through the green door, which now stood wide open, and into my new home.

# CHAPTER 6

I was woken the next morning by the sun streaming in through the little window. I lay there for a while, all warm and cosy, and thought about Tony. I hoped that he'd got home all right. I wondered what Mum said when he turned up at the door. I had a feeling that part of her would be pleased to have him back; she wouldn't be alone. Olive was still fast asleep. She lay on her tummy, which is the way she always slept, her small hand cradling her face. I looked around the room – it was even prettier than I remembered from the night before. We were at the top of the house under the eaves. The sloping walls were white and there was a dark wooden beam running the length of the ceiling. The big bed took up most of the space; it was covered in a soft quilt of the palest blue with yellow flowers all around the border. Back home we slept end to end in one tiny bed – we had never had a big bed like this, or a lovely soft quilt. We had scratchy brown blankets and, when it was very cold, Dad would put coats on top to keep us warm. At least now I didn't have to sleep with Olive's feet in my face. On the wall opposite the bed was a picture of the Last Supper, with Jesus and the Twelve Apostles sitting around a long table eating their dinner.

I carefully pulled back the covers, got out of bed and went across to the window. The wooden floor was warm under my feet. I pulled back the curtains and looked out over the garden. It was full of tall trees and green lawns and flowers, and beyond the garden I could see the church.

Olive stirred. I turned around, and she opened her eyes and smiled at me.

'Mornin, sleepyhead,' I said.

'I forgot where I was for a minute,' she said, sitting up. She got out of bed and padded across to me. She slipped her warm little hand in mine.

'Is that the mister's church, Nell?' she asked, staring out the window.

'I think so.'

'Imagine owning a church.'

'I shouldn't think he owns it – in fact I'm not sure that you *can* own a church.'

'Because it belongs to God?' said Olive.

I had to think about that one. I suppose God did own it, because Father Devlin in our church back home always referred to it as a House of God; but then again, if he owned it, when did he collect the rent?

'I'm not sure, Olive,' I said.

'I'll ask mister,' she said.

We splashed water on our faces from a bowl that

stood on a marble table against the wall, threw on our clothes and ran downstairs.

The kitchen was warm and it smelled nice, like flowers and trees. There was a yellow couch against the window and a long table running down the middle of the room. The fireplace was enormous. There were logs piled up against the bricks and a fire burned and crackled in the hearth.

The missus was stirring something in a pot over the stove and the mister was reading a paper. He looked up and smiled.

'Sleep well?' he asked.

He was still wearing the white bandage, which I now realised wasn't a bandage at all – it was what vicars wore, just like our priest, Father Devlin, at home. I smiled back. 'Yes, thank you,' I said.

'Porridge and eggs?' asked the missus, smiling at us.

'Proper eggs?' said Olive.

'As proper as they come,' she replied. 'We have chickens out the back that very kindly give us lovely brown eggs every day. You can feed them later, if you like.'

We sat down at the long wooden table. The sun was warm on my back and the room felt so cosy I could feel myself relaxing. This was a good place; we would be safe here. The missus put two bowls of porridge in front of us. I took a mouthful; it was sweet and creamy.

'Mister?' said Olive, in between mouthfuls.

'Yes, dear?'

'Do you own the church?'

He laughed. 'I'm afraid we don't own anything, Olive. We work for God and he doesn't pay very well.'

'I think God pays Father Devlin loads of dosh, cos he's got a cook and a cleaner and a big shiny car, and he drinks beer down the Pig and Whistle.'

'And who is Father Devlin?' asked the mister.

'He's our priest back home,' I said.

'So you're a Catholic, Nell?'

'Sort of lapsed,' I said, grinning. 'Our church got bombed and the only other Catholic church is too far for us to walk to.'

'But you have faith?' said the missus.

'What's faith, Nell?' asked Olive.

'The missus wants to know if we believe in God.'

'Well, we says our prayers, don't we, Nell?'

'Course we do.'

'And we lights candles.'

I smiled and nodded.

'Then you have faith,' said the missus, smiling sweetly.

'Well, *we're* not Catholics,' said the mister, 'we're Methodists. There's a lot of Methodist chapels in Wales, but you would be made very welcome in our little church, if you would like to come.'

'We can't,' I said. 'It's a mortal sin to step foot inside a Proddy church.'

'We'd burn in the Fires of Hell for all eternity,' said Olive, very seriously.

'Golly,' said the missus. 'That sounds painful.'

'Bloody agonising,' said Olive.

'Olive!'

'Well, it is.'

'I know it is, but you don't have to swear.'

'Sorry.'

'Do you know what I think, girls? I think God would be happy wherever you choose to worship him and I'm sure he wouldn't mind if you prayed in our little church. We could sneak you in when the devil isn't looking. How about that?'

I grinned. 'Okay.'

'Is your father away at war, Nell?' asked the missus.

'He's in the Navy and we all miss him somethin rotten.'

'I'm sure you do.'

'Isn't there a war on here?' said Olive.

I'd been wondering the same thing myself. Back in London the air-raid sirens went off all the time but I hadn't heard one since we got here and none of the houses in the village seemed to have been bombed.

'Luckily, the Germans aren't very interested in us, Olive: it's Cardiff and Swansea that are getting the worst of it. Sometimes at night the sky glows red over Cardiff and we pray for them.'

'It's the same in London,' said Olive. 'Bloody bombs every five minutes.'

'Olive!' I said, glaring at her.

'Well, it is,' she insisted.

'I know it is, but you don't have to keep swearing. The mister is a vicar, just like Father Devlin. You wouldn't swear in front of him, would you?'

'No, cos he'd give me a bleedin great penance for me trouble.'

If Olive kept this up we could well find ourselves back in the village hall, but the missus didn't seem to mind. 'Leave her,' she said. 'Coming out of that sweet little mouth it somehow doesn't sound like an oath.'

'What's an oath, Nell?'

'It's a bloody swear word, Olive, and you've got porridge on yer chin.'

'You swore,' she said, grinning at me. 'You shouldn't swear in front of a vicar, Nell.'

With that we all burst out laughing.

'You know, Olive,' said the mister. 'You can call me by my name if you like. It's Dylan.'

We had never called grown-ups by their first name. I'd known Mrs Baxter all my life but I didn't know her name. My mum called her Mrs Baxter and her husband called her missus and Mrs Baxter called my mum Mrs Patterson.

He could see that we were worried. 'How about Uncle, then? Would that suit?'

The lady took our bowls over to the sink and replaced them with a lovely brown egg each, and thick slices of bread covered in creamy yellow butter. 'And you can call me Auntie Beth,' she said, smiling.

'Okay,' said Olive, looking pleased with herself.

'I shall call you Uncle Mister and Auntie Missus.'

'Perfect,' said the mister, grinning. 'Now tuck into that lovely egg and then you can go and thank our feathered friends for supplying you with such a nice breakfast.'

# CHAPTER 7

We were leaning on the gate at the bottom of the garden, looking out over the hills. There was so much space here – the patchwork of green fields seemed to go on forever, separated by old stone walls that were covered in moss and ivy. Beyond the fields I could see tall trees, loads of them, with hundreds of birds circling above, dipping and diving. I felt like running, I felt like running with my arms spread wide. I wanted to feel the wind in my hair. I wanted to be part of this beautiful place. My heart was bursting with joy. I put my hand inside my jumper and closed it around the locket.

I looked back at the house. It was so beautiful, nestling between the tall trees, that I felt like crying. It suited its name, 'long house in the hollow'. Mum deserved to be here, she deserved to be in a place like this, to breathe in this air that smelled of grass and trees and flowers and a sky that went on forever, instead of the smog and dirt of London. I hadn't thought that I would ever want to be anywhere but Bermondsey, yet standing here in this lovely place I felt as if I never wanted to leave.

'Mum would love it here, Olive.'

'Would Tony love it too?'

I nodded. 'Yeah, I think he would.'

A horse wandered up to the fence and leaned its head on the gate. I stroked its silky mane and it shook its head, then nuzzled its nose into my hand. There were flies buzzing around it and it was flicking them away with its tail.

'He likes you, Nell.'

'*You* stroke him,' I said. 'He won't bite.'

'That's what you said about the tallyman's horse and he nearly bit me bleedin hand off.'

'That's cos you stroked him while he was havin his grub; horses don't like to be disturbed when they're eating. Anyway, he never bit yer hand off, he just gave you a little warning.'

'Well, it felt like he was gonna bite me bleedin hand off.'

Olive climbed up on the gate and leaned over so that she could reach the horse.

'Hello, horse,' she said, stroking his ears. 'We live here now, with Auntie Missus and Uncle Mister. We'll come and see you every day. Won't we, Nell?'

'If you like.'

'I *would* like.'

'Then we'll come.'

'We could feed him. What do horses eat?'

'Grass, I suppose.'

'Well, there's plenty of that here.'

'And maybe apples,' I suggested.

'Let's see if we can find some apples, Nell.'

Olive jumped down from the gate and I followed her across the garden. At the side of the house there were rows and rows of trees, with little pathways running in between them. The trees were heavy with pinky white blossom clinging to the branches and drifting through the air, lying like a carpet on the ground, but there wasn't an apple in sight.

'Where's the bloody apples?' said Olive.

'I dunno.'

'Let's ask Auntie Missus.'

We ran into the kitchen.

'Have you said hello to the chickens yet?' asked Auntie Beth, wiping her hands on a cloth.

'Not yet,' I said. 'But we met a horse.'

'That will be Toby.'

'So it's a "he" then?' said Olive.

'It is.'

'We wanted to feed him some apples but there ain't none on the trees. Where have they all gone?'

'It's the wrong season for apples, Olive. I'm afraid we don't get apples in the spring.'

'Oh.'

'You will have to wait for autumn; so will Toby.'

'He'll have to make do with grass then, I suppose,' said Olive, looking disappointed.

Auntie Beth went into the larder and came out holding a carrot. 'Toby likes carrots,' she said, smiling. 'Will that do?'

Olive took the carrot. 'Ta, Auntie Missus,' she said, running back outside.

'I'll try and get her to call you Auntie Beth,' I said.

'I don't mind,' she said, smiling. 'I think that Auntie Missus is very sweet and very Olive.'

I started to walk towards the back door then turned round. 'We like it here, me and Olive, we like it. Thanks for choosing us.'

'We haven't been blessed with children of our own, Nell, so having you and Olive here is a blessing.'

'Didn't God give you any?'

'I'm afraid not.' She gave a sad little smile. 'But he sent you to us, didn't he?'

'And he sent us to you,' I said, grinning.

Auntie Beth walked across to me, smoothed my hair and tucked it behind my ear. 'Aren't we the lucky ones?' she said, smiling down at me.

I put my arms around her waist. She didn't smell of home but she *did* smell of love.

'When you've finished playing outside you must write to your mum to let her know that you are safe and well.'

'And happy,' I said.

I walked to the end of the garden, where Olive was standing on the gate, looking over the field.

'Where the bleedin hell's he gone then?'

'Call him,' I said.

'Toby,' shouted Olive. 'Toby, I've got a carrot

for you. I tried to get you an apple but it's the wrong bloody season.'

'Olive?'

'Mmm?'

'Do you think you could swap the bloodies and bleedins for somethin else?'

'Like what?'

'Do you have to swear at all? Can't you just say what you want to say without swearin?'

'But *you* swear and Tony swears and the tallyman swears and the coal man swears and—'

'I know, but that's in Bermondsey – everyone swears in Bermondsey. I just don't think it's right to swear here.'

'I'll try not to.'

'Good girl.'

'Can I eat the carrot then?'

I was gazing out across the fields. I couldn't get over how green they were.

'Nell!'

'What?'

'Can I eat the bloody carrot or not?'

So much for no swearing. 'If you like,' I said.

We wandered back to the orchard and Olive sat down on the grass and leaned against a tree. I lay down beside her and gazed up through the branches at the blue sky. Then I closed my eyes and let the warm breeze play across my face. I felt so happy here and that made me feel guilty, because Mum and Tony and Freddie were still in London and London was dangerous. I hoped they would come soon.

'Has the mister and missus got kids of their own, Nell?'

I opened my eyes and sat up. 'God never sent them any.'

'Even though they work for him?'

'That's what I thought; don't seem very fair, does it?'

'God's like that sometimes though, isn't he?' said Olive, biting into the carrot. 'I mean, he must have known that Mr Baxter needed two legs and not one.'

'Father Devlin says that God works in mysterious ways,' I said.

'Maybe there weren't enough one-legged men in Bermondsey and he had to make up the numbers. Do you think that's why he done it, Nell?'

'You don't half ask some funny questions, Olive.'

'It's me age,' she said, taking another bite of the carrot.

'Shouldn't you wash that carrot before you eat it? Mum always washes em first.'

'It ain't gonna kill me, Nell,' she said.

'No, I don't suppose it will,' I replied, grinning.

Olive took another bite of the carrot. 'How old am I, Nell?'

'Yer five.'

'Why?'

'What do you mean, why?'

'Why am I five?'

Sometimes it was hard to keep up with Olive and all her odd questions. 'Cos you was born five years ago,' I said. 'You've been on this earth for five years.'

She seemed satisfied with this answer and went back to eating her carrot.

I lay back down and closed my eyes again. I loved the feel of the sun on my face. It must have been sunny in Bermondsey, we must have had days like this, but I couldn't remember any. I could remember the heat all right, and the dust and the smell, but this was different, this was lovely.

'Nell?'

'What now?' I said irritably.

'How old are you?'

I shook my head but I smiled at my sister; it was hard to be cross with her. 'I'm nearly fourteen,' I said.

'That's pretty old, Nell. You'll have to get married soon.'

I sat up again and pulled her close to me. 'Do you know how much I love you, Olive Patterson?'

'To the moon and back?'

I nodded. 'To the moon and back.'

'I love you too, Nell.'

'Good,' I said, kissing the top of her head. 'Because I would feel very sad if you didn't.'

'You don't need to feel sad, Nell, because I'll never stop loving you.'

'Come on, let's go indoors and write to Mum – she'll be wanting to hear from us.'

I held Olive's hand as we walked back to the house.

We were sitting at the kitchen table writing a letter to Mum to let her know where we were.

*Dear Mum,* I began.

*I am writing to let you know that me and Olive are well and happy. We are staying in a vicarage with a vicar and his wife and they are very nice. Their names are Mr and Mrs Morgan but we call them Auntie and Uncle.*

'Tell her about the horse, Nell,' said Olive, nudging my elbow.

*Olive wants me to tell you that we met a horse called Toby today.*

'Tell her I stroked him.'

*She says to tell you that she stroked him.*

*I hope that you and Freddie and Tony are okay and I hope that you can join us soon because it's lovely here.*

Olive nudged me again. 'Tell her about the eggs we had for breakfast, Nell.'

'For Gawd's sake, Olive, why don't you write your own letter?'

'Sorry, Nell.'

'I'll send her yer love?'

'Yes, but don't forget the chickens.'

'Olive!'

I finished the letter with:

*We both love you all and miss you. Please come soon.*

*Love Nell and Olive xxx*

Then I felt bad that I'd snapped at Olive and added:

*Mr and Mrs Morgan keeps chickens and me and Olive had lovely fresh brown eggs for our breakfast xxx*

'I told Mum about the chickens and the eggs, Olive.'

'Good, I think she'd like to know that, Nell. Best not to tell her about the Proddy church, though.'

'I didn't.'

'Good, cos we don't want her worrying about us burnin in the Fires of Hell for all eternity.'

I raised my eyes to the ceiling and noticed Auntie Beth grinning at us.

# CHAPTER 8

Me and Olive would be going to the same school. In London we went to different ones because of our ages but this was a tiny place and there was only one school in the village. I didn't mind too much because it meant I could keep an eye on my little sister. I would be turning fourteen in a few weeks so I could have left school but Auntie Beth thought it would be better to join Olive and maybe make some friends, and I was happy with that – I wanted to find a friend.

The school was only a short walk from the vicarage but on our first morning Auntie Beth wanted to take us there.

Olive insisted on saying goodbye to the chickens. She'd given all the chickens names; Ethel was her favourite one. 'I think Ethel looks like Mrs Baxter,' she said.

I stared at the chicken but I couldn't for the life of me see any resemblance to Mrs Baxter.

Next, she ran down to the bottom of the garden to say goodbye to Toby the horse. 'I'll be back later, Toby,' she said, stroking his silky nose, 'and

I'll feed you a nice carrot if I can get hold of one. Okay?'

It was a beautiful spring day as we started our walk down the lane that ran from the vicarage to the centre of the village.

Olive was holding Auntie Beth's hand and chatting nineteen to the dozen. I was walking a little behind and was silent because there was so much to look at and I felt as if my eyes couldn't take it all in.

The main thing was the colour: the sky was blue and the fields were green and the grass on the banks either side of the lane was green, but a different green, a bright green so juicy it made my mouth water. And amongst the green were dots of colour – white, yellow, pink and blue – and these were wildflowers. You didn't get wildflowers in Bermondsey. Nettles, sometimes, and the odd straggly weed growing out of a gutter, but they weren't bright green; more of a grey colour. My dad took me to the pictures to see *The Wizard of Oz* for my eleventh birthday and now I felt like I was Dorothy, moving from a world of black and white into one of colour. It was amazing.

Apart from the blue sky and the white clouds and the green grass and the wildflowers, there was the pale yellowy-pink of the blossom, great armfuls of it covering the branches of the cherry tree at the side of the lane – so pretty, prettier than anything I'd ever seen before in my life. Amongst the branches of the trees were birds: a blackbird with glossy blue feathers and little birds that Auntie Beth said were called 'tits' – that made Olive giggle. They had yellow tummies and blue caps on their heads. And there were butterflies, white butterflies like pieces of paper caught in the air, and bees and dragonflies with shiny green bodies.

Sheep were grazing in the fields beneath the branches of huge old trees, heavy in leaf, and the leaves caught the sunshine and moved it about so it was as if the trees were playing in the golden light. The mother sheep were big, covered in browny-white fleece that looked like it needed a good wash, but the lambs were either perfectly white or perfectly black. They had long, bouncy legs and little black noses and they jumped and played. Auntie Beth picked Olive up so she could look over the fence and watch them. Olive shrieked with laughter at their antics. I could tell from the brightness of her eyes that she, like me, couldn't believe all the things she was seeing.

There was always a lot of noise in London – people yelled a lot and laughed a lot, and the boats on the River Thames hooted their horns and the big cranes creaked as they swung over the river. The dockers swore a lot and whistled and groaned when they heaved the sacks of sugar onto their broad backs. Women shouted at their kids and babies in prams yelled for their mums. People in London yelled a lot.

At first I thought that the countryside was silent

but it wasn't. You could hear the birds twittering in the bushes and the trees swishing as the breeze caught their branches. You could hear the tractors going backwards and forwards across the fields and furry rabbits dashing in and out of the hedgerows. This was the sound of growing things and new life and I loved it.

As if all this wasn't wondrous enough, I could see the lane winding down ahead of us, two strips of brown where the car wheels went, with a green strip in the middle. It led down into the village beside the church where Uncle worked and beyond it was a cluster of pretty little houses. Washing was hung on the clotheslines, blowing in the breeze – flowery dresses billowing out and shirts hanging by their tails, and trousers and socks and underthings – over gardens full of plants that were just coming into flower; jewelled colours, creepers climbing the walls.

There was even a duck pond. A duck pond, bright blue, same colour as the sky – only there were pink lilies floating on it, sitting on green lily pads. I thought I should ask Auntie Beth if I could borrow some crayons and draw a picture when I got home from school, a picture that I could send to Mum and Tony.

'Are you all right, Nell?' asked Auntie Beth, turning round. 'You're very quiet.'

I nodded, too full of emotion to speak.

'What are you thinking?'

'That it's perfect. It's more perfect than anything

71

I've ever seen, Auntie. Better than anything I've seen even in a book.'

She smiled. 'It's nice on a day like this, not so pretty when it's raining.'

'I wouldn't care if it was raining,' I said. 'I'd love it this much just the same.'

I gave a little skip to catch up with Auntie Beth and she hitched Olive a bit higher on her hip.

'Look at that sheep, Auntie Missus!' cried Olive. 'Look at it! It's doing a bleedin poo!'

My beautiful little sister was a lost cause.

The school was tiny, a low stone building with a big brown door in the middle.

The playground was filled with children of all ages. The girls were skipping with a long rope and chanting a song I didn't know, in a language I had never heard before. The boys were kicking footballs to each other and play-fighting, tumbling on the ground, all bare legs and short trousers.

I felt Olive's hand slip into mine.

'Isn't it lovely?' I said.

Olive didn't look too sure. 'Is it?' she said, in a quiet little voice.

'You'll make new friends, won't that be nice?'

'Will it?'

'Of course it will, and when we write to Mum and Tony, we can tell them all about it.'

Olive's eyes were filling with tears. 'I miss Mum,' she said.

'I know you do, but you have to be a brave girl

and make her proud. She will be here soon and so will Freddie and Tony, and then you can show them around.'

'Okay, Nell,' she said.

I looked at the small building and all the children who were strangers to me. Then I closed my hand around the pink shell in my pocket and wished that Angela was here because I was actually feeling just as nervous as Olive.

A lady noticed us and walked across the playground. 'Hello, Beth,' she said. 'I heard that you had taken in two evacuees.'

Auntie smiled at her. 'This is Nell,' she said. 'And this is her little sister, Olive.'

'Welcome to our school,' said the lady, smiling at us. 'I'm sure you will be very happy here.'

'I dunno about that,' said Olive, looking anxious.

'She's only five,' I said. 'And she's a bit nervous.'

'There's nothing to be worried about here, Olive,' said the lady. Then she called across the playground. 'Aggie.'

A little girl, who looked the same age as Olive, ran over to us.

'Aggie, this is Olive. She's new and I think she would like a friend to show her around. Would you like to do that?'

The girl nodded and smiled at Olive. 'Wanna play hopscotch?'

Olive looked up at me. 'Would you like to go with Aggie?' I said.

'Okay.'

The two tiny girls held hands and ran across the playground.

'She'll be fine,' said the lady, smiling. 'My name is Mrs Rogers. Welcome to our school, Nell.'

'I'll be here when you come out, Nell,' said Auntie.

She kissed my cheek and I watched as she walked away. At the gate she turned around and waved. I had a warm feeling inside. Me and Olive couldn't have come to a better place; we would be loved and cared for. Bermondsey seemed like another life, far away from this little village school and the rolling hills beyond.

I looked across the playground and there was Olive playing hopscotch with Aggie. We were going to be all right.

# CHAPTER 9

As the weeks turned into months, the little village of Glengaryth became like a second home to us. We both benefited from the good food and fresh air. Olive's cheeks grew rosy and I wasn't as skinny as I used to be.

Bermondsey became a distant memory. Of course we missed Mum and Tony and the baby and I missed my good friend, Angela, but without the constant threat of air raids and the fear of a bomb dropping on our heads we were able to relax and run free in the fields and lanes. Sometimes in the evenings we all stood in the garden and watched the red sky over Cardiff, and were reminded that there was still a war on.

Olive and Aggie became great friends and played together every day after school, either at the vicarage or in the sweetshop, where Aggie was billeted.

Olive said that Aggie came from a place called Coventry that seemed to have been bombed almost as much as London.

'Aggie wants to live here forever,' announced Olive one day. 'And I don't blame her. Imagine livin in a sweetshop.'

'You'd end up with no teeth, Olive,' I said.

'Yeah, but I'd get more, wouldn't I?'

'Oh, Olive!' I said, grinning at her.

'I would, though.'

'I suppose you would, but you'd look a bit of a sight while you were waiting for em.'

'She gets sweets every Friday and she shares them with me. I love Aggie, Nell.'

'She's a sweet girl,' I said.

'That's cos she lives in a sweetshop.'

'Clever dick!' I said, grinning.

There was no one of my age at the school so I envied Olive her little friend. I had missed having someone to talk to and share things with. That was until the morning I walked into the classroom and saw a tall slim girl standing at the front of the class, grinning like a Cheshire cat. Her hair was dark, almost black, and she wore it in two shiny plaits that hung down either side of her head. She also wore little round glasses that she kept pushing up her nose. I immediately liked the look of her and hoped that we could perhaps be friends.

'This is Lottie Lovejoy,' said Mrs Rogers, our teacher. 'She is an evacuee from Brighton, which is by the seaside.'

I'd heard of Brighton – it wasn't very far from London. I'd never been there but I knew that posh people went there for their holidays. Our tallyman and his missus went there every year.

'On *our* money,' my mum had said.

It was hard to tell what age Lottie was but she looked about the same age as me. I grinned at her across the classroom.

'Welcome to our little school, Lottie,' said Mrs Rogers. 'Why don't you sit next to Nell?' She pointed to the seat beside me. Lottie walked towards me and sat down. She looked at me and grinned. I grinned back at her.

At playtime we sat on the wall surrounding the playground and got to know each other.

'What a dump!' said Lottie, looking around. 'I can't understand what half of them are saying.'

'It's not a dump,' I said, smiling at her. 'You have in fact landed in paradise.'

'Says you.'

'Trust me, you're going to love it here.'

'Well, at least I can understand what *you're* saying and that's a plus.'

'That's cos I'm from London, so I'd be a bit worried if you didn't.'

'I've been to London – my father was in a play up there and my mother and I went to watch him.'

'Your dad's an actor?' I asked, impressed by this piece of news.

She nodded. 'That's why I'm called Lottie, after a music hall star called Lottie Cherry.'

'Funny sort of name.'

'It wasn't her real name, it was her stage name.'

I didn't know anything about that sort of stuff. I thought that when you were given a name you were stuck with it, even if you didn't like it. I had no idea that people got to change their names.

'She also ran the Alhambra theatre in Brighton, so that was the connection,' continued Lottie.

'It's a really pretty name,' I said.

'So's Nell.'

'Thanks.'

'You're welcome.'

'Who are you staying with?' I said.

'Some old biddy called Eliza Strut. She's a perfectly frightful woman. Spends all day Sunday in church and I'm left to starve. She doesn't cook on a Sunday, says it's a sin against God. Personally, I think it's a sin against me, I'm the one that's bloody starving!'

'Sounds rotten. I'll tell you what, I'll ask Auntie Beth if you can have your Sunday dinner with us at the vicarage. She's lovely – I just know she'll say yes.'

'Really?'

'I'll ask her.'

'Thanks, Nell, you're a pal.'

'You're lucky this Eliza Strut doesn't make you go to church with her.'

'She did try – she said she had a duty to look after my soul as well as my body. I was tempted to tell her that she wasn't doing much of a job with my body and I wasn't about to let her get her hands on my soul. Instead, I told her I was an agnostic.'

'What's that?'

'It means I haven't made my mind up yet.'

'About what?'

'About anything really and religion in particular.'

'And what did she say to that?'

'If I remember rightly, I believe she very nearly choked on a decidedly unappetising excuse for a sausage.'

I'd never met anyone like this girl in my whole life. It was as if she'd landed from another planet. Imagine deciding to be an agnostic. My mum and dad would have thought I was losing my marbles. She talked different to me and Olive and the people we knew back home. I suppose we would have called her posh, but I thought she spoke lovely. I watched her mouth open and close and I was mesmerised by the stuff that came out of it.

'My father says that I am far too young to decide which faith I want to follow,' she continued. 'He said that wisdom and time would decide for me and if I decided that I didn't believe in any of it, then that was my decision.'

'Blimey!'

'I mean, it doesn't make much sense to me to pour water over a baby's poor little head and decide for them what they are going to believe. How can a baby know what it's going to believe in? What faith are you, Nell?'

'Catholic.'

'And do you absolutely believe in the teachings of the Catholic Church?'

79

I stared at her – no one had ever asked me that before.

'There, you see,' she said, rather smugly. 'You don't know, do you?'

'I've never given it much thought,' I said.

'Well, you can now.'

I sat on the wall swinging my legs and thought about our church in Bermondsey before it got bombed: the candles and the smell of incense and the lovely statue of the Virgin Mary and the baby Jesus tucked up in the manger at Christmas. It's what I knew and it's what my mum and dad believed, so that made me feel kind of warm and cosy about it.

'I've made up my mind, Lottie.'

'Crikey, that was quick,' she said.

'I like being a Catholic.'

'Well, at least I made you think about it.'

'Yes, you did, Lottie Lovejoy, and I shall be eternally grateful to you for that.'

At which point we burst out laughing.

'Tell me if I go on a bit, Nell. My father says I do – he says that's why I'll probably end up on the stage.'

'Don't worry, I'll tell you. I've got a tongue in my head too, you know.'

'That's why we're going to be the best of friends, Nell,' said Lottie, linking her arm through mine.

I told Auntie Beth about Lottie and how she was an agnostic and lived with Eliza Strut, who was a perfectly frightful woman, and she got no dinner on a Sunday because Eliza Strut was in church all day.

'So I was wondering if Lottie could come here for her Sunday dinner, Auntie Beth.'

'Of course she can, Nell, and I'm so pleased you have a friend.'

'Me too,' I said. 'She's a bit odd though, but, you know, nice odd.'

'We happen to like odd around here,' said Auntie Beth, smiling.

'You're gonna love Lottie Lovejoy then,' I said, grinning back.

We didn't know the kids from the village very well because we evacuees were in different classes.

'This is a Welsh-speaking school,' explained Mrs Rogers. 'So we decided that it was best to put you in separate classes, otherwise you would find the lessons difficult to understand.'

I thought that made a lot of sense and so did Lottie.

'School is boring enough,' she said. 'Without having to cope with a different language as well.'

'Don't you like school then?'

'Only ever went for one week.'

'One week!'

'Yes, and it was a bloody disaster.'

'Why, what happened?'

'They called my parents in and complained that they couldn't teach me because I refused to stay in my seat and wandered round the classroom all day.'

'What did your mum and dad say?'

'They told me to collect my coat from the cloak-room and then we left and never went back.'

'Blimey, didn't you miss being with kids your own age?'

'I find that most kids of my age are totally immature.'

'I'm not.'

'No, I can see that, and that is why we'll be friends.'

'How do you learn things then, if you don't go to school?'

'Well, my parents teach me and I read a lot.'

'So your parents don't mind you not going to school then?'

'No, they are all for free expression.'

'What the hell's that?' I said.

'Well, it means you learn what you are inter-ested in and not what someone *decides* you're interested in.'

'Isn't it the law though, to go to school?'

'Some old bloke comes round every now and again to make sure I'm not falling behind other kids of my age. He comes on a bike and he sniffs a lot and smells fishy. My mother opens all the windows once he's gone.'

'And are you?'

'Am I what?'

'Falling behind?'

'No, I'm streets ahead of them. I'm probably streets ahead of him as well; he never stays long. He just sort of mumbles and scratches his head and all this white stuff comes out of his hair.' Lottie shivered. 'Gross little man! Then he says, "Keep up the good work," picks up his grubby old briefcase and shuffles off till the next time.'

I'd never met anyone who didn't go to school and I had a sneaky feeling you had to be rich to get away with it.

'You don't have to sit in a stuffy classroom all day to find out what you want to know,' Lottie went on. 'There are libraries full of books and they're free. I choose what I want to learn about, then I go down to the beach and sit on the pebbles and listen to the sea and breathe in good clean air, not farty air from a room full of smelly boys.'

I grinned at this funny, quirky girl. 'You're a right card, Lottie Lovejoy.'

'What's a card?'

'It means you're perfect.'

'I do my best,' said Lottie, grinning.

Although I couldn't understand the Welsh language I loved the way it sounded, like a song or a lovely melody, soft and sort of sing-songy. Is sing-songy a word? Anyway, that's how it sounded to me.

'It's purported to be the oldest language in Britain,' said Lottie.

'What does pur . . . pur . . .?'

'Purported?'

'Yes.'

'It means they say it is, or they claim it is.'

'Oh, right.'

'It's a Celtic language, like Irish and Scottish.'

'Blimey, you learned a lot of stuff sittin on them there pebbles!'

'My point exactly.'

I couldn't get enough of my new friend; I wanted to know everything about her. 'Tell me about your home, Lottie,' I said.

She tossed one of her shiny plaits over her shoulder and said, 'Well, I think it's perfect but of course that's only my opinion. I live in a white house on the seafront in Brighton. It has big bay windows and when you walk into a room you feel as if you are part of the sea, like you're on a yacht, surrounded by water. And every day it's different, depending on the weather and the seasons. Sometimes the sea will be a greeny-blue and sometimes grey. Some days it can be angry, splashing over the promenade, and other days it's as calm as a mill pond with little waves lapping at the shore. My favourite part is in the early evening at low tide when the sand is wet and shiny. I can't tell you how beautiful that is, Nell. It looks like wet silk, with little rivers of silver water trickling back to the sea.'

I was hanging onto every word that was coming out of Lottie's mouth – she made me feel as if I was there.

'I told you to shut me up if I went on too much.'

'I don't want you to shut up, because it sounds so lovely. I've never seen the sea and you just made it come to life for me.'

'God, Nell, how bloody awful!'

'I live in Bermondsey, we don't have the seaside, just the river.'

'Close your eyes, Nell.'

'Why?'

'Just close them.'

I closed my eyes and waited for Lottie to speak.

'When all this is over,' she said softly, 'you shall come and stay with me in Brighton and we'll sit on the pebbles with our backs to the old stone wall and we'll listen to the sea rolling into the shore. We'll eat fish and chips out of the paper and then we'll tuck our knickers in our skirts and paddle into the water up to our knees. I'll show you the sea, Nell.'

I sighed and opened my eyes. 'That sounds like heaven,' I said.

Just then the bell went. 'Back to farty land,' said Lottie.

'Race you,' I said.

# CHAPTER 10

I thought that living in the countryside would be boring but it wasn't, not one bit. Every Saturday night there was a dance in the church hall. Uncle Dylan played all sorts of records and me and Lottie danced away to the music and so did Auntie Beth and Uncle Dylan. The couple from the sweetshop came as well, and Olive and Aggie just ran around the hall with the younger kids from the village.

Once a month we got to see a film on an old projector that kept breaking down, but we didn't mind. We watched *The Thirty-Nine Steps* and *The Good Companions* and we giggled at George Formby and Laurel and Hardy. It was packed the night *How Green Was My Valley* was on, because it was set in Wales and everyone in the village wanted to see it. There weren't enough seats, so Uncle Dylan put the film on for two nights, and me and Lottie went twice. We wept both nights when little Hugh's father died in a disaster down the pit. There was plenty of sniffing going on so I guess it affected a lot of people – even some of the men had glassy eyes. The boys liked the Westerns best and they screamed and booed the baddies as they chased Hopalong Cassidy and his faithful horse Topper across the screen. Afterwards they ran around outside shooting each other and pretending to fall down dead.

'Infantile,' pronounced Lottie, raising her eyes to the heavens.

Me and Lottie loved those evenings, sitting in the dark in the little hall, sharing Aggie's sweets. It was even better on the grey days, when the rain hammered down on the roof and we were all warm and cosy inside.

Every Sunday morning, we walked down the lane to the chapel. I don't think God minded much that there were a couple of lapsed Catholics and an agnostic in the congregation. It was a very simple place, unlike the Catholic church in Bermondsey, which was full of ornate statues and gold pillars. The only thing I missed was the statue of the blessed Virgin Mary. Uncle Dylan didn't wear a fancy costume or preach hell and damnation from the pulpit; he preached love and forgiveness. He not only prayed for our boys who were fighting in the war, he also prayed for the enemy, who he said were just young lads like our own. They were someone's son, someone's brother, someone's beloved grandchild. They were loved and if they lost their lives fighting for their country they would be mourned, in exactly the same way that our lads would be mourned. He said they deserved our prayers.

Lottie and I joined the church choir and we sang hymns in Welsh. It didn't bother me that I didn't have a clue what we were singing about because the Catholic Mass was in Latin and I didn't have a clue what that was about either.

Spring gave way to summer and we ran the hills and lanes around Glengaryth. We knew how lucky we were to have found this place in this lovely land. Me and Olive had been taken in by strangers who had opened up their home and their hearts to us. I would never forget this wonderful summer when we were free from harm and we could just be children.

The only thing that was causing us sadness was that Mum, Tony and Freddie hadn't yet left Bermondsey. If Mum could only see this place, if she could see how healthy we both were. We had filled out, Olive's skin glowed from being outside all the time, and we weren't pasty-faced like everybody at home anymore. If she would just get on the train and come she would see for herself how wonderful it was. But all she ever said in her letters was that Freddie was a sickly baby and they couldn't travel yet.

One afternoon me and Lottie wandered down to the pond and sat on the grass.

'It just doesn't make any sense to me, Lottie,' I said. 'I mean, if Freddie is sickly then this is the perfect place for him to be, isn't it? Away from that damp flat and the smog and the bombs. Why won't she come?'

'Grown-ups can be tricky creatures, Nell,' said Lottie, taking off her glasses and polishing them on the hem of her skirt. 'It's fear of the unknown, I expect. My dad says the best thing you can do in this life is to embrace new beginnings, take every new opportunity you can. Face your fears and do it anyway.'

'We don't even think like that where I come from, Lottie. In fact, everyone seems to enjoy being scared of something or other. Our neighbour, Mrs Baxter, is terrified of thunder and lightning, so she leaves her poor one-legged husband on his own and hammers on our door, weeping and wailing. Then she dives under the table and stays there until it's over. We have to eat our food with her underneath us. I think if we told her to face her fear and do it anyway she'd likely clobber us. I don't know why she couldn't dive under her own table.'

'I know I'm lucky to have parents that encourage me to think for myself,' said Lottie. 'I'm not saying they love me more than your parents love you, of course I'm not, Nell. But they have taught me not to let fear get in the way of what I want and to stand up for what I believe in.'

I nodded. 'We definitely come from different worlds, Lottie, but I think that I am learning things from you that I like and they are things I would never have learned if we hadn't met.'

Lottie put her arm around my shoulder. 'And I am learning things from you, Nell. So aren't we the lucky ones?'

'Yes.'

'And I'm sure your mum will soon pluck up the courage to get on that train.'

'I hope so, because Olive has stopped mentioning her – she'll be calling Auntie Beth "Mummy" at this rate.'

'Then you'll just have to remind her, won't you? That she has a mummy in Bermondsey who loves her.'

My fingers closed around the locket.

'That's lovely,' said Lottie.

I opened it and showed her the photographs inside.

'Your parents?' she asked, smiling.

I nodded. 'On their wedding day.'

'A very handsome couple, but they look as if they are about to be executed.'

'My mum said they were terrified.'

'Is your dad away at war?'

'Isn't everyone's dad away at war?'

'Sort of.'

'What do you mean?'

'Well, my father is certainly overseas but not in a fighting capacity.'

'What other capacity is there?' I asked.

'He's entertaining the troops.'

'Oh.'

'He's part of a concert party. My father doesn't

believe in killing another human being, Nell, and I'm pretty sure if he wasn't in a concert party he would be in prison. But as he said to me and my mother, he would rather be locked up than take the life of another person.'

'Well, I should think the soldiers need a bit of entertainment.'

Lottie looked out over the pond. 'He's not a coward, you know?'

'Of course he's not, Lottie. I think he sounds like a wonderful dad.'

Lottie smiled at me. 'He is.'

Suddenly we heard a low throbbing sound. We looked up and saw to our horror that there was a plane coming in low over the houses, just skimming the trees.

Lottie grabbed my hand and we started running but we didn't know where to run to for safety.

The noise of the plane was getting louder and it was now making a sort of *put-put* sound.

'It's going to crash, Nell!' screamed Lottie.

A boy shouted to us from across the street. 'Over here! Quickly.'

We ran across to him and he guided us through the bakery and out the back to an Anderson shelter.

Mr and Mrs Evans, who owned the bakery, were huddled together on a bench and the rest, mostly young boys, were sitting on the floor. We squashed in beside them as best we could, grateful to have got to safety.

'Thanks,' said Lottie to the boy.

'Didn't want our little evacuees getting squashed, did we, my lovely?' he said, grinning.

Lottie immediately took offence. 'For a start, I'm not your "lovely" and I think you will find that, on the nationwide percentile scale, we are both, in fact, taller than average for our ages.'

The boy didn't get a chance to answer as a tremendous explosion rattled the Anderson shelter and shook the ground beneath us. Mrs Evans made the sign of the cross. 'Oh, dear God,' she said. 'Some poor soul is on his way to heaven, Mr Evans.'

'Well, let's hope he's German,' said one of the boys.

'Daffyd Wynne!' said Mrs Evans. 'Did our good vicar not teach you that we are all God's children, no matter where we come from or what our beliefs are?'

The boy in question looked suitably shamefaced. 'Sorry, Mrs Evans,' he said.

'I should think so as well.'

'They *were* Germans,' said another boy quietly. 'That plane was a Heinkel.'

'Well, whoever they were, they didn't deserve to die like that,' said Mrs Evans.

'Where do you think it landed?' said Daffyd.

'Hopefully in a field,' said the other boy. 'We should see if anyone needs help.'

'I should think they are past all help,' said Mr Evans. 'I don't think you should go out there, Gerraint, you don't know what you might find.'

'I'll be careful,' said the boy.

Gerraint seemed to be the leader of the group. He got up and moved towards the entrance, and the rest of us followed.

When we got outside we could see thick smoke and flames billowing up beyond the trees. People had started running towards it. Gerraint turned to us. 'I think you should stay here,' he said. 'God knows what we are going to find over there.'

A police car came roaring down the street and screeched to a halt outside the bakery. A policeman got out and started yelling at people to stay back. 'Leave this to the professionals,' he shouted.

'God help us, Glyn Thomas, if we left everything to you,' said Mrs Evans. 'What took you so long to get here, anyway?'

'I was sitting down to my dinner, Mrs Evans.'

'And I'm sure you had every morsel eaten before you got in your car.'

'You know how Alice feels about wasting food.'

Mrs Evans folded her arms and glared at him. 'There are times, Glyn Thomas, when I wonder what ever possessed you to become a policeman.'

'I had a calling, Mrs Evans.'

'I doubt that, but you're here now so do your job, man.'

'I'm on my way.'

Mrs Evans looked in the car window at the other policeman. 'And your sidekick?'

'His wife gave him a sandwich to keep him going.'

Mrs Evans raised her eyebrows and stalked into the shop. 'God give me strength,' she said over her shoulder.

'Best get the job done, Glyn,' said Mr Evans. 'I'll come with you. Gerraint, you come too.'

'What about the rest of us, Mr Evans?' said Daffyd.

'You stay here – and it wouldn't hurt to say a few prayers, because I think it will need the Almighty's intervention to save these poor souls.'

Me and Lottie walked home, both of us lost in our own thoughts. The war had come to Glengaryth and we were both shaken by what had happened.

'You just don't know what's going to happen next, do you? I miss my parents, Nell, I really miss them.'

It was hard to see Lottie like this; she was always so sure of herself. She had an answer for everything, but this terrible thing had affected her badly. It made her seem more human somehow, a bit more like the rest of us.

I held her hand. 'My dad used to say that sometimes bad things happen to good people and there is nothing you can do about it. He said sometimes you just have a bad day.'

'I wonder what they are like,' said Lottie. 'I wonder how old they are. I wonder if they have a girlfriend or a wife waiting for them.'

'Or children,' I said.

'Their families will never know, will they? They're going to spend the rest of their lives hoping one day the door will open and they will come back to them. I think that's the saddest bit of all,' said Lottie, 'not knowing, always waiting.'

'I think I'd know,' I said. 'I think I'd know if someone I loved was dead.'

'Do you know what, Nell?'

'What?'

'You're the first person besides my parents that I've ever been able to talk to like this. Thank you for being my friend.'

We stopped walking and just stood there in the lane wrapped in each other's arms, crying our hearts out. That was how Uncle Dylan and Auntie Beth found us.

'Thank God you're both all right,' said Auntie Beth, running up to us.

'It was bloody awful,' said Lottie.

'But you're safe now,' said Uncle Dylan. 'You're safe.'

The two German pilots were buried in the little graveyard in Glengaryth. Nearly everyone in the village turned out, only a few stayed away. The service was a simple one. We sang hymns and we prayed for the two young men who had lost their lives fighting for their country. We prayed for the families who had lost their loved ones and would never know what had happened to them. Everything had been burned, so there was nothing to tell us who they were, but they were given a Christian burial and the village paid tribute to two men who were someone else's sons but who deserved to be laid to rest with dignity and compassion. And that's what the people of Glengaryth did that day.

# CHAPTER 11

Mum still hadn't come and I didn't know why. There was nothing to keep her in Bermondsey, she would be safe here and so would Tony and the baby. I wrote to her, urging her to come soon. A couple of weeks later, she sent a letter. Olive was at the sweetshop with Aggie so I took the letter upstairs. I sat on the bed and started to read.

*Dear Nell,*

*I know I promised you that I would come to Wales but I can't.*

*I've thought about it a lot and I want to stay here, Nell, in our home. I know this is not what you want to hear and I'm truly sorry. Freddie is a lovely baby, you would love him and so would Olive. He looks a bit like Tony except his hair is more the colour of Olive's, but he isn't strong like the rest of you and I just want to take care of him here, in surroundings that I know, with people who will look out for us. You know how good everyone is in the flats. We all pull together and help each other out. I know Tony should have gone with you the day you left and it was wrong of him to run home the way he did, but he is a great help to me, Nell. In fact, I don't know what I would do without him.*

*It helps to know how happy you and Olive are at the vicarage and how kind Mr and Mrs Morgan have been to you both. Your safety and happiness mean everything to me.*

*Keep writing to me, Nell, I love getting your letters.*

*Your loving mother*

*xxx*

I ran downstairs and showed the letter to Auntie Beth. She sat down at the table and read it.

'I don't know what to say, Nell. She seems to have made up her mind, doesn't she?'

I felt angry – she'd promised, and we wouldn't have left if we'd known she wasn't going to join us. 'But why?' I said. 'She knows they will all be safer here. All she has to do is get on a bloody train, that's all she has to do – how difficult can it be? Freddie would get strong, I know he would, and Tony would get used to it here. It doesn't make any sense.'

'I tend to agree with you, Nell. Would it help if I wrote to her?'

'Would you?'

'Of course, I'll do it right away.'

'Please tell her how lovely it is here and tell her

there's no smog, just fresh air that will make Freddie strong.'

'I'll be sure to tell her all those things, Nell.'

I wandered outside. I felt so angry. Mum had always told us that a promise was a binding thing, that a man was judged by his word. She said that if you promised to do something then you must always stick to it, unless there was something stopping you that was out of your control, and now here she was, breaking her promise. I walked around the side of the house to the orchard and sat down against a tree. Maybe she didn't miss us as much as she said she did, maybe Tony and Freddie were enough for her, maybe she didn't care. I closed my eyes tightly as angry tears ran down my face. But it didn't take long for me to come to my senses. What was I thinking? Of course Mum loved us, of course she missed us, so that left only one conclusion: something was stopping her, something that was preventing her from leaving Bermondsey, and I had a feeling it wasn't Freddie.

A couple of weeks later, I was surprised to see Uncle Dylan and Auntie Beth waiting for us at the school gate.

'I thought we'd go for a milkshake, Olive,' said Uncle Dylan, 'just you and me. Would you like that?'

'I'd like that a lot, Uncle Mister. Can Nell come too?'

'Nell and Auntie Missus have women's business to attend to.'

'Okay,' said Olive.

I watched Olive and Uncle Dylan walk away. I was puzzled; I couldn't think what women's business we had to attend to.

Auntie Beth took my hand and said, 'Let's walk, shall we, Nell?'

I now had a feeling of dread in my stomach: something wasn't right. I just knew it. 'There's something wrong, isn't there?' I said.

'I heard back from your mum, Nell.'

'Is it Freddie?'

'No, my darling.'

'Tony?'

She shook her head. 'I'm afraid it's your father.'

I thought I was going to be sick. 'He's not dead, is he? My daddy's not dead?'

'He's missing, Nell.'

'What does that mean?'

'It means they don't know where he is.' Auntie Beth took hold of my hands. 'It doesn't mean he's dead.'

'Where the bloody hell is he then?'

'He could be injured, he could be in a hospital somewhere. Lots of people go missing in the war and lots of them make their way home.'

Tears were streaming down my cheeks. 'He's not dead, I'd know if he was dead.'

Auntie Beth took a hankie out of her pocket and very gently wiped away my tears.

'That's the real reason your mum is staying in London. She wants to be there when your daddy comes home.'

'She didn't tell me the truth then?'

'I think she was trying to spare you the worry.'

'Yeah, she would. Auntie Beth?'

'Yes, dear?'

'Promise you won't tell Olive.'

'Of course, dear.'

'She's too young to be told something like that.'

'Would you like to go to the church and light a candle for him, Nell?'

I nodded and we walked up the lane towards the church.

It was cool inside – the only warmth was the sun coming through the long window over the altar. Auntie Beth knelt down, closed her eyes and joined her hands in prayer. I knelt beside her, but I couldn't pray. My mind was a jumble of thoughts. Mum held great store by St Anthony, the saint of lost things. Once we lost one of Olive's shoes and she couldn't go to school so we all prayed to St Anthony and we found the shoe under the bed, then went down to the church and lit a penny candle to his statue and thanked him. Mum said when something is lost, it doesn't mean that it is lost forever, it's out there waiting to be found. I had to find him, I had to find my daddy. That's what I had to do, but where was I supposed to look? I couldn't think straight. Was he in Germany? Was that where he was? I wanted to go there right

101

away and search every inch of that foreign land and bring him home. Maybe his boat sank – was he in some deep grey ocean, all on his own? He could be anywhere, but one thing I was sure of was that he wasn't dead. I'd know if he was dead – that's what I'd told Lottie and that's what I believed. If my daddy was dead something inside me would have died too and it hadn't: he was alive and he would come home.

# CHAPTER 12

We had come to Glengaryth in the spring and now it was December and everyone was looking forward to Christmas. The pond had frozen over and those brave enough skated and slithered across the ice. Gerraint and the other boys urged me and Lottie to join in the fun. I would have liked to, but I couldn't chance Olive following my lead and getting hurt if the ice cracked. I knew that Lottie was itching to join them as well, but she understood my concerns. Instead, we watched from the edge of the pond. Lottie had become a good friend to me and the boys had become friends to us both. We borrowed old bikes and cycled through the many winding lanes that circled the village. We swam in icy-cold rivers and walked for miles across the fields and into the woods that I'd seen from the bottom of the vicarage garden. We drank delicious milkshakes at the back of Mrs Evans's bakery and every Saturday we went to the village hall and listened to records on Uncle Dylan's record player.

Back home, Angela was my only close friend but here I was, for the first time in my life, part of a group of young people, and I loved it. I loved this life that I was leading. I knew that the day would come when I would have to leave this lovely place but for now it was home and I was going to make the most of it.

I missed my family but there were days when I looked out over the snow-covered hills and thought that I could happily live here forever. I loved everything about this new life. I loved the vicarage and the little chapel that Olive and I continued to sneak into when the devil wasn't looking. I loved the changing of the seasons, which I hadn't really noticed in Bermondsey. There were days back home when the smog and the mist off the river obliterated the sun and the sky seemed always to be grey. There were no flowers to herald in the spring, no leaves changing from green to brown, falling from trees and crunching under our feet. And as for summer, that was just muggy. There was one tiny window in the flat and there were days when you felt as if you couldn't breathe. It seemed as if there was no room between the tall tenements for the air to get through. Sweat rolled down the backs of the dockers as they worked bare-chested on the river, heaving the heavy sacks onto the boats. They kept bits of old rag in their pockets to stop the sweat running into their eyes; some of them tied the rags around their heads, which made them look like pirates. People became irritated with each other. Kids got walloped more and husbands were nagged more. And everyone swore more than usual. There was a lot of swearing in Bermondsey in the summer.

Maybe it was all too good to last – isn't that what people say? Was it a premonition? Or was it just that I couldn't believe how lucky we had been to have come to this place, miles away from all we knew, and to be with two people who loved and cared for us as though we were their own.

My fears came true one evening when we raced into the kitchen with the exciting news that there was to be a Christmas fair at school.

Auntie Beth and Uncle Dylan were sitting at the table.

'And we must make cakes. Can we make cakes, Auntie Missus?' said Olive.

But she didn't answer and I could sense there was something wrong.

'Sit down, girls,' said Uncle Dylan.

Olive was still chattering away. 'There is a prize for the best cakes. Will you help me make them, Auntie Missus?'

'Shush, Olive,' I said.

'I'm telling Auntie about the fair and the cakes.'

'I know you are, love, but you need to be quiet for a bit.'

'We have some news to tell you,' said Uncle Dylan.

'Are you having a baby? Oh, I hope you're having a baby! I love babies. I could help look after it,' said Olive, jumping up and down.

Auntie Beth looked sad. 'We aren't having a baby, Olive.'

'Oh, that's a shame,' said Olive.

Auntie Beth gave a sad little smile. 'Yes, it is, isn't it?'

'I thought perhaps God had changed his mind and sent you one.'

'Olive, you have to stop talking,' I said. 'And sit down.'

Uncle Dylan looked down at the table; he didn't speak right away. Auntie Beth reached across and took hold of his hand. He took a deep breath and looked at us. 'We have been told today that we have got to leave the vicarage.'

'Why?' I said, frowning.

'Because we are needed in the city, where we can do more good, where people are more in need of our ministry.'

'But you're needed here. Who's going to look after the church? And who's going to work the record player and the projector?'

'There is a war on, Nell, and everyone has to make sacrifices. People in Cardiff have lost their homes and their loved ones and they need God's word to comfort them.'

'So we've all got to move to bloody Cardiff?' said Olive.

'Not all of us, darling,' said Auntie Beth. 'Just me and Uncle Mister.'

'What about us? Why can't we go with you?' cried Olive.

'Because it's too dangerous. You have been sent here to the countryside for your safety. We could never take you with us, even if we were allowed to.'

'So what's going to happen to us then?' I asked.

'I'm sure you will be found another home with people who will love you as much as we do.'

At this Olive's eyes were filling with tears. 'But I don't want another home, I want to stay here with you and Uncle Mister.'

'I know you do, and if it was safe to take you with us, we would.'

'Of course we would,' said Uncle Dylan.

'Well, we won't go. Will we, Nell? We won't bloody well go!'

'It looks as if we're going to have to, Olive.'

Olive was glaring at us. 'What about Toby and the chickens? Who's going to look after them?'

'Toby doesn't belong to us, Olive. He will continue to live in the field and be looked after by his owner and I'm afraid we will have to give the chickens away.'

Olive jumped up from the chair, which fell backwards and clattered to the floor.

'Just like you're giving us away!' she screamed, and ran up the stairs.

'She's just afraid and sad,' I said. 'She doesn't mean to be rude.'

'We know that,' said Auntie Beth. 'I feel like throwing a chair over too.'

'It's not easy working for God, is it?' I said.

'He certainly tests us,' replied Uncle Dylan.

I stood up. 'I better check on Olive.'

I went into our lovely little bedroom. Olive was lying on her tummy, sobbing. I sat on the bed and rubbed her back.

'I don't want to go anywhere else, Nell, I like it here.' She gulped.

'I know you do, but we don't have any choice and neither do Auntie and Uncle. It's not their fault, Olive, and you need to say sorry for knocking over that chair.'

'The chair knocked itself over, Nell, it had nothing to do with me.'

'Is that right?' I said, smiling.

'Maybe it did have something to do with me.'

'Perhaps it was a bit of both.'

Olive wiped her eyes and sat up. 'Yes, I think it was a bit of both – but I think it was more the chair's fault. I mean, it's their job not to fall over, isn't it?'

'I suppose so.'

'Will we be able to stay in the vicarage, Nell? We could keep the chickens and eat eggs every morning and you're big enough to look after us.'

'I don't think it works that way, Olive. There are rules when it comes to children. You have to be looked after by a grown-up.'

'Well, you're as tall as Mrs Evans,' said Olive, warming to the idea.

'I don't think it goes by height, Olive.'

'We *will* be able to stay in the village though, won't we?'

'I should think so – I hope so, yes. I'm sure we can, they just need to find someone to take us in.'

'Shall we go round the village and ask?'

'That would be rude.'

Olive pulled a face. 'I don't see how that can be rude.'

'I don't want you worrying about it, Olive. I'm sure it will all work out.'

'It bloody better,' she said.

'Olive! What have I said about swearing?'

'These is desperate times, Nell, and they call for desperate measures.'

'Where on earth did you hear that?'

'From Aggie.'

'And where did she hear it?'

'Gawd knows.'

I was as sad as could be, but I burst out laughing. My little sister always managed to make me laugh.

# CHAPTER 13

Uncle Dylan wrote to the Bishop and asked if they could postpone the move to Cardiff until after Christmas. We all waited anxiously for the reply and were overjoyed when the letter came to say that we could stay in Glengaryth until after the New Year and have our Christmas celebrations here in the vicarage.

Auntie Beth called me and Olive into the kitchen one day and handed us some money.

'I thought you might like to buy some Christmas presents for your friends and family,' she said, smiling.

'I'm not sure that Mum would want us to take money from you, Auntie Beth,' I said.

'Oh, she wouldn't mind, Nell,' said Olive, reaching out her hand and taking it. 'Thanks ever so, Auntie Missus, we'll get something for you and Uncle Mister as well.'

'Olive!'

'What?'

'You can't just take money from people.'

'Auntie Missus isn't "people", Nell. Auntie Missus is . . . Auntie Missus.'

'Please take it, Nell,' said Auntie Beth.

'I think Olive already has,' I said, grinning. 'Thank you ever so much.'

'You have given us such joy, girls, that it's a pleasure.'

Apart from the butcher's, the baker's and the post office, there was a general store in the village and this is where we went to buy our gifts.

'Can I get something for Aggie, Nell?'

'Of course you can, and I want to get something for Lottie. We can get something for Auntie and Uncle between us.'

'What about Mum and Dad and Freddie and Tony?'

'I'm not sure we will have enough for that, but we could get them a lovely Christmas card.'

'Okay.'

The shop was owned by Mrs Llewellyn, who was a widow. Mrs Llewellyn knew about everything that went on in the village. Mrs Evans from the bakery said that she knew when someone had died before the person who had died knew. She could also tell you the weather forecast and how the war was going and whether we were winning or not.

'Do you think she's a witch?' asked Olive.

'Of course she's not a witch,' I said.

'How come she knows all about the weather then?'

'Do you know what, Olive?'

'What?'

'I don't think she does.'

Olive nodded and put on her wise face. 'Still, if it keeps her happy.'

'Exactly,' I said, grinning.

We were standing in the shop, looking at all the things on the shelves. There were lots of Christmassy things, like glass baubles and felt robins and paper lanterns, but nothing really special.

'I can tell you what the vicar's wife would like,' said Mrs Llewellyn.

*Well, there's a surprise*, I thought.

'She likes a good romantic novel. The slushier the better. Lots of trembling lips and sideways glances from under heavy lashes. You know the kind of thing: "his eyes fell to the floor and his breath came in short pants."'

I didn't dare look at Olive.

'What do you mean, his breath came in short pants?' she said. 'How can someone's breath come in short pants?'

'You're too young to understand, Olive,' said Mrs Llewellyn, searching under the counter. 'Now, I've just finished this book, it's like new because I took it off the shelf and I made sure that I didn't drop my dinner on it. You can have it for half price, will that suit?'

'I think that will suit fine,' I said.

'What's it about?' asked Olive.

'Well,' said Mrs Llewellyn, leaning on the counter. 'It's about a handsome lord who falls in love with a poor servant girl and his father won't give his permission to let them marry, so the lord gives up all his wealth and marries her, and they live in a humble cottage out on the moor. Then it turns out she's not poor at all, she was swapped at birth and she's really high-born.'

'What, she's tall?' said Olive.

'No, she's of the aristocracy.'

'So does the lord's father give him his money back?' said Olive, hanging onto every word that was coming out of Mrs Llewellyn's mouth.

'He does, Olive, and they live happily ever after.'

'I wouldn't mind reading that meself,' said Olive.

'You're too young,' said Mrs Llewellyn again. 'It gets a bit racy towards the end.'

'Don't even ask,' I said to Olive.

'Anyway, like I said, it's good as new and there's enough trembling of lips to keep the vicar's wife going for a while.'

'Thanks,' I said. I started looking around for something to give Lottie.

'What are you looking for, Nell?'

'Something for Lottie, Mrs Llewellyn.'

'I know just the thing,' said Mrs Llewellyn, going out through the back of the shop.

'She's a witch,' whispered Olive, 'she's a bloody witch!'

Mrs Llewellyn came back, holding something in her hand. She held it out for me to see. 'I think your young friend would like this.'

It was a snow globe and inside the glass was a

sweet little deer coming out of a wood. I shook it and watched the snow fall over his ears and over the trees. Lottie was going to love it. 'It's perfect,' I said.

Mrs Llewellyn looked pleased. 'I have a nose for that sort of thing,' she said. 'Now, how about you, Olive?'

'I want to get something for Aggie – have you got something up your nose for her?'

I groaned.

'Now, your little friend Aggie could do with a lovely pink ribbon to keep that hair of hers out of her eyes. It would be nice to see her eyes now and again, wouldn't it?'

'Yes, it would, Mrs Llewellyn. I think a ribbon would be just the thing. But could you make it yellow? Aggie likes yellow.'

'Yellow it is then,' she agreed.

'What about Uncle Mister?' said Olive.

'The vicar is partial to a bit of treacle toffee,' said Mrs Llewellyn, 'but you will have to go to the sweetshop for that.'

Olive was looking at Mrs Llewellyn in complete wonderment. 'You're bloody marvellous,' she said.

'Thank you, Olive,' replied Mrs Llewellyn.

Olive swore a lot – she just did – but what amazed me was that no one commented on it, no one seemed to mind. Maybe when you were as beautiful as Olive you could get away with it. Maybe when you were beautiful, people treated you differently. I had no chance.

Our presents were carefully wrapped up in proper Christmas paper and we left the shop delighted with our purchases.

'Happy Christmas, girls,' said Mrs Llewellyn as we left the shop.

'Happy Christmas, Mrs Llewellyn,' we called back.

We got the treacle toffee in the sweetshop. Aggie actually weighed it out and put it in a paper bag. Then she slipped us two pieces for ourselves. 'The missus won't mind,' she whispered. 'She does it all the time for her special customers.'

'I wish I could work in a sweetshop, Nell,' sighed Olive, as we walked down the road.

'If you worked in a sweetshop, Olive, there'd be no sweets left to sell.'

Olive thought about it and then said, 'I think you're right, Nell.'

Our last port of call was the post office, where we chose a beautiful card for Mum, Tony and Freddie. It had a house on the front that looked just like the vicarage. There was snow on the roof and a snowman in the garden with a scarf around his neck and a carrot for his nose. We wrote the card in the shop and posted it. Olive kissed the envelope before it went in the box.

'Happy Christmas, Mum,' I whispered.

On Christmas Eve, me and Olive walked down the lane with Auntie Beth and collected armfuls of holly. It was bitterly cold, with a sharp wind blowing across the fields. Our hands were freezing and our noses were red, but we didn't mind. Olive skipped ahead of us, her beautiful eyes bright with excitement.

'Why didn't Uncle Dylan come with us?' I asked, rubbing my hands together.

'Ah, he's on a secret mission, Nell.'

'What's the secret,' I said, grinning.

'Well, it wouldn't be a secret if I told you that, would it?'

We piled the prickly holly with its shiny red berries into a big basket and started walking back to the vicarage.

That evening we all went to Midnight Mass. Lottie came as well, even though she was an agnostic and she hadn't made her mind up yet. The little church was ablaze with candles; it was so beautiful I thought my heart would burst with happiness.

Uncle Dylan told the story of that first Christmas in a land far, far away. We prayed for our soldiers and for all the young men who were plunged into a war they didn't want. We prayed for their mothers and wives and sisters, who waited and hoped.

We sang 'Silent Night', 'Away in a Manger' and 'The First Noel'. I closed my fingers around the locket and prayed for my mum, Tony and Freddie, and I asked God to put his arms around my daddy and to carry him safely home to us.

Afterwards we walked across to the little side altar and knelt in front of the Nativity scene. Mary was kneeling down beside an empty manger; Joseph was standing beside her.

'Where's Jesus?' said Olive. 'And the shepherds and the angels?'

'It's not Jesus's birthday till tomorrow – they'll all be there then.'

'Well, technically it *is* his birthday,' said Lottie, 'because it's gone twelve o'clock.'

'Someone better get him quick then, hadn't they?' said Olive.

'I'm sure they will,' I said.

Lottie was spending Christmas at the vicarage because the frightful Eliza Strut was spending the day with her sister, who, according to Lottie, was equally frightful. 'I'd rather spend Christmas on my own than spend it with those two,' she said.

We walked home through the frosty night. Uncle Dylan carried a sleepy Olive on his back. The sky was inky black and there were so many stars it felt like a sparkly blanket above our heads.

'I'll always remember this Christmas, Nell,' said Lottie.

'So will I,' I said.

We held hands as we walked home.

# CHAPTER 14

The next morning I woke up before the others. Lottie was fast asleep beside me. Her long dark hair was loose, spreading across the pillow and her face. One arm was stretched out over my tummy; I liked the feel of it there.

I hated the thought of leaving the vicarage but at least I would still have my friend Lottie. I looked down at Olive, who was on a makeshift bed on the floor. As usual she was lying on her tummy, her face turned away from me, and she was making little squeaking noises like a kitten. I lay there thinking about my family in Rannly Court and how I longed to be with them on this Christmas morning. I knew they would be missing me and Olive as much as we would be missing them.

Lottie stirred and opened her eyes, then smiled at me. 'Happy Christmas, Nell,' she said.

I pulled myself up in the bed. 'Happy Christmas, Lottie.'

I leaned over and gently shook Olive. 'Wake up, sleepyhead, it's Christmas.'

She groaned and pulled the blankets up around

her neck. 'I'm tired, Nell,' she said, giving a huge yawn.

'I know you are, love, but you don't want to sleep Christmas away, do you?'

'No, but my eyes won't open, I think they're still asleep.'

'Come on, girls, I can smell bacon and eggs,' I said, pulling back the covers and getting out of bed.

We dressed quickly and ran downstairs. There was a fire burning in the grate and in the corner was a beautiful Christmas tree that filled the room with the sweet smell of pine.

Olive's eyes were like two saucers. 'Where did that come from?'

'Uncle Mister got it yesterday,' said Auntie Beth.

'Was that the secret mission?' I said, grinning.

She nodded. 'We wanted it to be a surprise.'

Olive walked across the room and looked up at the tree that almost reached the ceiling. She touched its bright green leaves. 'I miss my mum,' she said, and burst into noisy sobs.

Auntie Beth gathered her in her arms and together they sat on the floor. She rocked her gently until her sobs subsided, then kissed the top of her head. 'I'm sure your mum will be missing you as well, darling.'

I looked across at Lottie, whose eyes were filling with tears. We were in a lovely place but we all wanted to be at home with our families.

'Well, we're a happy lot,' I said, which made us all laugh.

After breakfast Lottie and I went for a walk into the village while Olive helped Auntie Beth prepare the Christmas dinner. Uncle Mister was in the church doing his preaching.

We'd arranged to meet Gerraint and the other boys outside the bakery.

'You like Gerraint, don't you?' I said.

Lottie didn't answer; she just smiled at me.

'You *do*, don't you?'

'I might,' she said, grinning.

'Do you like him, like a boyfriend? Or just a friend, friend?'

'I'm not sure there's much of a difference, is there?'

'I think there probably is, Lottie, not that I'm an expert on that kind of thing.'

'Neither am I. I've never had a boy who's a friend, *or* a boy who's a boyfriend. I just like him, that's all, and believe me, Nell, that's a miracle in itself.'

'I've never had a boyfriend either,' I said.

'You've got plenty of time for that.'

'I know.'

'I've got something for him,' said Lottie shyly.

'You have?'

She nodded and produced a card from her pocket.

'You're giving him a card?'

'And I've written my address inside.'

'What, old Ma Strut's?'

'No, my Brighton address.'

'Blimey, Lottie, that's almost a marriage proposal,' I said, giggling.

She punched me playfully on the arm. 'Remember what my father said, Nell?'

'Your father said a lot of things.'

'He said you must face your fears and do it anyway. So I wrote my address in the card and I put a kiss at the bottom.'

'You put a kiss?'

'And now I'm wondering if that was a step too far.'

'No, I think your dad's right about facing your fears and all that stuff. I should think Gerraint will be really pleased to get a kiss on Christmas morning.'

'Do you think so?'

'Yes, I do. I mean, who wouldn't want a kiss on Christmas morning?'

'Depends who's doing the kissing, I suppose,' said Lottie.

The bakery was closed and the boys were shivering in the doorway. As well as Gerraint and Daffyd, the other boys there were Reese, Effan and Aled. I thought they were lovely names – they made the names of the boys back home in Bermondsey seem rather dull. There was our Tony, of course, short for Anthony – named after Mum's favourite saint. Then there were Tony's friends, Dennis, George and Billy, and Angela's two brothers, Robbie and Stanley. I decided that if I ever had a son of my own I would give him a Welsh name. I definitely would.

We all wished each other a happy Christmas and walked down to the pond. It was freezing cold but we were young and we didn't care: it was Christmas.

Lottie and Gerraint wandered off on their own while the rest of us sat on the bench.

'Should we catch them up?' said Aled.

'I don't think they want us around,' said Daffyd.

Aled looked puzzled. 'Why not?'

Daffyd took off his hat and threw it at Aled's head.

The snow had started to fall softly around us as we walked back up the lane towards the vicarage.

'Well?' I asked.

'Well what?' said Lottie, grinning.

'Did you give him the card?'

'I did.'

'And?'

'He returned the favour.'

'He gave you a card too?'

'No, he gave me a kiss.'

I pulled her arm and made her stop walking. 'A proper kiss? A kiss on the lips?'

'Oh, Nell, it was . . . it was . . .'

'Nice?' I prompted.

Lottie's face was flushed and her eyes sparkled. 'Perfect, Nell. It was perfect.'

'Gosh.'

Lottie started to run and I ran after her, laughing. 'Perfect!' she shouted into the wind. 'Amazingly, utterly, mind-blowingly perfect.'

It seemed my friend had fallen in love with a Welsh boy called Gerraint. Blimey!

Christmas in the vicarage was wonderful. Auntie Beth had changed into a beautiful emerald-green dress, the fine woollen fabric falling in folds to just below her knees. She had curled her hair and it tumbled softly around her shoulders. I thought she looked lovely. The long wooden table looked just like the kind of Christmas tables you see in books. Beautiful crystal glasses sparkled in the glow of the many candles placed around the room, and there was a colourful paper cracker next to each plate.

'That's not Ethel, is it?' said Olive, pointing to the cooked bird in the centre of the table. 'Cos if it's Ethel I don't want any, thanks.'

'It's a turkey, Olive,' said Uncle Dylan, laughing.

'That's all right then,' said Olive. 'I don't know any turkeys.'

Uncle Dylan said grace. We pulled crackers and put on funny paper hats and read out silly jokes and then we tucked into the delicious food.

After we'd eaten and helped Auntie Beth clean up the kitchen, we sat by the fire and exchanged our gifts.

Auntie Beth loved her book. 'How clever of you,' she said, going a bit red in the face. 'How did you know?'

'Mrs Llewellyn,' said Olive. 'She knows everything.'

Auntie Beth smiled. 'She does seem to, doesn't she?' she said.

'And she said you'd like this, Uncle Mister,' Olive added, giving him the bag of treacle toffee.

'My favourite,' he said. 'Thank you, girls.'

Auntie Beth went over to the cupboard and handed Lottie, Olive and me a parcel each.

Lottie undid her parcel and inside was a beautiful red scarf and gloves. 'I thought they would look lovely against your dark hair, Lottie,' said Auntie Beth.

'Oh, I love them,' said Lottie, 'thank you so much.'

Auntie Beth smiled at her. 'I'm glad you like them.'

I had the same as Lottie but mine were lilac. There was also a book called *Anne of Green Gables*.

'It has always been my favourite book, Nell,' said Auntie Beth. 'It's about a funny little orphan girl who has all sorts of adventures. I hope you haven't read it.'

'We never had any books at home,' I said, 'but I love reading. Thanks ever so much.'

'Happy Christmas, Nell,' she said.

We were all staring at Olive.

'Aren't you going to open yours?' I asked.

Slowly and carefully, Olive began to tear the paper away from the box. She lifted the lid and tears started pouring down her cheeks.

'Oh, Olive,' I said, putting my arm around her shoulder. 'Why are you crying?'

She looked up at me. 'It's a . . . Oh, Nell, it's a . . .'

I looked in the box and there, nestling in snowy-white tissue paper, was a beautiful doll. It had golden curls and a sweet face. Its bonnet, dress and little booties were of the palest blue. I understood why Olive couldn't speak: she had never owned a doll, and neither had I. Dollies were for rich kids, not for the likes of us.

'Do you like it, Olive?' asked Auntie Beth.

'Is it mine?' whispered Olive.

'Of course it's yours,' she said.

'To keep?'

'Forever,' said Auntie Beth, smiling.

Olive gently picked the doll out of the box and held it to her chest. 'You're mine,' she said. 'And your name is Auntie Missus, because I love Auntie Missus and I love you.'

'Good choice of name, Olive,' said Lottie.

Olive walked across to Auntie Beth and threw her arms around her neck. 'It's the best present I ever had in all my life ever since I was borned,' she said. 'Thank you, Auntie Missus. Thank you, Uncle Mister.'

'You're very welcome, Olive,' said Uncle Dylan. 'We're glad you like it.'

'I love it and I will love it till the day I die,' she said, with a very serious look on her little face.

Lottie had presents for all of us. A box of

Cadbury's Milk Tray for Auntie Beth and Uncle Dylan, and a pink felt purse for Olive.

She handed me a small box. 'This is for you, Nell,' she said. 'Happy Christmas.'

Inside was a blue glass brooch that sparkled in the glow of the candles. I pinned it to my cardigan and smiled across at her. 'It's beautiful,' I said. 'I shall wear it always.'

I handed her the snow globe. 'Happy Christmas, Lottie,' I said.

She shook it and we all watched the snow cover the trees and fall gently over the little deer. 'It's perfect,' she said.

As the fire crackled in the hearth and the tree sparkled with silver tinsel, I looked around the room. Auntie Beth and Uncle Dylan were carefully choosing a chocolate from the purple box. Lottie kept turning the globe over and watching the snow falling again and again, while Olive was rocking the doll backwards and forwards in her arms. I felt as if I was going to burst with happiness. Olive and I had been so lucky. Auntie Beth and Uncle Dylan could have chosen two other children; Lottie and Aggie might not have been evacuated to Glengaryth.

The angel on top of the tree looked down at us and the snow blew softly against the window. And I knew that I would never forget this special, special Christmas Day.

# CHAPTER 15

On New Year's Eve we sat together in Uncle Dylan's church and listened to the bell-ringers welcoming in 1943. I thought about my family and I thought about my daddy who was lost, and I prayed that God could watch over him and guide him safely home to Rannly Court, where Mum and my brothers were waiting for him. As we walked back home up the little lane I thought about how different this was to New Year's Eve in Bermondsey. Back home the streets would be alive with people. Someone would have dragged a piano out into the square and men would be falling out of the Pig and Whistle roaring drunk, singing 'Auld Lang Syne' at the tops of their voices. Bells would be ringing out from the churches all over London and the boats on the Thames would be hooting their horns. Perhaps this gentle New Year's Eve was how it should be. It allowed you to think about the people you loved. It made you think about all the families that were separated by war and the boys and men who would never come home. Auntie Beth held my hand as we walked to the vicarage through the dark night and I wanted to tell her that I loved her and that I'd miss her. She squeezed my hand as if she already knew what I was thinking.

It was sad watching Auntie and Uncle packing all their stuff into cardboard boxes. It made it all seem very real. I kept hoping that someone would knock on the door and say that the village needed them and they could stay but it never happened.

Lottie and I were sitting at the far end of the garden. There was a cold wind blowing off the fields and we were shivering. 'You *will* be able to stay in Glengaryth, won't you?' said Lottie, blowing on her hands. 'Because I absolutely cannot stay here without you. You're the only thing that makes living with Eliza bloody Strut bearable, and what about my Sunday dinner, for God's sake? Am I supposed to starve again?'

'You should tell someone about that, Lottie, because I'm sure she's supposed to feed you every day, even on a Sunday. I mean, what makes her think that your appetite is any smaller on a Sunday?'

Lottie sighed. 'Why does everything go wrong just when it's all going right? My dad says that we are masters of our own destiny but we're not, are we? Other people decide our destiny and there's nothing we can do about it.'

'I just wish someone would tell us where we're going, because I'm fed up with Olive asking me every five minutes as if I know the answer to everything, when I don't.'

'That would be far too easy, Nell. Children aren't supposed to have feelings, you know.'

'Olive says she's taking the chickens with us.'

'That should be interesting.'

'I didn't want to leave Bermondsey but now, I don't want to leave *here*.'

'I know what you mean. I gave my parents a really hard time when they said that I had to go away. I said "so much for self-expression", when my wishes were being totally ignored. I feel bad about that now.'

'What did they say?'

'They said that there were times when they had to be my parents and not my friends and this was one of those times.'

'I suppose they were right, though.'

'Of course they were right, but I wasn't about to give in without a fight. It's their own fault, they were the ones that taught me to think for myself.'

'I never told you this, Lottie, but my brother Tony was supposed to be evacuated with us – he even got on the train but he jumped off just as it was leaving the station.'

'Blimey, did he go back home?'

I nodded.

'And didn't your mum mind?'

'Let's put it like this, I don't think she would have been surprised. I thought that it was a miracle that he'd got on the train in the first place.'

'He sounds a bit like me.'

'Tony's a one-off, you never know what he's

going to do next. Actually, I think it's easier without him, because as much as he's my brother and I love him, he can be a bit of a bugger.'

'So can I,' said Lottie, grinning.

Three days before we had to leave the vicarage, Mrs Jones, the welfare lady, came round. She looked all flustered and apologetic – she was fanning her face as if it was the middle of summer instead of the middle of winter. I knew instantly that it was going to be bad news.

We all sat down at the kitchen table and waited for her to speak.

She took a deep breath and said, 'I've tried everyone in the village and no one has room to take the girls.'

'Are you sure?' said Auntie Beth. 'They are settled here. They've made friends, they are doing well at the village school . . .'

'Well, I can't magic a room for them out of nowhere, Mrs Morgan, and believe me I have tried.'

'We're not doubting that,' said Uncle Dylan. 'But to move the girls now would be unsettling for them.'

Mrs Jones shrugged her shoulders. 'There is a war on, vicar, and all we can do is our best, and the best I can do at such short notice is a farm in Pontbryn.'

'But that's more than twenty miles away,' said Uncle Dylan, 'surely you can find somewhere closer?'

You could see that Mrs Jones didn't know what to say, she was going red in the face and tugging at the collar of her coat. She spoke slowly and deliberately, as if we were all deaf. 'If there was somewhere closer, vicar, I would have put them somewhere closer.'

Olive was glaring at the welfare lady and I was worried about what was going to come out of her mouth. I kicked her under the table. She scowled but didn't say anything.

'Still,' said Auntie Beth, smiling at Olive. 'A farm, eh? That's exciting. I bet there will be cows and pigs and chickens, maybe even a horse – you'd like that, wouldn't you?'

'I've got a horse here,' said Olive quietly. 'And I don't like cows.'

'Well, I'm afraid you will have to get used to them, dear,' said Mrs Jones, getting up from the table. She dropped her handbag in her haste to get out of the door. 'I shall collect them the day after tomorrow and take them to the farm.'

'And does this farm have a name?' said Uncle Dylan, looking cross.

'Hackers,' she said, bending down and picking up her bag. She started to walk towards the door, then turned around. 'If it's any consolation, I'm not happy about them going there either and as soon as a place becomes available in the village, I will do my best to move them back here. I get no pleasure from delivering news like this, you know. I have hundreds of children that I have placed with families and I am under no illusion that they have all been as lucky as these girls. Some have made their way back home.'

'I wish someone in Glengaryth would,' said Olive.

Uncle Dylan got up and put his arm around Mrs Jones. 'You are doing a marvellous job,' he said.

'Thank you,' said Mrs Jones, sniffing.

Once she had gone we all sat there feeling miserable.

'What about Aggie?' asked Olive, her eyes filling with tears.

'Come here,' said Auntie Beth, and she sat Olive on her lap and kissed the top of her head.

'We will just have to be brave soldiers and trust that God will take care of you in your new home,' said Uncle Dylan.

'I won't hold me breath,' said Olive.

It was a Saturday so me and Olive walked down to the village. I dropped Olive off at the sweetshop so that she could say goodbye to Aggie. 'Don't forget to get Aggie's address in Coventry,' I said.

'I won't.'

I met Lottie at the duck pond. We sat on the wooden bench looking out over the water.

'This is bloody awful news,' said Lottie, when I told her we had to leave the village.

'I know, but at least you'll still have Gerraint and the boys.'

'But I won't have *you*, Nell.'

'I don't know what this Hackers farm is going to be like. What if they don't *like* us? What if we don't like *them*?'

'We'll write to each other, Nell, and you can tell me all about it, but I'm sure it will be fine. How could they not like you? You're utterly marvellous.'

I smiled. 'You're pretty marvellous yourself, Lottie Lovejoy, and I'm going to miss you something rotten.'

'I'm seriously thinking of writing to my parents and telling them to come and collect me. Eliza bloody Strut has redoubled her visits to the church. I don't know why she doesn't just bloody well move in! Honestly, Nell, if I stay there much longer I shall fade away and die an agonising death and end up being eaten by dogs.'

'What dogs?'

'Just go with this, Nell, I'm on a roll.'

'Sorry.'

'Even when she does deign to cook it's practically inedible,' she continued. 'Every Friday she insists on cooking fish and I'm not exaggerating, Nell, when I say that it tastes as if it's been left over from the Last Supper.'

'You really should tell the welfare lady, Lottie.'

'I did.'

'And what did she say?'

'She said that I was lucky to be living with such a good Christian woman who has a love of God

133

and all his teachings. Pity she doesn't have the same love for children. If God moved in with her, I'm pretty convinced that he'd starve to death as well. I think she just wants the people in the village to tell her she's a bloody saint or something. Either that or she fancies the vicar.'

I grinned. 'The vicar at her church is ninety if he's a day.'

'So's Eliza bloody Strut.'

I slipped my arm through hers. 'What am I going to do without you?'

Lottie sighed. 'Perhaps we should just run away and beg to be taken in by someone else. Preferably someone who can cook.'

'I'll write to you,' I promised. 'We'll keep in touch.'

'Of course we will,' said Lottie. 'And one day when this bloody war is over we will stand at the water's edge and I shall show you the sea.'

Me and Olive sat in silence in the back of the car, watching Glengaryth slowly disappearing behind us. We drove past the school where we had been so happy. The duck pond where Lottie and I sat and chatted and the café where we had sat with our friends. As we passed the sweetshop I heard Olive whisper, 'Bye bye, Aggie.' She held Auntie Missus, her doll, against the window so that she could say goodbye too.

This all seemed so unfair – Lottie had been right when she'd said that no one listened to children. It was as though we didn't have a voice. We were being made to go somewhere that we didn't want to go and to leave people we cared about, and there was nothing we could do about it. I knew there was a war on and we must all do our bit and make sacrifices, but we'd already left our home and our family; why did we have to do it again?

Breakfast had been a sad little affair. Every time I looked at Auntie Beth and Uncle Dylan I felt like crying, but I was trying to be strong for Olive. Auntie Beth's eyes were red, as if she'd been crying all night. None of us could eat anything, not even Olive.

Uncle Dylan was trying to cheer us all up. 'You'll upset the chickens if you don't eat their lovely brown eggs,' he said.

'And we don't want to upset the chickens, do we?' said Auntie Beth, trying to smile but failing miserably.

Olive had slid from her chair and stood next to Auntie Beth, who lifted her onto her lap. Auntie Beth wrapped her arms around her and Olive buried her face in her neck and started sobbing. This was awful – I almost wished that Mrs bloody Jones would arrive and put an end to it.

We'd stood in the porch waiting for the car to arrive, our bundles on the floor beside us. Leaving the vicarage had been almost as bad as leaving Bermondsey. We had loved it here. Auntie Beth and Uncle Dylan had become like family to us and we would never forget them or the kindness and love that they had shown two little strangers, who they had treated like their own.

The journey seemed endless and, to add to our misery, it was pouring with rain and blowing a gale. It reminded me of one of Mrs Baxter's sayings: 'Wrap up warm, girls, there's a wind out there that would take yer nose off.'

Mrs Jones was yapping on about how lucky we were to be going to live on a farm and how she was sure that we would love it there.

'Have you seen it?' I said.

'Not exactly,' said Mrs Jones.

*Well, either you've seen it or you haven't,* I thought.

'How do ya know we're gonna love it then?' said Olive. 'You have to see somethin before you decide whether someone's gonna love it or not.'

*Good old Olive,* I thought, smiling to myself.

Mrs Jones turned around and attempted to smile at us. The car almost veered off the road and you could see her panicking as she tried to right it. Me and Olive didn't bother smiling back. We were both miserable and we weren't about to pretend that we weren't.

We passed lots of pretty villages that looked nice, but she kept on driving. On and on we went until we had left all the houses behind us and there was nothing but endless fields, all brown and muddy and chopped-up, and barns that looked as if they were falling down. It was nothing like the green fields around Glengaryth. We were driving into the back of beyond, or as my daddy was fond of saying, 'The arse end of the Piccadilly line.' I hadn't known what he meant at the time but now I did: we were indeed heading for the arse end of the Piccadilly line.

We eventually turned off the road and drove for what seemed like miles along a bumpy dirt track full of holes and muddy puddles that sprayed against the windows as we were thrown around the back of the car like a couple of parcels. I had a bad feeling about this. I hoped that I was wrong; perhaps we would be greeted at the door by a rosy-cheeked farmer's wife holding a plate of freshly baked Welsh cakes.

After what seemed like forever, we stopped at an open gate. There was a sign hanging by one nail that said: HACKERS FARM. We had to lean sideways to read it.

We drove through the gate and into a yard.

'This is it, girls,' said Mrs Jones, sounding relieved.

She got out of the car and nearly slipped over. I jumped out and caught hold of her arm.

'Thank you, dear,' she said.

Olive joined me and we looked in dismay at the scene in front of us. We were standing in what can only be described as a river of mud. We were wearing our school shoes and white socks. We looked for a dry path that would take us to the front door but there wasn't one – the only way was through the mud. The house itself was awful – it looked more like a shed than a home. Dirty bits of net hung at the windows. Paint was peeling off the door and everything was splattered in mud. Olive was hanging onto my coat.

'You can't leave us here,' I said.

'I've got no option,' said Mrs Jones, barely able to look us in the eye.

'I don't like it,' whispered Olive.

I felt angry. 'That's because there is nothing to like, Olive,' I said. 'There must be somewhere better than this, there *has* to be.'

'Well, there's not,' Mrs Jones snapped. 'Perhaps if you had been willing to be separated we might have found somewhere in the village.'

'Well, maybe that would be better than this.'

'No,' said Olive, 'we have got to stay together.'

'But if being separated means we could go back to Glengaryth . . .'

'If you think that I'm driving you all the way back to Glengaryth, you can think again. I'm going to visit my sister, who lives in the opposite direction. I'm exhausted and fed up with everyone blaming me when they don't get what they want. Mrs Hacker and her son are expecting you. They have already been reimbursed and that, I'm afraid, is that. You have been given aspirations above your station living in that vicarage and, in case you've forgotten, there's a war on. Now stop whining and follow me.'

We trudged behind her through the mud, which

covered our shoes and our white socks and splattered up our legs. Mrs Jones nearly fell over a couple of times but I didn't go to help her again. She couldn't wait to dump us in this godforsaken place and drive to her sister's – no doubt mud-free – house. In that moment I almost hated her and wished that she would fall arse over tit and stay there all night.

Having almost killed ourselves getting there, Mrs Jones banged on the door, but there was no response. Good, perhaps they had moved out or drowned in the mud and been eaten by Lottie's imaginary dogs, and we could get away from this awful place. No such luck: the door opened a couple of inches and a wizened face peered out at us.

'What?' it said.

'Ah, Mrs Hacker,' said Mrs Jones, smiling. 'I've brought the girls who you so kindly agreed to take in.'

'Did I?' the face croaked.

'Yes, you did, Mrs Hacker.'

Mrs Jones fished around in her now mud-spattered handbag and took out a piece of paper, which she shoved through the slit in the door.

There was silence as the woman read the piece of paper. It didn't seem to be bothering her that it was pouring with rain and we were getting more soaked by the minute.

'You better come in then,' she said reluctantly, opening the door wider.

We stepped inside. If at all possible, the inside was worse than the outside. The poky little room was dark and cold. The windows were tiny, hardly letting in any light. There was a meagre fire burning in the grate and on either side were a couple of threadbare chairs. A long table took up most of the space and something that smelled like a dead dog was cooking in a large pot over the stove. The woman herself was rough-looking; she had long lank hair that looked as if it had never been washed. Over her clothes she was wearing a dirty apron. She reminded me of the witch in the fairy tale of Hansel and Gretel. My vision of a rosy-cheeked farmer's wife disappeared out of the door and into the river of mud.

Mrs Jones looked uncomfortable and I hoped that she'd at last realised that she couldn't possibly abandon us here. I couldn't believe it when she smiled at us and said, 'Now be good, girls, and behave yourselves. I'm sure you will have a lovely time here.' Without another word she turned around, opened the door and was gone.

The woman stared at us. 'I'm Mrs Hacker,' she said. 'I'll get Jimmy to show you where to put your stuff. Jimmy?' she yelled.

A young boy came into the room. He looked a bit older than me.

'Show these two their room,' she barked.

The boy opened a door beside the fireplace. Behind the door was a staircase and he nodded to us to follow him. Clutching our parcels, we climbed up the narrow stairs after him. At the top, he opened another door.

'You're in here,' he said.

We walked into the room. It was freezing cold and it smelled horrible. There was a single bed pushed against the wall. I thought about our big bed at the vicarage with its lovely soft blue-and-yellow quilt and I could feel my eyes filling with tears.

'It's not much, is it?' said the boy.

'Did something die in here?' I said, putting my hand over my nose.

'No, just a lot of bed-wetting from the last lot of evacuees. I'd open the window but it's cold enough already in here.'

I didn't answer him. 'Are you her son?' I asked.

'No, I'm not,' he shot back, as if I'd insulted him. 'I'm an evacuee like you.'

Olive was hiding behind me. I knew that she was as frightened as I was in this strange place.

'What's she like?' I asked.

'A miserable old cow,' he replied.

'She won't hurt Olive, will she? Because if I thought for one minute that she would, I'd walk out right now.'

'I've never seen her hit anyone and the last lot were a nightmare – she just moans a lot and she's a lousy cook.'

The boy was about to go out of the door when he turned and said, 'Have you got anything of value on you?'

I put my hand inside my coat and fingered the locket. 'What's it to you?' I snapped.

'You better give it to me,' said the boy.

'I'm not giving you anything,' I said, glaring at him.

'If you don't give it to me she'll take it and you'll never see it again. You don't know me from Adam but you're going to have to trust me. I'll hide it for you and keep it safe.'

I looked at the boy and something about him told me that he was telling the truth. He seemed gentle and he had nice eyes. I reached behind my neck and undid the locket but still I didn't hand it over.

'I promise that I will take care of it for you,' he said.

I handed it over and he slipped it in his pocket.

'What about that?' he said, pointing to the glass brooch I had pinned to my coat.

'It's glass,' I said. 'It's not valuable.'

'Old Ma Hacker is like a magpie, she likes sparkly things.'

I unpinned it and handed it over. I still wasn't sure that I could trust him; I'd only just met him. But it seemed I hadn't got much choice.

'What are your names?' he asked.

'I'm Nell and this is my sister, Olive. Patterson,' I added.

'Jimmy Morris,' he said. 'Just do as you're told and you'll be okay. Don't worry, I'll look out for you and I promise I'll keep your stuff safe.'

That's when I smiled. We might have landed at the arse end of the Piccadilly line but we had an ally and for now that was the best we could hope for. Anyway, with a bit of luck we would soon be moving back to Glengaryth. We were just going to have to make the best of it. Maybe things wouldn't be so bad.

At least that's what I thought until I met Albert.

# CHAPTER 16

Albert was Mrs Hacker's son and she treated him as though the sun shone out of his rear end. Her eyes lit up whenever he walked into the room. I hated him on sight; I knew the type. I was an East End girl and I had learned early on which men you could trust and which you couldn't, and I didn't trust Albert Hacker as far as I could throw him. My job from then on was to make sure Olive was never left alone with him.

The first morning we came downstairs we both learned what would be expected of us while we lived under Mrs Hacker's rotten roof.

We sat down at the long table. She plonked two plates in front of us that each held a greasy fried egg and a piece of bread. The bread was hard and the egg was a congealed mess.

This feast was accompanied by a mug of black tea that had neither milk nor sugar in it.

'I hope you've brought your ration books,' she barked.

I handed them to her.

'Because I can't be expected to feed you on nothing.'

I remembered that Mrs Jones had said that she had been reimbursed for taking us in, so I knew she was lying.

Jimmy came into the kitchen and sat down with us. He smiled and I smiled back.

'This is a farm,' said Mrs Hacker, slamming down an equally gross egg in front of Jimmy. 'So we all have to pitch in. Jimmy sees to the animals – you can help him, he'll show you what to do. If you don't work, you don't eat. That's the way it works round here.'

I couldn't help wondering what her beloved Albert did. Nothing probably.

'And in case you're wondering, my Albert's in charge. You mind what he says, see, you do what he tells you to do.'

Just at that moment the golden boy walked into the kitchen. He scraped his muddy boots on an iron thing that stood just inside the door. Then he sat down at the end of the table and rolled up his sleeves, exposing fat, hairy arms. His mother set a plateful of food in front of him and ruffled his filthy hair.

'What about school?' I asked.

Mrs Hacker stared at me with her mean little eyes. 'You're too old for school,' she snapped.

'I'm talking about Olive.'

'There won't be no school,' said Albert.

'She has to go to school,' I said, glaring at him.

'Does she now?' he said, sneering at me.

'Yes, she does.'

'Well, if you're willing to walk ten miles there and ten miles back every day then by all means take her.'

'Don't you have transport of some kind?'

'Not for that, we don't.'

'I have to go to school,' said Olive in a quiet little voice. 'I have to learn me lessons.'

'Tough,' said Albert, wiping the bread around his plate and stuffing the food in his mouth.

I stared at him in disgust as the egg yolk dripped down his chin.

'Look,' said Mrs Hacker. 'This is a working farm and I can't spare Albert to go gallivanting round the countryside' – she nodded in the general direction of Olive – 'just so that *she* can learn her lessons. Albert never went to school and it never did him any harm.'

Jimmy made a face at me and Albert cuffed him round the head.

'What you making faces about, yer little runt?' he snarled.

Jimmy ignored him and got up from the table. He put his plate in the sink and said, 'I'll show you around if you like.'

I was glad to get out of the kitchen and away from these awful people, and anyway, I needed some fresh air – the egg had made me feel sick in my stomach. We put on our coats and our wet, muddy shoes and followed Jimmy outside.

'I'll do for him one day,' said Jimmy, walking across the yard.

'I'll help you,' I said.

'And *I* will,' said Olive. 'I'll help you an all.'

'Thanks, Olive,' said Jimmy, smiling down at her.

'You're welcome,' she said.

It had stopped raining but it was cold. Even if it had been a warm day I think I would still have felt cold.

We walked across to an old barn and went inside, Jimmy shutting the door behind us.

I counted five cows in the stalls, big black-and-white creatures. I had only ever seen cows from a distance; I hadn't realised until now how big they were.

'These are my friends, Olive,' said Jimmy, stroking the broad back of one of them. 'Come closer and say hello, she won't hurt you.'

Olive didn't move. 'They're bloody big,' she said, eyeing them up.

'But they're very gentle. This is Martha – she has lovely brown eyes, just like you.'

Olive edged closer.

'She likes you,' said Jimmy, 'look at the way she's staring at you.'

'That might be because she wants to bite me hand off.'

Jimmy laughed. 'Now why do you think she'd want to do that?'

'Cos she's a bloody big cow,' said Olive. 'The tallyman's horse nearly bit me hand off once. I reckon animals can be a bit tricky.'

'You'll get to like them,' said Jimmy.

'I'm not sure we're going to be staying around long enough to get to like em,' I said.

'You'll be okay if you keep yer head down.'

'Unfortunately I have a habit of not keepin me head down and so has Olive. We're from the East End, where no one keeps their head down – it's a survival thing.'

'I hope you stay, it's nice to have someone to talk to for a change.'

'Well, I can't promise anything,' I said, 'but I suppose we'll have to give it a try.'

'Good,' he said, smiling.

I watched him gently stroke Martha's ears. 'Where are you from, Jimmy?'

'I'm from Cardiff.'

'But that's not far away, is it?'

'Not really.'

'Why don't you go back, then? I mean, it's bound to be better than here, isn't it?'

Jimmy leaned his head against Martha. 'I've got nothing to go back to, Nell.'

'What about yer mum and dad?' asked Olive.

'Never had a mum and dad.'

'What, never?' I said.

Jimmy shook his head.

'How did ya get borned then?' said Olive, looking puzzled.

'I haven't got a clue, Olive. I think that perhaps I just arrived one day in a spaceship.'

'Imagine that!' said Olive, her eyes nearly popping out of her head.

'You're an orphan then?' I said gently.

'That's me,' he said, grinning.

'Oliver Twist was an orphan,' said Olive. 'An he done all right in the end. He didn't do too good in the beginnin and the middle bit was iffy, but he did all right in the end, didn't he, Nell?'

'Is this Oliver bloke a friend of yours then?'

'Don't be daft, Jimmy, he's in a book what me teacher at school read to us,' giggled Olive.

'And this Oliver turned out all right in the end, you say?'

'Yeah, the upshot was that he actually belonged to some posh people. Didn't he, Nell?'

I smiled and nodded. I loved listening to Olive gabbling on as if she hadn't landed in the worst place in the world.

'An he lived happily ever after.'

'Maybe that's what's gonna happen to me.'

'You have to live with a mean old man called Fagin first.'

'Well, that can't be much worse than livin with a mean old woman called Hacker.'

'I think it's really sad that you're an orphan,' said Olive.

'Oh, you don't have to feel sorry for me, being an orphan suits me fine. I'm a free spirit and I'll make me own luck.'

'You'd like my friend Lottie then,' I said, 'cos she's a free spirit an all.'

'Best way to be,' he said. 'This place might be a dump but it suits me for now and when it stops suiting me, I'll find myself a good stout stick and a spotted hankie and go and explore the world.'

'I like you,' said Olive suddenly.

'And I like you an all,' said Jimmy.

Hearing Olive say that she liked Jimmy was enough for me to decide to stay for a while.

# CHAPTER 17

I suppose that you can get used to most things and we soon got used to the farm. As long as we saw to the animals, Mrs Hacker pretty much left us alone and that suited us fine. Olive loved helping Jimmy and grew to love the cows, but the pigs were her favourites; she spent ages talking to them.

'What are their names?' she asked one day, when we were throwing slops into the trough.

'They haven't got names, Olive,' said Jimmy.

'Everyone should have a name,' Olive insisted. 'The cows have got names.'

'The cows are different.'

'Why? Why are the cows different?'

'All I'm saying is it's best not to get too attached to them. That's why I never named them.'

Jimmy looked at me and raised his eyebrows; I knew what he was talking about.

'The pigs might not hang around, Olive,' I said.

'Where are they going then?'

'Look, Olive, people have pets, don't they? Like cats and dogs,' said Jimmy.

'Old Mr Roberts has got a dog and he's a bugger.'

'Well, Olive, farm animals aren't pets.'

'What are they then?'

This was a nightmare. How could I tell a little girl that the pigs were for eating?

'There are some things, Olive, that it's best to just accept.'

'Like the Holy Trinity?'

'Got it in one.'

'I'm gonna name em anyway.'

'Suit yerself, love,' I said, smiling at her.

'I'm gonna.'

Jimmy tried to show me how to milk the cows but no matter how hard I tried I just couldn't get the hang of it. Martha didn't like me; she stamped her feet and kept turning round to glare at me with her big brown eyes. Jimmy laughed at my efforts. He was a natural, though. He spoke to them lovingly, as if they were real people instead of animals, all the time gently squeezing their udders. Me and Olive watched in wonder as warm white milk poured into the bucket.

'What's that coming out of her titty?' asked Olive.

'It's milk,' said Jimmy.

'Milk comes in bottles, don't it?'

'No, Olive, milk comes from cows,' I said, smiling.

Olive screwed up her face. 'That's not milk, it's wee. I ain't drinking that!'

'I think you and me need a chat, Olive.'

'Okay,' she said. 'I'm gonna name them pigs now.' And she ran out of the barn.

'She's a gutsy little thing, isn't she?' said Jimmy, grinning.

I nodded. 'Always has been.'

'I'd like to have had a brother or a sister – you're lucky to have her.'

'I've got two brothers as well. They stayed in London with me mum.'

'You must miss them.'

'I do.'

'You'll see them again.'

'Who did you live with in Cardiff, Jimmy?'

'I lived in an orphanage.'

'Was it okay?'

'Well, it was better than here.'

'Will you go back there after the war?'

'They chuck you out when you're fifteen and I'm sixteen now, old enough to take care of myself.'

'So what will you do?'

'I dunno, maybe I'll go to London and seek me fortune.'

'What's left of it,' I said.

'How old are you, Nell?'

'I'm almost fifteen.'

'You're tall for your age.'

'I get that from my dad.'

Jimmy picked up the bucket and we started walking back to the house.

'What did you do with my locket?' I said.

'I buried it up in the field under the old oak tree. Don't worry, I put it in a tin so it will be good as new when we dig it up. It's important to you, isn't it?'

'My mum gave it to me before we left Bermondsey so yes, it's very important.'

'Well, it's safe where it is, so you've got no need to fret. I'll show you where it's buried if you like.'

'Thanks, Jimmy,' I said, smiling at him.

'You're very welcome, Nell.'

Days on the farm were long: we were up before six helping Jimmy with the animals. By the evening Olive could barely stay awake long enough to eat her dinner. Once I'd taken her up to bed and read a bit of *Anne of Green Gables*, me and Jimmy spent the evenings together. At first I had worried about leaving Olive on her own but with Mrs Hacker downstairs I felt that she would be safe. Albert's bedroom was off the kitchen so he would have no excuse to go upstairs.

The more I got to know this sweet, gentle boy the more I grew to like him. Neither of us wanted to spend time with the Hackers, so on those cold winter evenings we'd sit in the barn. We talked about everything. I told him about Bermondsey and Rannly Court, my mum and Tony and Freddie. I told him about my best friend Angela and the bombed-out house that we loved to spend time in. I told him about the River Thames rolling past the back of the flats and my daddy who used to be a docker.

'Is he away at the war?'

I was silent.

'He's not dead, is he?' he asked gently.

'Missing,' I said. 'But Mum's sure that he's alive. She was supposed to join us here but she wants to stay where she is for when he comes back.'

'You have to have hope, Nell.'

'Most of the time I do,' I said, 'but sometimes I think I might never see him again.'

Jimmy smiled at me. 'Let's hope he comes back then, eh?'

I nodded. 'Let's hope.'

'This war can't last forever, Nell, and then you can go home and I can travel the world.'

'And what are you going to do when you've done that?'

'I'm going to buy a farm, a dairy farm, and I'm going to specialise in Friesians – they're the best milking cows. I'll own acres of fresh green pasture where the cows can roam free, not like this dump.'

'You like cows, don't you?'

'They're the most gentle creatures. I took to em right away – I like em better than most people I've met. I guess they're the reason I stay here. How about you, Nell? What do you want to do?'

'Go back home, I suppose, and work in the sugar factory.'

'Is it nice there?'

I shrugged my shoulders. 'I've never really thought about whether it's nice or not, it's just somewhere to work.'

'I could never be shut up in a factory all day,'

said Jimmy. 'I think I'd go mad and I couldn't work for anyone else either.'

'I hope you get your farm, Jimmy,' I said.

'I have to make my fortune first, Nell, but I will, I'll make my fortune.'

'I don't doubt that for one second, Jimmy,' I said, smiling at him.

Winter gave way to spring and life became easier. For a start we weren't freezing cold and wet all the time. As long as we saw to the animals and kept out of Albert's way, things weren't too bad. I wrote letters to Mum and Lottie. I told Lottie all about the farm and grumpy Mrs Hacker and horrible Albert and the lousy food. I also told her about Jimmy and how nice he was and how much I liked him. I didn't tell Mum how awful the place was because I didn't want her worrying. Instead I told her how Olive loved chatting to the pigs and stroking the big gentle cows, so I didn't exactly lie to her, I just made it sound a lot better than it was.

Once Olive was asleep, Jimmy and I would sometimes walk into Tyford, a small village that boasted a post office and a pub. It was a five-mile walk there and back but it was great to leave Hackers farm for a few hours and I didn't trust Albert to post my letters.

It was lovely to see the spring flowers growing wild in the fields and hedgerows. The grassy banks were ablaze with bright yellow daffodils and purple and yellow crocuses. It reminded me of the fields and lanes around Glengaryth. Hackers farm was a bit like Bermondsey; nothing seemed to grow there. In fact it was a wonder me and Olive grew, but surprisingly we did; in fact we had never been so healthy.

Jimmy and I walked across fields and climbed over wooden stiles. We'd sit quietly on the old stone bridge that spanned the little stream with our legs dangling over the side, watching the water flowing beneath us. I didn't care that we didn't talk much – it didn't matter somehow. I just liked being close to him. One day as we were walking back to the farm Jimmy held my hand, just like that, as if it was the most natural thing in the world to do. I didn't say anything but my heart missed a beat and I'm sure my face went red. His hand felt rough and strong in mine and it made me feel safe and cared for. I had never experienced feelings like this before and it was all a bit confusing. If Lottie had been here we would have spent hours talking about it and that would have been fun – she would have had something very wise to say or she might have quoted something her dad had said – but in a way I was glad she wasn't. I liked keeping these new feelings to myself; I liked lying in bed at night beside a sleeping Olive and going over it all in my mind. It was my secret and I hugged it close to my heart.

The post box was at the end of the track next to the gate. Olive and I used to run down there every morning to see if there were any letters for us. One day there was a letter from Lottie. It was easy to recognise her handwriting – it was very loopy and she dotted her 'i's with complete circles. I put it in my pocket and didn't read it until the end of the day, when I could be on my own.

After work I walked to the top of the hill and sat down on the grass. The farm looked a bit better from up here. The early evening sun was still warm and I suddenly realised that, despite being away from my family and living in this dump of a place, I was happy. I took the letter out of my pocket and started to read.

*Dear Nell,*

*Hackers farm sounds utterly bloody awful. I do hope you are keeping your chin up and not letting it get you down. I'm glad that you have a good friend in Jimmy and that Olive is enjoying the animals.*

*I'm leaving Glengaryth, Nell. My mother is collecting me at the weekend. It turns out that we are going to stay with some acting friends of my father's who live in Cornwall. They have a cottage by the sea and it sounds idyllic. I shall be glad to be near the sea again. I don't know how long we are going to stay there, maybe till the war has ended but I'm not sure. In many ways I shall be sad to leave. I know I will be sad to leave Gerraint but I am looking forward to seeing my mother.*

*We mustn't lose touch with each other, Nell,
because I really value our friendship. I have
never had a proper friend. I always thought it
didn't matter and that I was quite happy on
my own, but meeting you has made me realise
what fun it is to have someone special to talk
to and to share things with.*

*I shall think of you when I see the sea again
and hope that one day you will come to
Brighton and we can stand at the edge of the
ocean together.*

*Take care, my darling friend, give Olive a
big hug from me and know that I shall be
missing you until we meet again. I shall send
my address as soon as I know it. Please keep
writing.*

*With love always,
Your good friend Lottie Lovejoy
xxx*

I folded the letter and put it back in my pocket.
I was glad that Lottie was going to see her mum
and I knew that one day I would see her again.
I'd go to Brighton and find the white house on
the seafront and we'd stand at the edge of the
ocean together.

If Mrs Jones turned up now and said she had
found us a place back in Glengaryth I would say,
*No thanks, we're happy here* and I wouldn't be lying.
The freedom we had suited us both and as long

159

as we did our work and steered clear of Albert, we were okay. I knew that Olive missed Aggie but she didn't seem to miss going to school.

And me? I wanted to stay with Jimmy as long as I could.

# CHAPTER 18

What began as an ordinary kind of day ended up as a nightmare. The weather had suddenly changed and there was driving wind and rain blowing across the yard and teeming down the hillside. I had to borrow an old pair of Albert's rubber boots, which were miles too big for me. Mrs Hacker threw a pair of thick socks across the kitchen.

'They'll stay on with these,' she said.

I hated wearing anything that had touched Albert, but there was no way I could help Jimmy with the cows wearing my school shoes.

'I think Olive should stay here,' I said, pulling on the horrible smelly socks.

'A bit of rain's not gonna kill her,' said Mrs Hacker, glaring at me.

'She hasn't got the right clothes – she'll catch her death.'

'In case you hadn't noticed, girl, this is a farm and the animals have to be seen to, whatever the weather's like. Do you think the cows wait till the sun comes out before they're milked?'

'Me and Jimmy can do it together.'

'I'm not having her under me feet and that's that.'

Olive came downstairs wearing a thin little dress. I took her hand and together we went back up the stairs. I stomped all the way up.

'Why are you angry, Nell?'

'It's that bloody woman, she's enough to make a saint angry.'

'You swore, Nell.'

'I couldn't help it, so it doesn't count.'

I opened the drawer and put as many clothes on her as would fit under her coat.

'I can hardly move, Nell.'

'Better than catching a cold.'

'I don't mind, Nell.'

'Well, I do.'

'I feel fat,' said Olive, struggling down the stairs. 'I feel fat, like a fat person.'

I grinned at her. 'You *look* like a fat person, Olive.'

Jimmy came into the kitchen. 'Ready?' he said.

I nodded.

'Hang on, Jimmy,' said Mrs Hacker, opening a drawer in the dresser. She threw a pair of gloves across the room. 'No point in havin cold hands,' she said.

Jimmy picked up the gloves and pulled them on. 'Thanks,' he said.

We walked outside. The rain was driving across the yard, making it almost impossible to see anything.

'Nice boots,' said Jimmy, grinning.

'Very funny.'

'Do I look fat, Jimmy?' asked Olive, smiling up at him.

'You look as if you've eaten too many pies.'

'I'm a fat person today, that's what I am.'

'I can't believe she gave you a pair of gloves to wear,' I said.

'She loves me really,' said Jimmy, grinning.

I wondered for a minute whether Mrs Hacker actually *did* like Jimmy. It made her more human somehow.

The three of us started trudging across the field to where the cows were lying close together on the ground.

'Haven't they woken up yet?' said Olive.

'They always do that when it rains,' said Jimmy. 'In fact they know when the rain is coming so they prepare for it.'

'Why?' asked Olive.

'So that they have a dry place to lie down in.'

'Clever that, isn't it?' said Olive.

'Cows are much cleverer than people give them credit for.'

Between us we gently poked and prodded the big creatures, but today they were having none of it; even Martha was refusing to budge.

'Come on, girls,' said Jimmy. 'Don't you want to go into a nice dry barn?'

The wind and rain were racing across the field and we were all dripping wet.

'You and Olive go to the barn, Nell, they'll move soon,' said Jimmy. 'There's no point in all of us getting soaked.'

The rain was lashing my face and running into the tops of the boots.

I could see Olive mouthing something to me but the wind was so loud I couldn't hear what she was saying. 'What?' I shouted.

'I said I'm bloody freezing,' she yelled.

'Go to the barn, Olive, we'll be there in a minute.'

'Okay,' she said.

I watched her running across the field, then turned back to help Jimmy.

We pushed, we prodded, we whispered words of encouragement, and when that didn't work we started yelling at them, but they didn't move a muscle – these cows were going nowhere.

'Have they done this before?' I asked, shivering and wiping the rain out of my eyes.

'If Martha moved, the rest would follow,' said Jimmy. 'I'm wondering if there's something wrong with her.'

He knelt down beside her. 'Not feeling so good today, girl?' he murmured, smoothing her wet back. Martha looked at him with big, sad eyes. 'You need to find Albert, Nell,' he said.

I could hear the urgency in his voice and it scared me.

'Get him up here quick, I think there's something wrong with her.'

I stumbled across the field in the bloody boots,

falling a couple of times in my haste to get back to the farm. I knew how much Jimmy loved that cow; he would be heartbroken if anything happened to her. I hoped it was nothing serious.

I opened the gate and ran into the yard. The wind was picking up bits of straw and muck and rattling the metal urns that were lying around, and there was another sound, a kind of whimpering. I stood still and strained my ears. There it was again, and it was coming from the barn. The door was slightly open; there was just enough room for me to slip through without making a noise. As my eyes adjusted to the dark I saw them. Olive was cowering in the corner. She looked terrified. Her doll was lying on a bale of straw as if she had been playing with her. Albert had Olive's arms pinned against the barn wall so that she couldn't move. Then I saw one of his hands slide down and lift up the edge of her skirt. I picked up the first thing I saw – it was a spade leaning against some old machinery. I swung it back with all my might. The sound as it hit the back of Albert's head made me feel sick. He fell forward and landed on top of Olive. She scrambled out from under him and ran to me.

I was frozen to the spot, I literally couldn't move. All I could do was stare at Albert's body lying on the barn floor.

Olive was whimpering beside me and I looked down at her. Her face was the colour of chalk. I knelt down beside her and took her in my arms;

she was shaking. We clung to each other. I couldn't believe what had just happened.

Tears were streaming down her face. 'Albert,' she whispered.

'Hush now, it will be all right,' I said. But I knew it wouldn't, it wouldn't ever be all right again. I hadn't meant to hit him so hard – my only thought had been to get him away from Olive.

'Have you done him in, Nell?'

I walked across and prodded him with my foot but he didn't move, he was like one of the cows up in the field – except that he wasn't a cow, he was a person, and I'd killed him. I had, I'd killed him.

'What are we going to do?' said Olive, staring at me.

I kept looking at Albert's body, hoping to see some movement, willing him to move, but he didn't.

'Nell?' whispered Olive.

I shook my head and pushed my wet hair away from my face.

'We should tell Jimmy, Nell, that's what we should do. We should tell Jimmy that you've killed Albert. Jimmy will know what to do.'

'Yes, Jimmy,' I said.

Olive picked up her doll and we ran out of the barn and up to the field. I was screaming Jimmy's name over and over. He started running towards us. When he reached me I fell into his arms, pulling him down with me onto the wet grass.

'I didn't mean to, Jimmy,' I said, clutching at his coat. 'I didn't mean to, I didn't, I didn't.'

'Didn't mean to do what?'

'She killed Albert, Jimmy, Nell killed Albert,' sobbed Olive.

Jimmy was looking between me and Olive.

'You've killed Albert?'

Olive nodded.

'Are you sure?'

'He's dead all right, Jimmy, he ain't movin. Nell whacked him with a shovel and killed him. I ain't never seen such a dead person before.'

'Olive, you've never seen *any* dead person before,' I sobbed.

'I know, but if I had, they wouldn't have been any deader than Albert.'

I clung to Jimmy as if my life depended on it. I was terrified – did they hang children? I was fourteen; maybe I wasn't even a child anymore. 'What am I gonna do, Jimmy? What am I gonna do?'

'We have to go. We have to get away,' he said.

'*We?*'

Jimmy touched my cheek. 'Do you really think I'd let you go alone?'

'But it's not your problem, you don't have to get involved.'

'I'm already involved, Nell.'

'But what about Martha?'

'Let's concentrate on getting away from here, eh?'

I looked down at Albert's old boots. 'I won't get far in these, Jimmy.'

'You'll have to go back down to the farm.'

'I can't.'

'Yes, you can. You need a change of clothes and so does Olive. If old Ma Hacker's around, put all your stuff in a pillowcase and throw it out the window. You can do this, Nell, and the quicker you are, the quicker we can get away. Go now.'

'You'll come back, won't you?' said Olive, looking terrified.

I took a big breath. 'Course I will, daft, I'll be back before you know it. You stay here with Jimmy.'

'Okay, Nell.'

# CHAPTER 19

The rain had eased off by the time I reached the yard. I walked quickly past the barn, not daring to look in. I'd killed someone, I'd actually ended the life of another person. I'd hated Albert but I hadn't meant to kill him. It had happened so quickly, as if it was happening to someone else, as if I was watching a film, like it wasn't really true – but it was, wasn't it? I'd picked up a shovel and I'd killed Albert Hacker. There was a bit of me that was saying good job an all, he got what he deserved; someone would have done away with him in Bermondsey, that was for sure. Well, there was nothing I could do about it now: Albert Hacker was dead and that's all there was to it.

I looked in the kitchen window. I couldn't see Mrs Hacker but it was so dirty, it was hard to see anything much. Perhaps she'd already found Albert; perhaps she was at the end of the lane this very moment, waiting for the police car to arrive. I opened the door as quietly as I could. It creaked – I'd never noticed it creak before. I guess it had never really mattered before whether it creaked or not. The kitchen was empty. I ran up the stairs and started stuffing clothes into a pillowcase. Should I throw it out the window? What if Mrs Hacker was down there somewhere? But then again, she could have come into the kitchen and I would have to walk past her with a pillowcase full of clothes. I decided to throw it out the window and just hope that it wasn't going to land on her head. I opened the window and let it fall.

Someone must have been looking out for me because when I crept downstairs the kitchen was still deserted.

There was a loaf of bread and some cheese on the table. I had no idea when our next meal would be so I grabbed the food and stuffed it under my coat. There was knife on the side so I took that as well and, for good measure, I added a couple of tin mugs.

There was no one in the yard when I got outside, so I picked up the pillowcase and started running towards the field.

'Let's go,' said Jimmy as I reached them. 'We have to run, Olive, okay?'

'Yes, Jimmy, I can run.'

'Good girl.'

We'd been running for about ten minutes when I stopped. 'Jimmy?' I shouted.

He turned around. 'What?'

'My locket, I have to go back for my locket.'

'You can't,' he said. 'You'll get caught.'

'I have to, I promised Mum. I promised her I'd give it back the next time I saw her.'

I could see Jimmy's mind ticking over.

I stared at him. 'I have to get it.'

'Okay,' he said. 'But *I'll* get it, you keep running.'

'But—'

'If I don't catch you up, there's an old abandoned barn a couple of miles away. Keep going straight and you'll find it. Wait for me there, I'll come as soon as I can.'

I hadn't moved.

'Run,' he said. 'I'll find you.'

I didn't want to let Jimmy go but I grabbed Olive's hand and we started running.

Jimmy's couple of miles felt more like ten and we kept stopping to rest. I stared across the fields hoping to see Jimmy but there was no sight of him. The rain was now a relentless drizzle that soaked our already sodden clothes.

'Auntie Missus is getting wet,' said Olive sadly, 'and she doesn't like it.'

'Here,' I said. 'Put her in with the clothes, right in the middle where she can keep dry.'

Olive handed me the doll. 'Me legs are hurtin, Nell. I don't think they want to go any further.'

'It can't be far now,' I said, 'then we can rest in a nice dry barn. That'll be good, won't it?'

'Maybe you shouldn't have killed Albert, Nell.'

I swung round and held her shoulders. I was cold and wet and angry. 'How did Albert know you was in the bloody barn anyway?'

She mumbled something that I couldn't hear.
'What?' I shouted.

'I wanted to play with Auntie Missus so I went and got her. When I come downstairs Albert was sittin at the table and I got scared so I run into the barn.'

'And he followed you?'

There were tears running down Olive's face and I gathered her into my arms. 'I'm sorry, love, I'm sorry I shouted at you. None of this is your fault.'

'If I hadn't gone and got Auntie Missus . . .'

'He would have tried it on some day, Olive, he was just waitin for his chance.'

'Cos he's a bugger?'

'He's the biggest bugger I ever met.'

Olive wiped the rain and tears away from her face and grinned up at me. 'He's a dead bugger now though, ain't he?'

I shook my head. 'You'll never go to heaven, Olive Patterson,' I said.

'Course I will, God will understand – he forgave that robber bloke so he's bound to forgive me for saying bugger.'

'I'm sure he will,' I said. But I couldn't help wondering if he would forgive *me*.

It felt as if we'd been walking for ages, but at last we came over the crest of a small hill and down below us I saw a large building, half hidden amongst a copse of towering beech trees. It had to be a barn. I hoped it was the right one. We stood still for a moment or two as I shielded my eyes with my hand and gazed around. There were no other buildings that I could see, save a sprawling farmhouse in the distance, a jumble of outbuildings.

'That's it,' I said to Olive. She looked up and smiled at me. Her face was pale and tired but her eyes were hopeful. 'Come on,' I said, 'not much further.'

We walked down the hill towards the barn. It was very large. A sloping roof was supported by wooden walls and facing us were rickety old doors. The roof was uneven, dipping in parts as if it was about to cave in, and it was covered in moss and ivy.

The track leading up to the barn was rutted and stony. Small heaps of dried cow pats spotted the ground and there was a haze of midges, nettles and cow parsley as high as my shoulder.

The closer we got to the huge building, the more nervous I felt, but I kept my chin up, determined not to show any fear to Olive.

'Look!' she cried, pointing at something scuttling along the edge of the bales. 'A mouse!'

It wasn't a mouse, it was a rat. And if there was one rat, there would be others. I swallowed hard and pushed open one of the wooden doors. It creaked terribly and pigeons roosting on the rafters flapped up in a panic and rushed at us to get away. Olive screamed and hid behind me. I ducked my head and covered my hair with my hands but the birds were soon gone, disappearing into the afternoon, and quiet descended on the barn. It was dark apart from the area immediately beyond the door, which was full of soft sunlight. Motes of dust and tiny pieces of straw floated in the light. A small, grey feather drifted. I took a deep breath. Now all we had to do was wait for Jimmy.

# CHAPTER 20

The first thing that hit me was the smell, but it wasn't an unpleasant smell. It was must and dust and old hay, and then the sharp tang of oil and metal and rust. As my eyes grew accustomed to the dark, I saw an old abandoned tractor in the corner. Above it was a loft with a wooden ladder leading up to it, half the rungs missing. In the far corner of the barn, well away from the hay, were the remains of a fire and some empty cans, so I guessed that it had sheltered others looking for some place to rest before us.

Tarpaulin was bundled in one corner, along with spades and scythes and giant pitchforks: the farmer's tools.

I stepped forward. The floorboards were wide and old. The inside of the barn felt safe, like a sanctuary. I looked up at the roof, high above us, the light shining through it.

'It's like a church,' said Olive.

'You know what?' I said. 'You're right.'

We sat down in one of the stalls, which was dry and warm. We took off our wet clothes and hung them over the wooden partition, then put on the dry ones from the pillowcase.

'I'm hungry,' said Olive.

I took out the bread and cheese and divided some of it between us. 'We must save some for later,' I said.

With dry clothes on our bodies and food in our tummies we began to feel better.

'Now lay down and have a kip,' I said.

Olive went to sleep almost immediately. I stared down at her. What had I done to put her in such danger? I got up quietly and went to the door. I scanned the fields, willing Jimmy to appear, but there was no sign of him. I had no plan, just an urgency to get away from the farm. It hadn't seemed to matter when Jimmy said he was coming with us but now I felt sick and scared. Maybe I should just hand myself in and be done with it, but that scared me even more. I lay down next to Olive and cuddled close to her for warmth. What if Jimmy didn't show up? How could I do this without him? I suddenly felt so very alone. I wanted my mum, I wanted my dad, and I wanted Jimmy. But there was one thing I knew for sure: if we could make it back to Bermondsey we would be safe because Bermondsey took care of its own.

I lay there listening to the sounds of gentle rustling in the hay – mice or, God forbid, rats, but I guess they had as much right to be there as we did. I didn't expect to sleep but surprisingly I did. A deep, deep sleep that lasted until morning.

The first thing I did when I woke up was look around for Jimmy. I felt sure that he must have come in the night. I looked in all the stalls but he wasn't there. I got up and went outside. The sun was shining but I felt cold and shaky. I looked around the barn and over the fields but there was no sign of him. I couldn't understand it. He'd said he'd come so why wasn't he here? Were we in the wrong barn? Was there another barn just across the next field where Jimmy was waiting for us? Maybe he didn't want to leave Martha – but that meant that a cow was more important than me and Olive. But I knew in my heart that Jimmy wouldn't choose Martha over us, however sick she was. No, something had prevented him from leaving and I dreaded to think what that was.

I heard Olive calling me and went back inside the barn.

'Is Jimmy here?' she said, rubbing her eyes.

I shook my head.

'What are we going to do then?'

'I haven't got a clue, Olive.'

'Well, that's a nice bloody kettle of fish then, isn't it?'

'Language, Olive,' I said automatically.

She stood up and looked around her. She looked over the wooden partition, she looked up at the rafters and she spun around.

'What are you doing?' I asked, confused.

'I'm looking for the vicar, Nell.'

'Uncle Dylan?'

'That's the feller.'

'But Uncle Dylan's not here, is he?'

'Exactly,' she said, grinning at me. 'So how come I have to stop swearing?'

So there we were in an abandoned barn, with very little food and no idea what to do next, and we were bent over double, laughing our heads off.

'Oh, Olive,' I said, wiping my eyes. 'What would I do without you?'

'Gawd knows,' she said, grinning.

Olive took Auntie Missus out of the pillowcase and rocked her in her arms. 'She could have suffocated in there, Nell. Did you nearly suffocate in there, Auntie Missus?'

'She's a doll, Olive, not a person.'

'She might not be a person to you but she's a person to me,' said Olive, smoothing the doll's hair.

I smiled. 'Of course she is, Olive, I'm sorry.'

'I forgive you, Nell, because you don't understand how much I love Auntie Missus.'

'You're probably right,' I said.

'She's thirsty, Nell, and so am I.'

I was thirsty too. I took the two tin cups out of the pillowcase and we went outside. It had been raining so much the previous day that I knew there must be fresh water somewhere. We found a barrel just outside the door and I dipped the cups in it, hoping there was nothing awful lurking at the bottom. Olive sat down on an old bench and I went back inside and got the bread and cheese. The bread was a bit hard but at least it was food.

We sat together in the sunshine and ate our meal.

'I think we should stay here another day and if Jimmy hasn't come by tomorrow we will have to go without him,' I said.

'Go where?'

'Home.'

'To the farm?'

'The farm isn't home, is it? Anyway, we can't go back there, can we?'

'Where are we going then?'

'We're going back to Bermondsey, Olive. We'll be safe there.'

'Do you think Mum will be cross that you've killed Albert?'

'I don't think it'll make her day.'

'Still, there's worse things you could have done.'

'Like what?'

Olive was concentrating very hard. Then she said, 'Nothing springs to mind, Nell, but I'm sure there's something.'

'That's made me feel a lot better, Olive.'

'Good,' she said, smiling.

We spent the day exploring the barn. The tarpaulin bundled up in the corner was dry, so we dragged it across to one of the stalls and laid it down, then gathered armfuls of straw and piled it on top.

'That should be more comfortable,' I said.

'We're good at this, aren't we?' said Olive, lying down and testing it out.

'Good at what?'

'Runnin away.'

'Are we?'

'Yep, we've got food and we've got water and we've got a nice soft bed. All we need now is Jimmy.'

'I'm not sure that Jimmy is going to come, Olive.'

'We'll just have to manage without him then, won't we?'

'I suppose we will,' I said sadly.

We walked to the top of the hill and looked out across the fields. We waited and we waited, but he didn't come and I had to accept that he was never going to. We had no food left; tomorrow we would have to leave. We would have to find our way home.

# CHAPTER 21

We left as soon as the sun came up over the hill. I wanted to get as much distance between us and the farm as I could. I had no idea which direction we should be going in, so I just made a decision and started walking. We had to find food and we had to find a village or a farm; that's what we had to do. The sun was warm on my back as we walked and there was a soft breeze ruffling my hair. Olive skipped ahead of me, Auntie Missus dangling from one arm as if she was on some kind of holiday, instead of on the run from the law.

Despite the sun I was cold and numb inside. I couldn't wait to get back to London, to the flats and the river and everything I knew. I never wanted to see another cow or chicken or sheep as long as I lived. I wanted the smog and the damp, I wanted to be amongst my own kind. I wanted to sit on the old bed in 59 Edison Terrace with my friend Angela and watch the kids climbing over the rubble. I wanted to watch the girls from the custard factory shaking the clouds of yellow dust from their headscarves. But most of all I wanted to be back in Rannly Court with my family. This place that I had fallen in love with had become a prison that I had to escape from. All the good things that had happened here were soured by what I had done.

I'd slept badly, vivid dreams that took me to terrifying places. One minute I was living at the vicarage, only in my dream it was owned by Mrs Hacker and it was dark and dirty. Then I was watching the German plane flying low over the cottages in Glengaryth, but this time the plane didn't land in a field, it landed on top of Lottie, and I burnt my hands trying to drag her out from underneath it. I tried to scream for help but no sound came out of my mouth. I waved to Gerraint and the boys, who were standing outside the bakery, but they just turned away laughing. I tried to run after them but, although I was running as fast as I could, I was getting nowhere; it was as if I was running backwards. And then the blood – rivers of it flowing from Albert's head, running out of the barn, covering the yard. I woke up shaking, covered in sweat, and knew that I had to get away from this place as fast as I could.

We walked all day. Olive kept asking questions and I was irritated by her – I didn't want to talk, I just wanted to get as far away as we could. I knew she was hungry and thirsty and the responsibility of caring for her was dragging me down.

Olive was running ahead of me. 'There's a house down there,' she shouted.

I caught up with her and stared down at the little white cottage nestling between the trees. It was pretty – all that was missing was the roses round the door. Otherwise it looked as if it had just jumped out of the pages of a storybook. I took Olive's hand and we ran down the hill.

We stood in the shadow of a tree while I decided what to do. I couldn't see any movement but that didn't mean there was no one there. We approached the cottage slowly.

'You have to be very quiet, Olive,' I said, crouching down and peering through the fence.

'I will,' she whispered.

'And if we get caught, don't tell em anything, okay?'

'Don't worry, Nell, I won't tell em you bashed Albert over the head with a shovel and he's a deader. Me lips are sealed.'

'Good girl,' I said.

I opened the gate and we crept into the garden. Running down one side was an allotment full of fruit and vegetables. My mouth watered. Olive put Auntie Missus on the ground and we started filling the pillowcase with carrots, tomatoes, lettuce and rhubarb. We desperately needed water – my mouth felt dry and my lips were sticking to my teeth. I looked around and spotted a tap under the window. I knew I was taking a chance – we could run now before we were spotted – but we weren't going to get much further without water.

I grabbed the tin mugs.

'Stay here, Olive,' I said, 'and keep down.'

She nodded and I walked towards the window. I turned on the tap and filled each mug to the brim, drank mine quickly and filled it again. I'd just started walking back towards Olive when I saw the woman. She was kneeling on the ground in front of Olive and she was smiling. She stood up when she saw me.

'We were hungry,' I said quietly. 'I'm sorry we stole your stuff.'

'You're welcome to it,' she said. 'I've got plenty, you'll be doing me a favour.'

'Oh well, that's all right then,' said Olive, taking the mug of water and gulping it down in one go.

'You should drink more slowly,' said the woman. 'Or you'll get a tummy ache.'

I didn't like how familiar she was with Olive – I was the one who looked after her, not this stranger.

'She's fine,' I said.

I can't explain the look the woman shot at me then. Was it anger?

And then her face changed and she was smiling. 'Of course she is,' she said.

For some reason I wanted to put the food back. I couldn't understand why I was feeling like I wanted nothing from this woman. I mean, I knew nothing about her and I suppose she'd actually done nothing wrong; maybe I was just finding it hard to trust anyone.

'Would you like to come inside?' asked the woman.

'Yes, please,' said Olive, skipping up the garden path towards the front door. But I stood where I was.

The woman turned back. 'There's just me,' she said. 'You'll be quite safe here.'

What made her think we needed to be safe? Had Olive said something?

'Well, it looks as though the little one has already made up her mind for you.'

I was being silly; here was someone happy to share her food with us. I was going to have to trust people some time – London was a long way away and we were going to have to rely on strangers to help us.

'Thank you,' I said.

Olive was waiting for me by the door. I took her hand and together we followed the woman into the cottage. It was lovely inside, just like you would imagine a cottage to look like. The walls were white and the curtains were cornflower blue with a scattering of white daisies. There was a window seat in the same fabric. Sun was streaming through the windows, making the room look light and bright, and there was a vase of flowers on the table.

'Please sit down,' said the woman, 'and I'll get you something to eat.'

I put the pillowcase on the floor and sat down at the wooden table. Olive stood beside me, looking warily around the room. I put my arm around her.

'My name's Clodagh,' said the woman, smiling.

I decided not to tell her our real names. 'I'm Angela,' I said. 'And this is my sister Aggie.'

'What?' said Olive.

I gave her a warning look and luckily she understood. It was reassuring to know that there was still a bit of Bermondsey left in her: she knew when to keep her mouth shut.

The woman started putting food on the table. A big loaf of crusty bread, a wedge of cheese and a bowl of red tomatoes. There was yellow butter in another dish. It looked and smelled lovely. I could sense that Olive wanted to dive in but I nodded at her to wait.

'Don't wait for me,' said the woman, sitting down with us. 'I've already eaten.'

It was the best food that I had ever tasted. The bread was soft and delicious; I smothered it in the creamy yellow butter. The cheese crumbled in my mouth and the tomatoes were sweet and crisp. Where did she get all this lovely food? There was a war on and everything was rationed, wasn't it? The food at the vicarage was yummy too, so I guessed that things must be different in the country. I had a weird feeling that the woman had been expecting us, but I knew that was daft because of course she couldn't have known we were going to come here.

'Can I ask why you're both so hungry, Angela?' said the woman.

Before I could stop her, Olive said, 'Cos we're on the run.'

'That sounds very dramatic.'

'Not really,' I said quickly, glaring at Olive, who went red in the face. 'We're evacuees, we just weren't happy in the place we were staying. We're making our way home.'

'Home?'

'London,' I said.

'Can I have some water, please, missus?' said Olive.

'Wouldn't you rather have milk, Aggie?'

'Yes, please.'

The woman filled a glass with milk. 'Here you are,' she said, putting it in front of Olive.

Olive gulped it down so fast that it dribbled over her chin. She grinned and I could see a white moustache on her upper lip.

'Gosh, you were thirsty, do you want another one?' said the woman, who seemed to be hovering over her.

'One's enough for her, thanks,' I said.

'Milk is good for her, Angela.'

'It makes her sick,' I said.

'Well, we don't want that, do we?' said the woman, barely looking at me.

'You won't tell the coppers about us, will you?' said Olive.

'I'm not a snitch,' she said, winking.

I thought that was an odd thing to say, because most adults would have been worried for our safety and felt it was their duty to let someone know about us.

'Do you promise?' said Olive.

'I promise.'

'Cut yer throat and hope to die?' said Olive.

The woman was staring at Olive as if she couldn't get enough of her; she barely paid me any attention at all. 'Cut my throat and hope to die,' she said, smiling.

I should have felt relieved but the nagging feeling that something wasn't quite right was still niggling away in my head.

'Have you had enough to eat?'

We both nodded. 'That was the best food ever,' said Olive, wiping her mouth with the back of her hand.

The woman picked up our empty plates and took them over to the sink. 'Why don't you stay the night? Have a little rest before you go on your way.'

Olive's eyes lit up. The thought of sleeping in a proper bed was pretty inviting but I just wasn't sure.

'Just one night,' said the woman. 'I have two spare rooms, it would be no trouble.'

I looked at Olive, who had a pleading kind of look on her face. 'Do you want to stay, Aggie?'

'Yes, Angela,' said Olive, emphasising the word 'Angela'. 'I'd really like to stay.'

'Okay,' I said, 'but just for one night.'

'Why don't you go into the garden while I get the rooms ready.'

Me and Olive went outside and sat on a bench.

The sun was still warm and the garden smelled of flowers and fruit and vegetables. The fields and hills stretched away in front of us.

'She's nice, isn't she, Nell?'

'Try not to use my name, love.'

'Sorry, Nell, but she's nice, isn't she?' said Olive, skipping down to the bottom of the garden.

It was so peaceful here, I should have felt safe – but I didn't. I listened to Olive chattering away to Auntie Missus. She looked so happy now that her tummy was full of the good food, so why didn't I feel happy too? I couldn't put my finger on what was bothering me. It was perfect here. Maybe that was the trouble, maybe it was too bloody perfect. Maybe that was it.

We waited in the garden until the woman came to get us. 'All ready,' she said, in a sing-song voice.

The three of us went back into the cottage and followed her upstairs. She opened a door and said, 'This is your room, Angela.'

I put my head round the door. There wasn't much furniture in the room, just a bed and a small chest of drawers. She closed the door quickly, walked along the landing and opened another door. 'And this is your room, Aggie, right next to mine. I hope you like it.'

I could see at once that it was a child's room, a little girl's room. The walls were pink and the small bed was covered in a pink bedspread. There was a white bookcase with lots of colourful books in it and sitting against the cushions was a brown teddy bear.

I looked around the room. 'Have you got a little girl?' I said.

'No, no, I haven't.' She didn't say anything else, she just stood there looking at me. I got the feeling that she didn't like me, that she wished I wasn't there.

Olive picked up the teddy and stroked its fur.

'Do you like him?' said the woman.

Olive nodded. 'But not as much as I love Auntie Missus.'

Normally I would have told her that that was a rude thing to say, but I didn't.

'Perhaps Auntie Missus would like to sit with teddy,' said the woman, reaching for the doll.

Olive backed away from her and clutched the doll close to her chest. 'I have to keep Auntie Missus with me in case she gets lonely.'

'Why do you call your doll Auntie Missus, Aggie?' asked the woman, kneeling in front of Olive. 'That's a very unusual name.'

'The lady we were staying with gave this to Aggie for Christmas, she was very fond of her,' I said.

I could see by the look on the woman's face that she didn't like that.

'I didn't just like her, Nell – I mean, Angela – I loved her.'

'Why are you running away then,' asked the woman. 'If you loved her so much?'

I could see that Olive didn't know what to say.
'It's a long story,' I said.

'Well, perhaps Aggie will tell me one day,' she said, ignoring me and smiling at Olive.

There was something wrong here: why did she say 'one day'? There wasn't going to be another day. I wanted to grab Olive and run. 'Anyway,' I said. 'Aggie sleeps with me.'

The woman's face was like thunder when she looked at me.

'Wouldn't you like to stay in this lovely room, Aggie?'

Olive looked down at the floor. 'I sleep with . . . um . . .'

'Have you forgotten your sister's name?'

'Of course she hasn't,' I said. 'She's just tired.'

'Then perhaps you should both have an early night,' she snapped.

We walked out of the room and she slammed the door behind us. Without another word she stomped down the stairs, leaving us stood on the landing.

We went into my room and sat on the bed. It was still light outside and far too early for sleep.

Olive's eyes filled with tears. 'You know I said I liked her, Nell?'

'Yes, love?'

'Well, I don't.'

'Neither do I, that's why we're going tonight.'

'I'm frightened.'

'There's nothing to be frightened of, Olive, I'll

look after you. Now I think we should try and sleep, then when we know she's gone to bed, we'll leave.'

We lay in the bed wrapped in each other's arms. Olive soon fell asleep. Her breath was warm against my cheek. My eyes were starting to feel heavy but I was too scared to close them, my ears alert to every sound in the house. I didn't trust the woman downstairs one bit. *Oh, Jimmy, where are you? Why didn't you come? If you were here, you'd know what to do. I don't know what to do.*

I must have fallen asleep because I suddenly woke with a start. I didn't know what time it was, but it was dark outside. Olive was fast asleep; I would have to wake her soon. I got out of bed and put my ear to the door but I couldn't hear anything. I went back to the bed and gently shook Olive. She opened her eyes and I put my finger to my lips. We put Auntie Missus in the pillowcase and tiptoed towards the door. I turned the handle as quietly as I could but it didn't open: the door was locked.

# CHAPTER 22

When I woke up again the sun was streaming through the window and I could hear noises coming from downstairs. I couldn't believe we'd been daft enough to walk calmly into the house of a mad-woman, because there was no doubt in my mind that she was mad. There were quite a few mad people in Rannly Court and Mum said they were more to be pitied than judged, but this was no time for pity. Clodagh wasn't going to just let us go, of that I was sure. She wanted something and that something was lying asleep beside me. I shook Olive gently and she opened her eyes. I put my arms around her and she cuddled into me. I kissed the top of her head – her hair smelled a bit musty, which wasn't surprising given that we hadn't had a proper bath since we'd left the vicarage. I had to keep her safe; that was the main thing. I had to get her away from here. I felt hot tears behind my eyes. I wanted my mum's arms around me, I wanted her to tell me that everything was going to be all right. I wanted to lay my head on her shoulder and smell home. I placed my hand where the locket used to be – how I longed to see my parents' faces. I swallowed the lump in my throat. This wasn't the time to feel sorry for myself – I had to be strong, I had to find a way out.

Olive looked up at me. 'What are we going to do, Nell?' she whispered.

'I'll tell you exactly what we're going to do, Olive. We're going to act normal. You can do that, can't you?'

'I'll try.'

'You have to do more than try, love. If we're going to get away from here you're going to have to put on the performance of your life.'

'What have I got to do?'

'You have to look happy, as if you love it here; she mustn't suspect that we know about the locked door, okay?'

'Okay.'

'Tell her that you want to stay here a bit longer.'

'But I don't.'

'Neither do I and we're not going to, but she has to think we want to. I don't know how we're going to get away but I want you to keep Auntie Missus close to you, because if we get the chance to run, we won't be able to come back for the pillowcase.'

'Okay.'

I turned the handle on the door; to my relief it opened easily. 'Now remember, Olive, look happy,' I said.

Together we went downstairs and into the kitchen.

Clodagh was cooking something over the stove. 'Good morning, sleepyheads,' she said.

'Something smells good,' I said, forcing my face into a smile.

'Are you hungry?'

'Yes,' said Olive, '*really* hungry.'

'Good,' said Clodagh, smiling. 'Now sit yourselves down.'

She'd lit a fire in the grate and the room felt lovely and warm. She was humming away as if she was a kindly aunt or something, instead of someone who had locked us in our bedroom. Somehow that made her all the more scary.

'Can we stay with you a bit longer?' Olive asked suddenly.

Clodagh turned around and gave her a big smile.

'Oh, Aggie, that would make me very happy.'

I smiled at Olive; she was doing a great job.

'And can I sleep in my own room tonight?'

'Of course you can, darling,' said Clodagh, putting a pile of pancakes on the table and adding a jug of yellow honey.

'And once you've had your breakfast we can all go out into the garden and play a lovely game. Would you like that?'

'I'd love that,' said Olive.

'Could I have a drink of water, please?' I asked.

'Of course,' replied Clodagh, turning her back on us and going over to the sink.

'Hide and seek,' I mouthed to Olive.

Clodagh came back with a glass of water and put it down in front of me.

'My favourite game's hide and seek,' said Olive.

'That was Christine's favourite game too,' said Clodagh.

I gave Olive a warning look and she didn't ask any questions, but I was pretty sure that the pink bedroom up the stairs had once belonged to a little girl called Christine, and this madwoman wanted to replace her with Olive. Well, that would be over my dead body lady.

The three of us poured the golden honey over the pancakes. Clodagh giggled as it ran down her chin. 'Isn't this yummy?' she said, smiling.

I nodded.

'Yummy,' said Olive.

After we'd eaten, we went out into the garden. It was a beautiful day, the sun was warm and there was a hazy mist drifting down over the hill. A swarm of midges hovered above our heads. It was a perfect early summer's day – except there was nothing perfect about it.

'Okay,' I said, 'I'll close my eyes and you two hide.' I closed my eyes and started counting to a hundred. The first thing we had to do was gain her confidence, so we would have to play the game until she trusted us. 'Coming, ready or not,' I shouted. I could hear rustling in the bushes; Olive had never been very good at hiding. I parted the bushes and took her hand, and we started to look for Clodagh. I had the feeling we were being watched, as if Clodagh was testing us, so I winked at Olive and said, 'Are you enjoying yourself, Aggie?'

'Oh, I wish we could stay here forever, Angela.'

'Perhaps we can,' I said. 'Would you like me to ask Clodagh?'

'Yes, please.'

We looked all round the garden but there was no sign of her. Then I heard a noise behind me as Clodagh ran through the garden and touched base.

'I won!' she shrieked, as if she was six years old and not a grown-up woman.

'It's your turn to count now,' said Olive. 'Because you won.'

Clodagh looked wary, as if she was deciding whether that was a good idea or not.

'That's the rules,' Olive insisted.

Clodagh closed her eyes and started to count. We hid in places where she could easily find us. She was jumping up and down with excitement. 'Isn't this fun?' she shouted.

'My turn,' said Olive.

Clodagh grabbed me and pulled me behind the shed. I hated the feel of her hand in mine, it made my skin crawl. 'I'm having the best time,' she whispered, as we crouched down together. 'Aren't you?'

For a moment I almost felt sorry for her. I guessed she'd been lonely but this was no time for pity. She was beginning to trust us; it wouldn't be long now.

Then it was Clodagh's turn to count again. 'Can we hide in the house?' I asked.

'What a wonderful idea,' said Clodagh. 'Of course you can.'

She had her back to us and she was counting out loud. 'Sixteen, seventeen, eighteen . . .'

It was now or never.

We tiptoed towards the gate, opened it as quietly as we could, and started running.

# CHAPTER 23

We ran and ran, keeping to the edges of the fields. We pushed our way through brambles and we climbed over stiles. I kept looking back to make sure Clodagh wasn't following us but there was no sign of her. I began to relax.

'I'm tired, Nell,' said Olive. 'And so is Auntie Missus.'

'I know you are, Olive, but we need to get as far away from Clodagh as we can. We'll find shelter soon,' I said. 'Then you can rest.'

'I can run a bit further,' said Olive.

'Good girl.'

The light was beginning to fade from the sky by the time we spotted the building.

We walked towards it – it was some sort of outbuilding, maybe another barn. It looked abandoned but we stood outside for a while until we were sure that there was no one around.

'Come on,' I said.

It was pretty much the same as the barn where we had waited for Jimmy. It felt cold inside, as if it had never known sunlight. I shivered – we weren't dressed for this. If only we could have brought our coats with us. Above us was a loft with a ladder leading up to it. I remembered Daddy once telling me that heat rises. I didn't remember what we'd been talking about, but I remembered him telling me this.

'We should go up into the loft, Olive,' I said. 'It will be warmer up there. Do you think you can manage the ladder?'

'Of course I can, I'm not a baby, you know. And neither is Auntie Missus.'

'Of course you're not. Give her to me – it will be easier for you to climb.'

Olive handed me the doll and started climbing. I went up after her. Daddy had been right; it was warmer up there.

As we had nothing to eat or drink, there was not much for us to do. 'We might as well sleep,' I said. 'Then we can make an early start in the morning.'

Olive yawned. 'I'm not a bit tired, Nell.'

'Just try,' I said, lying down beside her, 'and tomorrow we'll find some food.'

I put my arms around her and stared up at the old beams above my head. Olive was soon breathing steadily and it wasn't long before I joined her.

I was woken by a deafening sound that seemed to be coming from directly over my head. I looked at Olive, who was still asleep. I climbed down the ladder and went outside. Four planes were zooming low across the fields and disappearing over the hill. I couldn't tell if they were ours or the enemy's but it brought home to me the fact that there was still a war on.

I felt wide awake as I gazed up at the sky, which was full of stars. It was beautiful and for a moment I felt a sense of peace that I hadn't felt in a long time. I knew it wouldn't last but I wanted to hold this feeling inside me for a little longer. I sat down on the ground and leaned back against the wooden barn. I thought about Mum and Tony and little Freddie. I thought about my good friend Angela and Mrs Baxter. I wondered if Lottie was happy in Cornwall and I wondered when I would see her again and when we would stand together at the edge of the ocean. And then I thought about Jimmy. Was he still at the farm, or had he run away to make his fortune? Would I ever see him again? How was he going to explain to Mrs Hacker what had happened to Albert? Mrs Hacker might not have been my favourite person in the whole world but Albert was her son and she loved him and she was going to be heartbroken.

I wished for the millionth time that I hadn't killed him. I still couldn't believe that I had actually ended the life of another human being. Did I have to kill him? I could have just threatened to tell his mother, but when I saw what he was about to do to innocent little Olive, I saw red. I was angry, angrier than I had ever been in my whole life and, yes, in that moment, in that barn, I wanted him dead. I wanted him splattered on the ground. I wanted to bash his brains out, that's what I'd wanted to do. We think we know ourselves, don't we? But we don't. We judge the murderers and the thieves and the beggars without knowing their stories. We judge them because we think we're better than they are, that we're the goodies in the white hats and they're the baddies in the black ones. But now I knew that underneath my hat I was as capable of killing and thieving as the worst thugs in Rannly Court. So much had happened since we'd left Bermondsey, it felt like another life. I was just an ordinary kid when I'd said goodbye to Mum in the flat but now I was a murderer and I was on the run from the law. How the bloody hell had that happened?

We set off the next morning just as the sun was coming up over the hill. It was harder to walk fast today. Olive wasn't running ahead of me like she was yesterday. We were both hungry and thirsty; we had to find food and water.

'Do you know how proud I am of you, Olive?' I said, as we walked along.

'Why are you proud of me, Nell?'

'Because you're brave and strong and you deserve to be wearing that white hat.'

'What white hat?' she asked, puzzled.

'The one that no one can see.'

'You're funny, do you know that?' she said, giggling.

'I do my best.'

'You need some food, Nell, cos I think you're going doolally.'

'Do you know what, Olive?'

'What?'

'You've stopped swearing.'

'I don't think it will last, Nell, it's just what my mouth seems to do.'

'You make me happy, Olive.'

'Well, that's good then, isn't it?' she said, grinning.

Eventually we came to a row of cottages. There was a girl of about my age hanging out some washing in one of the gardens. She had clothes pegs between her lips.

'Excuse me?' I said.

She looked at us and took the pegs out of her mouth. 'Can I help you?' she questioned.

'Some water, if you can spare it.'

She walked across to us.

'You're not spies, are you?'

'No, we're not spies,' I said.

'You can't be too careful these days.'

'We're definitely not spies,' I said. 'We're just thirsty.'

'No. You don't look like spies, but then again how are we supposed to know what a spy looks like?'

'Tricky,' said Olive.

She must have decided we weren't spies because she said, 'You can come in if you like, me mum's not here.'

'We'd rather not if you don't mind,' I said.

'We're not good with cottages,' said Olive.

'Fair enough,' said the girl, grinning. 'Well, come into the garden at least.'

I opened the gate and we went in.

'Are you hungry?' she asked.

I nodded.

'Okay, wait here.'

We watched her walk into the house. 'Do you think she's okay?' said Olive. 'She's not going to come back out with a shotgun, is she?'

'You've got a very vivid imagination, Olive.'

'After what we've been through I don't trust anyone, Nell. Especially people what live in cottages.'

'Perfectly understandable,' I said.

'Best be on our guard,' said Olive seriously.

The girl came towards us carrying a tray. To our delight there was bread and cheese, Welsh cakes and two cups of water.

'Mam made these cakes before she went out,' she said, grinning.

'What's your name?' I said, taking the tray from her and putting it down on the grass.

'Annadwen,' she said.

'Anna what?' said Olive, screwing up her nose.

'I know, bloody awful, isn't it? I don't know what my mother was thinking. It means "goddess of poetic inspiration". Never read a poem in my life!'

'Well, maybe you should start,' said Olive. 'You might turn into a goddess. I wouldn't mind being a goddess.'

'Well, I think it's pretty,' I said.

'Thanks, but I prefer Annie.'

We all sat down on the grass and started to eat. Olive bit into the bread. 'I wonder what my name means,' she said.

'My mother has a book all about names and their meanings. I can get it, if you like.'

'Yes, please,' said Olive. 'I might be a goddess as well.'

Annie went back into the cottage and after a few minutes came out, carrying a book. She flicked through the pages. 'Olive,' she said, reading aloud. 'From the Latin, meaning "symbol of peace".'

'Not as good as a goddess though, is it?' said Olive, looking disappointed.

'I think that's lovely, Olive,' I said.

She thumbed back a few pages. 'Want to know the meaning of yours?' she asked, smiling at me.

'Okay.'

Annie turned another few pages. 'Nell,' she said. 'Meaning "bright and shining light".'

'I prefer yours, Nell,' said Olive.

'Well, I think they're both nice,' said the girl.

The food was just what we needed and it would give us the strength to carry on walking.

'Where are you going?' said the girl.

'We're going home,' said Olive. 'To London.'

'You won't tell anyone you saw us, will you?' I said.

'Of course I won't,' said the girl. 'I guess you're evacuees then?'

I nodded.

'Don't worry, I won't tell a soul.'

'Do you know the woman who lives in the white cottage?' I pointed across the fields. 'A couple of miles over there.'

'Clodagh Price?'

I nodded.

'Everyone knows her. She's been a bit odd ever since she lost her daughter.'

'What did she die of?' I asked.

'Oh, she didn't die,' said Annie. 'Her husband ran off with her and they were never seen again. It was in all the papers at the time. She never got over it, poor woman. Do you know her then?'

'We stayed there last night.'

'She locked us in the bedroom,' said Olive.

'Blimey, why'd she do that?'

'We didn't hang around to find out,' I said.

Annie shook her head. 'As me mum would say, there's none so queer as folk.'

'She was queer all right,' said Olive. 'Frightened the bloody life out of us, she did.'

Annie grinned at her. 'Has anyone ever told you, you've got an old head on young shoulders?'

'People tell me lots of things – I don't take much notice of most of it.'

'Good for you,' said Annie, smiling.

It was so peaceful sitting on the grass in the sunshine with this sweet girl. I wished we could stay longer.

'Could we take the cakes with us, instead of eating them now?' I said.

'Of course you can, and I'll get you some more bread and cheese.'

'Won't your mum mind?'

'I'll tell her there was a starving beggar at the door. She's big on the Good Samaritan story; she'll help anyone, my mother.'

'She sounds kind,' said Olive, her eyes suddenly filling with tears. 'I've got a kind mum an all.'

I put my arm around her shoulder. 'We'll see her soon,' I said.

'I miss her, Nell,' she said, wiping her face on the sleeve of her cardigan.

'I know you do, darling. So do I.'

Annie pointed to Olive's doll. 'Has she got a name?'

'Her name's Auntie Missus,' said Olive. 'My mum hasn't met her yet.'

'I bet she'll love her.'

Olive smiled at her. I really liked this girl; she reminded me a bit of Angela.

'Are we going in the right direction?' I said.

'Keep going the way you're going and you'll come to Cardiff. Keep away from the docks if you can, they're getting bombed something awful.'

'We will,' I promised.

'Pick some fruit and veg and I'll get something to put them in. I'd like you to stay and meet my mum but grown-ups have a habit of doing the right thing. She might feel the need to dob you in.'

'Don't worry, it's time we were on our way.'

Annie went back into the cottage and returned with a bag full of bread and cheese and a bottle of water. We added carrots and tomatoes, lettuces and the cakes.

She handed me a grey blanket. 'I thought you could use this,' she said.

'You're an angel,' said Olive. 'A proper angel.'

'If my mum heard you say that she'd laugh fit to bust,' she said, hugging Olive. 'I hope you get home okay.'

'We will,' I said. 'And thank you ever so much.'

'You saved our arses,' said Olive.

Annie put her arms around me and we hugged. 'Keep safe,' she said.

I kissed her cheek. 'We will.'

We waved to Annie until she was just a speck in the distance.

'I really liked her, Nell. Did you really like her?'

'I thought she was lovely,' I answered.

'Just goes to show,' said Olive, 'not everyone what lives in cottages is barmy.'

'It does, doesn't it?'

For the next few days we walked, we ate and we slept, finding shelter wherever we could. In sheds, under bushes and once in a derelict house that still had running water, where we were able to refill the bottle. The nearer we got to Cardiff, the more we were made aware of the war. The sky in the distance was often bright red as if it was on fire, and we could hear the occasional muffled explosion. We were walking into a war zone but there was nothing we could do about it – it was the only way back to London.

'Are you scared, Olive?' I asked.

She shook her head. 'Not really, Nell, cos it reminds me of home.'

'I hadn't thought of that,' I said, smiling at her.

We had eked out the food and the water and now we had to find more. Meeting Annie had given me hope that maybe there would be more people like her along the way.

The closer we got to Cardiff, the more anxious I got. The bombing raids seemed nearer and sometimes the air was thick and smoky and full of debris, just like Bermondsey. How awful to have come so far only to get killed. Mum would never know what had happened to us. As it was, we hadn't been able to write to her since leaving the farm. There seemed to be so much to worry about that there were days when I wondered if we would ever get back home.

I'm not sure when I started to feel ill. At first it was just my legs – they felt heavy, I was dragging myself along. It was like walking through treacle. Then, even though it was warm and sunny,

I started to shiver – even my teeth were rattling. 'I don't feel so good, Olive,' I said, sitting down on the grass.

'Is it the scarlet fever, Nell? Is that what you've got?'

'I hope not,' I said.

'Do you want a drink of water?'

'I think we should save it, there isn't much left.'

'Well, I think *you* should have a drink of water, Nell. You might not have the scarlet fever, but it could still be something deadly like . . .'

'Like what?' I said, looking up at her.

'I dunno. Just somethin deadly. You know, somethin you die of, a deadly sort of thing.'

'Thanks for that, Olive.'

'You're very welcome, Nell.'

My head started to pound; it felt as if someone was hammering inside my skull. 'Can you run up ahead, Olive, and see if there's somewhere I could rest for a bit,' I said.

'I'll leave Auntie Missus here, she's not feeling very well either – I think she must have caught it from you.'

Olive laid the blanket down on the grass. 'Lie down on that, Nell.'

I took the doll from her and lay down on the blanket. The shivering had stopped and now I felt as if every bit of me was on fire. I tugged at my clothes, I wanted to rip them off. I pulled myself up and looked across the fields to see if Olive was coming back but everything was fuzzy. I lay down again. I had never felt so ill in my life; I felt as though I was floating. It was a nice feeling, kind of peaceful. I closed my eyes and gave into it. That was the last thing I remembered.

# CHAPTER 24

There's a halfway place between being awake and being asleep and I kept finding myself drifting through this place.

One moment I was lying in the field with the grass so close to my face and the sky above me, and the world felt as if it was tilting and I was going to fall off and spin out into the universe. And the next I was awake; at least, I thought I was awake. When I opened my eyes I was back home, in my own bed, in the flat. The light coming through the window was very bright, so bright it hurt my eyes, and I could hear Mum humming and the rattling of pots and pans that meant she was making supper, and I felt so happy. I'd never left home. Me and Olive hadn't ended up at the farm and I'd never killed anyone; it had all been a dream. But then the humming and the rattling drew away from me and the brightness faded and I felt as if I was falling again, falling back into sleep.

Next time I thought I was awake, I felt very warm and comfortable but when I opened my eyes I was in an unfamiliar room, or was it a room I recognised? I didn't know and I thought perhaps I was back in the cottage with mad Clodagh, and I cried out and someone's hand was on my forehead. I thought it must be Mum, only it was a rough hand, like a man's hand, and I started to fall again, sliding sweetly downhill into the darkness.

Once I woke and I saw Olive. I saw her clearly, kneeling on a seat underneath a window. Her chin was in her hands, her elbows on the window ledge, and she was looking out the window and laughing to herself. I thought: *Oh, that's all right then, we're safe,* and that time I slipped back down into unconsciousness feeling as if a weight had been lifted from my shoulders. I remembered a flannel on my face, the smell of coal tar soap, a towel on my arms and voices: Olive's chattering and a lower, gruffer voice, a man's voice. I felt a weight on the bed, by my legs, something warm pressed up against me.

The next time I opened my eyes it was light. I could see bright sunshine filtering into the room through a gap in the curtains. Under the window was a seat, so I hadn't imagined it. I looked around the room and winced; my head felt too heavy for my body. The room was unfamiliar to me but I was relieved to see that it wasn't Clodagh Price's cottage.

I closed my eyes again. I had never felt so tired in my life. I was happy just to stay like this, warm and safe. I didn't much care whose house I was

213

in, I didn't much care about anything – it was the strangest feeling.

I must have slept again and the next time I opened my eyes I saw Olive. She was on the window seat again. Her legs were spread out in front of her, with Auntie Missus lying on her lap.

'Olive,' I croaked.

She spun round, jumped down from the seat and came across to the bed.

'You woke up?' she said, smiling.

I nodded.

'I'll get the mister,' she added, running out of the room.

She came back almost at once, followed by an old man.

'So you've come back to us,' he said, smiling down at me.

'I think so,' I said.

'Good,' he said.

'How did I get here?'

'The mister carried you, Nell, and I helped him.'

'I was walking Henri—' began the man.

'That's his dog, Nell, and he's really friendly and he likes me,' interrupted Olive.

'—when I saw this young lady running towards me. You gave her quite a fright, you know. She was yelling something about her sister having the scarlet fever.'

Olive's eyes filled with tears. 'I thought you was a goner, Nell.'

I reached for her hand. 'I'm sorry, Olive.' My

eyes felt heavy again and I rubbed at them, trying to keep them open. 'I'm so tired,' I said.

'Sleep is what you need right now,' said the man gently. 'You sleep as much as you can.'

'But she's been asleep for bloody years!' Olive protested.

I closed my eyes and smiled: Olive was swearing again.

One morning I woke and decided that I wanted to get up. I swung my legs out of the bed but, as soon as I tried to put some weight on them, I collapsed in a heap on the floor. The noise brought Olive and the old man running up the stairs. Between them they helped me back onto the bed.

'My legs feel wobbly,' I said.

'I should think they do,' said the old man. 'You haven't used them for a long time.'

'How long?'

'Bloody years, Nell!'

I looked at the man. 'I haven't been asleep for years, have I?'

'No,' he said, smiling. 'I think perhaps your little sister likes to exaggerate.'

'Well, it seems like bloody years,' said Olive. 'I thought you were never gonna wake up.'

'Almost three weeks,' said the man.

I couldn't believe it. 'I've been asleep for three weeks?' I said.

The man nodded. 'Quite the little sleeping beauty.'

'What's been wrong with me then?'

'In my very humble opinion I'd say you were exhausted, both physically and, I'm afraid, mentally.'

'You'd had enough,' said Olive, very seriously.

'Thank you for taking care of me, mister.'

'I'm glad I could help,' he said. 'And my name is Yann, Yann Kovak.'

'Yann?' I said.

'It means "God is gracious",' he said.

'Well, I don't know about that,' said Olive. 'We've had one hell of a time and we haven't come across much graciousness from God or any other bugger.'

'But he guided us here, Olive,' I said gently.

'I suppose he did,' she agreed reluctantly.

'So what would you like to call me?'

'We'll call you Yann,' said Olive, smiling at him.

'I'm not sure we should, Olive.'

'Oh, I don't mind,' he said. 'I happen to quite like the name.'

I could tell by the way he spoke that he wasn't English and he definitely wasn't Welsh.

'I'm Polish,' he said, as if he knew what I had been thinking.

'Our neighbour, Mr Gavlick in Rannly Court, is Polish,' I said.

'He hasn't got a dog, though,' said Olive.

'So, you feel strong enough to get up, do you?'

'I thought I did.'

'How about if I put a chair by the window so that you can see outside? Would you like that?'

'Yes, I would,' I said, smiling.

Yann pulled a chair across the room and helped me out of bed. This time I leaned on him as he lowered me into the chair.

'Now, Olive,' he said. 'Shall we make some good soup for your sister, to make her strong again?'

'Okay,' said Olive. 'And try not to go to sleep again, Nell.'

Yann winked at me. 'You sleep as much as you like,' he whispered, placing a rug over my knees.

Just as Olive was about to go out of the room she turned back to me and said: 'Am I still six, Nell?'

'No,' I said. 'You're seven.'

'When did that happen?'

'At the farm.'

'I thought I felt bigger,' she said, running down the stairs.

# CHAPTER 25

As the days and weeks went by I began to feel stronger – at least, my body did – but I still felt oddly detached from everything. I watched Olive playing in the garden with Henri and I ate a little of the food that Yann prepared for me. I felt at peace living here but I had lost something; I had lost something of the girl I used to be. I barely thought about all that had happened – if it crept into my mind, I pushed it away. I had even stopped wanting to return to London. The thought of taking to the road again and having to look for food and shelter made my head hurt, so I pushed it to the back of my mind. I knew that the time would come when we would have to leave, as we couldn't stay here forever; we couldn't expect Yann to continue to feed us and put us up in his house. But for now we would stay where we were. I couldn't think beyond today.

Yann asked no questions and I was relieved because I wasn't ready to give him any answers. This gentle man just accepted that me and Olive needed him and so he looked after us as if we were his own.

In the evenings he read to us, lovely stories that I'd never even heard of. My favourite was *Wuthering Heights* by Emily Brontë. Somehow it touched something inside me; maybe it was the wild and lonely moors, which reminded me of Jimmy. It was a love story but it wasn't slushy, not like the ones that Mrs Llewellyn and Auntie Beth liked to read. I would sit in a comfy chair beside the fire, close my eyes and listen to Yann's soft voice. Often I would feel tears running down my cheeks. I cried a lot these days over the silliest of things, like watching Olive curled up with the dog, or the smell of roses, or the soft morning mist that hovered like a cloud over the hillside. No one said anything, they just let me cry.

One morning I asked Yann for some paper and a pencil. I sat at an old wooden desk by the window, and a beam of sunshine fell onto the page as I wrote. Even this small task of putting pencil to paper was almost too much for me, but I let Mum know where we were and that we were safe, and I told her how much we both missed and loved her. Yann and Olive walked into the village to post it.

As I sat in the little garden on my own I wondered again why Jimmy hadn't met us in the barn. I'd grown so very fond of him while living in that horrible place and I knew that he felt the same about me. I'd only been fourteen but sometimes when I looked at him I'd felt something inside that I had never felt before. I'd trusted him and I'd known that he would never do anything to hurt me.

In Bermondsey, sex was talked about all the time. The women would stand in huddles in the square, their arms folded, their laughter loud and raucous, echoing around the tenements. While babies and toddlers played at their feet, they discussed in vivid detail what their old men had got up to the night before. They never said that they were carrying a child, they would say they were 'up the spout again' and someone would reply, 'You should tell him to tie a knot in it.' Boys would shout rude things as the girls walked by and the girls would simper and make eyes at them. Sex in Bermondsey was a crude thing, a thing to be laughed at, a thing to be whispered about and giggled over. That wasn't how I felt about Jimmy. What I felt was gentle and precious, the beginning of something that I didn't really understand, something that lay soft as a feather inside my heart, the promise of something in the future that I would dream about in bed at night.

And so autumn came, in all its glorious colour. I had grown to love this season, more beautiful somehow than the promise of spring or the brightness of summer, a gentle pause before winter set in.

One morning I decided to join Yann and Olive on their daily walk with Henri. It felt strange to go beyond the garden and my place of safety.

The leaves above me as we walked down the lane were a vivid mixture of browns and reds and golds, like a multi-coloured umbrella touching the blue sky, then drifting like gentle rain from the trees, forming a bright carpet under my feet as I walked. There was a chill in the air and the acrid smell of smoke from a bonfire, mixed with the dry, sharp, prickly smell of damp and dying things.

I let them walk ahead of me; my steps were slower these days and I was less confident, somehow. Yann said this feeling wouldn't last and I wanted to believe him.

I watched as Olive kicked up the leaves and I listened to her laughter as she let them drift down over her head. I noticed that she was getting taller, her legs strong and straight as she raced after Henri. It was hard to believe that she was only seven. She had been so brave on this journey we had shared, never complaining, always managing to find something to laugh about and to make me laugh in the darkest of times.

I watched Yann throwing a stick for Henri, then throwing it again as the dog retrieved it and came running back to him. It was hard to tell Yann's age – his hair was white but there were no lines on his face. His eyes were a grey-blue and kind, always kind. I knew if I told him what I had done he would understand, I knew he wouldn't judge me. I had a feeling that he also had a story to tell and maybe one day I would get to hear it.

I learned that he had been a teacher in Poland and, on hearing that Olive hadn't had any schooling for almost a year, he began to teach her. Every morning they would sit together at the kitchen table. Yann made it fun and Olive soon caught up with the lessons she'd missed. I would sit by the fire watching them, one white head and one auburn one bent over the books. Most mornings the house would be filled with the sound of their laughter.

It had been weeks since Yann and Olive had posted my letter to Mum, but I still hadn't heard from her.

'The war has disrupted everything, Nell, including our wonderful postal system,' Yann explained. 'The reality is that she may not even have received your letter. Be patient, dear, and try not to worry. I'm sure you'll hear from her very soon.'

And so as autumn gave way to winter, I waited. I grew stronger and I smiled more, but I never heard from Mum and I kept trying to push away the thought that something was wrong. We'd got letters from her at the vicarage and at the farm, so why not here? It didn't make any sense.

'Why don't you write to her again?' said Yann.

And so I did, but the months passed with no reply.

It was nearly Christmas and snow had been falling for weeks. Yann and Olive still walked Henri every day and returned with red cheeks and noses.

Henri would bound into the house, wagging his tail and shaking snow from his fur, which flew all over the room, then he would flop down in front of the fire, filling the house with the smell of wet dog.

One morning Olive decided to build a snowman.

'Wanna help me, Nell?' she asked.

I shook my head.

'Still feeling under the weather?'

I nodded. 'I'm much better though,' I said, smiling at her.

'These things take time,' she said very seriously.

'Who told you that?'

'Yann did, and he should know, he's a teacher.'

'I'll watch you from the window,' I said.

'Okay,' she replied happily, and ran out into the garden with Henri bounding behind her.

I watched her for a bit, rolling the snow into a big snowball, then lifting her face up to the sky and letting the flakes fall onto her tongue. Henri was racing round her like a mad thing and rolling over and over.

'He still thinks he's a puppy,' said Yann, coming into the room carrying an armful of logs.

I turned around and faced him. 'I think something's happened to my mum,' I said.

Yann bent down and put the logs in a basket beside the fireplace.

'Maybe we should ask the authorities – they might know something,' he said.

'NO!' I screamed. 'You can't do that, promise

you won't do that, you have to promise, Yann. You *have* to promise.'

Yann walked across to me. 'Hush now,' he said. 'I won't do anything you don't want me to do, Nell, you have my word.'

My heart was beating so loud I felt sick. I put my head in my hands and sobbed, great heaving sobs. I hadn't been able to feel anything for months but now it poured from me, filling my chest so that I could hardly breathe.

Yann knelt down at my feet until the crying eased, leaving me gulping for air.

'Better?' he asked softly.

I nodded.

'Sometimes it helps to talk, you know. I think that you are holding onto an awful lot of pain in that little body of yours. This is a place of safety, Nell. These walls won't talk and neither will I.'

I looked into his eyes and whispered, 'I killed someone, Yann.' The relief once I'd said it was overwhelming.

'Do you want to tell me why?'

And so as Olive built her snowman and the fire crackled away in the grate I told my story. When I had finished, Yann took hold of my hands and said, 'I also killed a man, Nell, and like you, it was to protect someone I loved.' He gently wiped away my tears. 'I couldn't save my wife but with the help of strangers I came here, I found this place. It was a wreck when I moved in so I got it cheap and then I made it into a home. The physical work helped me to cope with my grief and my guilt. We are not bad people, you and I, but we have both encountered evil and we both did what we had to do. I understand, dear girl, and I will hold your secret in my heart as I know you will hold mine.'

Just at that moment Olive ran into the kitchen. 'I need a carrot for his nose and coal for his buttons and a hat and a scarf, and I'm starving! What's the matter with you two?'

'Nothing at all,' said Yann, smiling. 'There is nothing wrong with us at all.'

When I woke on Christmas morning something felt different – not just the bright light that flooded the room but also the strange silence. I got out of bed and went across to the window. The hills were covered in a blanket of new white snow. I suddenly wanted to be part of it, the newness of it, the freshness of it. I looked across at Olive, who was still fast asleep.

I dressed quickly and went downstairs. Henri was lying in front of the fire. He raised his head and wagged his tail as I entered the kitchen. Yann was peeling potatoes at the table.

'Happy Christmas, Nell,' said Yann, smiling.

'Happy Christmas,' I said.

'No Olive?'

'She's still asleep.'

'Would you like some porridge?'

I shook my head. 'Is it okay if I go for a walk?'

'Take Henri with you,' he said.

I took my coat down from the peg, jammed a woollen hat over my ears and opened the kitchen door. 'Come on, Henri,' I called.

I walked down the lane. Henri raced ahead of me, delighted at this unexpected walk. He ran through the trees and snuffled in the hedgerows. Every so often he ran back to me bearing gifts of snowy twigs and bits of undergrowth, as if he was making sure that I was all right. His nose was white and blobs of snow clung to his fur like soft balls of cotton wool, making him look like some alien creature.

Each step I took made a new footprint, as if I was the only person in the world, as if no one but me had ever walked this way before.

I was glad to be alone on this Christmas morning, glad to be here in this lovely place, the silence broken only by the distant sound of a church bell and the soft flurry of snow as it drifted like white powder from the branches of the trees.

I leaned on the fence and looked out over the snowy hills, sparkling like a million diamonds in the early morning sun, and I felt something change, as if the ice that had formed around my heart was beginning to thaw, like the warmth of a summer's day. There was a stillness inside me and a feeling of calm that I hadn't felt for so long. It was as if I was waking from a long sleep and I felt thankful to be here on this perfect day, in this beautiful place. And something else: I wasn't afraid anymore. It was time to go back home to Bermondsey, it was time to be with my family. I called Henri and together we walked back to the house, not slowly this time, but with a determined stride. My legs ached from so little use but I knew that they would grow stronger. They would carry me through the lanes and over the hills; they would carry me home.

# CHAPTER 26

I kept these feelings to myself until the New Year, when I told Yann that it was time for us to go.

A few days later I broke the news to Olive. Henri was asleep under the kitchen table and she was absentmindedly stroking his fur with her foot.

'But we *are* at home,' she said, looking confused.

'This isn't our home, Olive,' I said gently. 'This is Yann's home. Our home is Rannly Court, with Mum and Tony and Freddie.'

'Have we got to go on the run again?' she asked, looking worried. 'I don't think I want to do that, Nell.'

'It will be different this time,' I said.

'How will it be different?' said Olive.

'Because this time you will be going on a train,' said Yann, smiling at her.

Olive's eyes filled with tears. 'We won't have to sleep in no more barns?' she said.

'No,' said Yann. 'No more barns.'

Olive grinned and jumped down from the table.

'Where are you going?' I asked.

'To tell Auntie Missus,' she said, grinning. 'She needs to know these things.'

'Of course she does,' I said. 'And do you think she'll be pleased?'

'I think she'll be pleased when I tell her we don't have to sleep in any more bloody barns!'

'Oh, Olive,' I said. 'You do make me laugh.'

'Have you got a spare pillowcase, Mr Yann?'

'Why on earth do you need a pillowcase, Olive?'

Olive raised her eyes to the ceiling. 'To pack our stuff in, of course.'

'I think we can do better than that,' said Yann. 'I'm pretty sure I have a proper case somewhere.'

'Well, that's a relief,' said Olive, 'cos I don't think all our stuff will fit in a pillowcase anymore.'

Olive was right. A few months after we'd got here Yann had gone into Cardiff and bought us new clothes, including a red coat for Olive and a navy blue one for me. He also bought us under-wear and jumpers, skirts and good strong boots. I can remember him coming home with them. I was sitting by the fire, still weak and unwell, when he came into the room carrying loads of bags.

'I had to guess your sizes,' he said. 'I hope they're okay.'

I, of course, immediately started to cry. Olive, on the other hand, proceeded to give us a fashion show, where she pranced around the kitchen in all her finery. This man had been so kind to us and I would miss him terribly, but now it was time to go home.

After Olive had gone upstairs with Henri at her

heels I looked around the room. We had been so happy here. I smiled at Yann. 'I don't know how we can thank you enough,' I said. 'For all you've done for us.'

'It's me who should be thanking you, Nell. I hadn't realised how lonely I was until you came. I've loved having you both here.'

'But won't you be lonely again when we've gone? I would hate to think that you were lonely.'

'Maybe it's time for me to reach out, Nell. People have tried to befriend me, it's me that's pushed them away.'

'I wish you would,' I said. 'I'd feel better knowing that you had friends.'

'There's a man I see sometimes when I walk Henri – he has a dog too and Henri likes to play with him. I get the feeling he is also alone. I know where he lives, so maybe I'll pay him a visit.'

'That would make me very happy.'

'There is a passage in the Bible, Nell, that I have always loved. It goes, "There is a time for every purpose under heaven". Maybe it's my time to say hello to the world again.'

I stood up and put my arms around him. His face felt rough against my cheek. 'I love you, Yann,' I said. 'You saved my life.'

'And I think, my dear child, that you have perhaps saved mine,' he said.

It was the beginning of spring when we finally set out on our journey home. We had to get a bus to

Cardiff; Yann came with us. As we got closer to the city we could see the damage that had been done. We passed bombed-out buildings, piles of rubble, houses with walls and chimneys gone, just like the one me and Angela used to sit in. There was a church with its spire missing and sandbags piled up against the front doors. We passed a beautiful castle perched on the top of a grassy hill.

'Does the King live there?' asked Olive.

'Not the King, no,' said Yann. 'It is owned by the fourth Marquess of Bute – he inherited it from his father.'

'Is he a good man?' said Olive.

'I believe that he has done a lot for the people of Cardiff, Olive, so yes, I think he is a good man.'

Out of nowhere, an air-raid siren sounded. I felt sick; I'd forgotten that horrible noise and how terrified it used to make me feel. Olive buried her face in my lap. 'I'm scared, Nell,' she said. 'I think we should go back home.' It made me realise how Yann had put himself in danger to buy our new clothes. I hadn't thought about it at the time. I hadn't thought about much at the time.

The conductor hurried everyone off the bus and we followed him and the driver across the grass towards the castle. More people were hurrying behind us.

'Where are we going?' I asked.

'There's a shelter inside the ramparts that surround the castle, we will be safe there,' explained Yann.

Just at that moment there was a loud explosion, which shook the ground beneath our feet. Olive screamed and Yann pulled us both down onto the ground; people around us were doing the same. I lay there, my heart pounding in my chest and Olive whimpering beside me. Maybe she was right – maybe we should go back with Yann. We were safe in the country, that's why Mum had sent us away. Would she be cross with me for endangering Olive's life like this?

After the explosion everything went quiet and you could have heard a pin drop. We stayed flattened against the grass; the all-clear hadn't yet sounded so there could be more bombs. Eventually people started to stand up. I looked back at the city. Smoke and flames were rising up above the buildings, filling the air with that horrible acrid smell that caught at the back of your throat and made you want to throw up. That horrible smell which reminded me of home.

The siren continued to whine and people started running again. 'Give me Auntie Missus, Olive,' I said. Olive gave me the doll and I tucked her under my coat.

We reached the castle walls and were ushered inside by a warden. We followed him along tunnels, loads of them. We passed a table with a woman serving tea; there was a menu on the wall, telling you what you could have to eat.

'Hungry?' asked Yann.

'A bit,' I said.

'Starving,' said Olive.

There were benches all along the walls that were quickly filling up with people.

'Grab a seat,' said Yann, 'and I'll get us something to eat.'

We sat down beside a lady holding a little baby. She was feeding it with her titty, milk trickling down its chin. The baby was concentrating very hard, its tiny fists pummelling the woman's breast. I smiled at the woman and she smiled back.

'Thank God for the Marquess,' she said. 'He is a saint.'

'Is he?' asked Olive, round-eyed.

'He is,' said the woman. 'He takes good care of the common people.'

'Are we common, Nell?' whispered Olive.

'Probably,' I said, grinning back at her.

Yann brought back three cups of tea and some spam sandwiches.

'Would you like a cup of tea and a sandwich?' he asked the woman, in his gentle voice.

'I'd slit me throat for a cuppa,' she said, smiling up at him.

'There'll be no need for that,' said Yann, laughing.

As he went to get her tea the all-clear sounded.

'Don't worry about the tea,' shouted the woman, unlatching the baby none too gently from her breast. 'I've got a nice bit of tripe and onions back in my kitchen. That's if I've got a kitchen left!' For some reason this made her laugh fit to bust, her mouth wide open, revealing more gums than teeth.

Yann picked up the case and we followed a line of people shuffling towards the exit.

As we walked across the grass Olive said, 'Why was that woman laughing when she thought her kitchen might be bombed?'

'Maybe if people didn't laugh, they'd cry,' I replied.

# CHAPTER 27

The station was crowded with people. There were lots of soldiers walking about with kit bags slung over their shoulders and WRVS women handing out tea. Some of the soldiers didn't look much older than Jimmy; they looked weary, as if they'd had enough and seen too much. We boarded the train and Yann put our case in the rack above my head, then spoke to a soldier sitting by the window.

'Are you going to London, young man?' he asked.

The soldier nodded. 'Yes, sir, I am.'

'Would you mind keeping an eye on my girls?'

'Of course,' said the soldier.

*Why do we need someone to keep an eye on us?* I thought. *We've done all right on our own so far.* But I didn't say it out loud.

Yann enfolded me in his arms. I pressed my face against his coat and breathed in the musty smell of it. I wanted to remember the smell; I wanted to remember Yann. I didn't want to leave him.

'We'll come back one day,' I said.

'I shall look forward to that, my dear.'

Olive's eyes were filling with tears. Yann noticed and knelt down in front of her. He cupped her face in his hands and said: 'You will soon be with your family, little one, and knowing how happy you will be makes me happy too. We will miss you, Henri and I, and we will think of you often.' He wiped away the tears that were now running down Olive's cheeks. He touched the doll's head. 'We shall miss Auntie Missus as well,' he added.

We waved out the window until Yann was just a speck in the distance.

I sat back and watched the fields and villages racing past. We had come to Wales in the spring of 1942 and we were returning home to London in the spring of 1944. Tony would be thirteen and Freddie wouldn't be a baby anymore. So much had happened since we'd left Bermondsey. We had encountered the best of people and the worst. Olive and I had made wonderful friends that I knew would stay in our hearts forever. Auntie Beth and Uncle Dylan, Lottie and Aggie and Jimmy and Yann.

The soldier looked across at me and smiled. 'Going home?' he said.

'Yes,' I said, 'we're going home.' I smiled and closed my eyes. *We're going home.*

As the train approached the outskirts of London, my heart felt as if it was bursting out of my body. I was excited, scared, worried and every other emotion it was possible for one person to feel. I couldn't wait to be in Mum's arms, just to rest my head against her, to hear her telling me how much she loved me. I wanted to be someone's child again. For so long I'd felt like Olive's mum. Maybe that was why I had been content to stay with Yann for so long, because in his quiet way he had taken the responsibility of my little sister off my shoulders. I'd been allowed to be a young girl again.

As the train raced towards London and home I thought about what my future would bring. Perhaps I'd get a job in the sugar factory; maybe Angela was already working there. Or maybe the custard factory. I didn't care where I worked as long as I was at home.

London looked even worse than I remembered. There was a feeling of dread inside me as we passed whole streets of houses that had been totally demolished.

Had Mum got my letters? And if she had, why hadn't she written back? Was she okay?

Of course she was okay, of course she was. There was a war on, wasn't there? Yann had said that was why we hadn't heard from her. I was praying that he was right.

'Are we nearly there?' asked Olive, kneeling up on the seat.

'Almost,' I said.

'Will my mummy be meeting us at the station?'

'She doesn't know we're coming, Olive.'

'Is it a surprise?'

'Kind of.'

'Does she know how old I am?'

'Of course she does.'

'Is that cos she borned me, Nell?'

I nodded.

'Are you going to tell her that you bashed Albert's head in?'

I looked across at the soldier. He had his eyes closed and I hoped he was asleep. 'Shush,' I said.

'Are you going to tell Mummy that you bashed Albert's head in?' she whispered again.

'I don't know,' I said.

'I shouldn't bother if I was you, Nell. No good will come of it.'

Olive's little sayings always seemed to come out of the blue and I hadn't a clue where she got them from. 'We'll see,' I said. 'Hush now.'

'Am I getting on yer nerves, Nell?'

I smiled at her. 'A bit.'

'I thought I was.'

As we pulled into Paddington station I looked across at the soldier; he was still asleep. I leaned across and nudged him. 'We're here,' I said gently.

He jumped as I touched him and his arm swung out, almost hitting me.

'Oh God, sorry,' he said, pulling himself up in the seat. 'Did I hit you?'

'No,' I said, smiling, 'you missed.'

'I seem to go into a dead sleep these days and when I wake up it takes a minute to come to.'

'I just thought you'd want to know we'd arrived.'

He yawned and rubbed at his chin. 'Thanks, I might have gone all the way back to Wales,' he said, smiling. He stood up and stretched. 'I'll get your case down for you.'

'Thanks.'

'Have you got far to go?'

'Bermondsey,' I said. 'It's only about five miles, we'll take the Tube.'

'Well, good luck,' he said, opening the carriage door.

'Good luck to you too.'

I watched him walk away. I hoped he would be all right – I hoped he would make it through this horrible war alive.

I held Olive's hand as we walked across the crowded station towards the Underground.

'It smells of home,' she said.

I took a deep breath and inhaled the smog of London. 'You're right, it does,' I agreed.

'Am I still seven?' she said. 'Cos I feel like eight.'

'You're almost eight.'

'That explains it then.'

I laughed. 'Let's go home.'

We'd been waiting ages for the Tube to turn up when an announcement came over the loudspeaker telling us there were delays on the line and the next train would be in about an hour.

'Let's get a cup of tea and something to eat, shall we?' I said.

We went back up to the platform and Olive

skipped ahead of me towards the waiting room. There was a lovely fire burning in the grate and the tea urn was making a bubbling noise; it felt warm and cosy in there. It was mostly filled with soldiers and their girlfriends but there was an empty table by the window.

I left Olive with the case and went over to the counter. 'Tea and buns for two, please,' I said.

'Buns are off, ducky,' she said.

'Off?'

'Yes, ducky, all gone, none left.'

I pointed to the two buns in the glass cabinet next to the till. 'What about those?' I said.

'They're for Bert – he wouldn't be happy if I sold those.'

I didn't ask who Bert was. 'What have you got left then?' I asked.

'Sausage rolls, Battenberg and fruit cake.'

'I'll have two pieces of fruit cake then, please.'

'Only got one left, ducky.'

'I'll have one Battenberg and one fruit cake then.' Mum was going to laugh about this when I told her. Oh, I wished I was telling her now, I wanted to be home. I just wanted to be home.

I carried the tray back to the table and sat down. 'Battenberg or fruit cake?' I asked.

'You know I don't like marzipan, Nell,' said Olive, turning up her nose.

'Have the fruit cake then,' I said.

'It feels nice, doesn't it?' said Olive, biting into the cake. 'This bloody cake's hard as rock.'

'What feels nice?'

'What?'

'You said it feels nice.'

'London,' said Olive. 'It feels nice, doesn't it?'

I nodded. 'Yeah, it does,' I said, smiling. 'It feels really nice.'

After making the tea and cake last as long as we could, we made our way back down into the Underground. At last the Tube came rattling through the tunnel and we jumped on. We were nearly there, we were nearly home.

I sat studying the Tube map on the opposite wall; I knew every station on the Underground. Me and Tony used to play a game to see who could remember the most stations.

We changed Tubes at Baker Street – nearly home, nearly home. I hoped Angela was in. I couldn't wait to sit on the old bed in 59 Edison Terrace and tell her everything that had happened since I'd left home.

We were soon pulling into station. I picked up the case and we made our way up the escalator and into the open air.

We were hurrying now, along Jamaica Road, through the park, past the pawn shop and the Spread Eagle and Crown. We waved to the pretty ladies leaning against the walls. Hurrying, hurrying towards home and Mum.

As we turned into Rannly Court I started to scream.

# CHAPTER 28

It was gone. There was nothing but rubble where the flats had once stood. I dropped the case, my knees buckled and I fell to the ground. I was aware of being held, of people touching me, holding me, but I struggled against them. Olive was clinging to me, I could hardly breathe, I was gulping for air, I wanted to die. They were gone, my lovely mum and Tony and baby Freddie, they were all gone. I wanted to die.

'Hush now, hush now.' It was Mrs Baxter.

'Mummy?' said Olive.

Mrs Baxter sat on the ground and gathered us both into her arms, rocking us as if we were babies. My screams had turned to gut-wrenching sobs that seemed to come from the very bottom of my stomach. I felt as if I had been cut in two, the pain was so bad.

'Tell me they're all right, Mrs Baxter, please tell me they're all right. They can't be dead, they *can't* be. Please tell me they're all right, please, please, *please*.'

'I believe they are alive, Nell.'

'Really?'

'I believe they got away.'

Olive was as white as a sheet, tears streaming down her face. I took a deep breath. I had to pull myself together – she only had me now and I couldn't fall apart. I had to believe that our family were alive. Olive was too little to believe anything less. 'I'm here, Olive, I'm here. Nell's here.'

Mrs Baxter helped me to my feet. I was shaking so much I could hardly stand. I took hold of Olive's hand and helped her up too. 'It's going to be all right, Olive,' I said through my tears.

'Mummy's not a deader?' she said.

'It's going to be all right,' I said again.

'Come along with me,' said Mrs Baxter, taking charge.

We walked across the square to the block opposite where Rannly Court used to be. The block of flats where Angela lived.

'The council gave me this flat, Nell,' she said, as we climbed up the stone steps.

The flat she showed us into was almost exactly the same as her old one. Me and Olive sat side by side on the couch, while Mrs Baxter went into the kitchen to make tea for us all.

'I've put plenty of sugar in it,' she said, coming back. 'For the shock.'

I cupped my hands around the hot mug. I was still shaking and I felt sick in my stomach.

I didn't want to ask any more questions in front of Olive, I didn't want to scare her.

'Try to drink it, love, it will make you feel better,' I said.

'Where's Mr Baxter?' said Olive, looking round.

'I lost him a year ago, Olive.'

'How did you lose him?' asked Olive, looking confused.

'I think he died, love,' I said gently. 'Did he die, Mrs Baxter?'

'He did, Nell.'

'I'm ever so sorry,' I said.

'Was it the scarlet fever?' said Olive.

'Consumption,' said Mrs Baxter. 'All I have left of that dear man is his wooden leg.'

'Well, at least you've got something left of him,' said Olive very seriously.

'It helped me through those early days, Olive,' said Mrs Baxter. 'I took it to bed with me every night. It was a great comfort.'

'Auntie Missus has been a great comfort to me an all, Mrs Baxter, cos we've been through some pretty bad times too.'

Mrs Baxter was looking confused. 'Her doll,' I explained, sipping the hot tea.

'You've grown, Olive,' said Mrs Baxter, smiling at her.

'That's cos I'm nearly eight,' said Olive. 'I used to be six and then I was seven, but I didn't know I was seven until Nell told me, and now I'm almost eight.'

She said all this without seeming to take a breath.

'So that's why I've grown, Mrs Baxter, cos I'm nearly eight.'

'You're a funny little thing, Olive,' said Mrs Baxter. 'And a brave one by the sound of it.'

'I don't know what I would have done without her,' I said.

'Your mum will be proud.'

It made me feel better that Mrs Baxter was talking about my mum as if she was alive. I was beginning to feel calmer sitting in her little flat but I needed to see my family – I had to find them.

'It must have been terrible,' I said.

'I've never been so scared in my life, Nell. I fled with nothing but Mr Baxter's wooden leg.'

'I'm sorry about your home.'

'Yes, I was very sad at the time. I lost everything. I'd just bought a new frying pan on the never-never; I'm still paying for it. There were lots of happy times in that little flat but I still have my memories in here,' she said, touching her heart, 'and I still have his leg. The Germans couldn't take that away from me.'

'I'm glad about that,' said Olive. 'I still have Aggie in my heart.'

'And who's Aggie?'

'She's my best friend and she lives in a sweetshop in Glengaryth.'

'Well, I'm sure you'll see her again one day.'

'Oh, I will, we're going to live together when we're grown up, we made a promise.'

'I'm glad you found a friend, Olive.'

'So where do you think our family are?' I asked.

'I wish I could tell you that, Nell, but I don't know.'

'Do you think they were evacuated, Mrs Baxter?'

'We'll go down the town hall tomorrow and see if they know anything.'

I looked at the tea in my hands. 'I can't go to the town hall, Mrs Baxter.'

'Can't you?'

I shook my head.

'You see, we're on the run from the old beak,' said Olive.

Mrs Baxter took my hands in hers. 'Do you want to tell me about it?' she asked gently.

'I did a very bad thing, Mrs Baxter.'

'Well, if I know you, Nell, I'd say you had a good reason to do whatever you did.'

My eyes filled with tears. 'I killed someone.'

Mrs Baxter nodded – she didn't look shocked.

'She bashed Albert over the head to save me,' said Olive.

'So you see, I can't go down the town hall. No one must know that we're home.'

'Then I'll go on my own and I'll see what I can find out. You're amongst your own now, Nell, you have nothing to fear.'

'What about Angela?' I said, suddenly remembering my friend.

'Angela has joined her brothers and sister in the country.'

'But what about her mum and her granny?'

'Her granny, poor soul, passed away about a year ago now. It was a blessing in the end. Angela loved her gran but I think she was worn out with the worry of it all. In my opinion it was all too much for such a young girl.'

'And her mum?'

'They took her away, Nell. I visit when I can – she's slowly getting better. I think she's in the right place and she's happy enough.'

I'd been looking forward to seeing my friend Angela but at least she was safe and maybe now she could be a young girl again without having to take care of her mum and her granny.

Me and Olive stayed indoors while Mrs Baxter went down to the town hall.

I looked out the window to where our flat used to be. It made me sad thinking of how happy we had been there. Mum in the kitchen cooking our dinner and Daddy warming his back against the fire and Tony being sent outside to get the mud off his legs. I watched as the big machines rolled backwards and forwards over the rubble, flattening what was left of Rannly Court. I couldn't think that my family might be under there, I had to believe they were safe somewhere.

Olive joined me at the window. 'What are they doing, Nell?' she asked.

'Just clearing the stuff away, Olive.'

'What about the tallyman's horse? Do you think he's under there?'

'I shouldn't think so.'

'I hope he's not – even though he bit me I wouldn't like to think he got squashed.'

'Try not to worry about it, love,' I said.

Mrs Baxter's flat was a lot brighter than the flat we'd lived in. I'd mentioned it to her.

'It's cos Rannly Court's gone, Nell,' she'd said. 'It's let the sun in. Some silly cow said the Germans had done us a favour. I sent her off with a flea in her ear, I can tell you.'

'I suppose Tony and Freddie have changed a lot since we've been gone.'

'Your Tony's like a beanpole, not a bit of fat on him. I'd say he's taller than you now.'

'And Freddie?'

'Full of mischief. He's a dear little chap, walking now, of course, follows Tony everywhere.'

I wanted to ask Mrs Baxter if Mum had heard from my daddy but I couldn't do it in front of Olive.

After Mrs Baxter left I walked over to the window. Now that Rannly Court had gone you could see the river, my very own ocean. Only it didn't look as magical as I remembered; it looked black and murky and unwelcoming. It wasn't an ocean at all – it was just a dirty old river that seemed to hold secrets that scared me.

'Can we go out, Nell?' said Olive.

I turned away from the window. 'We have to stay here – we can't let anyone know we're home.'

'Cos of Albert?'

I nodded.

'I'll suffocate from lack of fresh air.'

'No, you won't.'

'I will, I think I'm suffocating already. Have my lips turned blue, Nell?'

'Your lips look perfectly fine.'

'I'm not so sure about that, Nell.'

'Come over here and I'll open the window.'

'Good idea, Nell, it might save me life.'

I opened the window and we leaned out as far as we could.

'That's better,' said Olive. 'I think I'll live.'

'You should go on the stage,' I said.

'Nah, me and Aggie are going to buy a shop.'

'What sort of shop?' I asked, grinning.

'A bread shop – me and Aggie like bread.'

'Well, I wish you both luck,' I said.

'We don't need luck, Nell, we've got God.'

'And who better to have on your side than God,' I said, smiling.

Eventually Mrs Baxter returned. 'No luck,' she said, taking off her coat and hanging it behind the door. 'But as the welfare lady said, so many people left London around that time that it had become hard to keep track of them all.'

'What can we do then?'

'I'm goin to ask round the neighbours and see if anyone saw them, but if that draws a blank, I don't think there's much more we can do, Nell, other than wait. I'm sorry, love.'

'Thanks anyway, Mrs Baxter, it was good of you to try.'

'I'll scoot round the neighbours in the morning. You never know, duck, someone might have seen them.'

We put Olive to bed early – we'd had a long day and she looked fit to drop.

Once she was asleep me and Mrs Baxter settled down in front of the fire and I asked her what had happened.

'There'd been a raid on the docks, so people had already started to leave the flats before the siren went off. Everyone helped everyone else. I have never been so proud to call myself a Londoner.'

'And didn't you see Mum at all?'

Mrs Baxter shook her head. 'Everyone was running for the shelters and I ran with them. I didn't see your family, Nell, I'm sorry.'

'But you think they got out?'

'I hope they did, that's all I can say.'

I sat looking into the fire.

'How long ago did it happen?'

'I reckon it must be six months ago now, and the council have only just got round to clearin it up.'

*So that's why Mum never answered any of my letters,* I thought.

'It must have been awful.'

'It didn't feel real at the time. It was only afterwards that it sunk in, what had happened. We were numb. People were stood in the yard, looking at what had been their homes. We'd lost everything, it was heartbreaking.'

'I'm so sorry, Mrs Baxter.'

'Mr Baxter got over losing his leg and I'll get over this.'

'What about me and Olive? Where are we going to live?'

'I've been thinking about that, Nell. If you stay here they're sure to put you both into care, or send you away again. I'm leaving London; I can't bear to look at the ruins of my old home every day, it hurts too much. I'm going to stay with my sister in Eastbourne until the war is over. You and Olive best come with me.'

'Won't your sister mind?'

'No, she runs a guest house so there's plenty of room. It means you'll have to get a job though, Nell, to help pay for yours and Olive's keep, but you'll be safe there. There's no point in trying to find your family now. Anyway, you've been through enough by the sound of it.'

'You don't know the half of it, Mrs Baxter,' I said.

'How about we have a nice cup of tea and some bread and dripping, and you can tell me all about it?'

As I drank the sweet tea and ate the bread and dripping, I told Mrs Baxter everything that had happened to us since we left Bermondsey. I told her about Auntie Beth and Uncle Dylan and how kind they'd been to us. Then I told her about the horrible farm and why I'd killed Albert.

'I'd ave killed him an all, dirty bugger,' said Mrs Baxter.

'I didn't mean to – at least, I don't think I did.'

'You did what you had to do, Nell, and you saved your little sister – that's reason enough for me.'

Then I told her about mad Clodagh Price and how we'd had to escape.

'Blimey, Nell!' she said. 'I guessed you'd been through it, but I hadn't realised it had been that bad.'

'If I'd known what was ahead of us there's no way we would have left Bermondsey. But do you know what, Mrs Baxter? Even though some of what happened to us was awful, I'm not sorry we went. I think we both grew up in ways we never would have if we had stayed at home. Before we left, Olive had just been my little sister, but she became my best friend; I never realised what a brave little girl she was. There were times when she seemed older than me and I depended on her. I'm so proud of her.'

'It doesn't surprise me, Nell. There's always been something special about that little girl.'

'I realise that now.'

'Your poor mother would have been worried sick if she'd known. It made her so happy to know how well you had settled at the vicarage and then how much Olive loved the farm. You didn't tell her how bad it was, did you?'

'I didn't want her worrying.'

'You've gone through so much, Nell, and then to get home and find the flats had been bombed . . .' She shook her head. 'You poor girl.'

Mrs Baxter picked up a poker and rattled the coals. Warm air rushed into the room.

'Do you think they're alive, Mrs Baxter?'

'All we can do is live in hope, ducks, that's all we can do for now.'

'How will Mum know where we are if she comes home?'

'I've let Mrs Ryan know where we're going.'

'Can we trust her?'

'Her husband's no better than he should be and her boys are a nightmare. Mrs Ryan knows how to keep a secret – she's been keeping them most of her life. She'll swear she knows nothing on the life of her poor departed mother if she has to.'

'And my dad?'

'No word yet, but as they say, no news is good news.'

'I hope so.'

'We have to keep our spirits up, Nell, that's all we can do for now.'

'It's Eastbourne then, is it?' I said.

'A nice dose of fresh sea air will do us all the world of good.'

'Is it anywhere near Brighton, Mrs Baxter?'

'Right next door.'

I thought of my friend Lottie and smiled.

'I'd like to say goodbye to Mrs Ryan, would that be okay?'

'I'm sure she'd be tickled pink to see you, Nell. You know where her flat is.'

I walked along the corridor to Mrs Ryan's flat

and knocked on the door. Her face broke into a huge smile when she saw me standing there.

'Come in, come in,' she said.

The tiny flat was full of stuff: there were piles of it on the floor, on the chairs and sliding off the table.

'Don't mind the mess,' she said, dumping an armful of clothes off the couch and onto the floor so that I could sit down. 'I keep trying to tidy it up but it just doesn't seem to want to be tidy, so I've decided it's not worth losing any sleep over.'

'Well, I think it's very cosy,' I said.

'So do I,' said Mrs Ryan, looking around the room.

'And that's all that counts, isn't it?' I said.

We didn't speak for a bit, then Mrs Ryan said: 'I'm sorry you lost your home, love.'

'I still can't believe it's gone,' I said. 'We were really happy there but I'm more worried about my family than the flat.'

'Of course you are.'

'Do you think they got out? Mrs Baxter feels sure that they did.'

'I agree with her, Nell. We had plenty of warning that the planes were on their way. Mr Ryan was on holiday at His Majesty's pleasure and I was here with my Tommy. He's a bit of a rogue is Tommy, but I was so proud of him that day, Nell. He helped the wardens get the old people to safety with no thought for himself. I saw him in a whole different light. There might be some good in him after all.'

'I always liked your Tommy, Mrs Ryan.'

'Oh, he's likeable enough, when he's not being a little git.'

I grinned, knowing all Mrs Ryan's sons were little gits but she'd kill anyone who hurt them.

'So if all the old uns got out, I'm sure your Tony would have got your mum and little Freddie to safety.'

I nodded. 'I have to think that, don't I?'

'You do, girl, you do.'

'So you didn't see them afterwards?'

'It was mayhem – everyone was running for the shelters. I wish I could put your mind at rest, Nell, but I'm as sure as I can be that they're all right.'

'It must have been terrible, Mrs Ryan.'

'You just don't think it's going to happen on your doorstep, but I suppose being right next to the docks it was bound to happen sooner or later. The saddest thing is that a whole community has been lost – even if they rebuild Rannly Court it will never be the same.'

'Do you think they *will* rebuild it?'

'Who knows, who knows?'

'Mrs Baxter told you the police were after us, didn't she?'

'She did, and your secret's safe with me, girl, you can depend on that.'

'Thank you, Mrs Ryan.'

'You're very welcome, Nell.'

I leaned back against the chair and closed my eyes. I suddenly felt overwhelmingly tired – I could have stayed in Mrs Ryan's messy little flat all night.

'Best get yourself off to bed, ducks. You look all done in.'

I stood up and stretched. 'I think I will.'

'Rest assured, the only person I'll give your whereabouts to is your mum when she comes back – and I'm sure she will come back, Nell.'

I walked across and kissed her cheek. It was warm and soft and she smelled of lavender.

'Enjoy the seaside, Nell,' she said, smiling.

# CHAPTER 29

Mrs Baxter's sister was called Mrs Wright and she was lovely; she welcomed me and Olive with open arms. The guest house was called Sea View, which I thought was pushing it a bit as the only way you were likely to see the sea was by hanging out of the attic window with someone holding onto your legs.

'I don't think it matters, do you?' said Mrs Wright. 'I mean, two doors down is called Downs View and you'd have to stand on the roof with a pair of binoculars to see the Downs. I think Sea View sounds nice, don't you? Actually, seeing the sea is neither here nor there – it's the expectation that you might that counts.'

I smiled at her. 'I think you're right,' I said.

Sea View was a tall building on three floors. It was painted white; parts of it were peeling off, leaving yellowy patches on the walls.

'It's the salt that does that,' explained Mrs Wright. 'Not much point keeping painting it cos the sea always wins in the end.'

There didn't seem to be any evidence of a Mr Wright and he was never mentioned. When I asked Mrs Baxter about him, all she said was: 'Mr Wright turned out to be Mr Wrong and in my opinion she's well shot of him. He got his just deserts in the end though, but I'm not one to speak ill of the dead, so enough said.' Then as an afterthought she added, 'Miserable, philanderin git!'

I didn't like to ask what exactly his just deserts were but they seemed to make Mrs Baxter happy.

Me and Olive shared a pretty bedroom at the top of the house and we each had our own bed with matching blue eiderdowns. It reminded me of the vicarage in Glengaryth.

I often thought about that little village, how happy we'd been there. I thought about how lucky I was to have met my lovely friend Lottie. If we had stayed there all through the war, how differently things would have turned out. I could wish that we had never gone to Hackers farm, that I'd never met Albert, but then I'd also never have met Jimmy. I wondered where he was now – still at the farm or off to seek his fortune? – but wherever he was and whatever he was doing, I knew that he would be thinking of me as I was thinking of him. We hadn't known each other for long, but it was long enough to realise that we had grown to care for each other. It had been the beginning of something sweet and wonderful.

I wrote to Yann to let him know we were safe and to tell him what had happened to us. I got a letter back to say that he missed us both and so did Henri. He wrote:

> *I plucked up the courage to visit my neighbour. I was right, he is a widower and lives alone. We walk the dogs together and we play cards and drink too much beer. I have you and Olive to thank – you made me want to step out into the world again. Maybe one day you will visit me. Until then stay safe.*
> *With love from your good friend*
> *Yann.*

I wondered if I would ever see him again.

The ocean was everything I thought it would be. Stretching far out towards the horizon and touching the sky. Me and Olive leaned on the old railings and stared out over the grey water as it rolled towards the shore and tumbled over the pebbles.

We couldn't walk on the beach because it was out of bounds but I knew that one day I would stand at the water's edge with Lottie and together we would run into the cold water. I was content to wait for that day.

'Why does it stop when it reaches the edge?' asked Olive.

'What do you mean?'

'Well, why doesn't it just keep going and cover the town and the shops and Mrs Wright's guest house?'

'I dunno,' I said. 'I've never seen the sea before, have I, so I don't know how it works.'

'I'll ask Miss Timony, she knows everything,' said Olive.

'Good idea,' I said.

Miss Timony lived in Sea View permanently – not just for her holidays but all the time, every day.

'She's a retired headmistress,' said Mrs Wright, 'and she has neither kith nor kin. I owe her everything.'

I didn't know whether I was supposed to ask what exactly she owed her, so I waited for her to continue.

'When the war came, Nell, people weren't interested in coming to Eastbourne for their holidays anymore. You see, they couldn't go on the beach or the pier, so it lost its appeal. My guests got fewer and fewer, until all I had left was Miss Timony and a few travelling salesmen. It got to the point where I knew I would have to sell up. I felt bad telling Miss Timony that she would have to find other accommodation because I knew that she was happy at Sea View.'

'She's still here though?' I said.

'She is indeed. And do you know why?'

I shook my head.

'She suggested we run the place together, with her as a sort of sleeping partner, and I have to say the arrangement has worked very well. She said she was doing it for purely selfish reasons because she was settled here but I think it was out of kindness. Eastbourne is full of hotels and guest houses, most of them more modern than my one, you know, more mod cons and such. She could have had her pick, but she did that for me. Sometimes it's the kindness of strangers that surprises you most.'

I nodded, thinking of Yann and all he had done for two young girls who needed his help. Yes, the kindness of strangers could indeed surprise you.

Eastbourne had been badly bombed – in fact, we learned from Mrs Wright that it was the most raided town along the Sussex coast. Lots of children had been evacuated there but as more and more bombs fell on the town it became apparent that it was no safer than London and they were sent further into the countryside.

'Oh, Nell,' said Mrs Baxter. 'Maybe it wasn't such a good idea to bring you here.'

'We had nowhere else to go, Mrs Baxter, and like you said, we would have been taken into care. You did the right thing.'

'I hope so, Nell.'

'You did,' I said, kissing her cheek, 'and we love it here.'

'As long as you're happy, Nell.'

'Oh, we are.'

We had known very little about how the war was going when we were in Wales, but Mrs Wright took it upon herself to give us daily updates every morning at breakfast. On Tuesday, 21 March, she told us that eighty-two German fighters were destroyed and forty-three US bombers were lost.

'But,' she added, 'sixteen were saved and landed safely in Switzerland, so that was nice, wasn't it?'

The next day she told us that Germany had invaded Hungary and she was going down to the church to light a candle and pray for 'those poor unfortunate people'.

We learned of the successes and the losses; we were spared nothing. It was easy to tell when the war was not going in our favour as Mrs Wright forgot to cook tea because she was on her knees down at Holy Cross church.

Me and Olive had taken to walking round Eastbourne, getting to know it. So much of the town had been damaged and many of the shops were boarded up. One afternoon after our walk, Mrs Wright informed me that Miss Timony would like to see me in her room.

I ran a comb through my unruly hair and went upstairs.

The first thing I'd noticed about Miss Timony's room was the number of books she had. They were stacked in untidy piles against the walls. They slid off tables, they occupied footstools, they covered the floor, they bulged out of bookcases and they surrounded Miss Timony's armchair. In fact, there was very little else in the room. No ornaments, no clock, no plants, nothing. Just hundreds of books. Yann would have loved it.

'Ah, my dear,' she said, when I tapped on the door and went in. 'I was wanting to speak to you, if you have the time.'

'Of course I do,' I said, stepping over the books and making my way to a little velvet stool, where I sat down in front of her.

She pushed her glasses down her nose and looked at me. 'Mrs Wright tells me you are going to need a job.'

'I am,' I said.

'And do you know what you want to do?'

'I've never had a job before but back home I always thought I'd like to work in the sugar factory or the custard factory with my friend Angela.'

'I think you can do better than that, my dear.'

'But I'm not trained to do anything, Miss Timony. I couldn't work in a shop or an office or anything like that. I think I'd be happy in a factory.'

'How about a hotel, Nell?'

'A hotel?' I said.

'A very dear friend of mine is the proprietor of the Strand Hotel on the seafront. I've spoken to him and he'd like to meet you.'

I could feel myself getting hot and pulled at the collar of my blouse. 'But what would I have to do?'

'Do you think that you could serve people tea and cakes?'

'I don't know.'

'Well, I do, and it will be a lot nicer than working in some godforsaken factory, where you never see the light of day. Sunshine is good for our wellbeing, Nell.'

'Is it?'

'It is, my dear. Our bodies produce vitamin D when our skin is exposed to the sun, which is essential for our bones. Children who spent their days down the mines often came up short. There are a lot of short-statured people in Wales, so I'm told.'

I wasn't convinced – I hadn't noticed any particularly short people in Glengaryth.

'Isn't it posh girls that work in hotels and serve people tea and cakes?' I said.

'You are a bright girl, Nell, and may I say a very pretty one.'

I couldn't help thinking that Miss Timony needed new glasses.

'You don't believe me, do you?'

I shook my head.

'And that is where your beauty lies. There is a sweetness about you, Nell, that is very becoming.'

'Gosh,' I said.

'So will you give my dear friend Mr Costos and his hotel a chance?'

I nodded my head and grinned. 'Well, I suppose I've got nothing to lose,' I said.

'Except your chains,' said Miss Timony.

'Pardon?' I said.

'It is a very famous quote, Nell, by an inspirational man called Karl Marx. "Workers of the world unite, you have nothing to lose but your chains."'

I didn't know what she was talking about but I thought it sounded nice.

'Don't mind me, Nell, I read too many books. So, shall we pay dear Mr Costos a visit in the morning?'

'Why not?' I said. 'Oh, and by the way, Olive wants to know why the sea stops at the edge of the shore.'

'Send her up, dear, send her up.'

I was grinning as I ran back downstairs. *Imagine the likes of me working in a hotel! I wish Angela was here – she'd be dead impressed.* I straightened my shoulders. I could do this. I mean, how difficult can serving tea and a lump of cake be? And Miss Timony had said I was pretty. I wondered if Jimmy had thought I was pretty; I hoped so.

# CHAPTER 30

My newfound confidence disappeared in a puff of smoke as I stood next to Miss Timony, looking up at the Strand Hotel. I'd been kidding myself to think that Mr Costos would actually give me a job in this beautiful place.

'I'm not sure about this,' I said, hanging back.

'Not sure about what?'

I made a face.

'Remember the words of Mr Karl Marx.'

I had to think for a minute. 'About the chains, you mean?'

Miss Timony nodded. 'The only chains holding you back, Nell, are those of your own making.'

I didn't have a bloody clue what she was on about – I wished she'd talk normally. I didn't even know this Karl Marx bloke; in fact, I thought he sounded like a bit of a smartarse.

'Come on, Nell, shoulders back. Mr Costos is expecting us.'

I reluctantly followed her up the steps.

If I was worried outside the hotel, I was terrified inside. I had never been in such a beautiful place in my life. Even if I didn't get a job here I could tell Angela what a proper posh hotel looked like.

Even though it was still morning, all the lights were on. A beautiful chandelier hung from the centre of the ceiling, throwing light and shadow across the room and bouncing off the huge mirrors and glass tables. Deep blue velvet sofas were placed around the walls and beside the white marble fireplace. Paintings in ornate gold frames hung on the honey-coloured walls.

I was just about to tell Miss Timony that I had decided to hang onto my chains and work in a factory when the low moan of a siren interrupted my thoughts.

'Follow me,' said Miss Timony, taking my arm.

'Where are we going?' I said.

'To the cellar: chop, chop!'

I quickly chop-chopped after Miss Timony, followed by a trail of people hurrying through the hotel doors from the street outside. We quickened our step as the first bomb fell; it sounded horribly close. I put my hands over my head and hurried towards the cellar door. There was a man guiding everyone down the narrow stairs.

'Good morning, Miss Timony,' the man said, smiling.

'Good morning to you, Mr Costos,' she replied.

'Be careful on the stairs.'

'I most certainly will,' said Miss Timony, smiling at him.

I imagined the cellar would be a dark, gloomy

place, but it wasn't. The walls were painted in the same honey colour as the walls upstairs and, to my amazement, a smaller chandelier hung from the centre of the ceiling. A chandelier in a cellar! I couldn't wait to tell Angela.

'Where have all these people come from?' I asked, looking around. 'Are they all guests in the hotel?'

'No, dear, Mr Costos has opened his doors to anyone who needs shelter.'

'That's good of him,' I said.

'He's a good man, Nell.'

We stayed until the all-clear sounded and then made our way back upstairs.

Once everyone had gone back out into the street, Mr Costos came across to us.

'Shall we sit?' he said, motioning towards one of the beautiful sofas.

I followed Miss Timony and we sat down. Mr Costos sat opposite us, smiling.

I thought he was very handsome. He was tall and dark, with black shiny hair that was smarmed down with so much Brylcreem it looked like a little cap on top of his head. Above his lip was a thin moustache that turned up a bit at the ends. In Bermondsey he would have been called a dandy. I thought he looked like Clark Gable. It was hard to tell his age.

'So, you are little Nell,' he said, taking my hand, 'who my dear friend Miss Timony has said so many nice things about.'

I shook his hand and nodded.

'And you need a job, yes?'

'Yes,' I said shyly.

'And I need a waitress, so we will be doing each other a favour.'

I looked at Mr Costos's smiling face and I felt the chains slowly fall from my shoulders.

Maybe that Karl Marx bloke knew what he was on about – there was nothing to be scared of here.

'I have someone to cover breakfasts so I will need you to work every day from eleven o'clock in the morning until five in the afternoon, with Wednesdays off. I will also need you to work every other weekend. Will that suit you?'

'Yes, Mr Costos, that will suit me fine.'

'That's settled then. You will be my little cockney waitress and I'm sure you will be happy here.'

'Thank you, Mr Costos,' I said, smiling.

'You are very welcome, little Nell.'

Just then a young man literally burst through the hotel doors.

'You can't imagine what I've just been through!' he said. 'That bloody bomb nearly blew me off my feet – my whole life flashed before me. I thought I was going to die.' He sat down next to Mr Costos and wiped his forehead with a hankie. 'And there are bits of my life, Gino, that I wasn't that keen on remembering.'

'Breathe, dear boy, breathe,' said Mr Costos, patting his knee.

'I'm still shaking,' said the man, holding out his hands to prove it.

'Were you close to the bomb when it fell, Philip?' said Mr Costos, gently.

'Not exactly, but I might have been and that's almost as bad.'

'You've had a nasty shock, dear boy, but you're safe now.'

The man seemed to recover pretty quickly. 'And who's this wondrous girl sitting in front of me?' he asked.

'This is Nell, who Miss Timony told us about. She has agreed to work for us in the tea rooms. Isn't that splendid?'

He was staring at me so intensely that I was beginning to feel uncomfortable. He made a square shape with his hands, as if he was taking a photograph of me.

'You look like a young Fanny Cornforth, my dear. Don't you think so, Gino? Don't you think she looks like a young Fanny? With all that fabulous Titian hair.'

Miss Timony looked at me and smiled. 'It's a compliment, my dear.'

Mr Costos raised his eyebrows. 'Don't let my friend scare you, Nell, he's given to flights of fancy.'

'You're a philistine when it comes to art, Gino. You don't have an artistic bone in your body and you, an Italian – your forefathers would be ashamed.'

'My forefathers, as you well know, were goat herders and I don't need artistic bones to run a hotel.'

270

Mr Philip leaned forward, his elbows on his knees.

'Have you heard of the artist Dante Gabriel Rossetti, dear girl?'

'I'm afraid not,' I said. 'Sorry.'

'He was a great artist, Nell, of the Pre-Raphaelite movement. One of his muses was a young girl called Fanny Cornforth – she was also his mistress. Unfortunately she got rather fat and ended up in an insane asylum in Chichester. You have her beautiful hair but let us hope you have a less dramatic life.'

'Why don't you go and rest after your shock,' said Mr Costos.

'I think I will, Gino, I'm still a bit shaky.' As he left the room he turned back and winked at me. 'Goodbye, Fanny, we shall meet again, I hope.'

I grinned at him; I'd never met anyone quite like him in my whole life.

After he'd left the room Mr Costos smiled at me. 'Philip can be a little dramatic at times but he is right about your hair, Nell, it is indeed beautiful.'

I could feel my face getting hot – I wasn't used to compliments. 'Thank you,' I said.

'You are very welcome. Now, why don't you and Miss Timony sample our tea and cakes? It will give you an idea of the work you will be doing.'

The tea rooms were situated right at the front of the hotel overlooking the sea.

It was a pity that the huge window was criss-crossed with white tape.

'It is in case the hotel gets bombed, Nell, and the glass shatters. So many injuries have been caused by shards of glass flying around,' Miss Timony explained.

I looked around the room; there must have been at least twenty tables. Sparkling cutlery and glasses were laid out on crisp white cloths. It was lovely. I couldn't believe that I was actually going to work here. If only I knew that my family were safe somewhere, my happiness would have been complete.

# CHAPTER 31

Olive started school at Holy Cross infants, which was attached to the church where Mrs Wright did her praying. There were just two classrooms, with a playground at the front and a lovely green field at the back, where the children were able to run around. So many children had been evacuated to the countryside that there were very few pupils left.

Olive loved her teacher, Miss Jolly. 'Don't you think that's a nice name, Nell?' she said.

'It's a good name if you *are* jolly, but a pretty unfortunate one if you're not.'

'Oh, she's jolly all right, Nell, and really pretty, and she says I'm a clever girl and I'll soon catch up.'

Miss Timony had gone to see the teachers before Olive started school to make them aware of the schooling she'd missed.

I didn't much care about that; I just wanted Olive to be happy. She had been through so much for such a little girl.

When we'd first arrived in Eastbourne she used to ask about Mum and Dad and Tony and Freddie, but she didn't mention them anymore. Miss

Timony said to leave her and she would open up in her own time. 'No point in pushing her, Nell,' she said.

'I won't.'

'And what about you?'

'I walk a lot, Miss Timony. I find it helps.'

'We all deal with grief in our own way, Nell, but I do think it's best to let it out if you can.'

'Do you think Olive is keeping it all inside?'

'I don't think so. Young children have a way of dealing with things they might not want to remember.'

'How?'

'They seem to be able to live in the moment, they don't dwell on the past. It's still there inside her head but she's tucked it away. In Olive's case I think that's a blessing.'

What Miss Timony said made sense because, while I couldn't stop thinking about all that had happened to us since leaving Bermondsey, Olive remained her usual cheerful little self. None of what had happened seemed to have affected her and I was thankful for that. I wished I could just turn my brain off in the same way.

Every morning before going to work I helped out at the guest house. I cleaned rooms and helped Mrs Wright and Mrs Baxter in the kitchen as they cooked breakfast. It was easy to see how close the two sisters were – they chatted and giggled as they threw eggs and bacon in the pan and buttered toast. I hoped that me and Olive would remain that close. There was always plenty of food because Mrs Wright got extra rations on account of running a guest house. I also met guests at the station and walked them down to Sea View. Mrs Wright said it gave her the edge on other guest houses, whose guests were left to make their own way there. Not that there were many guests to meet.

'I used to have to turn people away, we were so busy. I couldn't tell you the last time I had a "no vacancies" sign in the window. It was hard work, but I loved it. All those kiddies with their buckets and spades and little fishing nets, too excited to eat their breakfast – I just loved it, Nell.'

'But it will be busy again, won't it? Once the war is over?'

'I hope so,' she said. 'I do hope so.'

I didn't have to be at the hotel until eleven o'clock in the morning so I was able to walk Olive to school every day. I loved those times when we were on our own. I loved listening to her chatter as she skipped along the seafront, swinging her gas mask like a handbag.

'Have you made a new friend at school?' I asked.

'Yes, his name's Henry, the same as Mr Yann's dog.'

'Any girls?'

'Of course there's girls, Nell, but they're not my sort of girls. I like Henry best. Can I bring him home to tea?'

'We'll ask Mrs Wright. I'm sure she won't mind.'

'Nell?'

'Yes?'

'Can I write to Aggie at the sweetshop?'

'I'm afraid not, Olive.'

'Why not?'

'We can't let anyone in Wales know where we are.'

'Cos you bashed Albert over the head with a shovel?'

'Yes.'

'I miss her, see.'

'You can write to her when the war's over and she's back home in Coventry. You've got her address, haven't you?'

'Yes, and she's got mine, but Rannly Court's not there anymore is it, so how is the postie man meant to deliver the letter?'

'Does that make you feel sad, Olive? That Rannly Court's not there anymore?'

'A bit.'

'It's normal to feel sad and you can always talk to me, you know.'

'I don't think I want to talk about it just now, Nell, if that's okay with you.'

'Of course it is. Now, how about introducing me to this new boyfriend of yours?'

Olive started giggling. 'Henry's not my boyfriend, Aggie is.'

'But Aggie can't be your boyfriend, she's a girl,' I said.

Olive looked at me all wide-eyed and said: 'But she's *still* a person, Nell.'

Well, there was no answer to that one, was there?

I loved working at the Strand Hotel. I don't know what I was so worried about; it must have been those chains that Miss Timony was on about. I wore a black dress, a white apron with a frill round the bib, and a little white cap secured with a wide elastic band that went round the back of my head. When I caught sight of myself in a mirror, I didn't look like me at all – I looked like the kind of girl who worked in a posh hotel. Most days I worked with a girl called Jean; we got on like a house on fire. She was the only girl in a family of five boys. Her younger brother was the only one at home; the others, including her dad were all away fighting the war.

'Bertie has asthma so he didn't pass the medical. Mum knew he wouldn't but she had to let him find out for himself,' said Jean.

'Does he mind?'

'He minded a lot at first and some people were unkind to him.'

'That's horrible.'

She nodded. 'There are some horrible people around.'

'Is he okay now?'

'Yes, he joined the Red Cross and drives an ambulance. He never leaves the house without wearing his uniform.'

On my first day, I started clearing one of my tables and found some money on the tablecloth. I went across to Jean. 'Someone's left their money behind,' I said.

'That's yours, daft.'

'Mine?'

'Yeah, it's a tip.'

'What's a tip?'

'Bloody hell, Nell! Where have you been?'

I didn't know what she was on about. 'I haven't been anywhere,' I said.

'People leave money on the table for the waitress that served them. If they like you, they leave you a tip. That's why it's a good idea to be nice and polite. The nicer you are, the more money you get; that's how it works. Now, pocket it before someone else does.'

This was wonderful – not only did I get paid, I got tips as well.

When I'd lived in Bermondsey it would never have occurred to me to work anywhere but a factory. That's what girls like us did, we worked in the sugar factory or the custard factory or the sack factory down at the docks. It was only posh girls that worked in shops and hotels. Not that it bothered us much. Round our way it was called 'knowing your place' and 'not getting above your station'. Me and Angela had known our place from the moment we were born and if we had known what a station was, we certainly wouldn't have got above it. But here I was, working in a posh hotel, wearing a posh uniform, and I didn't feel out of place at all.

'All this talk of class is nonsense,' said Miss Timony one day. 'You are as good as the next person, Nell, and don't let anyone tell you you're not. I taught so-called educated girls when I was a headmistress and, believe me, some of them were completely clueless, without a decent brain cell between them. Never forget, cream always rises to the top.'

I loved listening to Miss Timony speaking. She had such a gentle voice and she came out with stuff I'd never heard before. I wished I could be like her.

'She's cultured,' said Mrs Wright. 'And a proper lady into the bargain. You don't get many like her; some of em think their bodily functions don't smell, but not Miss Timony. I bless the day she came to Sea View.'

I loved this new place I'd come to – it was so different from Bermondsey and Wales. The rolling hills of the Sussex Downs rose up behind the old town and on its doorstep was the sea, stretching out to the horizon and beyond.

I went up to the Downs as much as I could. I loved it up there; I loved the peace and quiet. I would stand very still and listen to the soft whisper of the breeze moving over the swaying grass. As I walked across the hills I thought of Mum and Daddy and Tony and Freddie and wondered if I was kidding myself in thinking they were still alive somewhere. I wished I still had the locket; at least then I could look at their faces.

I remembered the moment my mum had given it to me, and what she'd said as she put it around my neck. 'If ever you feel lonely, you can open the locket and see my face and you'll know that I am missing you as much as you are missing me.' *Well, I am missing you, Mum, and I hope at this moment you are missing me just as much.*

Was the locket still buried under the oak tree at Hackers farm? Or had Jimmy dug it up and taken it on his travels? I wished I knew why he hadn't met us at the barn – it hadn't made sense then and it didn't make sense now, because I knew that he would rather have been with me than the Hackers. I guessed I'd never know and I guessed I'd never see Jimmy or the locket again.

# CHAPTER 32

One day my walk took me up onto the Downs and across the fields to Beachy Head, the white chalk cliffs that skirted the coast and rose high above the beach. I stood at the edge and looked down over the sea and the lighthouse. Everything seemed so small from up here. My hair was blowing around my face. It was going to be hell to get the tangles out of it when I got home; I should have worn a scarf. But I loved the feel of the wind blowing through it. I sat down on the grass and hugged my knees. On this beautiful day in this beautiful place it was hard to believe we were at war.

I was reminded of it very quickly, when out of nowhere something shot through the clouds and roared towards the cliff. I jumped up and looked around me but there was nowhere to hide; I was a sitting duck. I started running away from the cliff, stumbling across the grass. I threw myself onto the ground as the bomb crashed into the cliff, shaking the earth beneath me. I lay there trembling, my heart beating out of my chest.

'Are you okay, miss?'

I raised my head and saw a man running towards me. He took hold of my hand and helped me up.

'This must have been your lucky day,' he said, grinning.

'Call that lucky?' I said.

'I sure do – that Doodlebug hit the cliff before it could hit you.'

'Is that what it was?'

'Yep.'

'It wasn't a plane then?'

'It was a kind of plane, a PAC. A pilotless aircraft.'

'You called it a dood . . .?'

'Doodlebug. It's a nickname the Americans gave it because the roar it makes sounds like the midget racing cars they drive on speedway tracks.'

'Are you an American?'

'No, Canadian. I'm stationed at the base on the other side of the Downs.'

He held his hand out towards me. 'Robert Kellerman, Canadian Air Force, at your service.'

'Nell Patterson,' I said, shaking his hand. 'I hope you don't mind me saying but you look very young to be a pilot.'

'I'm twenty,' he said. 'Not that I feel that young anymore.'

We stood quietly watching the grey-black cloud of smoke billowing up over the cliff edge. Then we walked together back over the fields.

'Are you from round here?' he asked.

'I'm from London but I'm staying here with friends.'

'Do you like to dance, Nell?'

I thought of the dances at the village hall in Glengaryth and nodded. 'I'm not very good though,' I said.

'Me neither, two left feet, but I like to listen to the music.'

'I have to go this way,' I said. 'It was nice meeting you.'

He started to walk away, then turned back. 'Listen, there's a dance on Saturday night at the Grand Hotel. Would you come, Nell?'

'Oh, I don't know,' I said.

'Well, I'll leave it up to you but I think it'll be fun.'

'Can I bring a friend?'

'Sure you can.'

'I might see you then.'

'I hope so. Goodbye, Nell.'

'Goodbye, Robert.'

I watched him walk across the field, then made my way home.


'A dance with a bunch of Canadian airmen? Of course I want to come,' said Jean, grinning. 'I have dreams about marrying an American but a Canadian will do.'

'He didn't mention marriage – he just asked me to a dance.'

'All the best romances start with a dance.'

'I'm not looking for a romance, Jean.'

'Why not?'

'Because I'm only sixteen.'

'What better age? You're young, you're beautiful and you're available. You *are* available, aren't you?'

I thought about Jimmy, about how I'd felt that spring evening when he'd held my hand as we walked through the fields.

'Well, are you or aren't you?' said Jean impatiently.

'I suppose I am.'

'You don't *know*?'

'Okay, yes, I am.'

'Good. Now what are you going to wear?'

My heart sank. 'I haven't got anything suitable for a dance,' I said.

'Then we'll go shopping.'

I don't think that I had ever gone shopping for clothes in my whole life. Mum had always bought mine and Olive's clothes off the tallyman. He'd come into the flat with a suitcase and spread the stuff out on the kitchen table, then gone outside while we tried them on. There was never much choice but we didn't mind; it was just exciting to get new clothes. Mum couldn't afford to go to a proper shop because you had to pay up front, whereas with the tallyman you got to pay a bit every week. But I was earning money now; I could afford to buy something for the dance.

'I'd love to go shopping,' I said.

'Are you working Saturday?'

'No, it's my weekend off.'

'Mine too – we'll have a great time, Nell.'

'I'll have to ask Mrs Wright and Mrs Baxter if I can go to the dance first.'

'Why on earth do you have to get their permission?'

'Because I can't expect them to look after Olive while I'm out. Olive is my responsibility, Jean, not theirs. It would be taking advantage if I didn't ask.'

'Okay, but just make sure they say yes.'

I really wanted to buy new clothes and go to a proper dance, I really, really did.

'Fingers crossed,' I said.

'Of course you can go,' said Mrs Baxter, 'and it was nice of you to ask us first, wasn't it, Mary?'

'Very nice. Olive's not a bit of trouble, you go and enjoy yourself, girl.'

'Where's it being held?' asked Mrs Baxter.

'The Grand Hotel,' I said.

'I went there once,' said Mrs Wright.

'Was it nice?' I asked.

'It was a long time ago, Nell, I expect it's changed a bit since then. It was like stepping into another world.'

Mrs Wright stopped talking and her eyes filled with tears.

'What's the matter, love?' asked Mrs Baxter.

'Isn't it funny,' said Mrs Wright. 'A man can make your life hell, he can knock you about, flirt with other women, but when he goes, all you remember are the good times. Just a few times when he was kind – because that's all there was, Nell, just a few times. One of them was when he took me to tea at the Grand Hotel for my birthday. I was young and pretty then and I was in love.'

'You're still pretty,' I said.

'Not like I was then.'

'She was a beauty, Nell, she could have had her pick.'

'And I picked all right. I picked the meanest, laziest, no-good son of a— Well, let's just say I picked the wrong one. But that day in the Grand Hotel, I was happy and I like to think that he was too.'

Mrs Baxter smiled at her. 'I guess he wasn't all bad, it just seemed that way at the time.'

'Anyway, enough about me, Nell. You go to that dance and you have a lovely time. Olive can help me bake some cakes while you go shopping with Jean.'

'Thanks,' I said.

I ran upstairs to my bedroom and looked in the mirror. Was I pretty? Miss Timony said I was and so did Jean, and Mr Philip said I looked like Fanny something or other and Miss Timony said that was a compliment. But I'd never been the pretty one; Olive was the beauty of the family, everyone said so. I'd just accepted that I was the plain one. I touched my hair. Mr Costos said that my hair was beautiful. I studied my face; all I could see was what I had always seen. I squinted to see if I could make out what they saw, but no, it was just

286

the same old me. Mad hair, old eyes and thin as a beanstalk. But I was going to a dance in the Grand Hotel and I was going to buy a frock in a proper shop. I grinned into the mirror. Maybe things were about to get better.

# CHAPTER 33

Jean decided that we should go shopping in Brighton because the clothes shops in Eastbourne weren't modern enough.

'It's all old ladies' stuff here,' she said. 'We need to make an entrance, Nell, and we're not going to make one if we shown up in stuff our mothers wear.'

I didn't know anything about fashion. I always thought that the pretty ladies who stood on the street corners back home looked lovely but my mum said they looked cheap. Well, given that our clothes came from the tallyman and theirs must have come from a proper shop, I found that hard to understand. I wasn't completely stupid – I knew those ladies were doing something that people only talked about in whispers – but I liked them because they were kind and cheery and they weren't mean to anyone.

We caught the bus into Brighton. I was so excited to be going to Lottie's hometown.

'Do you think she'll be there?' Olive had said that morning.

'I shouldn't think so,' I'd answered. 'It sounded as if she and her mother would be seeing the war out in Cornwall.'

'Will you try, though? Will you knock on her door just in case?'

'I might as well.'

'I think you should, Nell, because you just never know, do you?'

'It would be wonderful, wouldn't it?' I'd said. 'If she opened the door.'

'I'd try if it was Aggie. Me and Auntie Missus would try every day if it was Aggie.'

'I'll try then.'

'How far away is Coventry, Nell?'

'Best ask Miss Timony, she'll know.'

'I'll ask her.'

'Will you be okay today?' I'd said.

'Yes, me and Mrs Wright are cooking cakes. I think I'd like to be a cooker, Nell. I think I'd be a good cooker.'

I smiled at her. 'I think you'd be good at anything you put your mind to, Olive.'

'I think me and Aggie might open a cooker shop, Nell. Aggie likes eating.'

'I think you mean a bakery,' I'd said.

'That's the one, a bakery – I think we'll open a bakery. Or a tea shop, I'm good at making tea.'

Olive was so definite about what she and Aggie were going to do when they were all grown up; it just never occurred to her that they might never see each other again. I envied her – I wished I felt that sure about Jimmy.

The bus took us all the way along the seafront, past towns and villages with names like Seaford and Newhaven, Peacehaven and a sweet little village called Rottingdean. There was also a little train whose tracks ran along the front of the beach.

'It's called Volk's railway, it's been there forever,' said Jean. 'My parents took me and my brothers on it once as a treat – it was the best day of my life. It's not in use at the moment because of this bloody war.'

As the bus pulled into Brighton we could see how much damage had been done to the town. Beautiful buildings had been ripped apart, some reduced to just a pile of rubble. I wondered if people had been killed in there, or if they'd managed to get to safety. As we got closer to the pier I could see rolls of ugly barbed wire and concrete barriers lining the beaches, just like in Eastbourne. There was a ship way out on the horizon, just a misty shape in the distance. I wondered if it was a Royal Navy ship guarding the coast from the enemy. It made me think of my daddy; he would have been on a ship like that. I swallowed down the lump in my throat. I mustn't feel sad today – this was a happy day out with my friend Jean, and anyway, I had to keep faith that he was all right, that's what I had to do.

The sea looked calm today, hardly moving at all.

Dark seaweed was draped in long, shiny strands across the pebbles. This was the beach where Lottie used to come and read her books. I couldn't wait for this war to be over, when I would see my friend again, when we could stand together hand in hand and watch the water lap the shore.

'So, shall we shop first and *then* look for your friend's house?' said Jean.

I nodded. 'Okay,' I said. 'Let's shop.'

We walked up the hill to the town. Jean seemed to know where she was going.

'Do you know Brighton well?' I asked.

'Pretty well. I've got an aunt who lives in Hove, just along the coast. I would have taken you to Hanningtons but it was bombed. You would have loved it, Nell. We couldn't have afforded to buy anything in there but it was lovely just to look around. You *have* got your ration book with you, haven't you?'

My ration book was probably still at Hackers farm. 'I lost it when me and Olive were evacuated,' I said.

'Bloody hell, Nell! You won't be able to buy anything without your coupons.'

'Hold yer hair on, Jean. Mrs Baxter gave me hers.'

'That's all right then, you had me worried there for a minute.'

We walked along the road past large department stores with mannequins standing in the windows wearing the latest fashions. It all looked lovely and

I wanted to go into every one of them, but Jean just kept on walking.

'Where are we going?'

'To Madam Eleanor's shop in Bond Street. I've never been in there but I've always wanted to.'

I hurried after her as we turned off the main road and into a narrow street. I could smell the sea and taste the salt on my lips in the warm air blowing up from the promenade.

We stopped outside a little shop. Over the door it said: GOWNS OF DISTINCTION.

'Here it is,' said Jean, going into the tiny building. A bell tinkled above our heads as I followed her inside.

'It looks expensive,' I whispered.

Before Jean had a chance to answer me, a woman appeared from behind a curtain. I thought she looked very smart. She was wearing a lovely cream costume with a pale blue scarf draped around her shoulders. Her hair was almost white; soft waves fell gently around her face. I thought she could have been an actress.

'Good morning, ladies,' she said, smiling at us. 'And what can I do for you today?'

'We're going to a dance tonight and we need to buy a dress,' said Jean.

'I'm sure we can find something nice for you,' she said, flicking through the rails of dresses. She stared at me for a moment as if she was sizing me up. 'Green, I think, to set off your hair.' Then she looked at Jean. 'And blue for you.'

'This dance is at a posh hotel,' said Jean, 'not a church hall. I'd like red, please.'

'Well, if you're sure, dear.'

'Oh, I am,' said Jean. 'I want to make an entrance and I won't make much of an entrance wearing blue, will I?'

Madam Eleanor turned back to the rows of dresses. 'It all depends on the kind of entrance you're planning on making,' she said, a bit sharply.

Jean looked at me and rolled her eyes. I grinned at her.

Madam Eleanor handed us both some dresses to try on and we went behind a flowery curtain. I was having so much fun.

Jean helped me into an emerald-green dress. The material felt so cool as it slipped like silk over my body. I'd never worn anything like it in my life. I suddenly wished that my mum was here – she deserved to have a day out like this and to be dressed in these beautiful clothes that came off a hanger and not off the tallyman.

I looked in the mirror; I hardly recognised the young girl looking back at me. The dress looked as if it had been made just for me. It had a sweet-heart neckline and little capped sleeves, then it nipped in at the waist and fell in soft folds to just below my knees.

'Blimey!' said Jean. 'You look, I dunno, but good. You look good, Nell.'

Madam Eleanor had been right about the

colour – it brought out the green of my eyes and highlighted the red in my hair. She had been right about Jean's dress as well. She didn't suit the red one at all but she looked beautiful in the sky-blue dress that she eventually chose.

Madam Eleanor carefully folded both the dresses in tissue paper and put them in two bags that had 'Madam Eleanor's Dress Emporium' written across the front in gold lettering.

'Do come again, ladies,' she said, as we left the shop.

We thanked her and started to walk down the road towards the seafront.

'What's the address?' asked Jean.

I took the piece of paper out of my purse and handed it to her.

'Glebe Villa, Kingsway,' she read. 'No number?'

'Sorry, that's all Lottie wrote down.'

'Kingsway's a long road; it could be the Hove end.'

'No, Lottie said it was near the pier.'

'Which one? There's two.'

'What are they called? I might remember.'

'The Palace pier and the West pier. Ringing any bells?'

'It's the Palace pier.'

'Let's start at the West pier and walk along until we find it.'

So that's what we did. We walked past hotels and guest houses and private houses. Some had been damaged; one guest house with cardboard at the window had a sign saying: STILL OPEN FOR BUSINESS.

I stopped outside a hotel and looked up. It must have been at least seven storeys high.

'These buildings are so beautiful, Jean,' I said.

'They're Regency,' said Jean. 'Named after the Prince Regent, who came to Brighton to take in the sea air.'

'No wonder Lottie loved living here so much.'

'I think this is it,' said Jean.

I looked up at the beautiful white house. It had a huge bay window on the first floor. I could almost imagine Lottie standing there, pretending to be sailing on a boat out at sea.

'Blimey, your friend Lottie must be worth a bob or two! Do her parents own the whole house?'

I'd been thinking the same thing. Why did Lottie want to be my friend? We were from different worlds – she was rich and I was poor. Her parents wouldn't want a kid from Bermondsey as a friend for their daughter. I realised then that Lottie had only befriended me because there was no one else of the same age in Glengaryth. All that stuff about standing next to the sea together was just lies.

'Let's go,' I said.

'Aren't you going to knock on the door, Nell? You never know, she might be there.'

I shrugged my shoulders. 'I just want to go home,' I said sadly.

I didn't say much on the bus back to Eastbourne.

I felt angry inside, and stupid and let down, but most of all I felt sad. Jean didn't seem to notice though, she was too busy talking about the dance and how we'd be the best lookers there, and that we'd knock everyone's socks off when we walked into the Grand Hotel wearing our new frocks. I just muttered yes and no in all the right places and that was all she needed from me.

Olive was in the kitchen when I got back to the guest house and so were Mrs Wright and Mrs Baxter. I hadn't eaten since breakfast and the sight of the cakes and biscuits spread out on a metal rack made my mouth water.

'Have one of my cakes, Nell,' said Olive, picking one off the rack and holding it out to me. 'I made them all by myself, didn't I, Mrs Wright?'

'She's a good little cook,' said Mrs Wright, smiling fondly at her.

I took a bite. The cake tasted sweet and delicious.

Mrs Baxter looked at the bag I'd put down on the floor. 'Found something then?'

I nodded.

'Put it on then and give us a look.'

'Yes, Nell,' said Olive. 'Put your new dress on.'

I went upstairs to my bedroom, got undressed and slipped the beautiful green dress over my head. Then I brushed my hair and ran downstairs.

Nobody said anything for a minute – they just stared. Olive walked across to me and gently touched the silky fabric.

'You look like a proper woman, Nell,' she said softly.

'I'm still Nell,' I said.

'But you look different.'

'Olive's right,' said Mrs Baxter. 'That dress does something for you. I don't know if it's the colour or the cut, but it's perfect. You're growing up, Nell.'

'Into a beautiful young woman,' added Mrs Wright.

'You should go and show Miss Timony, Nell,' said Olive. 'I think she'd like to see your new dress.'

'Oh yes, do,' said Mrs Wright. 'She'll be tickled pink.'

I still felt sad when I thought about my friend Lottie, but it was hard to stay unhappy around these three. I walked upstairs and tapped on Miss Timony's door.

'Come in,' she called.

I walked into the room. 'I thought you'd like to see the new dress I bought for the dance,' I said.

Miss Timony took off her glasses and put the book she'd been reading down on the table next to her chair.

'You chose well, my dear,' she said, smiling at me. 'You look charming.'

'It was the lady in the shop that thought I'd look good in green.'

'It makes such a difference when you are served by someone who has an eye for colour.'

I nodded.

'So what is troubling you, Nell? Because I can see that something is.'

I stepped over the books and sat down on the little velvet stool. 'It's Lottie.'

'Your friend from Wales?'

'Yes.'

'Has something happened to her?'

'Not exactly.'

'Do you want to tell me?'

My eyes filled with tears and everything came tumbling out of my mouth.

'She pretended to be my friend, Miss Timony, she said that one day we would stand at the edge of the sea together, that she valued our friendship, but she lied because she lives in this big house on the seafront, a whole house, not a flat, which means she's rich, like, really rich . . .'

'And what has this got to do with your friendship?'

'Why would she want to be my friend, Miss Timony? I'm just some poor kid from Bermondsey, I ain't got nothin that she wants.'

'Except perhaps love and loyalty and friendship.'

'But she can get that from anyone.'

'Can she? I very much doubt that, Nell. All the money in the world isn't going to buy her those things.'

I wanted to believe her but I couldn't: I'd made up my mind and that was that.

'Forgive me, Nell, but you are behaving like the worst kind of snob.'

'What do you mean?'

'You are judging Lottie purely on her social standing and not on the unique person she is. From what you've told me about your friend I'd say she has a mind of her own. She's been brought up by liberal-thinking parents, who have taught her to think for herself. You are doing Lottie a great injustice, Nell, if you think she was using you because it suited her at the time.'

I could feel my face going red. *Was Miss Timony right?*

'And if you have just been to see her house then I presume she gave you her address. Am I right?'

'Yes,' I said quietly.

'Would you give your address to someone you never wanted to see again?'

'No.'

'Well then.'

'I've been wrong about her, haven't I?'

'I'm afraid you have, Nell.'

'I feel really bad.'

'Think of it as a lesson learned. I doubt you will be so quick to judge someone because of their social status again, will you?'

I smiled. 'Thank you.'

'Now, go and enjoy this dance, Nell, I'm sure you'll have a wonderful time. I wish I was young again – I loved to dance.'

'I'll tell you all about it tomorrow.'

'I shall look forward to it. Now, what shoes are you going to wear with that beautiful dress?'

I looked down at the black lace-ups I wore for work and groaned; I hadn't given a thought to the shoes.

'I suppose I'll just have to clean these up.'

'You can't wear black lace-up shoes with that dress, you simply can't!'

'But they're all I've got, Miss Timony. I'll *have* to wear them.'

'What size do you take?'

'I haven't a clue.'

Miss Timony slipped her foot out of one of her slippers. 'Try this,' she said.

I stared at her as if she was mad.

'I'm not suggesting that you wear my slippers, Nell, I was just wondering if we are perhaps the same size.'

Well, that was a relief. I slid my foot into the slipper. 'It fits well,' I said.

'Then you shall go to the ball, Cinderella,' said Miss Timony, smiling.

# CHAPTER 34

I met Jean outside the pier and we made our way along the seafront to the Grand Hotel.

'Nice shoes,' said Jean.

'They belong to Miss Timony,' I said, looking down at the pretty cream shoes. 'I only had a pair of black lace-ups – I completely forgot about shoes.'

'I just presumed you had some,' said Jean.

'I don't have much of anything,' I said. 'If it wasn't for our uniform being free I don't know what I would have done.'

'Some hotels make you pay for them, you know. They take a bit out of your wages every week. But Mr Costos isn't like that.'

'Is he married?' I asked.

'There's a mystery there, Nell, because you might have noticed that he wears a ring on his wedding finger, but I've never heard him mention a wife.'

'I suppose she could be back in Italy,' I suggested.

'I think we'd have heard about her by now, don't you? I mean, she would have shown her face at some point, wouldn't she? And I can't remember the last time Mr Costos went to Italy.'

'Perhaps she's dead and he still wears the ring.'

'Perhaps,' said Jean, but she didn't look convinced.

'And what about Mr Philip? Where does he fit in?'

'Another mystery we are destined never to know, Nell, and that's so bloody annoying.'

We stood looking up at the Grand Hotel. There were a lot of young people running up the steps and through the doors. The girls all wore pretty dresses and the boys looked smart, with slicked-back hair and nice suits, and then there were the servicemen. The sailors in navy blue, the airmen in a lighter blue, and then the khaki uniforms of the Army. I was trying to spot Robert but he wasn't amongst them. I could hear music coming from inside and my tummy felt as though it was full of frogs. It wasn't just me that was nervous, Jean looked pretty overwhelmed too. I took a deep breath. 'Come on, Jean,' I said, sounding braver than I felt. 'Gird yer loins, as my mum used to say.'

'Never heard that one,' said Jean, laughing.

'Maybe it's a Bermondsey thing.'

We linked arms and ran up the steps. The foyer was full of young people laughing, chatting and calling out to each other. It was all lovely and exciting and I couldn't wait to get into the ballroom.

'I've got to go,' said Jean.

'But we've only just arrived.'

'I don't mean *leave*, I mean *go*, you know, to the lavvy. It always happens when I'm nervous, sorry!'

We manoeuvred our way through the crowd towards the cloakroom. Loads of girls were jostling for space at the long mirrors that ran the full length of the room. They were giggling, fiddling with each other's hair. The room smelled sweet, like lavender and talcum powder. Jean went into a cubicle and I leaned against the wall and waited for her. I looked at the girls in their pretty dresses with crimson lips and pink cheeks. I'd never worn make-up; maybe if it hadn't been for the war and I'd stayed in Bermondsey, Angela and I might have tried it. I'd never even seen lipstick on my mum, but I guessed she just never had the money to spend on herself. The only women I knew who wore lipstick and rouge were the pretty ladies in Bermondsey who stood on the corners chatting and winking at the men. But even though I wasn't all dolled up, it didn't matter. I was wearing my lovely green dress and Miss Timony's shoes and I didn't feel out of place at all.

'That's better,' said Jean, coming out of the cubicle, 'I'm ready to gird my loins now.'

Back in the foyer we paid our two-shilling entry fee and went through the big double doors.

The room we entered was enormous. Huge chandeliers hung from the ceiling, twinkling like a thousand stars. A blue haze of smoke drifted above our heads. Tables were grouped around a shiny wooden dance floor, where a few couples were already dancing. At the far end of the room was a raised platform, where musicians were sitting on chairs playing violins and trumpets and saxophones and instruments that I didn't know the names of. They wore black suits and white shirts and dickie bows, and they sounded lovely. Jean and I stood just inside the door, completely terrified.

'Do you think we should sit down?' she whispered.

'I don't know *what* we're supposed to do,' I said, looking around.

We were saved by Robert, who was making his way towards us across the dance floor. He kissed my cheek and said, 'I'm so glad you came, Nell, I wasn't sure that you would. And this is . . .?' He smiled at Jean.

'My friend Jean,' I said.

'Would you ladies like to join me and my friends?'

I nodded and we followed him across the room. As we approached a table, three very handsome young men stood up and shook our hands. They introduced themselves as Eric, Bryan and Tom. All three had crew cuts, just like Robert, and they all wore the distinctive blue Canadian Air Force uniforms.

'Lemonade?' offered Tom, smiling.

'Yes, please,' I said. 'Jean?'

She nodded and Tom went to get the drinks.

'They're all gorgeous,' whispered Jean. 'And so polite. You can tell they're not English, can't you?'

'I suppose you can,' I said, grinning.

The one called Eric was smiling at Jean across the table and she was smiling back at him. He moved seats so that he was sitting next to her. They started chatting straight away.

'Do you want to give it a go?' said Robert, nodding towards the dancers.

'I'm not very good, remember?'

'And neither am I,' he said, grinning, 'but who cares?'

He took my hand and we walked onto the dance floor. Then he put his arms around me and I leaned into him. He smelled nice, like newly mown grass and soap, and his face was soft against mine as we started to move. The band was playing something beautiful that I'd never heard before. 'What are they playing?' I asked.

'"Moonlight Serenade" by Glenn Miller – it's great, isn't it?' said Robert.

'I could listen to it forever,' I said.

Tonight, everything felt magical and special. The lights, the music, the way my new green dress swished softly around my legs and the way Miss Timony's cream shoes managed to take me around the dance floor as if I had danced in them all my life. I felt like a different person, not the old Nell. It was like these last few years had never happened – Auntie Beth and Uncle Dylan, the Hackers, Clodagh Price, Annie and Yann were like ghosts drifting above my head, like the smoke from the cigarettes. Except for Jimmy; he was still too real to be a ghost. Even in Robert's arms, Jimmy was still as real to me as the day I'd trusted him with my locket.

'You look lovely, Nell,' Robert whispered in my ear.

'So do you,' I said, because I didn't know what else to say.

'I don't think anyone's called me lovely before,' he said, grinning. 'Handsome, maybe, but not lovely.'

We danced till we could dance no more, then made our way through the dancers and sat back down. Robert lit the candle that was stuck in a wine bottle in the middle of the table. I sipped my lemonade and smiled at him.

'Do you mind if I smoke?' he asked, taking a packet of cigarettes out of his jacket pocket.

'Not a bit,' I said. 'My dad is a smoker – my mum was always nagging at him to give it up, but he never did.'

Robert flicked the lighter, then cupped his hand around the flame until it caught. He inhaled deeply and stared at me through the smoke.

'So, tell me about yourself, Nell. You said you were from London – what brings you to Eastbourne?'

'The war,' I said.

'Well, I'm not sure you're any safer here.'

'I know, but I'm happy. I've got a good job and

my little sister likes her school so I think we'll stay.'

'You have a little sister?'

I nodded. 'Her name's Olive.'

'And are your parents with you?'

I didn't want to tell him my story; I didn't know him and I didn't think he'd be interested anyway. 'My dad's at sea,' I said, 'and my mum stayed in London with my baby brother. What about you?' I quickly changed the subject.

'I'm from London too.'

'You *are*?' I said, puzzled.

'But not *your* London,' he said, smiling. 'I'm from London, Ontario.'

'Is that Canada?' I said.

He nodded.

I was just about to ask if he had a girlfriend back home when Jean plonked herself down next to me. 'I'm bushed,' she said, fanning her face with her hand.

'Where's Eric?'

'Getting some drinks in.'

'I'll help him,' said Robert, standing up.

I watched Robert as he walked away. He was tall, his shoulders were broad and he moved with confidence through the crowd. I thought he looked more of a man than Jimmy and it wasn't just because he was older, it was more than that. The word 'experience' popped into my head. Robert was fighting a war – he'd seen things that Jimmy had never seen. Maybe Jimmy just had a bit more growing up to do. But Jimmy was wise and kind and I wondered if Robert was too.

Jean sighed. 'I'm in love, Nell,' she said.

'With Eric?'

'Don't you think he's dreamy?'

'You can't be in love, Jean, you've only just met him.'

'Don't you believe in love at first sight, Nell?'

'No, I don't.'

'Well, I'm living proof of it. Do you think he likes me, Nell?'

'I'm sure he does.'

'No – *really* likes me. Really, *really* likes me?'

'From the way he was looking at you, I'd say he likes you very much,' I said, smiling at her.

'Do you think he'll ask to see me again?'

'He likes you, Jean, what more can I say? I'm not a fortune teller.'

'We should go and see a fortune teller, Nell, and find out what our future holds – you know, when we'll get married and how many kids we'll have.'

'I don't believe in all that stuff,' I said. I could almost hear Lottie's voice saying, *It's a load of old rubbish, Nell.*

'Would it be too forward if I did the asking?'

'There's a war on, Jean, I think all those sorts of rules have gone out the window.'

'I'd rather he did the asking though.'

'That would probably be better.'

'What about you and Robert?'

'I don't know.'

'But you like him, don't you? Oh *do* say you like him, Nell, we can go around in a foursome – wouldn't that be fun?'

I stared at her.

'What?' she said.

'Oh, nothing.'

'Don't tell me you've got someone else, Nell, that will spoil everything.'

'Just a friend,' I said.

The band was playing an upbeat number. I caught hold of Jean's hand. 'Come on, let's have a twirl together.'

'My feet are killing me,' she said, making a face.

'Tough,' I said, 'because I'm in the mood for dancing.'

'Okay,' she said, dragging herself up. 'But only one.'

I danced with Tom and Bryan and complete strangers who came up to the table with big smiles on their faces so that I couldn't refuse them, but I saved the last dance for Robert. The lights had been turned down and the orchestra was playing 'We'll Meet Again'.

'Can we?' asked Robert.

'Can we what?' I replied.

'Meet again,' he said, smiling into my eyes.

I nodded. 'I'd like that.'

At the end of the night the four of us walked home together through the dark streets. The only light to guide us was a watery moon and a sky full of stars. There was a warm wind blowing up from the beach and we could hear the soft swish as the sea pulled the pebbles from the shore. It had been a magical night, just like Mrs Wright's evening at the Grand had been. I couldn't wait to get back to Sea View and tell her all about it.

# CHAPTER 35

We spent most of that night in the cellar underneath Sea View as sirens continued to whine, hour after hour, starting low, getting louder, then lessening and getting louder again in waves that still put the fear of God into me. I had never got used to that awful wailing sound and I didn't think that I ever would. When the bombs started to fall poor Olive clung to me, whimpering.

Miss Timony had paid for bunk beds to be fitted, so at least we were able to lie down, but only Olive and two travelling salesmen managed to sleep. The men snored so loudly that we couldn't have slept even if we'd wanted to. The all-clear didn't sound until five o'clock in the morning, when we all trooped back upstairs, where I fell into an exhausted sleep. I was woken by Olive shaking me.

'Go away,' I said, 'I'm not working today.'

'You've got a visitor, Nell,' she said. 'You should get up.'

I groaned and pulled the covers up around my chin.

Olive shook me again. 'You have to get up,

Nell. There's a soldier waiting for you in the kitchen and he's really tall and he talks funny and I like him.'

'What are you talking about?' I mumbled.

'There's a soldier in the kitchen, Nell, and he hasn't come to see Mrs Wright or Mrs Baxter – he's come to see you. He wants to take you out for a ride in his car.'

I sat up and rubbed my eyes. 'Robert's downstairs in the kitchen?'

'Um, I don't know if his name's Robert. I think it might be Robert but he's in the kitchen eating toast and drinking coffee. I've never tasted coffee, Nell, have you ever tasted it?'

'Olive, can you please stop talking?'

'I don't think so,' she said.

'I suppose I'd better get up then.'

'Yes, you should, and you should put on your new green dress and Miss Timony's shoes.'

I reluctantly dragged myself out of bed. 'That green dress is for dancing in, Olive, not for wearing in a car.'

'Well, that's what *I'd* wear,' she said, 'if I got to go out in a car.'

'Tell him I'll be down in a minute.'

'Well, don't be long,' she said, 'because he's waiting for you and it's rude to keep people waiting.'

What was Robert doing here? He'd said he wanted to see me again but we hadn't made a definite date. I supposed that meant he must like me and suddenly I wasn't tired anymore. I washed and dressed and ran downstairs. He stood up as I went into the kitchen.

'I hope you don't mind, Nell,' he said. 'But it's a glorious day and I thought you might like to go out for a spin.'

'I'd love to,' I said.

'You have to take me to Henry's house first,' said Olive. 'We're having a picnic and Auntie Missus is invited as well. Auntie Missus is my doll,' she explained, smiling at Robert. 'But I think she's a person.'

'I guess she probably is then,' said Robert, smiling back.

'I'll go and get her then, shall I?'

'You do that,' he said.

'Can we go in your car?' said Olive. 'Auntie Missus likes cars.'

'Then we shall definitely go in my car.'

Olive turned around at the door. 'You should have worn your green dress,' she said. 'I wanted Henry to see it.'

'I shouldn't think Henry will care what I'm wearing,' I said.

'That's what *you* say,' she said.

I shook my head in despair; my little sister came out with the oddest things.

'Where are you intending to go?' asked Mrs Wright.

'Where do you recommend?' he said, smiling at her.

'Alfriston,' said Mrs Wright. 'It's such a lovely village and it's not far from here.'

'Alfriston it is then,' said Robert, smiling at her.

I could see by the way Mrs Wright and Mrs Baxter were gazing at Robert that he had won them over. It didn't surprise me because he was having the same effect on me. I wondered what Miss Timony would think of him. Something was telling me that she wasn't so easily charmed.

Olive chatted non-stop all the way to Henry's house; Robert was highly amused by her. Henry was waiting for her at the gate as we pulled up outside the house. Robert opened the glove compartment and handed Olive two bars of chocolate.

'For you and Henry,' he said, handing them to her.

Olive flung her arms around Robert's neck. 'Thank you,' she said. Then she whispered something in his ear that I couldn't catch.

We watched Olive and Henry walking up the path like an old married couple, each of them holding one of Auntie Missus's hands as if she was their child.

'That girl is going to be something wonderful when she grows up,' said Robert, laughing.

'She's pretty wonderful already,' I said. 'What did she whisper in your ear?'

'She said you should have worn your new green dress and it wasn't for want of trying on her part,' he said, grinning.

'I don't know where she gets it from,' I said.

It had been a warm summer and even though it was now almost September, the weather was still beautiful. We drove along the coast road – the sea looked so calm and inviting. I tried to imagine what it would look like without all the ugly barbed wire. I wondered how it would feel to run down the pebbles and into the cold sea.

We left the coast road and cut up through the villages towards Alfriston. I kept looking at Robert as he concentrated on driving through the narrow country lanes. He was so handsome that my heart missed a beat and I could feel my face going red. *For heaven's sake, pull yourself together, girl,* I thought.

'We don't have roads like this in Canada,' said Robert, breaking into my thoughts. 'Our roads are wide and straight, not nearly as interesting as yours.'

We eventually came to the village. It looked as if it had been torn from the pages of a child's fairy-tale book. It was how I imagined a perfect village to be. We parked the car and walked across the green. In front of us, set on a gentle slope, we could see the spire of a church rising up behind the trees.

'Let's take a look at it,' said Robert, catching hold of my hand.

As we got closer we could see that the church had been built in the shape of a cross. Bright green ivy trailed across the old stone walls and darker green moss clung to the red roof. Next to the gate was a wooden sign telling visitors about the history of the church. It was called St Andrew's.

Robert started to read it out loud: '"The custom was to bury local shepherds with a clump of sheep wool in their hand. The wool was supposed to signify to the gatekeepers in heaven that the dead man's poor record of church attendance was due to his obligation to his flock." Wow, how neat is that?'

'I wonder if it worked?'

'I guess we'll have to wait until we get to heaven and see how many shepherds made it through the pearly gates,' said Robert, grinning.

We opened the gate and walked up the path between ancient gravestones. Some of them were so old that they were leaning over and some had collapsed altogether; they lay cracked and broken on the ground. I supposed that anyone who had ever loved them was long gone and so the graves were left neglected and uncared for. On the newer graves stood jam jars filled with pretty flowers; sweet-smelling roses trailed across the grey stone, and white daisies and orange marigolds blossomed in the soft earth. We paused to read some of the inscriptions.

'Folk died young back then, didn't they?'

'I wonder why,' I said.

'Poverty and disease, I guess.'

I was standing in front of one grave where five children, all under ten, had been buried.

'How could their parents bear to lose so many of them? It's heartbreaking,' I said, my eyes filling with tears.

Robert took my hand. 'Come away, Nell,' he said. 'This isn't a day for sadness.'

'No, you're right,' I said, 'I'm sorry.'

'No need to be sorry – it shows me that you are a girl with a kind heart and that's a lovely thing to be.'

We walked away from the graves and went towards the church.

Beside the porch was a beautiful stone sundial.

'Have you ever seen one of those before, Nell?' asked Robert. 'Because I haven't.'

I placed my hand on the stone: it was warm and smooth. 'No,' I said.

'Do you think we can go inside?'

I pushed down the wooden latch and the big door creaked open.

After the sunshine it felt chilly inside the church. I shivered in my thin cotton dress. We walked down the central aisle, our footsteps echoing on the uneven stone floor. Coloured light from a beautiful stained-glass window fell across the wooden pews and flecks of dust danced in the rays of bright sunshine.

We walked across to a side altar and lit candles. I prayed to God to keep my family safe and to bring my daddy home to us, and I prayed that he would keep Jimmy safe, wherever he happened to be. I looked across at Robert, who had his eyes closed, and I wondered who he was praying for.

Once we were outside again I felt warmer. We walked around to the back of the church and there in front of us was a river. This had to be the most beautiful place in the world. We sat on the grass and watched the water flowing slowly past. Further along the bank I could see a stone bridge and it reminded me of another time and another boy. Memories of warm spring evenings when me and Jimmy would walk to Tyford to post my letters home to Mum, and then sitting on the bridge with our legs dangling over the side, watching the river roll beneath us and getting to know each other.

Robert broke into my thoughts.

'Are you hungry?' he asked.

'A bit,' I said.

We walked back across the green and into the village, and had lunch in a lovely old pub called The George Inn. We sat at a little table looking out over the pretty high street. The food was delicious and Robert was good company; he was easy to be with. I didn't feel the need to impress him.

'How is the war going?' I asked.

'The news is a bit sketchy but the last report we had was that the Americans are within a few miles of Paris and the Japanese are fleeing from advancing troops in Burma. What news there is coming through is encouraging.'

'Why aren't you fighting, Robert?'

'Oh, I will be – we had taken a bit of a battering, lost a few men. Some of us were sent here to regroup. I expect to be shipped out any time soon.'

'Are you scared?'

'It would be very unwise not to be, Nell, so yes, I'm scared – but I also want to be part of it. I want to be there when we defeat the enemy, but most of all I want to go home, knowing that I've done my bit.'

'We *all* want to go home,' I said sadly.

'And with God's help we will, little Nell,' he said, reaching across the table and holding my hand.

# CHAPTER 36

Summer gave way to autumn. The breeze blowing off the sea became crisper and the nights became cooler; you could see your breath in the mornings. Bonfires burned in back gardens and leaves turned from green to fiery red and russet brown, falling to the ground like multi-coloured drops of rain. They crunched under our feet as we walked across the Downs and they tangled our hair as they drifted from the trees.

On one of my weekends off, Robert took Olive, Henry and me to Cuckfield, where we picked big fat blackberries full to bursting with juice. Olive and Henry ate more than they picked but I didn't scold them – they were having a lovely time, running around the field looking for the ripest berries. Juice dribbled down their chins and stained their gas-mask boxes a deep purple. People were getting fed up with wearing the cardboard boxes around their necks all the time. There hadn't been a sniff of gas in all the years we'd been lugging them around. The ugly masks smelled of rubber and disinfectant and they made us feel sick. People were starting to leave them at home and women were using the cardboard boxes to carry their sandwiches and make-up instead. Men used them for storing their baccy and matches. Of course, if you were caught by a beady-eyed warden you were in deep trouble. Pillar boxes had been painted a yellowish green and they were supposed to change colour if there was a gas attack, but we were beginning to doubt that there ever would be one; not that we wanted one, of course.

We carried the fruit back to a delighted Mrs Wright at Sea View, who turned it into delicious blackberry jam.

I was spending a lot of time with Robert – he would often meet me after work and we'd walk hand in hand along the seafront or we'd go up on the Downs. When he could borrow the car, we went further afield to Chichester and the lovely village of Bosham. We'd sit by the harbour and watch the boats coming in and out. But it was to Alfriston that we went the most because it was so peaceful. This beautiful village became our special place. We sat on *our* bench, we trailed our fingers in *our* stream and we walked hand in hand amongst the old gravestones. One day I bought flowers and placed them on the grave that held the five little children. I wanted them to know that they hadn't been forgotten, even though they'd died so long ago.

Jean was still going out with Eric. He was a nice lad and the four of us often went to the pictures together, or up to Beachy Head, where Robert and I had first met.

In between customers at the tea room we would chat about the boys.

'What am I going to do when he's shipped out, Nell? I love him, I do. I really love him.'

'I suppose you will just have to be brave, like all the other women whose husbands and sons are fighting in the war.'

'I don't think I'm very good at being brave, Nell. I feel like crying every time I think about him leaving. Don't you feel the same about Robert?'

'I know I'll miss him,' I said. 'But I think I'll be okay.'

'You don't love him then? Not like I love Eric.'

'Sometimes I think that maybe I could.'

'That's a strange thing to say, Nell.'

'Is it?'

'Well, either you love him or you don't.'

'I like him a lot and I love being with him but he doesn't give much away. He never mentions his family or his life in Canada. Does Eric talk about his family?'

'All the time – I think they're very close.'

'That's what I'm talking about; Robert just never mentions his.'

'I'll ask Eric, he might know something.'

'Don't do that, Jean. I don't want him to think I'm prying into his life.'

'I'll tell Eric not to say anything.'

'Best not.' I said.

Jean sighed. 'Love is a very painful thing, isn't it, Nell?'

'Listen to you, you old drama queen! You never know, he might surprise you and pop the question.'

'Wouldn't that be great? I'd be Mrs Jean Kennedy.'

'Is that his name?'

'Yes, his great-grandmother was Irish. We could have our honeymoon in Ireland, wouldn't that be amazing?'

'Well, he couldn't marry a nicer girl than you, Jean.'

'Thanks, Nell. Do you know what would be great?'

'Tell me.'

'A double wedding: me and Eric and you and Robert.'

'I'm not even seventeen yet, Jean, and I have a lot more on my mind than weddings.'

Just then a family came into the tea rooms and Jean took her pad and pencil out of her apron pocket and went to take their order.

I leaned back against the glass counter and thought about Robert. Jean was so sure that she loved Eric, not a doubt in her mind; maybe there was something wrong with me in that department. Robert was kind and funny and caring, not to mention very good-looking.

One evening Mrs Baxter asked to speak to me. We sat on a bench in the back garden of Sea View. She was looking very serious and I wondered what was on her mind.

'This may have nothing to do with me, Nell,' she

said, 'but with your mum not here, I feel a responsibility for you. Can I ask, how old is Robert?'

'He's twenty,' I said.

'And you are?'

'Sixteen.'

'Do you think that perhaps he is a bit too old
for you?'

'I don't think so – is that what's worrying you
then?'

'What do you know about him, Nell?'

'Very little actually, except that he's kind and
polite and he wouldn't make me do something I
didn't want to do.'

'I suppose that's what I was worrying about.'

'You'll just have to trust me.'

'It's not you I don't trust, Nell, it's that handsome pilot of yours.'

'Don't forget, Mrs Baxter, I'm a Bermondsey
girl and it will take more than a pretty face to turn
my head.'

'Well, the best advice I can give you is, don't do
anything you wouldn't want your mother to see.'

'Don't worry, I won't, so you can stop worrying.'

'You're a good girl, Nell, and I wouldn't like to
see you get hurt.'

'It's nice that you care about me – it makes me
feel less alone. You and Mrs Wright have been so
good to us and I know my mum would be very
happy if she knew how kind you have both been
to me and Olive. I promise that if I have any
worries I'll come to you.'

'You didn't mind me saying, Nell?'

'Of course I didn't.'

That night I lay in bed and thought about Robert. Was I falling in love with him? Or had I left my heart in that faraway place with a boy who had nothing and yet dreamed of owning a farm of his own one day?

# CHAPTER 37

There was good news coming from the front via Mrs Wright but the flying bombs kept dropping, mostly under the cover of darkness, and then we had to drag ourselves out of bed and troop down to the cellar and spend the rest of the night on a hard bunk bed listening to the snoring salesmen. The flying bombs were horrible things – they made this awful roaring sound and then they went silent. That's when you had to run for cover because it meant they were about to hit the ground and explode.

Everyone was so used to the bombs and the sirens and the blackouts that it was fast becoming hard to imagine life without them. Nobody voiced what we were all thinking: what if we lost the war? What was going to happen then? Miss Timony said that we must have faith in our soldiers, who were risking their lives for our freedom, but it was a scary time and all everyone wanted was peace.

People carried on working, they got married, they had babies, they danced and they sang, they mourned for the ones they had lost and they held their loved ones tighter. Mrs Wright reckoned the war had brought everyone closer. Neighbours who had squabbled all their lives helped each other out; people became kinder. Miss Timony said it was a shame that it had taken a war to bring people together.

'Do you think it will last after the war?' I said.

'My limited understanding of people, Nell, is that they have very short memories.'

My memory wasn't short, though: I remembered everything. My daddy's ginger hair and sparkling blue eyes, the gentleness of my mum, Tony's bony knees and sweet little Freddie. I remembered our home in Rannly Court that was always full of love and laughter. I remembered the pawn shops, the tallyman, the pubs and the pretty ladies. I remembered the noise of the women and children and the smells coming off the river. I would lie awake at night and relive all those happy times and pray that one day we could all be together again, back in Bermondsey in my little part of the East End, which I loved.

Winter arrived with a vengeance. Gales battered the coast and sent angry waves bashing against the sea wall and spraying over the promenade. The blackout was difficult enough but the wet weather made it even more treacherous as we stumbled on the slippery pavements and grabbed onto complete strangers. I'd never said sorry to so many people in all my life. But I had a lot to be thankful for. I loved my job; Mr Costos was just about the best boss in the world. He always had a smile on his face and so did Mr Philip, who still insisted on calling me Fanny. They were so kind to me and Olive, and I knew how lucky I was. I was so grateful to Miss Timony for getting this job for me. I got to know the regulars who came into the hotel for their tea; I saw them in the town and they waved and smiled at me like old friends. These people had welcomed me and Olive into their lives and I would be forever grateful to them.

And then there was Robert, who I was getting closer to every day. I remembered Mrs Baxter's advice not to do anything I wouldn't want my mum to see and that was getting hard. I would be seventeen in a few months, and that is what Robert whispered in my ear one night when we were cuddled together in a shelter on the seafront. We had only kissed up till now but I knew what he was getting at.

'You do love me, don't you, Nell?' he'd said, brushing away my hair and gently kissing my neck.

'Maybe.'

'Only maybe?'

'You'll be going away, Robert, I may never see you again.'

Robert tipped my chin up and smiled. 'You've become special to me, Nell; I would never hurt you. I want something to remember you by when

I'm fighting this war. You do know that I love you, little Nell?'

'But you live in Canada and I live here.'

'I'll come back for you. We'll get married – would you like that? Please, Nell, I just want us to be closer. Is that such a lot to ask?'

I had this niggling little thought that Robert was being rather dramatic. His words were like a line from a movie, when the music swells up and the lovers walk hand in hand into the sunset.

'I'm not ready, Robert,' I'd said, and he'd gone a bit moody and didn't hold my hand on the way home. When we got to Sea View, he didn't kiss me goodnight like he always did, he just started to walk away.

'Robert!' I called after him.

He turned around and stared at me.

'You're not a child, Nell,' he said.

*Is that what I was being? Was I being a child?*

'You shouldn't start something if you're not prepared to see it through.'

'See *what* through?' I asked.

'Us,' he said.

Looking at Robert's face scowling back at me, I almost felt like laughing. He looked like a spoiled child who'd been denied a ride on the merry-go-round. Except that it wasn't a ride on the merry-go-round that he was asking for, he was asking for something much more precious and I wasn't ready to give it to him, however much he scowled.

'Goodnight, Robert,' I said, and went indoors.

I could almost hear Miss Timony saying, *Don't give in to blackmail, dear girl.*

I decided to talk to Jean about it.

It was a couple of days before we got the chance to see each other. I hadn't heard from Robert since the night on the seafront. Well, if he thought I'd give in just because he was acting like a spoiled child, he could jolly well think again.

Jean and I went to a little café opposite the pier. We waited until the waitress brought a big pot of tea and a scone each before we started to talk.

'I hope you don't mind me asking,' I said, 'but have you and Eric done more than just kiss each other?'

'Not really – we've decided to be strong, even though it's killing us.'

'And Eric is okay with that?'

'Of course he is! I imagine you're asking me this because Robert wants more than a kiss?'

I nodded.

'And is that what you want, Nell?'

'I don't know.'

'Well, I think if you really wanted to do it you'd know all right. Sometimes it gets so difficult when I'm with Eric that I feel quite unwell and I know it's the same for him. It's just that we've decided to wait. It sounds to me as if your Robert has other ideas.'

'Don't you like Robert, Jean?'

'Is that what it sounds like?'

'It does a bit.'

'Oh, I'm sorry, Nell. It's not that I don't like him, I just don't think he's being very careful with your feelings. He's handsome and he's charming and probably used to getting his own way, but you're only a young girl and he's old enough to know better. If he can't control himself that's his problem, not yours.'

'That's just what I needed to hear, Jean, because come to think of it, that's exactly how he's acting.'

'He'll come round, he likes you.'

'Does he?'

'Oh, he likes you all right.'

Jean was right; Robert did indeed come round. In fact, he came round with nylons for me, flowers for Mrs Wright and Mrs Baxter, and bars of chocolate for Olive and Henry.

'I've been an idiot,' he said, as we walked across the cliffs. 'Forgive me?'

We stopped walking and I put my arms around his neck. I looked into his handsome face. He was older than me, but sometimes he was like a little boy who wanted all the sweets in the sweetshop and knew that if he begged enough times he'd probably end up getting them. But I wasn't his mother and he wasn't going to get round me that easily. He'd chosen a Bermondsey girl and it was time he realised it.

That night in bed I thought about what Robert had said to me. He had as much as asked me to marry him; at least, I thought he had. But he hadn't actually *asked* me – he didn't say the words. I was trying very hard to remember what exactly he had said. Yes, I remembered now. He'd said, 'We'll get married – would you like that?' Only he hadn't waited for an answer; it was as if he hadn't needed one. The whole thing made my head hurt. Maybe it was a Canadian thing. Maybe they didn't bother going down on one knee and actually asking the girl; maybe that was it. I'd ask Jean.

It was pouring with rain and the wind was buffeting the coast and sending white froth over the sea wall, flooding the promenade and racing across the road. The tea rooms were almost empty.

'You'd think people would be even more in need of a nice cup of tea and a sticky bun to cheer them up, wouldn't you?' said Jean. 'God, I'm bored stiff!'

'Jean?' I said.

'Mmm?'

'This may sound like a daft question, but when a boy from Canada asks a girl to marry him, does he go down on one knee?'

'Oh my God, Nell, has Robert asked you to marry him?'

'I think so.'

'You think so?'

I nodded. 'He didn't say it in so many words, but he said that he would never hurt me and once the war was over, he would come back and we could get married if I wanted to. I suppose that's a kind of proposal, isn't it?'

'It sounds like a proposal to me, Nell – not the most romantic but definitely a proposal. What did you say?'

'I didn't say anything, because I'm not sure that he was looking for an answer.'

'A double wedding,' said Jean, grinning. 'Wouldn't that be the best thing?'

'I'm not sure that it would. I'm not sure that I'm ready to settle down and unless Mum is safe and finds us, Olive is still my responsibility.'

'Well, they'll be shipped out soon so you'd better make up your mind or it will be too late.'

# CHAPTER 38

Everyone noticed that Robert had stopped coming to the house but no one except Olive mentioned it.

'Why doesn't Robert come here anymore?' she asked one morning as I walked her to school.

'We had a bit of an argument.'

'You didn't bash him over the head with a shovel, did you?'

'Of course I didn't. I don't make a habit of bashing people over the head with shovels, Olive.'

'Well, that's a relief, because I don't fancy going on the run again, Nell, and I don't think Henry would be allowed to come with us, and I don't want to leave him.'

I took her hand and we crossed the road and sat in a shelter. It was freezing and the sea was grey and uninviting, bashing against the iron supports of the pier. The ugly barbed wire was still in place, moving and creaking in the cold wind blowing off the sea.

I looked down at Olive and smiled. 'We are never going to go on the run again, Olive Patterson, so you can stop worrying.'

'I'm glad about that. I had an argument with Aggie once.'

'You did?'

'Yes, and she played "In and Out the Dusty Bluebells" with Mabel Brown and they wouldn't let me join in, but we made up in the afternoon and Mabel Brown said she would never lend Aggie her skipping rope ever again. So, couldn't you make up with Robert, Nell?'

'It's not as easy as that, Olive. I don't think that we can ever be friends again.'

'Couldn't you just try?'

I shook my head. 'He's not the person I thought he was, love.'

'Does that mean he's someone else?'

'In a way.'

'Is he still called Robert?'

'What do you mean?'

'Well, if he's not the same person, then he must be a different person, and if he's a different person then he must have a different name.'

How could I explain any of this to my little sister?

'Let's just say he isn't as nice as I thought he was.'

'I like him a lot, Nell, and so does Henry. Henry says he's going to be a pilot and fly planes and wear a uniform just like Robert. He'll have to grow a bit, though.'

'You like Henry, don't you?'

'I like Henry a lot. Henry says he wants us to live together when we grow up.'

'Would you like that?'

'No, I'm going to live with Aggie, but I told him that he can cut the grass if he likes.'

I smiled. 'And what did he say to that?'

'He said he'd cut the grass but I don't think he will, Nell. I think he'll live with Malcolm Fenshaw, who can spit further than anyone else in the school, that's who I think he'll live with. Me and Aggie will just have to cut our own grass, but I don't think that Aggie will mind.'

I felt like laughing out loud as I listened to Olive, but she looked so very serious as she discussed Henry's living arrangements that I just squeezed her hand. 'Let's get you to school,' I said.

My heart wasn't broken but I was angry and I felt stupid – really stupid. I'd thought that Robert was kind and truthful. He'd been lovely to Olive and that hurt as well. She and Henry had looked up to him as if he was some sort of god, but he wasn't. He'd even won over Mrs Wright and Mrs Baxter; in fact, he'd made fools of all of us. I found out what he was really like from Jean.

She'd been quiet all afternoon; in fact, she could barely look at me and I couldn't think what on earth I could have done to upset her.

In between customers I asked her what was wrong.

'I need to speak to you, Nell, after work,' she'd said quietly.

'Sounds serious,' I said.

'It is.'

We were sitting in the café with two steaming coffees on the table in front of us.

'I'm all ears,' I said, grinning.

'Oh, Nell, I'm so sorry but you must believe me when I tell you that I've only just found out.'

'Found out what?'

'How can I say this?'

'I've always found it easiest to just say it, it gets it over with quicker.'

Jean stared out the window, took a deep breath then turned to face me. 'Robert is married, Nell. He has a wife back in Canada.'

I heard what she'd said but I couldn't make any sense of it. I watched the rain trickling down the windows, making patterns between the criss-crossed tape. I watched people scurrying past and a bunch of people huddled in the shelter on the seafront.

'Nell?' said Jean softly.

I turned and looked at her. 'A wife?' I said.

'Oh, Nell, he has a baby as well. I'm so sorry.'

'How did you find out?'

'I told Eric that Robert had more or less asked you to marry him. I couldn't understand why he was so angry. I'd never seen him like that before and that's when he told me. I was really cross with him for not telling me sooner, I could have warned you off. I'm still bloody fuming!'

'This isn't your fault or Eric's,' I said. 'I just feel like the worst kind of idiot.'

'You're not an idiot, Nell, you just trusted one. I could bloody kill him. I could – I could kill him!'

A week later I received a letter from Robert. It was in a blue envelope and my name was written on the front in capital letters that seemed to scream at me. I didn't want to open it; I wasn't interested in anything he had to say.

I was more angry than sad at what he had done and I was glad about that because I didn't feel as if my heart had been broken: it was my trust that had been broken. He had wanted me to give away something that was precious and he'd thought he could do that with a few slushy words and the promise of love, while all the time he was married with a baby. Well, I felt sorry for his poor wife, who was waiting for him to come home from the war. There was nothing he could say that would make this better. I never wanted to see him again and I didn't want to receive any letters from him in blue envelopes, so I didn't open it.

Jean and I went to the café after work and I gave her the letter and asked her to give it to Eric to return to Robert.

'Have you forgiven Eric?'

'Yes, I've made him feel so bad about not telling me earlier that he's falling over himself to make it up to me.'

'And what was Robert's reaction?'

'He's really angry with him for telling me and they're not mates anymore but Eric says that will all be forgotten when they are sent back to the war. He says you have to put your differences aside when you are fighting the common enemy. He told me a story about a pilot who had to fly with a chap who'd gone off with his wife. The plane crashed and he held that man who had betrayed him in his arms, until he drew his last breath. He held him in his arms and he said he forgave him for going off with his wife. I thought that was a really nice story.'

'I guess I can understand that, but I can't forgive Robert.'

'I'm not saying that what he did was right, Nell, but I bet it happens a lot. These boys are far from home and need the comfort of a woman.'

'Yes, and then they leave and the girl's left with a lot more than a broken heart to look after.'

'They're going soon, Nell. They don't know exactly when it will be but Eric says it's soon.'

'I'm sorry, Jean. I know how much you care for him.'

'We're going to get married, Nell, as soon as it can be arranged.'

'You're going to *marry* him?'

'Yes.'

'But what if . . .?'

'He gets killed?'

I nodded.

'It doesn't make any difference. He's the one for me, Nell. I know it in my heart and I'm not going to let fear stop me from marrying him.'

'What does your mum say?'

'She likes him and she trusts me to make up my own mind. Of course she is worried about the same thing you are, but it's what we both want and if we only have a few weeks together at least we can *be* together properly.'

I put my arms around her. 'I'm so happy for you, Jean. I like Eric a lot and I know he'll look after you.'

'I guess I picked the lucky straw.'

'I guess you did and I wish you all the happiness in the world. Where will you live?'

'Eric says it's up to me. Once the war is over we'll go to Canada together. Eric says I'll love it there, but I'm not sure. He is happy to live here in England if that's what I want.'

'He sounds like a great chap.'

'He is. I feel as if I've known him all my life, and do you know what, Nell? He loves me so much that I can hardly take it in. There is something wonderful about being loved that much. I'm sorry it wasn't like that for you and Robert.'

'I'll get over it, I had a lucky escape.'

'You deserve to meet someone like Eric.'

'Sometimes I think that I already have.'

'Really?'

'He's just a boy really, a kind, gentle boy.'

'Why aren't you with him then?'

'We lost each other along the way.'

'Well, if you love him as much as I love Eric, my advice is to jolly well find him!'

'Anyway, this is about you, not me,' I said. 'When is this wedding going to be?'

'As soon as possible. Do you think Olive would like to be my bridesmaid?'

'I think that she would love it – in fact, I know she would.'

'You'll ask her then?'

'I don't need to – she'll say yes all right, in fact we'll never hear the end of it. I don't know what she's going to wear though, she hasn't got anything fancy enough for a wedding.'

'Do you think if I bought some material someone might make her a dress?'

'I'll ask them at home, I bet they'd love to.'

'I wouldn't have met Eric if it hadn't been for you, Nell. I'll always remember that.'

'I guess you owe me one.'

'Cheese sandwich do?'

'Perfect.'

'Nell?'

'Yes?'

'You should definitely find that boy of yours.'

I smiled, thinking of Jimmy. He might not be as handsome as Robert but I knew that he would never hurt me and he would never force me to do something I wasn't ready to do. I realised in that moment that it was Jimmy I loved, and when the time came that I was ready to give myself to someone it would be Jimmy, and if I never saw him again then it would be someone like him. Someone kind and tender, who loved me just for myself. I didn't care that Robert thought I was being childish, because right now I was happy to wait and I would never again let another man make me doubt myself.

Jean and Eric got married on Christmas Eve in an old church on the edge of the Downs. It was the most beautiful and romantic setting you could wish for. Snow had been falling all night and now it covered the rolling hills as if they'd been painted especially for the occasion.

I'd walked up the path towards the church under a grey winter sky, between gravestones as silent as the snow that covered them. Olive looked beautiful in a white taffeta dress. Around her waist was a pale blue sash. Mrs Wright had been lovingly sewing the dress for weeks and it couldn't have looked any better if it had been bought in Madam Eleanor's Dress Emporium in Brighton.

Olive ran ahead of me up the path, Auntie Missus dangling from her hand. The doll was dressed in the same white taffeta complete with blue sash, which Mrs Baxter had made for her.

I left Olive in the porch to wait for Jean and went inside. The church was cool and dark. Motes of dust danced in the thin winter sun shining through the stained-glass window. Dark green holly and red berries, mistletoe and winter foliage were wrapped around the stone pillars and draped across the altar. Candles flickered in glass jam jars on the old stone ledges underneath the beautiful windows. It smelled of Christmas; it reminded me of home.

I slid into a pew next to Mrs Wright, Mrs Baxter and Miss Timony. Mr Costos and Mr Philip were behind us. Eric was sitting in the front row with Bryan, one of the lads we'd met at the dance. They both looked very handsome in their blue Canadian Air Force uniforms. I guessed that Robert would have been the one by Eric's side and that made me feel bad, as if the whole thing was my fault and I should have known better. Robert had been Eric's best friend and I knew Eric would have chosen him to be his best man if it hadn't been for me.

Just then the organ started playing 'Here Comes the Bride' and Eric and Bryan stood up and moved to the centre of the aisle. A hush of expectancy fell over the congregation as everyone waited for Jean to appear. My eyes filled with tears as she walked slowly down the aisle holding onto her brother Bertie's arm. She looked beautiful in a delicate ivory silk dress that fell in soft folds to her ankles. Her mother and her auntie had made the dress out of parachute material but nobody would have guessed it – she looked like a princess. She was carrying a posy of white winter roses. Olive followed slowly behind her, looking neither left nor right; she was taking her role as bridesmaid very seriously.

It was a beautiful, simple ceremony full of joy. We sang Christmas carols at the tops of our voices and when Eric kissed his bride everyone clapped and cheered.

It was late afternoon when we came out of the church, and almost dark. Someone produced a box camera and proceeded to take pictures of the happy couple under a tall oak tree, whose branches were weighed down with snow. It had been the most wonderful day and even the thought of what Robert had done hadn't spoiled it.

The reception was held at the Strand Hotel – it was Mr Costos's wedding gift to Jean and Eric.

'I'm the luckiest girl in the world, Nell,' she said.

'You deserve to be. I'm so happy for you both and you look beautiful, Jean.'

'Do you know what, Nell? Today I feel beautiful, even if I am wearing a parachute!'

We danced the night away to a trio playing Glenn Miller music, and even Miss Timony took a turn around the floor with Mr Costos. I did a quickstep with Bryan, who had two left feet, and a waltz with Mr Philip, who glided effortlessly around the floor as if he'd been dancing all his life.

By ten o'clock Olive was fast asleep on one of the blue velvet couches, her arm around Auntie Missus. Mr Philip covered her gently with a blanket.

We all waved the newlyweds off to bed at midnight; they were staying at the hotel. The rest of us started to put on our coats and gather up our belongings when an air-raid siren sounded.

And so Jean and Eric spent their first night together as a married couple in the cellar, with all the guests and a couple of inebriated sailors who had come in off the street.

# CHAPTER 39

Jean and Eric had to cut short their honeymoon on the Isle of White because the Canadians were moving out. The day before New Year's Eve, Jean handed me a familiar blue envelope.

'Robert asked me to give it to you,' she said.

I felt my tummy turn over at the mention of his name and that annoyed me because it meant that I could still be affected by him. I didn't want to know what he had to say, I didn't *care* what he had to say.

'I don't want it,' I said.

'I thought you'd say that. Look, Nell, I know he's behaved badly and I'm not going to try and justify what he did, but I believe that he is truly sorry. I know he's charming and he can spin a line but he has nothing to gain from this and you will never see him again. He's going to war and he wants to make his peace with you. Anyway, I've delivered the letter – I haven't a clue what it says but my guess is that he wants to see you before he goes. It's up to you, Nell, and no one would blame you if you didn't want to see him. I for one certainly wouldn't blame you.'

I took the letter and slipped it in my apron pocket. 'I'll think about it,' I said.

'Don't shoot the messenger.'

I smiled at her. 'It's okay,' I said. 'I'm not going to shoot anyone today.'

Jean looked relieved and I gave her a hug.

All afternoon I was aware of the letter. It felt heavy, even though it was just a thin piece of paper. There was a part of me that wanted to rip it up and throw it in the bin and another part that was curious to know what he could possibly say that could begin to justify what he had done. When my tea break came round, I left the hotel and walked across the road and sat in a shelter on the seafront. It was freezing cold and I wished I'd put my cardigan on. My hands were shaking as I opened the letter, as much from nerves as from the biting wind that was blowing off the sea.

Robert's handwriting was beautiful, neat and even as if every word had been measured. I started to read.

*Dearest Nell,*

*If you are reading this letter then thank you, that alone is more than I deserve.*

*I was an idiot and I treated you badly. I don't even have the excuse that my marriage is a bad one because it isn't. I've not only betrayed you but I've let my wife and son down as well and I'm truly ashamed of myself. I'm not the man I thought I was.*

*I don't make a habit of deceiving women. I've never done it before and believe me when I say that I will never do it again.*

*I have no excuses. I should have known better, I should at the very least have been honest with you.*

*Can you forgive this selfish man who found himself falling in love with you when he had no right to?*

*We are leaving soon and I would dearly love to see you before I go. I will be at the bar in the Grand Hotel tomorrow evening at nine o'clock hoping with all my heart that you will come.*

*Love*
*Robert x*

I folded the letter and put it back in my pocket. I was glad that I'd read it and I was glad that it wasn't full of excuses. In fact, I found it to be pretty honest and it showed a more vulnerable Robert than the one I had found myself falling for. But that didn't mean that I was ready to meet him. What if I'd given in to him? I could have been left with a baby; had he thought of that? Or had he only been thinking of himself and his needs? I felt so confused and muddled and I needed to talk to someone about it.

I was standing by the window in Miss Timony's room looking down on the street below. It was a

348

blustery day and there were very few people about. I waited patiently while she read Robert's letter – I needed someone to tell me what to do and I trusted Miss Timony's opinion. I knew she wouldn't just tell me what she thought I wanted to hear.

'Sit down with me, Nell,' she said at last.

I walked across the room and sat down in front of her on the little velvet stool. She folded the letter and handed it to me.

'I don't know whether to meet him or not, Miss Timony. I don't know what good it will do.'

'Well, I think it will do Robert a lot of good but it's how it will affect *you* that matters. What is your heart telling you to do, Nell?'

'It keeps changing – one minute I think I should meet him because he's going to war and he feels bad about what he did, and the next minute I get angry and I want him to suffer. Why should I make him feel better just because he's decided that that's what he wants? I mean, that's what this was all about, wasn't it? Robert getting his own way.'

Miss Timony took off her glasses and placed them on the table next to her. She reached towards me and held my hands.

'Matters of the heart are rarely black and white, Nell. I believe Robert when he says he is truly sorry – I think there is a sincerity in his letter. It's what *you* feel that worries me most. You are still carrying all this hurt and anger around with you, and that's not healthy. You have been left with an image of Robert as a selfish, cruel man – a kind of ogre, the proverbial bogeyman – when if fact he is just human like the rest of us, with all our faults and foibles. If you don't see him one last time that image will remain in your head and you may well judge others by his standards.'

'You think I should see him then?'

'It's not what *I* think, my dear, I can only give you my opinion. It's you who must make that decision. All I have done is tried to open your mind a little so that you can think more clearly.'

At nine thirty the next evening I found myself standing outside the Grand Hotel. I had changed my mind so many times about whether or not to come. I'd talked myself into it, then just as quickly talked myself out of it again. I still didn't know if I was doing the right thing. When Robert asked me to meet tonight it hadn't quite registered that it was New Year's Eve. The pavements were packed with people so that I had to walk in the road. It seemed the whole of Eastbourne was out in force. There was a feeling of excitement in the air, maybe even a feeling of hope.

There were people sitting on the steps leading up to the hotel entrance. They were laughing and singing and drinking beer from glass bottles. I was never going to find Robert in this mad crowd. I squeezed past them; men grabbed at me and tried to pull me down. I knew it was just high spirits and I laughed as I pulled away from them.

The foyer was jam-packed and the bar was at

least four deep with men all shouting at the same time and holding money up to the poor barman. Then I felt a hand on my arm and I found myself looking into Robert's handsome face.

He said something but all I could see was his mouth opening and closing. It was impossible to hear him above the noise of the crowd. He put his hand on the small of my back and gently guided me into the lounge. There were a few people round the piano but it was a lot quieter than the bar. We sat by the window on one of the couches.

I leaned back against the cushions. 'I couldn't hear what you said.'

'I said I didn't think you were going to come.'

'I nearly didn't.'

He nodded. 'I can understand that.'

I looked down at my hands. I didn't know what to say to him; I felt all wrong-footed. I looked up at him. 'I shouldn't have come,' I said.

He smiled gently. 'But I'm glad you did.' He stood up and held out his hand to me.

'What are you doing?'

'Well, if we can't speak, perhaps we better try singing.'

I grinned. 'Really?'

'Why not? It's New Year's Eve – let's jolly well sing!'

We walked across the room to the revellers at the piano. I was no singer but I joined in with the others, singing the songs we heard on the wireless: 'The White Cliffs of Dover' and 'We'll

Meet Again' – songs that gave me a lump in my throat so that I had to keep stopping. Robert didn't know many of the lyrics but he hummed along with the rest of us. I looked across at him and smiled – he looked so handsome and so young that my anger began to melt and my heart began to forgive.

As midnight approached we walked hand in hand across the road to the seafront and, as the boats tooted their horns and the church bells rang out the old year and welcomed in 1945, Robert kissed my cheek.

'Happy New Year, little Nell,' he said.

I looked out over the dark water and thought about my family. Were they safe? Were they celebrating the New Year somewhere and thinking of me and Olive? Oh, I hoped so. I missed them so much, I wanted to see them, I wanted to be in my mum's arms.

Robert put his arm around me and I leaned into him. His coat was rough against my cheek. I knew that I would never see him again but I was glad that I was here with him on this special night. I closed my eyes and prayed that he would make it through the war and return safely home to his loved ones.

# CHAPTER 40

In between frying eggs and bacon, Mrs Wright was glued to the wireless. One morning in March she informed us that Montgomery's men were crossing the Rhine.

'Monty says that the battle is going very well,' she said, as if she'd just spoken to him on the telephone.

Everyone was feeling hopeful that the war was finally coming to an end. The home guard had been disbanded and, as Mrs Wright said, 'That's telling us something, isn't it?'

'Can't count our chickens yet, though,' Mrs Baxter warned. 'Wars are tricky things.'

Olive nodded in agreement. 'So are boys,' she added very seriously, dipping soldiers into her boiled egg.

'Having trouble with Henry, are you?' asked Mrs Baxter.

'Not exactly trouble,' said Olive. 'But he keeps wanting to play kiss chase and his breath smells of pickled onions. Henry has a thing about pickled onions. His mum told me not to worry as he has eaten just about every pickled onion in the house and she isn't going to pickle any more until next Christmas.'

'Best give him a wide berth at Christmas then,' I said, grinning.

'I intend to,' said Olive. 'And when Henry gets married I shall warn his wife not to pickle any onions.'

'Very good advice,' said Mrs Baxter, looking fondly at Olive.

I missed my family but living with Mrs Wright and Mrs Baxter had been like having two mothers who truly cared for us. I would never forget their kindness to me and Olive. They couldn't have loved us more if we'd been their own.

Jean had said goodbye to Eric and we all tried our best to keep her spirits up. She was being very brave and I was so proud of her.

'I know he'll be all right, Nell, I just know he will.'

'Of course he will,' I said. 'He's got you to come home to now.'

'I'm glad you made your peace with Robert before he went.'

'I am too, and it wasn't as hard as I thought it would be.'

'If Robert hadn't been married I think it would have been a different story. Eric said that he had grown very fond of you and it had given him many a sleepless night.'

'But he *was* married, wasn't he? And I can't think about what might have been. Anyway, I'm a great believer in things working out the way they are supposed to, and Robert and I were not supposed to be together. And that, my friend, is that.'

'I had a letter from Eric and Robert asked him to pass his love on to you.'

'Are they friends again now then?'

Jean nodded. 'I thought they would be, I think their friendship is pretty strong.'

'I'm glad, I felt a bit guilty about it.'

'You have nothing to feel guilty about, it was his own silly fault. I just hope he learned his lesson.'

'Oh, I think he did.'

'I bet he doesn't tell his poor wife though. I'd never forgive Eric if he did that to me.'

'Eric wouldn't do that to you, Jean.'

'I bet that's what Robert's wife thought.'

Winter gave way to a spring that was welcomed in like a returning hero. The days were longer and the evenings warmer. Birds fluttered amongst the branches of the trees and everywhere there were signs of new life, a renewal, a new beginning. People seemed to walk with a spring in their step and hope in their hearts. Flowers bloomed in parks and gardens – they sprung up between potatoes and carrots as if to say, *What the world needs now is food for the soul, not the belly*. Yellow daffodils, purple crocuses and multi-coloured tulips vied with each other to be the best, the brightest, the most glorious. Tight buds clung to the branches, ready to burst into life.

There had been other springs but none that brought with them such a feeling of hope and new beginnings; none that stirred the heart like this one did.

Holidaymakers started returning to the town and Sea View became alive again. Tape was peeled from the windows and new curtains hung with great pride.

Miss Timony decided that Sea View needed a facelift.

'It's time for a new beginning,' she declared. 'And new beds and sofas will reflect that.'

As far as I could see, the beds were perfectly fine and so were the sofas. I didn't think that Sea View needed a facelift at all. I loved the old-fashioned cosiness of the guest house. There had been so many changes in my life in the last few years that I couldn't get excited about this one.

'Well, if Miss Timony feels the place needs a facelift I'm more than happy to go along with it,' said Mrs Wright.

'Mrs Baxter won't have to get rid of Mr Baxter's wooden leg, will she?'

'I shouldn't think that comes under "soft furnishings", Olive.'

'Well, that's a relief. I'll let her know, in case she's worrying about it.'

'You do that, my love.'

We all took turns meeting the new arrivals off

the trains and escorting them to the guest house. One day Mrs Wright asked me to meet some guests who were arriving on the four o'clock train.

'Take Olive with you,' she said. 'There are children arriving and I think it would be nice for her to meet them.'

'What about Henry?' I asked.

'I think just you and Olive would be best – we don't want to overwhelm them, do we?'

I picked Olive up from school and we walked to the station.

'Are the children my age?' asked Olive, skipping along beside me.

'I don't know, Olive, Mrs Wright just said there were children.'

'I hope there's someone of my age. How old am I now, Nell?'

'You know how old you are, Olive. Mrs Wright baked you a cake with nine candles on it.'

'I was just checking . . . Nell?'

'Yes, love?'

'Did I get a birthday card from Mummy?'

I crossed my fingers behind my back. 'There's no birthday cards until the war is over, it's the law.'

'Okay, Nell.'

We arrived at the station early, so I bought two bags of Smith's crisps and we sat on a bench to eat them. The crisp packets had little paper bags inside them that were filled with salt. You had to tear open the bag, then shake it hard so that all the crisps were covered in salt. Olive shook her bag so violently that half the crisps burst out of the top and scattered all over the station floor.

'Here, share mine,' I said, offering her my bag.

'Thanks, Nell, I don't know how that happened.'

'You shook them too hard, that's how it happened.'

'Blame Henry – that's what he does.'

'Well, tell him not to.'

'Okay, Nell.'

Once we'd finished the crisps we put the empty bags in the bin and walked across to the barrier.

'How are we supposed to know who we're meeting?' asked Olive, staring up the platform.

'Mrs Wright gave me a piece of paper with "Sea View" written on it – we have to hold it up.'

'Can *I* hold it up?'

'Of course you can, but make sure it's the right way up.'

'I'm not daft, Nell.'

I smiled at her. 'I know you're not,' I said, getting the paper out of my pocket and handing it to her.

'How come we've never held up a piece of paper before?'

'Mrs Wright said she saw another guest house doing it and she thought it was classy.'

We heard the sound of a train in the distance. There was a high-pitched whistle as it came nearer, then it shuddered and slowly screeched to a halt, belching out thick white smoke. Porters rushed past us, pushing two-wheeled trolleys.

'Okay, Olive,' I said, 'hold up the paper.'

There was a whirl of activity and noise as the train doors opened and slammed shut; people climbed out, stepping down onto the platform, passing bags and suitcases to the porters. Olive and I stood together, waiting for the smoke to clear. Then we scanned the faces of the people hurrying towards the barrier.

'Is that them?' said Olive, pointing to a family with three children.

She held up the paper but the family walked straight past us without so much as a glance.

More people passed us and then, as if in slow motion, I watched as a tall, thin boy helped a woman down from the train. She was holding the hand of a smaller child. I couldn't move. Tears poured down my face and then a scream tore from my throat: 'MUMMY!'

Olive clung to my skirt. I grabbed hold of her hand and started running up the platform. Tony got to me first and we clung to each other, laughing and crying. Mum had Olive in her arms, a much bigger Olive than the last time she had held her, and she smiled at me over the top of my little sister's head. I walked towards her as she put Olive down.

'My Nell,' she said, smiling – that smile that I had kept in my heart all these years and sometimes feared that I would never see again – but here she was, she had come back to us. Our arms went around each other and I breathed in the smell of home. I'd grown taller than Mum; her head was tucked under my chin. I wasn't a little girl anymore but in her arms that's how I still felt. I looked into her eyes and touched her hair; I couldn't believe it was really her. Freddie was tugging on my skirt. I wiped away my tears and knelt down in front of him. 'Hello, Freddie,' I said. 'I'm your big sister.' He stared at me, then hid behind Mum's skirt.

I turned to Olive. 'Do you remember Freddie, Olive?'

Olive frowned. 'Was he that thing in the drawer?'

'That's right, but he was a baby, not a thing,' I said, smiling.

Tony grinned. 'You're right, Olive, he *was* a thing and a very noisy thing at that!'

We were all laughing except Olive, who was standing very close to me and holding my hand tightly. I looked down at her and saw that she was crying.

'What's wrong, darling?' I asked.

'What about the people we were supposed to be meeting, the ones with the children?'

I took a hankie out of my pocket and gently wiped her eyes. 'Mrs Wright and Mrs Baxter played a trick on us – they knew we were meeting Mummy. It was a surprise, Olive, a wonderful surprise.'

Tony ruffled her hair and tried to lift her up but she pulled away from him.

'She'll come round,' I said. 'She just needs a bit of time.'

'We have all the time in the world,' said Mum. 'All the time in the world.'

I was so busy seeing to Olive that I didn't notice the tall man with the ginger beard walking towards us.

# CHAPTER 41

Olive held my hand all the way home. Freddie was on Tony's shoulders. Daddy and I kept smiling at each other. My heart was so full I could hardly breathe.

'Don't you want to hold Mummy and Daddy's hands?' I asked Olive.

She shook her head.

When we got back to the guest house there was a banner across the door saying WELCOME HOME and Mrs Wright and Mrs Baxter were standing underneath it, smiling and dabbing at their eyes. We were ushered into the house amid much laughter and tears. Olive hung back, looking sad and worried.

'Do you mind if me and Olive go for a little walk?' I said.

Mum smiled and said, 'You go.'

Tony stood up as though he wanted to join us but I shook my head and he smiled as if he understood.

We walked down to the seafront. The sea was so calm it looked like a sheet of glass, glistening right out to the horizon.

We sat quietly on a bench holding hands and then Olive spoke.

'Who's that man, Nell?'

She didn't remember him. It just hadn't entered my head that Olive wouldn't remember her daddy but, of course, why would she? She was only four years old when he went to war. I should have spoken about him, kept his memory alive in her head, but it just hadn't occurred to me that she would forget someone as big and strong and wonderful as her daddy.

I put my arm around her shoulder. 'He's your daddy, Olive, don't you remember him at all?'

She shook her head.

'Well, he's the bestest, kindest daddy in the whole world and he loves you very much. He used to work on the docks and I would wheel you down to the river in your pram to give him his lunch. You were such a beautiful baby, Olive, everyone used to say how beautiful you were and it made your daddy so proud – he loved to show you off to the other dockers. You are a lucky girl to have such a lovely daddy.'

'He sounds nice but I still don't remember him, Nell.'

'That's because he was in the Navy fighting the war. Don't you remember him at all?'

'No, I don't.'

'Never mind, you have lots of time to get to know him and love him, and you will, Olive, I promise you will, so don't worry about it. It will just happen without you doing a thing.'

'I remember Tony though, but he was smaller. He jumped off the train and went home, didn't he? Cos he was a little bugger!'

I laughed. 'That's right, he did and he *was* a little bugger! He may be taller but he's still Tony and I expect he's still a little bugger. And that baby in the drawer is your brother Freddie and you're his big sister.'

Olive didn't answer me – she seemed lost in thought and that was okay. I could hardly believe myself what had just happened and for my little sister it must be even harder. We hadn't seen our family in three years and Olive had only been five when we'd left Bermondsey. She was going to need time to get used to things and, funnily enough, so was I. I had cared for my little sister since the moment Tony had got off the train and left us alone. That responsibility wasn't mine anymore and I suppose it should have been a relief, and yet somehow it wasn't. What should have been the happiest day of our lives was leaving us both feeling worried and confused. I smiled down at Olive.

'Everything is going to be fine,' I said.

'But are you sure that man is my daddy, Nell?'

'I'm absolutely sure.'

'I think Henry will be surprised, because I told him that I didn't have a daddy.'

'Oh, Olive, you've always had a daddy!'

'But I didn't know that.'

'I'm sorry, love. You should have spoken to me about it.'

'I think you were too busy running away and sleeping in barns and getting locked in bedrooms and bashing people over the head with shovels to worry about whether or not I had a daddy.'

'You do make me laugh, Olive.'

'I guess that's better than crying, Nell.'

'I guess it is.'

'Can Henry come to tea and meet my new daddy?'

'Of course he can, he can come to tea any old time he likes.'

'Good.'

'Are you ready to go home now?'

Olive nodded. 'I need to tell Auntie Missus.'

'Of course you do.'

'I bet Mrs Wright has baked one of her cakes too.'

We walked hand in hand back to the guest house. We all had a story to tell and I couldn't wait to hear Mum and Dad's too.


Mrs Wright and Mrs Baxter had put on a delicious spread and we all tucked into it. Tony, as usual, was eating as if he'd never seen food before.

After we'd eaten, Mrs Wright and Mrs Baxter left us alone.

'We'll leave you to talk,' said Mrs Baxter, smiling at us.

'We owe you both so much,' said Mum. 'We can never thank you enough for taking care of our girls.'

Mrs Baxter's eyes filled with tears. 'They've been angels,' she said, hurrying out of the room.

'We're going to miss them,' said Mrs Wright, following her sister.

I had a sinking feeling in my stomach. 'We're not going back to Bermondsey, are we?' I asked.

'No, the council have given us a house in Hove – isn't it wonderful?'

'What, all of us?' I said.

'All of us,' said Daddy.

Olive stared at me; she had a panicked look on her face. 'NO!' she screamed. 'I have to stay here, I can't leave Henry and Auntie Missus doesn't want to move. Tell them I'm not going with them, Nell, tell them.'

There was a stunned silence in the room as everyone stared at Olive, whose little body was shaking with anger.

'But this isn't our home, Olive,' I said gently. 'We can be with our family now.'

Olive jumped up from the table, tears rolling down her cheeks. She glared at Mum. 'I won't go, I won't and you can't make me.'

Little Freddie's bottom lip was quivering – he knew that something was wrong – but it was the look on Mum's face that tore at my heart. Dad shook his head and held her hand. 'Give her time, Kate, this must all be very confusing for her.'

Olive had fled from the room. 'I'll talk to her,' I said, going after her.

This was awful; this wasn't how it was supposed to be. My heart went out to Mum and Daddy. I'm sure this wasn't what they had been expecting either. I went into the kitchen, where Mrs Baxter and Mrs Wright were sat drinking tea. 'Have you seen Olive?'

'Isn't she with you?' asked Mrs Baxter.

I sat down next to them and put my head in my hands. 'She's refusing to go to the new house. She was really rude to Mum, I feel awful.'

'I told you the shock would be too much for them to take,' said Mrs Wright. 'But would you listen? No, you wouldn't.'

'Oh dear, I was wrong, wasn't I? You always did have more sense than me, Mary.'

'Well, that's the first time you've admitted to that,' said Mrs Wright, smiling at her sister.

'I should have told you as soon as we knew your parents were both safe, but I thought it would be a wonderful surprise to meet them at the station. I was wrong – you both needed time to get used to it. I'm so sorry, Nell.'

'Please don't feel bad,' I said. 'It was a wonderful surprise, it truly was, but it was too much for Olive.'

'I didn't hear the front door open so I don't think she's gone outside,' said Mrs Wright.

'Oh dear, I do feel dreadful,' said Mrs Baxter.

'Please don't,' I said again. 'This isn't your fault.'

'I think perhaps it is.'

'Do you think she's with Miss Timony?' I said.

'If she's up there, send her down to us, Nell,' said Mrs Wright, 'and tell Miss Timony what's happened.'

I went upstairs and tapped softly on Miss Timony's door. I didn't want to wake her if she was resting.

'Come in, Nell,' she called.

I opened the door. Olive was sitting on the floor with her head on Miss Timony's lap. Miss Timony was gently stroking her hair.

'Oh, Olive,' I said.

Olive's tearstained face looked up at me. 'I'm not going, I'm not going,' she sobbed.

'It's okay, Olive, you don't have to go if you don't want to.'

She wiped at her eyes with the sleeve of her cardigan and looked up at me. 'I can stay here?'

I didn't know if I was doing the right thing. Where Olive lived wasn't for me to decide anymore but I'd looked after her for so long, I just couldn't bear to see her so upset and scared. 'Yes, love, you can stay here until you are ready to move into the new house. Mum and Dad and Tony and Freddie love you and they want you to be with them, but no one is going to make you move into the new house until you are ready.'

'Do you promise?'

'Yes, Olive, I promise. Now I want you to go

downstairs and say sorry to Mum and Dad for being rude to them. Will you do that?'

Olive nodded and smiled at me through her tears.

'Good girl,' I said, giving her a hug.

After she'd gone I could barely look at Miss Timony; I stared at a pile of books at my feet instead.

She reached out and held my hand. 'I would have said the same thing, Nell.'

I raised my head and looked at her – it was the last thing I had expected her to say. 'You would?'

'She's gone through too much in her little life to be expected to just do as she's told and go where she's told to go, by people she hardly remembers.'

'I'd dreamt of the day we would all be together again; I never let myself believe that they were dead. I imagined how it would be, how happy we would be, but that's not what's happened. Olive doesn't remember Daddy and she doesn't want to live with her family. In fact, I'm not sure she wants anything to do with them – it's almost as if they are strangers to her.'

'I suppose they are in a way. You were older when you left London – you remember everything about your life in Bermondsey but Olive has forgotten. This place has become home to her, she has her school and she has her little friend

Henry and, most importantly, she has you. And for good or bad you have become Olive's surrogate mother, and she doesn't think she needs another one.'

'But it's not the way I imagined it.'

'Life rarely is. The only happy endings one can truly rely on are in books. As you see, I surround myself with happy endings. If a book I'm reading seems to be heading for disaster I stop reading it. I've had enough sadness in my life to waste my time reading about someone else's misfortune. So there you have it, you have found me out. I'm not well read at all, I'm an old romantic; give me hearts and flowers any day.'

'Me too.'

I looked around the room at all the happy endings, in piles on the floor and spilling from the bookcases, and I was glad for Miss Timony because she was lovely and she deserved happy endings. But this wasn't a book, was it, and I had promised Olive that she didn't have to move to the new house. What were Mum and Daddy going to say? Would they make her go? Would I have to break my promise to her?

She had been so brave, hardly complaining. She'd played hide and seek in Clodagh Price's garden even though she must have been scared to death, and when I'd fallen ill she'd found Yann. She had trusted me even though I didn't really know what I was doing myself. I couldn't let her down now. If I had to fight my parents on this then I would. Olive must stay here, where she was happy, until the time came when she was ready to live with them.

'What can I say to my parents, Miss Timony?'

'You'll find the words, Nell,' she said.

I hoped with all my heart that she was right.

# CHAPTER 42

I dreaded going back downstairs; I didn't want to face my parents. Would they be disappointed in me, when I fought for Olive to stay here?

As it happened it was Tony who had done the fighting and I didn't have to say anything at all.

Olive was sitting on the floor with her head on Mum's lap when I went back into the room.

'We've had a little chat, Nell,' she said, smiling at me, 'and Tony has persuaded us that the best thing for Olive right now is for her to stay here. Isn't that right?' she said, stroking Olive's hair.

'And I said sorry, Nell. Didn't I, Mummy? I said sorry.'

'You did, darling,' said Mum.

'Thank you,' I mouthed to Tony.

'Mummy says that you and me can visit the new house, Nell.'

'That sounds good – does that make you happy?'

'Yes, it does. And Mummy says that Henry can visit as well and I can show him my new room, and Tony says he'll bake a chocolate cake. Henry loves chocolate cake but I told him not to buy any pickled onions.'

We all laughed and it was lovely to see Olive happy again.

'You can bake cakes?' I said to Tony, who had never so much as fried a sausage in his life back in Bermondsey.

'Tony is quite the little chef these days,' said Daddy.

I grinned at my brother. 'Really?'

Tony nodded. 'That's what I want to be, I want to be a chef.'

'Not a docker?'

'Can't think of anything worse,' he said, screwing up his face.

'Blimey, that's a change of heart, isn't it?'

'It took leaving Bermondsey to make me realise there was more to life than working on the river, lugging bags of sugar onto barges.'

I noticed that, even though Olive was leaning against Mum, her foot was touching Daddy's foot, and it gave me hope. I smiled at him. 'What about you, Daddy? Won't you miss the river?'

'Let's just say that I'm not the man I was, Nell.'

Mum seemed quick to change the subject. 'Do you want to know who taught Tony to cook, Nell?'

I shook my head.

'It was Beth.'

For a second I didn't know who she was talking about. 'Beth?' I said.

'The vicar's wife,' said Tony. 'At the vicarage, in Glengaryth.'

I couldn't believe what I was hearing. 'You've been to Glengaryth?'

'We've been living there,' said Mum.

'In Glengaryth?' I was beginning to sound like a parrot.

'Did you see Aggie?' butted in Olive.

'I did,' said Tony, grinning.

Olive's eyes were like two saucers in her head. 'You saw my Aggie?'

Now *Olive* was sounding like a parrot.

'Close your eyes, Olive,' said Tony.

Olive did as she was told while Tony rummaged in a bag. Then he took out an envelope and placed it in her hands. 'Okay, you can look now.'

Olive opened her eyes and looked at the letter. Tears began running down her cheeks as she traced her name on the front of the envelope with her finger. 'From Aggie?'

Tony nodded.

Olive stood up and walked over to me. 'It's a letter from Aggie, Nell.'

'Aren't you going to open it?'

'Not yet,' she said.

'Do you want to read it in private?'

'Just with you, Nell, because you haven't got a letter from Lottie so you can share mine.'

I hugged her to me – my little sister had such a big heart and I was so proud of her. I would love and protect her all the days of her life, I really would.

I was dying to know the rest of Mum's story but I knew how special this letter was to Olive. 'Shall we go up to our bedroom?' I said.

'I think that would be the best thing to do, Nell, because then Auntie Missus can listen as well.'

'Mum?' I said.

'You go and open that letter, girls, and I'll see if Mrs Wright has any more tea on the go.'

'Mrs Wright has always got tea on the go,' I said, grinning.

Olive went across to Tony and put her arms around him. 'My heart is full,' she said, very seriously. 'Thank you for my letter.'

'You are very welcome, Olive,' said Tony, smiling.

'Who's Auntie Missus?' asked Mum.

'My doll – I'll introduce her to you later.'

As we got to the door Olive looked back into the room. 'If she's up to it,' she added.

Together we walked up to the bedroom and sat on the bed.

Olive picked up Auntie Missus and sat her on her lap. With her finger she traced the writing on the front of the envelope again.

'Aggie wrote this,' she whispered.

'Do you want me to read it to you?' I said.

'Yes, please, Nell.'

I took the letter out of the envelope and started to read.

*Dear Olive,*

*You are my very best friend and I miss you a lot. I have been very sad since you left and nothing is much fun anymore. I wish I had a picture of you so that I could look at it when I am feeling lonely. I play with the other girls at school but it's not the same. I hope that I will see you again. Give my love to Auntie Missus and please don't forget me.*

*I love you.*
*From*
*Aggie xxx*


'Can I write back to her, Nell?'

'I'm afraid not – no one must know where we are. I'm really sorry, love.'

'How will we find each other then?'

'When the war is over you can write to her in Coventry.'

'Will the war be over soon?'

I nodded. 'Everyone seems to think so.'

'As soon as the war is over I'm going to write to Aggie and then can I go to Coventry to see her?'

'We'll work something out, Olive.'

'Aggie said she loves me, Nell. I'd like to tell her that I love her as well.'

'Do you know what, Olive?' I said, putting my arm around her shoulder.

'What?'

'I think she already knows.'

'Do you think so?'

'Yes, I think so.'

'Would you read the letter to me again?'

'Of course I will.'

Once Freddie and Olive were in bed we all settled down in the front room and told our stories. I had made the decision not to tell my family the whole truth. I might have told Mum about Albert if we'd been on our own but somehow I couldn't tell Dad and Tony.

'We just weren't happy there,' I said. 'So we decided to try to make our way home.'

'You just weren't happy there?' said Mum. 'Are you sure that's all it was? It feels like a pretty drastic thing to do just because you weren't happy.'

I could feel my face going red; I couldn't look at Mum.

'If I know you, Nell, I'm pretty sure you wouldn't have dragged Olive halfway across the country in the middle of a war just because you weren't happy at the farm.'

I decide to tell them half the truth. 'It was Albert,' I said.

'Albert?' asked Dad.

'Mrs Hacker's son.'

'Did he hurt you?' said Dad, looking angry. 'Did he hurt Olive?'

'No, but he would have done if we'd stayed.'

'So you ran away to protect Olive?' said Mum. I nodded.

'Then you did the right thing, Nell, and it was a very brave thing to do,' said Dad.

'I didn't have a choice.'

Dad stood up and walked across to the window. 'I feel like going to that godforsaken farm and teaching that boy a lesson,' he said.

*Well, he'd already been taught a lesson, hadn't he? Dad might have given him a good hiding but I'd killed him.*

'I should have come with you, Nell. It wouldn't have happened if I'd been with you,' said Tony.

'It wasn't your fault.'

'I just didn't think.'

'You were only eleven – you were just a boy.'

'I would have gone to Wales sooner if I'd known how unhappy you were. Why didn't you write and tell me, Nell?' asked Mum.

'Because I didn't want you worrying about us, and it wasn't so bad to begin with.'

'We went to that farm, Nell,' said Mum.

'You went to Hackers farm?'

Mum nodded. 'We hadn't heard from you for so long and I was beginning to think that something was very wrong, so when the flats got bombed that's where we headed for – we headed for the last place we'd heard from you, which was that awful farm.'

'Did you see Mrs Hacker?'

'There was a "For Sale" sign at the end of the drive; the whole place was deserted.'

'Didn't you see anyone at all? A young boy, maybe?'

'No one.'

'What did you do after that? How did you end up at the vicarage?'

'We walked to the next village, to see if anyone knew anything about you.'

'And did they?'

'No, but the postmistress told us that soon after her son died Mrs Hacker put the farm up for sale and no one had heard from her since.'

'Did she say how he died?'

'No, she didn't – at least I don't think she did. Do you remember her saying anything, Tony?'

My brother shook his head. 'I was too hungry to take in anything much.'

'We were a sad little bunch, Nell. We'd left Bermondsey with just the clothes on our backs and nothing else.'

'How did you get to Wales with no money?'

'We hitched rides, mainly with lorry drivers, who kindly shared their food with us.'

'Oh, Mum,' I said. 'It sounds as if you had a worse time than us.'

'I was foolish to leave the way we did but I wasn't thinking straight, I just knew that I had to find you and Olive.'

'And you did.'

'And all the while I was lying in a comfortable hospital bed with no idea of what my family were going through,' said Dad.

Mum smiled at him. 'You weren't to know, love.'

It had grown dark outside as Mum continued her story.

'Mrs Cooper from the post office took pity on us and took the three of us in. She fed us and gave us clean clothes. I remembered you saying that the vicar was a Methodist, so Mrs Cooper sent a telegram to the church in Cardiff to see if your vicar knew anything about you.'

'And did he?'

'No, but he sent money for the bus and told us to go to the vicarage in Glengaryth, where we would be taken care of, and that's what we did.'

'But they'd left the vicarage,' I said.

'Beth had come back – she was having a baby and it wasn't safe for her to stay in the city. She welcomed us with open arms.'

'Auntie Beth had a baby?' I said, grinning.

'A little girl, and she was glad of my help. I was useful, I could earn my keep. We stayed there until the vicar was able to come home, and then we went back to Bermondsey to look for you.'

'I'm so happy that Auntie Beth has a baby – she wanted one so badly.'

'And do you know what she named her? She named her Olivia Nell, after you and Olive. Wasn't that a lovely thing to do?'

'It really was,' I said, my eyes filling with tears. Somehow that meant a lot to me, it meant we hadn't been forgotten.

'And she's a beautiful little thing.'

'She's okay, for a baby,' said Tony, grinning.

'Did you like Glengaryth, Tony?'

'I hated it to start with – all those bloody sheep, I thought I'd go mad. I was all for running back to London but I don't think Mum would have been too happy.'

'You're right, I wouldn't,' said Mum.

'So I stayed and I learned to cook and I learned to love the countryside. And I knew that whatever happened next, I never wanted to live in Bermondsey again.'

'How did you find us, Mum?'

'Mrs Ryan – it was very clever of Mrs Baxter to let her know where you were going. If she hadn't done that, we wouldn't have known where you were. It was such a relief, Nell. We stayed with Mrs Ryan and I wrote to Mrs Baxter to let her know we were safe, and then I went to the council and asked if we could be re-housed in Sussex.'

'How did you find Daddy?'

'I went to see the welfare officer; it took a couple of weeks for them to track him down to a hospital in Kent. I always had hope in my heart, I never gave up, and I'm glad I didn't because from that day I knew we were going to be family again. We might have lost our home but not each other.'

'I'm sorry about Rannly Court, Mum, I'm sorry you lost everything.'

'I didn't lose the things that mattered, Nell,' she said, smiling at us.

# CHAPTER 43

The new house was lovely. It was on a council estate in Hove, just along the coast. Me and Olive went there on the bus. Some of the houses had been damaged and were boarded up but it was a lovely little road that curved round like a horseshoe.

We were standing in the front garden, looking up at it.

'My own front door, Nell,' sighed Mum. 'Did you ever see anything so lovely?'

'It's the most beautiful front door in the whole entire world,' said Olive.

'It is, isn't it?' said Mum. 'And there's a garden at the back as well, so your dad will be kept busy, and if that's not enough, we have our own shed. Can you imagine that? Our very own shed.'

Mum looked so happy I had a lump in my throat. She deserved a nice front door and a back garden and a shed. 'Oh, Mum, I'm so happy for you,' I said, hugging her.

'Now, do you want to see the rest of the house?'

'Of course we do,' said Olive, running round the side.

The house was much bigger than the flat in Rannly Court. It had a lovely kitchen with a table and chairs where you could eat your food. There was a bathroom off the side with a proper bath. When we'd lived in Rannly Court we had to fill a tin tub with water every Friday night and take turns washing ourselves. If you were last in the tub, the water would be stone cold.

Olive raced upstairs and I followed. As I admired the three lovely bedrooms I had the strangest feeling that I'd been here before. It was only when I went back downstairs and into the front room that I saw the sofa and I realised why: all the furniture had come from Sea View. I was guessing that Miss Timony had refurbished the guest house so that Mum and Dad could have the old furniture. How kind people had been to us on this journey of ours.

I'd hated the war, I'd hated leaving Mum and losing our home, but I'd also gained something that might never have happened if I'd stayed in Bermondsey.

I was more confident, I had a job in a lovely hotel and I didn't feel out of place; I was as good as the next girl that worked there. If I'd stayed at home I would have ended up in the sugar factory or the custard factory. I would probably have been happy enough, but now I knew there were better things out there for me and I could do anything I wanted to do. I wondered if leaving Bermondsey had changed Angela as well. I would love to see her again, to sit down and talk to her, to hear her story. We weren't thirteen anymore; we would both have changed but not in the ways that mattered. We came from the same place and Bermondsey would always be a part of us, but one thing I had learned was that it wasn't the whole of us.

We stayed at the house all afternoon. I left Olive playing with Freddie and went out into the back garden, where Dad was digging up the earth for a vegetable patch.

'Do you think you'll be happy here, Dad?' I said.

He stopped digging and leaned on the shovel. 'I wouldn't care where I was as long as you were all safe. There were times, Nell, when I didn't think I would ever see you again. So yes, I can be happy here.'

Nobody had told me what had happened to Dad and why he had been in hospital. 'Were you wounded, Dad?' I asked.

'I nearly drowned. I don't know how long I was in the water before I was picked up. I got pneumonia, Nell, and it's left me with a weakness.'

'Oh, Dad, I'm really sorry.'

'Don't be sorry, love, I was one of the lucky ones. A lot of my friends weren't as lucky as me.'

Just then Tony called to me.

'Tea and cake, anyone?'

'I can't believe the change in Tony.'

'Oh, he's a dab hand at the old cake baking; I'm going to get fat at this rate.'

I kissed his cheek. It felt rough to my lips. I loved

him so much, it was hard to believe that he had come safely home to us. I had so much to be thankful for. 'You could do with getting fat,' I told him.

'You really can cook,' I said, helping myself to another slice of Tony's fruit cake.

'Did you doubt me?'

'It's just that when we were kids all you ever wanted to do was mess around in the river, skipping school and making Mum worry herself silly.'

'What else was there to do round there?' said Tony.

'I suppose there wasn't that much, was there? But it was home and it was all we knew.'

'I still think about the river – that's where I was the most happy. I thought it was the best place on earth.'

'But now you're not so sure?'

'Now I know there's more.'

So I wasn't the only one who had been changed by the war.

'I'm going to have to look for a job to help Mum out. Is there anything going at that hotel of yours?'

'I'll ask Mr Costos, and if he hasn't got a vacancy he might know of another hotel that has. But wouldn't it be easier to try the hotels in Brighton and Hove?'

'I don't mind where I work as long as I can learn to become a proper chef. I want to open my own restaurant one day, Nell.'

I looked at my brother, so tall and grown-up, and I remembered the skinny kid with the muddy knees and the holes in his jumper. 'I'm so proud of you, Tony,' I said.

'So when are you going to tell me what really happened at that farm?'

'What makes you think anything happened?'

'Because I know you wouldn't have dragged Olive halfway across the country without a very good reason. Am I right?'

I nodded.

'So?'

'Maybe one day,' I said.

I put my arms around him and laid my head on his shoulder. It felt good to be in his arms; I felt safe.

He held me away from him and said, 'You can tell me anything, Nell, you know that.'

'I know,' I said, 'and maybe one day I will.'

We kissed Mum goodbye. I could tell that it was hard for her to see us leave; it wasn't what she had hoped for when she found us.

'We'll be back soon,' I said.

'If I come to live here can I have a cat?' asked Olive suddenly.

Mum smiled. 'You can have any old thing you like,' she said.

'A pig?'

'I'd rather we stuck with the cat,' said Mum.

'Perhaps I could call it Pig.'

Mum smiled at me and shook her head. 'She hasn't changed a bit, has she?'

'Not a bit,' I said

We waved goodbye to them until we turned the bend in the street and they were out of sight. It was a fine day as Olive and I walked back home along the seafront. We'd decided to walk as far as Brighton, then get a bus home from there.

'What did you think of the new house?' I asked.

'I thought it was really nice.'

'Do you think you might like to live there one day?'

'Maybe one day, but not yet. It might help if I had a cat called Pig. I'll ask Auntie Missus what she thinks.'

'You do that.'

It was lovely walking along the seafront with Olive; even the ugly barbed wire didn't spoil it. I loved living by the sea. I used to pretend that the Thames was my very own ocean but that was before I saw what a real ocean looked like. I supposed this was going to be our home now that Mum and Dad had been given a house here and I didn't really mind.

I stopped outside the tall white house on Kingsway. 'This is where Lottie lives, Olive,' I said.

Olive looked up at the four storeys. 'All of it?'

'That's what I said when I first saw it.'

'Bloody hell, she must be really rich, Nell! Poor people don't live in houses like this.'

'I thought that as well.'

'She's not a bit snobby though, is she? I think

387

she's really nice and it's not her fault that she's stinking rich.'

'No, it's not,' I said, grinning.

'I guess if we moved into the new house you could be close to Lottie. Would you like that, Nell?'

'Very much.'

'Do you think that Aggie will come and live here with me?'

'Perhaps when she's older. I don't think her parents would let her leave home at nine years old, do you?'

'Well, I don't fancy living in Coventry, Nell. I don't like the sound of Coventry. I'd rather live here by the sea and I think Aggie would too.'

'You've never even been to Coventry – how can you decide you don't like it?'

'It's just a feeling, Nell.' She put her hand on her heart. 'In here,' she added.

Then she put on her grown-up, serious face and shook her head as if she had the weight of the world on her little shoulders. 'And there's still Henry to worry about, Nell. I think he'd fall apart without me.'

Mum was right: Olive hadn't changed one little bit.

# CHAPTER 44

One morning Olive and I went down to the kitchen to find Mrs Wright and Mrs Baxter frying eggs and bacon with tears rolling down their cheeks.

'What's happened?' I asked, alarmed to see them both so upset.

'Berlin has fallen, Nell, and Hitler is dead – isn't it wonderful?'

'So why are you crying? That's good news, isn't it?'

'Not for Hitler, it's not,' said Olive, plonking herself down at the table.

'He was a bad man, Olive, he started the war,' said Mrs Baxter.

'Does that mean it's over then?' she asked.

'Does it?' I said to Mrs Baxter.

'Well, it's not official, Nell, but Mrs Wright and I are quietly optimistic.'

I walked over and gave them both a hug. 'This is a wonderful day, a really wonderful day.' And then I found myself crying as well.

'Bloody hell,' said Olive. 'I'd hate to see you lot when you get bad news!'

The tea rooms were buzzing with talk of peace; everyone had an opinion on when the war would finally end. The doom-mongers were predicting that it could drag on for years but the rest were full of excitement and hope.

Mr Philip was the most excited. He twirled round the tables even though there were customers in, but everyone was in such high spirits that nobody took any notice.

'Be careful, Philip,' said Mr Costos, smiling. 'We don't want you injuring yourself before the big day.'

'I can't help it, Gino, my heart is dancing out of my chest. No more ghastly air-raid sirens, no more blackouts and oh, Gino, we will be able to swim in the sea again.'

'If we can remember how,' said Mr Costos, smiling fondly at him.

Jean and I were leaning against the counter, listening to them.

'Do you know what?' said Jean. 'I don't think Mr Costos needs a wife.'

'I've been thinking that for a while,' I said.

'Funny old life, isn't it?'

'I suppose it is. If this really is the end of the war, when do you think Eric will come home?'

'That's all I think about, Nell. He said in his last letter that he'll be back as soon as he can but he has no idea when that might be. Oh, Nell, I can't wait to see him.'

'Have you decided where you want to live?'

'I'm happy to visit Canada and meet Eric's family but I can't imagine living so far away from home. Is that selfish of me, Nell?'

'Eric said he didn't mind *where* he lived so I shouldn't worry about it.'

'But *I* shouldn't mind where we live, should I? As long as we're together?'

'You read too many romantic novels, my friend. I'm not sure real life is that simple.'

'You sound very worldly wise all of a sudden, Nell. Is it because of what Robert did?'

'Not especially. I think maybe the last few years have made me see people in a different light, that's all.'

Just then Mr Philip came across to us. 'Gino says we can hang the Union Jack out of the top window. I think I'm about to burst with excitement.'

We grinned at him. 'We'll help you when the tea rooms close,' I said.

'You darlings! Now, I have to go before I get emotional and Gino gets cross with me.'

The rest of the afternoon was fun; it didn't feel like work. It felt like the week before Christmas when you could hardly wait for the actual day to come.

After much giggling and some pretty dangerous manoeuvres, we helped Mr Philip hang the Union Jack out the window and then I rushed home. It had been announced on the wireless that at seven o'clock there was to be an announcement from Mr Churchill, but when I ran in the door,

Mrs Wright said that she'd heard on the *Forces Programme* that he probably wouldn't speak until the next morning. Unconfirmed reports were coming in that Germany had surrendered. We had been half-expecting it but to actually hear the news was overwhelming.

'Quick, we have to get the flag out,' said Mrs Baxter.

'I think maybe a moment's silence first,' said Mrs Wright. 'For all those poor souls that didn't live to witness this day.'

'Wait,' said Olive. 'Auntie Missus lived through it as well, I have to get her.'

'You're right, Olive, she did,' agreed Mrs Baxter, smiling at her.

We waited while Olive raced up the stairs and came back with her doll, then we stood in silence, each with our own thoughts. I said a prayer for Jimmy that he was safe and well and that somehow I would see him again, and then I said a prayer for Albert, who I was beginning to regret bashing over the head quite so hard. I hoped he was now a nicer person than he had been when he was alive.

We had to wait until the next day to be told there was victory in Europe but already the people of Eastbourne were celebrating. There were Union Jacks everywhere. People were dragging chairs and tables into the streets for impromptu parties; it felt as though the whole of Eastbourne was having one big celebration.

Mum, Dad, Freddie and Tony came to Sea View to share in the fun. It was lovely to all be together on this very special day.

'I think we should take Mr Baxter's wooden leg with us,' said Olive. 'After all, it's got as much right to join in the celebrations as we have.'

'What a lovely idea, Olive,' said Mrs Baxter, smiling at her. 'It will be like a part of Mr Baxter is with us. I'll go and get it.'

We walked down to the seafront and joined a crowd of people around the bandstand. Someone had produced a barrel organ and people were singing and doing the conga up and down the prom.

At the end of the afternoon Freddie was getting tired, so Mum and Dad got ready to go back home. As they were leaving, Olive decided she wanted to go with them. I could see by the look on Mum's face how happy it made her.

'It's just for one night, Mummy,' said Olive. 'I have to give Henry time to get his head round it.'

At six o'clock Jean came round. 'Let's go to Brighton, Nell,' she said. 'There'll be more going on there.'

We went upstairs to my bedroom and got dolled up. We wore the dresses that we'd purchased from the little shop in Brighton. Jean produced a tube of lipstick and some rouge; I'd never worn make-up before and it all added to the excitement.

There didn't seem to be any buses running so we decided to thumb a lift. We didn't have to wait long before a car full of soldiers pulled up.

'Brighton, ladies?' said one of them.

'Yes, please.'

There was so many of them in the car that it didn't look as if there was room for us but they managed to squeeze us in. One of them tried to get a bit too friendly with Jean.

'Hands off, love,' she said. 'I'm a married woman.'

'And he's a married man,' shouted another soldier.

'Nice try,' said Jean, grinning and kissing his cheek.

'I shall never wash again,' he declared dramatically.

A couple of the soldiers threw their hats at him.

It was all in good fun and they were nice lads so we didn't mind their high spirits – they deserved to have a good time after what they'd been through.

We waved goodbye to them at the Palace Pier and were immediately caught up in an avalanche of people much bigger than the crowd in Eastbourne. I tried to hang onto Jean's hand but she slipped away from me. I started to panic; I felt as though I couldn't breathe and without Jean, I was scared. I managed to push through the crowd towards the railings, where I took in great gulps of sea air. I stayed there until I felt a bit better, then started smiling. After all I'd gone through, here I was, scared of a few people out enjoying themselves. *Pull yourself together, girl!* I scanned the crowd, trying to find Jean.

'Lost someone?' asked a young lad in RAF uniform.

'My friend,' I said.

He bent down. 'Here, climb onto my shoulders, you'll get a better view.'

I was just about to take him up on his offer when I heard my name being called.

'It's okay,' I said. 'My friend is calling me.'

'Then have a great time,' he said, kissing me full on the lips and disappearing into the crowd.

I was quite shocked for a minute; it wasn't every day that you got kissed by a complete stranger. But today wasn't any old day, was it? It was the end of the war and I guessed that normal behaviour just didn't apply. Today was a day of rejoicing and being carefree and kissing whoever you liked.

Jean called my name again and I shouted, 'Jean!' so that she knew what direction to go in.

Suddenly there she was, elbowing her way through the crowd – only it wasn't Jean at all.

The plaits were gone and so were the glasses but I would have known that smile anywhere. 'Lottie!' I screamed, falling into her arms.

# CHAPTER 45

We were both gabbling away at the same time – we couldn't get enough of each other – but there was so much noise around us that we could barely hear.

'Let's go to my house, where we can talk properly,' Lottie yelled.

'I came here with my friend Jean,' I yelled back. 'I can't just abandon her.'

'What is she wearing?' shouted Lottie, standing on tiptoes and scanning the crowd.

'What?'

Lottie mouthed the words to me as if I was deaf. 'What is she wearing?'

'A blue dress.'

The crowd seemed to have got even bigger and they were singing at the tops of their voices. Men were grabbing girls and swinging them around. Lottie and I were getting pushed in all directions.

'We can come back later and look for her, how's that?' Lottie shouted, taking my arm. 'I'm sure she's having a wonderful time.'

We crossed the road and walked the short distance to the big white house.

'This is it,' said Lottie.

'I know,' I said. 'I've been here before.'

'Really?'

'Yes, and I got all stupid about it.'

'Why?'

'I didn't know why someone who lived in such a posh house would want to be my friend.'

'You daft girl! And anyway, it's not that posh; the top floor is running with damp. We actually live in a hovel,' she said, grinning.

I didn't believe that for one minute – this house was beautiful.

'Anyway, Nell, shame on you for thinking that! I would have thought you'd got to know me a bit better.'

'It was just a silly thing and Miss Timony put me right – in fact, she made me feel a bit ashamed.'

'Good for Miss Timony, whoever she is.'

I followed her up the steps to the front door. She caught hold of my hand and pulled me along the hallway.

'Mum, look who I found,' she shouted.

A woman walked towards us. 'And who has my excitable daughter found?' she said, smiling at me.

'It's Nell, Mum. I found Nell, right here in Brighton, almost outside the front door.'

Lottie's mum came towards me. 'Oh, Nell,' she said. 'How delighted I am to meet you at last.'

'Do you mind if we go up to my room?' asked Lottie. 'We have rather a lot of catching up to do.'

'Of course you have,' she said. Then she reached

out and held both my hands in hers. 'I am so glad that you are safe and well, my dear, so very glad. My daughter was agitated the whole time we were in Cornwall, wondering if you were all right, and you are. What a joyous occasion!'

Lottie's mum was lovely, like a model, and she was sweet and kind and she spoke beautifully, just like Lottie. She was exactly how I had imagined her to be.

We ran upstairs to the bedroom, which was just how Lottie had described it to me. Beyond the big bay window was the sea and it really did feel as if you were standing at the front of a ship. I could almost feel the wind blowing through my hair. I took a big breath.

'It's beautiful,' I said.

'It is pretty amazing, isn't it?' agreed Lottie, standing beside me. 'Anyway, enough about the view. You're all grown up.'

'We're *both* all grown up.'

Lottie pulled me down on the bed. 'I want to know *everything*, every single thing. How on earth did you end up here, for a start? Tell me, tell me!'

'I don't know where to start.'

'I've always found that the beginning is a rather useful place.'

'The farm was awful.'

'It sounded awful.'

'So we ran away.'

'You ran away?'

I nodded.

'You just decided to run away? Just like that? How did you manage? Where did you sleep?'

'In barns mostly, once in a derelict house, once in a madwoman's house.'

'Oh my God, Nell! Couldn't you have just told the welfare lady how ghastly it was and got her to move you?'

'The welfare lady never came back to check on us, which didn't exactly surprise me considering she couldn't wait to be shot of us in the first place. Anyway, I wouldn't have known where to find her, so we just ran. I know it was a pretty daft thing to do but I wasn't thinking straight. I just wanted to get away from that place, it wasn't safe to stay there.'

'Did someone hurt you? Was it that bloody awful Albert?'

'Something like that.'

'But why Brighton?'

'Eastbourne, actually. We made it back to Bermondsey but when we got there, Rannly Court had been bombed and my family were missing.'

'Oh my God, Nell! I'm so sorry.'

'We didn't know what to do or where to go. Mrs Baxter, an old neighbour, was leaving London to live with her sister in Eastbourne and she said we could go with her.'

'Good old Mrs Baxter.'

'I have a job, Lottie. I'm working in a hotel on the seafront and loving it.'

'And what about dear little Olive?'

'She's happy at her new school and she's found a special friend called Henry.'

'And your family? Did you find them, are they okay?'

'That's the best bit. They are all safe – even my dad – and they are living very happily in Hove.'

'What an adventure you've had! I almost envy you. I was completely safe in the depths of Cornwall and bored out of my skull. I missed Glengaryth and I missed you, and believe me when I say there is absolutely nothing to do there, and the whole place smells of fish. Coupled with the fact that I had to share a bed with a rather obese girl, who smelled of cheese.' Lottie shuddered. 'Absolutely bloody ghastly!'

We lay back on the bed and held hands.

I giggled. 'Oh, it's so good to see you again, Lottie. You haven't changed a bit.'

'You too, and the timing couldn't be better, because I don't think I would have wanted to go back on my own. Now we can go together.'

'Go where?'

'To Glengaryth, of course.'

I let go of Lottie's hand and sat up.

Lottie was still chatting away. 'We can borrow Mum's car. I learned to drive while I was in Cornwall – there was sod all else to do there.'

I didn't answer her.

'What's wrong, Nell?'

I stood up and walked across to the window. 'I can't go back there.'

Lottie walked over to me. 'Because of your work?'

'It's not that,' I said quietly.

'Then what?'

I had kept it to myself for so long that I didn't know how to say the words.

'Whatever it is, Nell, you can trust me. It can't be that bad. It's not as if you've killed someone, is it?'

'But that's just it, Lottie, I *have* killed someone. I hit Albert on the back of the head with a shovel and I killed him.'

'No, you didn't.'

'I wish that was true, but I did. He was interfering with Olive, I wasn't thinking straight and I killed him – that's why we had to run away.'

Lottie grabbed my shoulders. 'Listen to me, Nell, you might have hit him but you didn't kill him.'

I stared at my friend. 'You weren't there, you don't know what happened.'

'How long ago was it?'

I tried to clear my head. 'It must be two years, maybe a bit less, I'm not exactly sure. What has that got to do with anything?'

'Because the ghastly Albert Hacker only died six months ago.'

'But that's not possible.'

'Well, it's true. Apparently he was cleaning a tractor, the handbrake slipped and the thing rolled over him. You might have given him a bad headache, Nell, but you certainly didn't kill him. It was an accident.'

I wanted to believe her, I really did, but I'd seen the blood and I knew he was dead. 'How do you know all this?' I asked.

'Mum and I drove to Wales before we came back here. I hadn't heard from you for so long, I just knew something was wrong. We found the gruesome farm – which has been sold, by the way – and we asked at a nearby cottage for any news of you. That's how we learned what had happened.'

I suppose I still didn't look convinced – I just couldn't take in what she was saying.

'What can I say to convince you it's true?'

'I don't know.'

'Look at me, Nell, why would I lie about something like this?'

'You wouldn't.'

'Exactly. Now repeat after me: Nell Patterson did not kill the utterly ghastly Albert bloody Hacker, even though she had every right to.'

I put my hands over my face. Lottie was telling me the truth, of course she was: I hadn't killed Albert. It was then that the weight I had carried around like an unwanted overcoat fell from my shoulders. Tears were pouring down my face.

'That's it,' said Lottie. 'You have a good old cry. According to my mum it's very therapeutic, as long as you don't indulge in it.'

And then I was laughing, with my head thrown back and my mouth open. I was laughing like a madwoman but I didn't care: I wasn't a murderer after all. I caught hold of Lottie's hands and swung her around the room, laughing and crying, then we collapsed onto the bed and she held me in her arms until I calmed down.

'So we can go to Glengaryth?' she said.

I smiled. *Glengaryth, that's where I've left a little piece of my heart, that's where I've left a young boy called Jimmy.* I thought that I could never go back but now I could. Jimmy might be long gone – in fact, if Mrs Hacker had sold the farm there would be no reason for him to stay there – but maybe the locket was still there, buried under the oak tree. I might not ever see Jimmy again, but I might find the locket.

'Yes,' I said. 'Let's go back to Glengaryth.'

'Fabulous,' she said, jumping off the bed, 'but first I think we'd better find your friend.'

'Oh God, I'd forgotten all about her!'

'Some friend you are,' said Lottie.

I stuck my tongue out and we ran downstairs.

# CHAPTER 46

I thought I'd been happy all this time but I hadn't, not really. It was always there, the guilt and the fear. Every time I saw a policeman I felt sick to my stomach because I thought they'd caught up with me and that I was going to go to prison. I hadn't exactly lied to the people who cared about me, I just hadn't let them into that dark place that I carried inside me, the place that I visited in my sleep. I had only let them in so far. Now it was different, *I* felt different: that's how I knew I hadn't been truly happy.

The first person I told was Olive. I met her from school and we walked up to the Downs. I took a blanket and some sandwiches Mrs Wright had made.

'Olive's going to love this, Nell, and don't forget to take Auntie Missus with you; she'll only make you come back for her if you don't.'

'A picnic?' said Olive, jumping up and down. 'Can Henry come?'

'Not today, love, this is just for me and you.'

'Okay, Nell,' said Olive, as she always did when I said no to something.

We walked over the fields to the cliffs and I spread the blanket on the ground. Olive sat Auntie Missus beside her. It was a beautiful afternoon and the sea sparkled below us under the bright sun.

'Now, what I'm about to say is very important, Olive, so I want you to really listen.'

'Shall I hold my ears, Nell? Because that's what our teacher makes us do.'

'I don't think there's any need to do that, Olive.'

'Okay,' she said, biting into a paste sandwich.

'You remember when I bashed Albert over the head with a shovel?'

'Mmm.'

'Well, it turns out that I didn't kill him after all.'

'Yes, you did, Nell, he was a deader all right.'

'No, I didn't, I only thought I had.'

'Did he come alive again then?'

'He wasn't dead, Olive.'

'So he's still alive then?'

'No, Olive, he's dead.'

Olive looked totally confused and who could blame her? 'Are you feeling all right, Nell?' she said.

I grinned. 'I'm not explaining this very well, am I?'

'Not really.'

'When I hit Albert I thought I'd killed him because he didn't move but it turns out all I did was knock him out.'

'You didn't hit him hard enough, Nell,' said Olive, looking suspiciously down at her sandwich. 'What paste is this?'

'It's sardine. You're not listening to what I'm saying, Olive, this is important.'

'It's just that I thought it was chicken but now I know that it's sardine it makes sense and I *am* listening.'

'Okay, what I'm saying is that Albert *did* die but not then, not there in the barn – he died much later. He was cleaning out that rusty old tractor and it rolled over him.'

'It's not many people who die twice, is it? This sandwich still tastes of chicken.'

'For heaven's sake, Olive!'

'Sorry, Nell. So does that mean we didn't have to go on the run?'

'After what he tried to do to you, I think we would still have run away, don't you?'

'Yes, I think we would . . . Nell?'

'Yes, love?'

'I'm glad it was the rusty old tractor that killed him and not you.'

'I feel the same way,' I said. 'Because I don't think I meant to kill him, I just wanted him to stop what he was doing to you.'

'Well, he's stopped now all right, hasn't he? He's stopped breathing and walking and eating and clipping Jimmy round the head. He's just bloody stopped and good job an all! Can I have another sandwich?'

'Of course you can. You do understand now, don't you, Olive?'

'Yep. You bashed Albert over the head with a shovel and he died and then he came alive again and the tractor rolled over him and he died again. Someone up there must have wanted him dead pretty badly, Nell.'

I laughed. 'I guess they did.'

The next person I told was Mrs Baxter, because she had had to keep the secret as well.

'That's wonderful news,' she said. 'I'd be lying if I said I'm sorry he's dead, Nell, but I'm glad that you don't have to feel scared anymore.'

'Thank you for keeping the secret, Mrs Baxter, and thank you for looking after us.'

'You and little Olive are lovely girls. If Mr Baxter and I had been blessed with children of our own I would have wanted them to be just like you two. And I know that Mr Baxter, God rest his soul, would have felt the same.'

I hugged her. 'You'll always be our second mum.'

Her eyes filled with tears. 'Now you've set me off, and not a child in the house washed, as my dear mother used to say.'

Yann and I had continued to write to each other and I now wrote to let him know that I hadn't killed Albert after all and that I was coming to Glengaryth and would be visiting him.

I decided not to tell my family about Albert; it would only cause them pain to know what we had been through and anyway, it didn't matter anymore. If Olive came out with it one day I'd deal with it then.

But I *did* tell them all that I was going back to Glengaryth with Lottie.

'Can I come with you, Nell?' asked Olive. 'Aggie might still be at the sweetshop.'

'The war is over now, Olive, Aggie will be back home with her parents.'

Olive looked disappointed. 'But she *might* be there, Nell.'

'Look, love, I'm only going for a couple of days, so why don't you write that letter to her while I'm gone and then we can post it together when I come back?'

'Okay, I'll write to her.'

'Good girl.'

'You *will* come back, won't you, Nell?'

'Of course I will. I wouldn't leave you, would I?'

'No, Nell, you love me too much. But I'll miss you.'

'Why don't you stay with Mum and Dad while I'm away?'

'I'll see what Henry says, Nell.'

'You do that,' I said, smiling at her.

When I thought I'd killed Albert I couldn't wait to get away from Wales. All the lovely memories I'd had were tainted by what I thought I'd done. Now I couldn't wait to go back to Glengaryth. I was longing to see Auntie Beth and Uncle Dylan and the new baby.

A week before we were due to go, an official-looking letter arrived in the post. It was addressed to me. If I hadn't found out about Albert's accident I would have been terrified.

'Who would be writing to me here?' I said to Mrs Baxter. 'No one knows where we are.'

Mrs Baxter looked at the letter. 'Well, it's been posted in Cardiff.'

'Maybe it's from Auntie Beth and Uncle Dylan,' I said.

'Well, the only way to find out is to open it, pet.'

I sat down at the kitchen table, took the letter out of the envelope and started to read. Then I put my head in my hands and sobbed.

'What on earth has happened?' said Mrs Baxter, sitting down beside me.

'My friend Yann has died,' I sobbed, handing her the letter.

She put her arm around my shoulder. 'Oh, Nell, I'm so sorry, love.'

'He was so good to us, Mrs Baxter.'

'Was he very old?'

'I think maybe he was – his hair was white but it was hard to tell his age and it wasn't something we talked about.'

'Do you want me to read what it says?'

I nodded.

She took the letter from me. 'It's from a firm of solicitors in Cardiff – Martyn, Hughes and Radcliff.'

'Solicitors? Why would solicitors be writing to me?'

'I think we're about to find out,' she said.

She read the letter slowly, running her finger under each line, then looked up at me. 'Well I never!' she said.

'What? What does it say?'

'He's left you his house, Nell. Your friend, Yann Kovak, has left his house to you and Olive.'

Mrs Baxter handed me the letter. 'Read it for yourself.'

I unfolded it and started to read.

*Dear Miss Patterson,*

*I am sorry to inform you that Mr Yann Kovak passed away peacefully in his sleep on Thursday, 10 May.*

*Mr Kovak came to see me a month ago. He knew that he was dying and he asked me to act on his behalf. He wants his house, known as Elena Cottage, to be left to you and your sister Olive. He also asked me to tell you and your sister that his beloved dog, Henri, will be living with his friend and neighbour Mr Percy Wakefield at Woodland View, should Olive wish to pay him a visit.*

*I am sorry to be the bearer of such sad news. I only had the privilege of meeting Mr Kovak on two occasions but I found him to be an extraordinary and fascinating man.*

*Can you please arrange an appointment at*

*your convenience to go over the details. I look
forward to meeting you both.*
  *Yours faithfully,*
  George Martyn

I put the letter in my pocket and walked down
to the seafront. The sea always calmed me. I felt
as though my heart had been ripped out. Yann
had been like a father to me and Olive when I
feared my own father had died. I thought that he
would always be there and now he was gone. I
closed my eyes and tried to picture his face, the
way his eyes crinkled up when he laughed and the
way they filled with tears when his heart was
moved by a piece of music or the sight of the first
crocus or fresh snow covering the hillside. I
remembered sitting beside the fire in the big
kitchen. I remembered the pretty bedroom where
I had been so ill. I remembered the lovely garden
that looked out over the hills. It all belonged to
me and Olive now, but it was hard to be excited
because Yann wouldn't be there: I would rather
have Yann than all the houses in the world.

I watched a group of soldiers dismantling the
horrible barbed wire. Soon the beach would be
open again and children would once more paddle
in the icy water and play in the rock pools. Soon
I would stand at the edge of the ocean with Lottie,
but I would never see Yann again.

# CHAPTER 47

The day before Lottie and I left for Wales, Olive and I decided to spend some time with our family. We hadn't spent a lot of time with them and I wanted Olive to start feeling at home in the new house. I knew it was what Mum and Dad wanted too.

It was lovely being together again. There was so much more room here than in the flat in Bermondsey and, with the furniture from Sea View, it was beginning to feel like home.

In the afternoon we all went for a walk along the seafront, Olive running ahead of us, holding onto little Freddie's hand.

'This is what I dreamed of, Nell,' said Mum as we walked along by the sea. 'All of us together. There were times when I feared it would never happen.'

'I felt the same, Mum,' I said. 'When Auntie Beth told me that Daddy was missing I was so scared, and then when we got back to Bermondsey and saw that Rannly Court had been bombed, I thought you were all dead; I thought I'd never see you again.'

'We've been blessed,' said Daddy. 'We must have had a guardian angel looking after us all.'

'I think we did,' said Mum.

Once we were back at the house we all sat round the table eating a lovely stew that Mum had made for us. We laughed and giggled at things that weren't even that funny because we were so full of happiness.

As darkness began to fall outside the window it grew chilly, so Tony made a lovely fire in the grate. Mum put little Freddie to bed and we sat around in chairs and on the floor, tired but contented and just happy to all be together at last.

Olive suddenly climbed onto Dad's lap and I could see his face light up to have his little girl in his arms again.

'What happened to you, Dad?' I asked gently. 'In the war. How were you injured?'

'Do you really want to hear this, Nell?' he said.

I nodded.

'I'd like to hear it as well,' said Tony.

'And me,' said Olive, looking up at him and then adding, 'as long as it's not too gory. I'm not into gory!'

Daddy smiled and took a deep breath. 'I was serving on a destroyer called the *Bedouin* when we were torpedoed by the Italians. A lot of the crew died but I was lucky and just took a hit to my leg and my back. The ship sank, but with the help of the officers and crew I survived. We were a sorry bunch. Me and some other chaps that were injured were put into the lifeboats and the rest were left hanging onto anything they could find to keep them afloat. We were cold, exhausted and covered in fuel oil. We were about a hundred yards away when the *Bedouin* went down. She'd been a good ship and many of those tough seamen were crying to see her disappear below the water. We drifted for what seemed like hours until we were rescued by an Italian hospital boat.'

'You were rescued by the same people that torpedoed you?' said Tony.

'We were. Two hundred and thirteen men were saved that night.'

'What happened then, Daddy?' asked Olive.

'We were taken to an island called Pantelleria and put in a prisoner-of-war camp.'

'Were they nice to you, Daddy?' said Olive, her eyes filling with tears. 'They didn't hurt you, did they?'

'No, my love,' said Daddy, kissing the top of Olive's head. 'We were treated well; the Italians were fair and not cruel. We stayed there for about ten days and then moved to another camp called Santa Ninfa.'

'Funny old names,' said Olive.

'They were,' said Daddy, smiling at her.

'We were to move camp another three times before we were eventually released and shipped back home.'

'And then you went to the hospital?' asked Olive.

'I had to have an operation on my leg, which

414

hadn't healed properly. But I was home and all I could think about then was getting back to you lot.'

'And Mummy found you?' prompted Olive.

'She did,' said Daddy, 'and then we found you.'

'So it wasn't so bad?' said Olive.

'Walk in the park,' said Daddy, laughing.

Early Saturday morning, Lottie pulled up outside Sea View in her mum's little black car. Mrs Wright had packed enough food to feed an army and Mrs Baxter had added blankets and a torch. You'd think we were about to scale Everest.

'Best be prepared,' said Mrs Baxter. 'You never know what you might encounter along the way.'

We were hugged and kissed and waved off at the door. As the car pulled away I looked back and I could swear that Mrs Baxter was dabbing at her eyes with a hankie. I owed these two women so much and I had grown to love them as if they were family.

The night before, Olive had decided to stay at Mum and Dad's.

'Will Henry be okay with it?' I'd said.

'Sometimes, Nell, you just have to do what's right. I mean, it's not going to kill him to do without me for one weekend, is it? He gets to see me every day but Mum and Dad and Tony and Freddie don't, do they? He has to understand that I must spread myself around. So Henry will just have to get over it.'

Sometimes my little sister was wise beyond her years.

We had left Eastbourne behind us and were soon speeding along the coast road. It was lovely.

'I can't believe you can drive a car,' I said.

'Like I said, there was sod all else to do down there.'

'No handsome Cornish fishermen?'

'Not my type.'

'And what's your type?'

Lottie grinned. 'Gerraint is my type, he's definitely my type.'

'Does he know you're coming?'

'I thought I'd surprise him. He knows I'm back in Brighton and he knows I've found you but I haven't told him about this trip.'

'And how do you think he'll react?'

'I think he'll hit me over the head with a club and drag me off to the nearest cave.'

'Sounds painful.'

'It wouldn't be true love if there wasn't a bit of pain involved.'

'I know what you mean.'

'What aren't you telling me, Nell Patterson? Have you had a secret affair?'

'Sort of.'

'And you haven't told me!' she screeched.

'It was a bit of a disaster, best forgotten really.'

'Let's stop and have one of Mrs Wright's sandwiches.'

'Already?'

'Other people's disasters give me an appetite. Besides, I need to be able to concentrate.'

Lottie pulled over and we unwrapped the sandwiches. 'Okay, tell me everything,' she said.

'Well, his name's Robert and he's in the Canadian Air Force.'

'Sounds promising.'

'It was to start with but he'd neglected to mention a wife and child waiting for him back home.'

'Oh, I'm sorry, Nell. Were you terribly heartbroken?'

'I was terribly angry.'

'Good girl.'

'I did forgive him though.'

'I wouldn't have expected anything less from you.'

'Well, he was going off to war and somehow it seemed the right thing to do.'

'You're a nicer person than I am, Nell. I would have let him go off to war with more than a flea in his ear.'

I grinned. 'I bet you would!'

'So you got over him? It didn't put you off men for life?'

'It's made me a bit cautious.'

'What about that boy, Jimmy, the one you talked about in your letters? It sounded as if you liked him.'

'He was lovely and I would love to see him, but if, as you say, the farm has been sold, he'll be long gone. He could be anywhere, Lottie. I doubt I'll ever see him again.'

'But you'd like to?'

I nodded. 'I'd love to.'

'Then we'll jolly well ask around – we'll be like two private detectives, we'll interrogate everyone who might have known him. We'll find him, Nell.'

'If he wants to be found.'

'You'll never find him if you think like that. You have to be positive, my friend.'

'I'll try.'

'My curiosity has been satisfied,' said Lottie, starting up the engine. 'Let's go find our men.'

'Yes, let's,' I agreed. I was so happy to be going back to that lovely little village with Lottie; it was so different from the first time. I had only been thirteen back then and Olive only five. It had been scary; we hadn't known where we were going to end up or what was going to happen to us.

I gazed out the window at the unfamiliar streets and houses. People were going about their Saturday morning business. A woman was pushing a pram along the pavement and a man cycled past on a blue bike. People with lives that I knew nothing about. I looked back at the woman. She was wearing a headscarf, even though the sun was shining and it was warm outside. Perhaps she'd just had her hair done and she was being taken out to dinner by an adoring husband. I smiled to think that she would never know that, for a few seconds, a complete stranger driving past her in a little black car had wondered about her life. We passed bombsites and bombed-out houses. Soon the task of clearing the rubble and rebuilding would start. I wondered if Rannly Court would one day rise out of the ruins.

'I can't wait to see Gerraint,' said Lottie. 'I mean, I've changed, I've got taller and so have you. I wonder if he'll still like me, or will he be disappointed?'

'How could he be disappointed? You're gorgeous, you were even gorgeous with the plaits and the glasses. He liked you then so he's going to adore you now.'

'You're right, Nell, we're both gorgeous. Glengaryth will think that we are visiting movie stars.'

'Didn't you see him when you were in Wales with your mum?'

'No, once we'd been to the ghastly farm and knew you weren't there, Mum just wanted to come home. It was a long journey and she was keen to make it back to Brighton before dark. It nearly killed me being so close to Glengaryth and not seeing him, but it was so good of Mum to go to Wales in the first place – I didn't want to push my luck.'

'It *was* good of her, wasn't it? I mean, she didn't even know me.'

'I've never had a best friend before. I suppose not going to school didn't help, so when I told Mum how worried I was about you, she was as anxious to find you as I was.'

'Well, I still think it was lovely of her.'

'She *is* lovely. I know she's my mother and I could be biased but she's one of the nicest people I know. She can't wait to see Dad; he's been entertaining the injured troops up and down the country and he's coming home next week. We're having a party – you must all come, Nell, even Auntie Missus.'

'I'm sure we'd all love to come.'

The journey was long but we had so much to talk about, we didn't mind. We had picnics on the way and managed to eat almost all the food. We only stopped once more, to fill the car up with petrol.

As the light faded from the sky we reached the Aust ferry that would take us across the river and into Wales. We would soon be in Glengaryth.

# CHAPTER 48

It was pitch-black when we arrived at the vicarage. The lights on the little car picked out the old house as we turned into the drive. We got out and I stood there looking up at the two tall chimneys silhouetted against the dark sky. It felt like a lifetime ago that I'd first stood here, a frightened girl, uprooted from all that I knew and loved and put down in this strange country. Me and Olive had been at the mercy of strangers and we had no idea what the future held for us.

Tonight the sky was full of stars and I felt at peace.

'It feels like a sort of homecoming,' said Lottie.

'It does, doesn't it?'

Just then the door was flung open, shedding a pool of light onto the garden. Auntie Beth came running towards us.

She threw her arms around us both. 'Come in, come in,' she said, smiling.

We walked into the kitchen, which was just as I remembered it. The long wooden table, the yellow couch under the window and the huge old fireplace.

My eyes filled with tears as I looked around. 'I'm so glad that nothing's changed,' I said.

'Oh, Nell,' she said, taking me in her arms. 'It's so wonderful to see you again.' She looked across at Lottie. 'And how you've both grown.'

'Where's the baby?' I asked.

'Would you like to see her?'

'Yes, please.'

'She's asleep, but come upstairs.'

The three of us stood gazing down at little Olivia Nell. Her eyes were closed, her dark lashes resting like feathers on two plump cheeks. Every so often her lips moved as if she was telling herself a story. 'She's beautiful,' I whispered.

'She is, isn't she?' said Auntie Beth, smiling fondly down at her baby girl.

Lottie didn't say much as Auntie Beth and I gazed down into the cot – I got the feeling she wasn't as captivated as we were.

Uncle Dylan came home later and we spent the evening eating and catching up with each other's lives. They asked about Mum and Dad and Tony and little Freddie.

'I don't know what I would have done if your mother hadn't turned up when she did. She was a godsend, Nell.'

'I don't know what *she* would have done without you – she wouldn't have known what to do or where to go.'

'I was eight months pregnant with Olivia and Dylan was working in Cardiff.'

'It was such a relief to know that your mother was here, Nell,' said Uncle Dylan. 'I tried to get back as much as I could but it wasn't enough and then your lovely mother and your family arrived. I truly believe that God answered our prayers.'

'And what about you, Lottie?' said Auntie Beth. 'I heard on the grapevine that you had left Eliza Strut's house.'

'My mother and I went to family friends in Cornwall. Of course, it was a terrible wrench having to leave the delightful Mrs Strut.'

'I bet it was,' said Auntie Beth, giggling.

Even Uncle Dylan was struggling to keep a straight face.

'She's a decent God-fearing woman, Lottie,' he said, 'and I'm sure that Jesus has reserved a special place for her at God's table.'

'As long as she's not sitting next to me,' said Lottie.

This time even Dylan was laughing.

The next morning after breakfast, me and Lottie helped Auntie Beth with the washing-up, then I played with the baby while Lottie went down the garden to pet the horse.

Olivia had just started to sit up but she kept falling back against the cushions and giggling. 'I'd never get any work done if she was mine, Auntie Beth, she's just adorable.'

'Do you know what, Nell? I think you're too old to be calling us Auntie and Uncle – why don't you call us Beth and Dylan?'

I'd been sort of thinking the same but I didn't want to be rude. 'Okay,' I said.

'That's settled then.'

'Do you mind if we walk down to the village?'

Beth smiled and put her arm around my shoulder.

'I can't tell you how wonderful it is to have you here again, Nell. I've missed you so much. Now, off you go before I get all teary.'

It all felt so familiar as Lottie and I walked side by side through the lanes. We cut across the fields past Dylan's little chapel and our old school. We stopped and looked at the small square playground.

'There should be a plaque on the wall that says, "This is where Lottie Lovejoy met Nell Patterson".'

'And another one that says, "This is where Olive met Aggie".'

'Absolutely,' said Lottie.

'It looks smaller than I remember,' I said.

'That's because we're bigger.'

We left the school behind us and walked down into the village square.

'Let's go and surprise Mrs Evans, shall we?'

'Oh, let's!' said Lottie.

We walked across the road to the bakery. Mrs Evans almost vaulted over the counter when she saw us.

'Oh my word, girls! Is it really you? All grown-up and looking like a pair of models.'

We each gave her a hug – we had grown so tall that she was like a child in our arms.

She dabbed at her eyes. 'The pair of you are a sight and no mistake; wait till Gerraint sees you. I presume he knows you're here?'

'No, he doesn't, I want to surprise him.'

'Then you've come to the right place,' said Mrs Evans, smiling. 'Him and the lads come in here every day for their dinner; you can surprise him then.'

'Perfect,' said Lottie. 'You are a darling, Mrs Evans. We'll be back later then.'

We walked across the road to the duck pond and sat on the bench just like we used to.

'I never thought I would ever come back here,' I said. 'I never thought that I would ever want to, but I'm so glad that we're here together.'

'It hasn't changed a bit, has it?' said Lottie, looking around.

'I remember when we all came down here and you and Gerraint went off on your own.'

'My first kiss,' said Lottie, sighing dramatically.

'Really? You never told me that.'

'Well, I was only fourteen! I'd hardly left a trail of broken hearts behind me.'

'And no one since?'

'Well, I had a near miss at a Christmas party in Cornwall. A ghastly boy asked if he could kiss me under the mistletoe.'

'And what did you say?'

'I told him I wouldn't kiss him under a general anaesthetic.'

I started laughing. 'I bet that didn't go down well.'

'No, it didn't – he told me he only asked because he felt sorry for me and I told him he smelled of gone-off trout. My mother thought it was hilarious when I told her.'

'So, Gerraint's the boy for you?'

'From the moment we met, actually, not a doubt in my mind. He became my best friend once you had gone away. We like the same things, Nell. We both want to see the world, maybe even live abroad for a while.'

'And get married?'

'Not high on the agenda. I have always thought marriage was a bit overrated. My parents aren't married, you know.'

I was a bit stunned – I just presumed that if you lived together and you had a child then you would be married.

'I've shocked you, Nell.'

'I suppose you have a bit, but not in a bad way. I've just never come across it before.'

'My parents view the whole love, honour and obey thing as rather bourgeois.'

'What does that mean?'

'Well, it's a French word meaning middle class, small-minded; trying too bloody hard to fit in. My parents have never done the fitting-in bit very well.'

I grinned. 'I think your parents are perfect.'

'I can't wait for you to meet my father. I respect him so much, Nell. He was called some terrible names when he refused to fight in the war – we even had a white feather posted through our door.'

'A white feather?' I said.

'It's a symbol of cowardice. But my father's not a coward, he's a pacifist, and he wasn't afraid to stand up for his beliefs.'

'And that's really brave, braver than the idiots who put a white feather through your door.'

Lottie put her arm around me. 'I love you as much as I love Gerraint, Nell.'

'That's a lovely thing to say.'

'It's true.'

'And do children figure in this great romance of yours, Lottie? Only you didn't seem terribly interested in baby Olivia.'

'My mother once told me that children are like farts: you can only tolerate your own. So we might do the whole baby bit, but only after we've seen the world.'

We sat side by side on the bench until Mrs Evans waved to us from across the road.

'They'll be here soon, girls,' she said as we got close.

We followed her into the bakery. She lifted up the counter flap and ushered us through. 'You can hide in my sitting room until they come in, and mind you stay as quiet as two little mice, my lovelies.'

We wandered around the little room, looking at all Mrs Evans's ornaments and family photographs.

'Oh, do look at this, Nell,' said Lottie, smiling. 'They were really quite handsome, weren't they?'

I picked up the framed photograph of Mr and Mrs Evans on their wedding day. 'Mrs Evans looks absolutely petrified,' I said.

'That's exactly how I'd look, Nell.'

'Oh, Lottie,' I said. 'Do you really not want the white dress and the bridesmaids and the yummy cake?'

'I can buy a cake anytime I want.'

'Shush!' I whispered. 'I hear boys.'

'Oh my God, Nell!' said Lottie. 'I feel quite ill.'

She was as white as a sheet.

'Are you going to be sick?'

'I sincerely hope not.'

Just then Mrs Evans put her head round the door. 'Gerraint's here,' she whispered.

'Are you sure you feel okay?' I asked.

Lottie took some deep breaths and nodded. 'As okay as I'm ever going to be. Let's do this, Nell.'

'Good girl,' I said, and we went into the café.

# CHAPTER 49

As soon as the boys saw us they started yelling our names, but not Gerraint. He just stared at Lottie as if he couldn't get enough of her. He walked around the table and took her in his arms and that's how they stayed, with their arms around each other, as if they were the only two people in the room. The boys had stopped making a noise – there was no silly cheering or whistling, just smiles. Lottie looked at me over Gerraint's shoulder. She looked so happy – she was where she wanted to be, they both were.

After a while they sat down with the rest of us and Gerraint gave me a big hug. 'It's good to see you, Nell,' he said. 'Thank you for bringing my girl back to me.'

'Oh, I didn't bring her back, she brought herself. I just tagged along for the ride.'

'The ride?'

'Your clever Lottie drove us here in her car.'

'You can drive a car?' he said, smiling at Lottie.

'Absolutely,' she said. 'Do you want to go for a spin?'

'Can I come too?' said Daffyd.

'Haven't you got to get back to work?' said Glyn.

Daffyd groaned. 'Spoilsport,' he said, making a 'poor me' face. 'It's all right for Gerraint, he works for his father.'

'It has its advantages,' said Gerraint, grinning.

Mrs Evans came across with a tray full of pasties. 'Tuck in,' she said.

'I'll tell you what,' said Lottie. 'You have your dinner and me and Nell will walk back to the vicarage and get the car.'

'Gerraint is even more handsome than I remembered,' said Lottie, as we walked back up the lane.

'I'm so happy for you,' I said.

She stopped walking and said, 'Now, what about you? What do *you* want to do?'

I knew exactly what I wanted to do. 'I want to go back to the farm,' I said.

'Consider it done,' said Lottie, reaching for my hand. 'We can ask around and see if anyone knows anything about your Jimmy.'

We stopped at Tyford, the little village where I used to walk with Jimmy to post my letters to Mum. I looked across at the old stone bridge where we used to sit on those warm spring evenings, getting to know each other.

'Let's try the pub,' said Gerraint. 'My guess is that most of the local gossip will go on in there.'

It was dark inside but we could see a few men

430

standing at the bar. They looked up and stared at us as we went in. Gerraint ordered three glasses of lemonade, then spoke to the barman.

'We're looking for a lad called Jimmy who lived at Hackers farm,' he said. 'Did you know him?'

'Sorry,' said the barman, shaking his head. 'I can't say I do. Lived with the Hackers, you say?'

'Yes,' I said, 'he was an evacuee.'

'He'll have gone home by now, won't he? That farm's been sold. Although why anyone would be daft enough to buy it, I don't know. The place is falling down.'

'You looking for Jimmy?' said a man sitting in the corner.

I turned to face him. 'Do you know him?'

'I knew *of* him,' he said.

'Do you know where he is?'

The man took a long swallow of beer. 'Last I heard he'd buggered off to London and good luck to him, I say. I'd have done the same if I'd lived with the Hackers.'

I felt sick to my stomach. 'Thanks anyway,' I said.

We left our drinks and went back outside.

'I'm sorry, Nell,' said Lottie.

'I didn't really expect him to be here but I had hoped he would have stayed in Wales,' I said.

She put her arm around me. 'Do you want to go home?'

'Do you mind if we still go to the farm?'

'Whatever you want to do, darling.'

Lottie stopped the car at the top of the hill and we all got out.

'You want to be alone, don't you?' she said.

'I think I do, yes.'

'Gerraint and I will go for a walk and meet you back here in about an hour. Will that be long enough?'

I nodded and watched them walk away hand in hand. I almost envied what they had and wondered if one day I would find that kind of love.

I stood on the top of the hill and looked down on the farm. I had good memories and bad memories of the place but I didn't feel scared. It was where I'd met Jimmy, so for every bad memory there was also a good one.

I walked down the hill and into the yard. Someone had been tidying up; it wasn't the mess that I remembered. I walked towards the house. The windows were sparkling clean so that I could actually see inside. All the furniture was still there: the wooden table, which looked as if it had been scrubbed clean, and the threadbare chairs on either side of the fireplace. All exactly the same.

I walked across to the barn and pushed open the door – I needed to rid myself of the image of Albert lying there as still as death. I spun around as I heard a movement, then laughed as I realised the noise was coming from two cows lying down in the stalls. Maybe the new owners had already moved in. I went back to the house and knocked on the door but there was no answer.

Next, I walked across the yard. The pigs were still snuffling around in their pens and when I looked up at the field I could see the rest of the cows. I screwed up my eyes against the sun and saw a figure up there.

It could be anyone, couldn't it? It could be the new owners. But something made me start running, through the gate and up onto the field.

'Jimmy!' I yelled as I got closer. 'Jimmy!'

He turned at the sound of my voice and started to run towards me. 'Nell!' he screamed.

I threw myself at him, almost knocking him off his feet. I was laughing and crying.

He held me away from him. 'I can't believe it's really you,' he said. 'I can't believe you came back.'

We started talking at the same time, barely taking a breath.

'They said you were in London.'

'I went looking for you but the place you told me you lived in had been bombed. I didn't even know if you were still alive.'

'We went to Eastbourne in Sussex.'

'You didn't kill Albert, Nell.'

'I know. But why didn't you meet us in the barn?'

'Because Albert wasn't dead – he wasn't dead, Nell. I had to get help and I had to blackmail him into not telling old Ma Hacker what you'd done to him. If she knew, she would have got the police onto you.'

'Why didn't you come after that?'

'It was too late, Nell. You were gone, I couldn't find you. I tried, Nell, I really tried.'

'Why are you still here, Jimmy?'

'I promised the new owner I'd stay on to look after the animals until he took over the farm.'

'And what are you going to do after that?'

'I'm going to get married,' he said, grinning. He kissed my cheek. 'I can't believe it's really you, Nell.' Then he walked away – just like that he walked away, down the field towards the house.

My cheeks were burning with embarrassment; I couldn't believe what had just happened. He'd looked as happy as I was but he'd walked away from me and, worse than that, he'd said he was getting married: he didn't love me at all. I'd waited so long for this moment, I'd dreamt about how it would be if I ever saw him again. But he loved someone else: my Jimmy was going to marry someone else.

With tears rolling down my cheeks I started back up the hill. I was running away again and I knew this time I would never come back. Then I heard him calling my name, but I kept running; I didn't want to face him. He caught up with me and spun me round.

'Where are you going?'

'Away from this place,' I said. 'And away from you.'

'But why, Nell? Tell me why!'

'Because I love you, Jimmy, and you are going to get married.'

He held my face in his hands. 'To *you*, Nell. If you'll have me, I'm going to get married to you.'

'But you walked away from me.'

'To get this,' he said, and he handed me a tin. I opened it up and inside was the locket and the little blue brooch.

He gently lifted the hair from the back of my neck and secured the clasp. 'Will you, Nell? Will you marry me?'

I didn't answer – I didn't have to. I just held him close and on that windy hillside I knew that this was a forever love that would last for the rest of our lives. And I couldn't wait for the journey to begin, the journey that would carry me home.

# EPILOGUE

I put the last of the dishes on the drainer to dry, wiped my hands on the towel and wandered over to the window. The farm was on the southern side of the Downs, the house built in a cleft between two hills, the back enclosed by a copse of tall old trees that protected it from the wind. From the window, I could see the glisten of sunlight on the sea in the distance, its blue haze merging into the sky so there was no horizon.

Closer than the blues were the greens of the fields, the grass growing now that May had arrived, the meadows full of wildflowers that helped feed our small herd of dairy cows. Jimmy was out there somewhere, checking the stock, seeing which had calved overnight and making sure that all was well with mother and baby. It was hard work, but it was his dream that had become our dream, and we loved it. Sometimes I had to smile to myself: who'd have thought it? Me, a girl from the East End, ending up here, a farmer's wife on the Sussex Downs!

I leaned my elbows on the window ledge and cupped my chin in my hands.

Closer still was the farm garden, a lawn surrounded by an ancient hedge woven through with brambles. Gnarled apple trees were in blossom and birds were nesting in the hedges; house martins darting in the sky above.

Our two precious boys, Ronan and David, were playing amongst the trees, seven-year-old David hanging off the branches, swinging, and his five-year-old brother on his hands and knees pushing a wooden tractor through the grass. Ronan saw me at the window and grinned, a gap in his teeth – his smile that reminded me so much of Olive's smile at his age.

Olive . . . my darling Olive. We had experienced something amazing, her and I. A journey that had made us stronger and braver, a journey that had made us who we were today. We shared memories that were ours alone. We didn't talk about them much but there were times when something would take us back and we remembered.

We sold Yann's cottage, which enabled Jimmy and me to purchase our farm and Olive and Aggie to buy a shop in Kemp Town that they turned into a tea rooms. They called their shop 'Auntie Missus'.

I walked across to the dresser and took down the framed photograph of her and Aggie outside their shop. They were smiling into the camera, Aggie with her arm around Olive's shoulder. When Olive was a little girl and she'd said that one day she and Aggie would live together I had put it down to childish talk; I'd never realised that the promise they made to each other all those years ago would be a promise that would last forever. Theirs was a different kind of beautiful and I was so proud of them both.

Lottie's dream of travelling the world with Gerraint had been halted by the arrival of their twin girls, Kitty and Selena, who they adored. Now their two little ones had become the only world they needed. And yes, one summer evening Lottie and I had eaten fish and chips sitting on the pebbles, and then hand in hand we'd stood together at the edge of the ocean, just as she had promised we would.

We lost dear Miss Timony three years ago. We were all heartbroken. I missed her wisdom and her patience, the way she never preached, just guided you to a place where you could think more clearly. She had touched us all in different ways and for a while our worlds were less bright. Mrs Baxter never returned to Bermondsey, she stayed with her sister in Eastbourne and they ran 'Sea View' together.

Tony fulfilled his dream of becoming a chef and was working in a prestigious hotel in London, and Freddie had passed the exam for the grammar school; it turned out that he was the clever one in the family.

Dad got stronger and Mum said that his beloved grandchildren had given him a new lease of life. They both adored them.

Jean sailed across an ocean to meet Eric's parents. She fell in love with Canada and only came home to say goodbye to us all. It was sad to lose her but she was so happy that I could only be pleased for her.

Mr Costos and Mr Philip continued to run the hotel and Jimmy and I often visited them.

Mrs Ryan wrote to let me know that my dear friend Angela never came home at all. She died in a hospital far from everything she knew and loved. She survived the war, but not the blood poisoning that took her life. I was heartbroken to lose my dear friend from those childhood days, when Bermondsey had been our whole world and a bombed-out house our playground. I keep the little pink shell she gave me on my bedside table and I say a prayer for her every night before I go to sleep.

I opened the back door to let in some air, just as Jimmy started to walk across the yard. He was holding his hat in one hand, a slight frown on his face, lost in thought. I watched as he approached, that familiar, long-legged, slightly loping stride, those broad shoulders, the untidy hair; his face already brown from being outside in all weathers. He must have felt my eyes on him because he looked up and grinned. He raised the hand holding the hat in greeting and I raised my hand in return. He quickened his pace and I met him at the door.

'Hello, missus,' he said.

'Hello, mister!'

He put the hat down on the dresser, took my face in his hands and kissed me. He smelled of the outdoors and of the animals and the sun and the hay. I loved the smell of him; I loved everything about him. It wasn't the same now as it had been when we were young; it was a less urgent, less anxious, more settled kind of love.

'Where are the boys?'

'Outside.'

We crossed to the window that looked over the garden and stood there with our arms around each other, watching our children play.

# LETTER FROM SANDY

Thank you so much for choosing to read *The Runaway Children*. For those of you who have read and enjoyed *The Brighton Girls trilogy*, I hope you enjoy Nell and Olive's story just as much.

I'd like to take this opportunity to thank all my readers for your ongoing support and wonderful reviews: it means a lot to me, you really are the best.

If you have enjoyed my story I would be very grateful if you could take a moment to post a short review, which may help new readers to discover my books.

I love hearing from you and I will always respond to your messages. I really do appreciate you all.

Thank you again.
Sandy x